DEAD GIRLS CAN'T LIE

Carys Jones

About *Dead Girls Can't Lie*

Best friends tell each other the truth – don't they?

When North Stone's best friend Kelly Orton is found hanging lifeless in a tree, North knows for certain it wasn't suicide. Kelly had everything to live for – a loving boyfriend, a happy life, and most importantly of all, Kelly would never leave North all by herself.

The girls have been friends since childhood, devoted to each other, soul sisters, or at least that's what North has always believed. But did Kelly feel the same way, or was she keeping secrets from her 'best friend' – deadly secrets…

When the police refuse to take North's suspicions seriously, she sets out to investigate for herself. But her search soon takes her to a glamorous world with a seedy underbelly, and before long North is out of her depth and getting ever closer to danger. Determined to find the truth, she soon wishes that dead girls could lie, because the truth is too painful to believe…

For my Mum, for teaching me that in life there are no limits just goals you've yet to achieve

1

Kelly didn't kill herself.

The message arrived shortly after midnight when North was caught somewhere between sleep and surrender. Blurry-eyed she stared at her phone, at the cryptic message from an unknown sender.

'I know,' she whispered to the device as she lay on her sofa, bathed in the glow from her television which was on its second run through of *Dark Crystal*. 'I know she'd never leave me.'

By dawn North was completely awake and the message was gone, wiped from her phone as though it were the fragment of a dream. But North didn't care. It had given her the impetus she needed to get out of her flat and prove the point which had been gnawing at her since her best friend's demise. She wasn't alone in her conviction. That was all that mattered.

*

'North Stone. That your name?'

'Yes,' North tightened her fingers which were clenched around her hands. It was cold in the interview room. Colder than she'd expected.

'North. That's an… interesting name.'

With a sigh she braced herself for the inevitable volley of questions which would now be flung back and forth across the table.

Why North?
Why did your parents call you that?
Where are your parents?

The conclusion to such questions was always the same; North was strange. Everyone in their small South Downs town knew it. Everyone except Kelly. And she was the reason that North was even here. They were supposed to be talking about *her*.

'My parents were mega into stargazing. I know, I know, I work in the local observatory the irony of which isn't lost on me. Yes they were lost at sea during a romantic adventure on board a yacht. No I don't expect them to ever return. It's been eighteen years, I'm pretty sure they're gone.'

The police officer's silver eyebrows dropped into a flat, sympathetic line. He was obviously old enough to know the notorious story of what happened to the Stones. He was asking about her name to be polite. Kind even. And North did not have time for either placation. She was here on urgent business.

'Look,' North unclasped her hands and lay them flat on the table as though she were showing her cards in a high stakes poker game. 'You're wrong about Kelly Orton. She would never kill herself.'

'Miss Stone—'

The officer hung a little too heavily on the *Miss* for North's liking.

'And on a *jogging trail*? Absolutely not! No way! For starters, Kelly never went jogging. Like, ever. We're both allergic to anything that makes you sweat. Seriously, Officer…' she lifted her ashen eyes to meet his.

'Childs,' he stiffly informed her.

'Officer Childs. You're wrong about Kelly. You guys shouldn't be ruling this as a suicide you should be launching a murder investigation.'

With a sigh, Officer Childs stood up, letting his chair grate noisily against the tiled floors. He walked over to the door to the interview room and opened it with one fluid motion, extending his body out into the hallway. 'Angie, can you get in here?'

A moment later he was joined by another officer, a woman with bright red hair which stopped suddenly at her shoulders. Her mouth lifted into a pitying smile the second she saw North hunched on the other side of the table.

The air in the little room managed to hold the years' old stench of stale cigarettes and coffee. A single strip light across the ceiling bathed everyone who sat in there in an unflattering light. Kelly would have hated it. She'd have tossed her golden hair over her shoulders and refused to sit in such a room. North twisted uncomfortably on her plastic chair.

'I'll handle this,' Angie whispered to Officer Childs who eagerly left as she slid into his vacated seat. 'So, Miss Stone.' Her tone was clipped and formal. She reminded North of some of her more competent teachers during her time at Millwater Secondary. But thinking about school made her think of the Kelly from the past and she couldn't do that. Not yet. Not when there were so many questions about the present left unanswered.

'As I was telling your colleague,' North adjusted herself to match the female officer in stature. Though she was much shorter than Angie, she could still push her shoulders back and lift her chin. She wanted to look confident. Especially when everyone was treating her like she was broken. 'Kelly Orton did not kill herself. It's impossible. Someone put her there. Someone killed her. This is a murder case.'

'Someone killed her?' Angie arched an eyebrow as she gave a sympathetic nod. 'Look, Miss Stone, I know that this must be an extremely trying time for you given how close you were to the deceased but—'

'She *never* went jogging.' North slammed her hands against the table, all pretence of appearing composed abandoned. This was her friend they were discussing. Her best friend in the entire universe. As soon as the news had come in, North knew it wasn't true. When her parents disappeared she'd felt it from the top of her head to the tips of her toes. But when they told her about Kelly being found on a jogging trail in some nearby woods, North felt nothing. There was no tingle of truth running through her body like some water diviner. 'You need to start looking for who did this to her. For who is to blame.'

'I could show you the pictures,' Angie cocked her head at her, her green eyes crinkling sadly at the corners. 'The pictures from the crime scene. Would that help you get closure?'

'What? No. I mean—'

'She was found hanging from a tree, Miss Stone. It appears that she laced the rope around the branch and executed her own intentional fall. Please excuse my bluntness but I fear that some of the facts might not be getting through to you. There was a rope around her neck marked with her own fingerprints. A dog walker found her at approximately five thirty-six a.m. The coroner's report claimed that Kelly had been dead for at least two hours prior to discovery. This leads us to believe that she visited the jogging trail during the cover of night to avoid being seen. Or stopped.'

'You're wrong,' North clung to her conviction, regardless of the evidence being thrust towards her via Angie. Since reading the grim details in an online newsfeed, North knew they were false; nothing about the discovery of her friend rang true with her. 'Kelly is the happiest person I know. She's the brightest star in the whole damn galaxy.'

'She was,' Angie quietly corrected her. 'I know how difficult this must be for you. Kelly was your best friend. In cases like these, loved ones are often wracked with guilt, wondering how they missed the signs, wishing that they could have done more—'

'Kelly *did not* hang herself. She *did not* go out to some piece of crap jogging trail in the middle of the night to end her own life. She just wouldn't do that.' North balled her hands up, letting the tips of her nails create crescent moons in her palms.

'People aren't deliberately leaving you.' Angie gave North a long, level look. It was a look North was used to seeing on the faces of teachers, then co-workers. A look filled with fear and sympathy. A look that said, *I'm sorry all this crap happened to you but I'm kind of glad it wasn't me.*

In Millwater, North was a cautionary tale. She was the girl whose parents went away and never came back. People liked to blame her preoccupation with the stars on a reluctance to accept her own dire reality. Kelly never felt that way. She admired North's obsession with all things celestial. And now she was gone and the whole world already believed it was suicide.

'This isn't about my parents,' North raged.

'I know that your grandmother died last year,' Angie kept her voice soft. 'You must be feeling pretty alone right now.'

'This is about Kelly,' North was on her feet. The rage setting her body on fire making it impossible to remain sitting down, to pretend to be civil. Here was an officer of the Millwater Police Department refusing to acknowledge that a terrible crime had been committed. Kelly Orton would never, *ever*, go jogging.

Not that Millwater PD had much experience in dealing with cases of this nature. Most people left the sleepy little town before they felt compelled to commit any sort of crime. Drug addicts moved on to bigger cities with stronger connections to the underworld and the wealthy flocked closer to London. Boasting a commute of two and a half hours into the capital, Millwater wasn't a favoured location for young professionals. The people who lived there were trapped in the middle of the road, stuck on a plateau reflected by their claustrophobic little town.

'Seriously,' Kelly had once said, mojito in hand, 'if you ever see me in a pair of leggings or jogging bottoms shoot me, North. Just shoot me.'

Kelly and North would hop on a bus and leave the dull confines of Millwater to go dancing. To the theatre. They'd change the lyrics to their favourite songs and plan out all the musicals that they'd one day write together. They ate pizza and drank cheap wine as they watched *Sex and the City*. They cried over *Titanic* and made a vow that they'd always make space for one another on that bloody door at the end. They were inseparable, their lives so fiercely intertwined that it made no sense that when Kelly's final breath had been squeezed out, North hadn't just dropped to the floor. Somehow a heart that was used to beating in tandem with another was managing to go solo. And North didn't understand any of it.

'If you won't believe me then I'll prove it myself,' North was marching towards the door.

'North, just listen—'

Spinning around, North faced Angie like a bull which had been shown a red flag. 'This isn't about me feeling abandoned. Or me struggling to grieve. This isn't even about my parents, or my grandmother. This is about Kelly. How she never would have done this. Somehow I'm the only one who gets that, which means it's up to me to figure out what really happened to her.'

'I'm sorry.' Angie's expression was kind, open. She wasn't trying to push North away.

'I don't need your pity.' North let the door slam behind her as she hurried out. Her phone buzzed in her pocket, hastily she pulled it out.

Kelly didn't kill herself.

The same message from the same unknown sender. This time North made sure to carefully save it before it could disappear again.

*

'The reason I called you all together is because there has been an exciting discovery.' Alexander Beckett stood before his workforce of fifteen. His soft Irish lilt bounced off the walls of the meeting room. In a crisp white shirt and jeans he looked effortlessly casual and devastatingly handsome. According to Kelly, he had a jawline you could cut cheese on. His eyes were bright as he addressed the assembled group.

'What we originally thought was the presence of a new star is actually—' he stopped short when he locked eyes with North.

She had slid into the back room, her cheeks still burning with outrage following her visit to the police station. Autumn winds had left her hair tangled madly atop her shoulders. She resisted the urge to shrink beneath the intensity of his gaze. Alexander Beckett had eyes as bright as any star. When they looked at you it felt like they were penetrating through your skin, your bones, looking right down to your core. North tried to channel Kelly, tried to think of what her beloved friend would do. Instead of nervously chewing her lip and sinking deep into her green hooded jumper, North stood up straight and met Alexander's gaze.

'You shouldn't be here,' the group parted like the red sea as he made his way through them, approaching her. 'North, I heard about what happened to Kelly. You should be with loved ones right now. You should be grieving.' He placed his hands on her shoulders and North wanted to scream. He wasn't supposed to be touching her. 'Go home,' Alexander urged, squeezing her shoulders tighter and lowering his voice. 'Take a few days. I can't imagine what you're—'

'Tell me about the star,' North ordered abruptly. She could sense people averting their gazes but still straining to listen. But she was no longer a source of intrigue for the office gossips. That time had passed.

'Look, North—'

'You claim it's not a new star. Then what is it?' Out of the corner of her eye she saw Elijah sidle up to her, his blue eyes dulled with concern.

'North, go home.' Alexander gave the order but didn't lift his hands from her shoulders.

'It's a supernova,' Elijah offered quietly, nervously pushing a hand through his dark curls. 'Celine spotted it last night.'

'A supernova?' North's voice caught in her throat. A supernova. The death of a star. Discovered last night. Just a few nights after Kelly had supposedly taken herself out to the woods, to the jogging trail and—

'Don't concern yourself with this, North. Go home. I insist.' Despite his insistence Alexander didn't move, nor did his hands.

'I want to be here, at work,' North told them sincerely. She could feel everyone watching her, assessing her face for signs of an imminent breakdown. Did they expect tears? Hysteria? She refused to give them the satisfaction. North had been perfecting public mourning since she was fourteen. She'd gone pro around the time she lost her grandmother.

'Go home,' Alexander repeated, a cool calmness lingering in his gaze but his tone sharpening as he delivered an order. He was reverting to being just her boss.

'Please,' North looked deep into Alexander's eyes, trying not to see what she normally found in them. 'I don't want to be alone right now.'

'You shouldn't be here,' he was leading her away from the group, towards the door, and for some reason she was letting him. 'The supernova will still be here when you get back.'

'You're going to study it?'

'Yes,' Alexander let go of her to scratch his perfect chin. He smelt of cologne mixed with the ocean. He must have gone running along the beach that morning. Now *he* was someone who went jogging. He had the washboard stomach to prove it. Alexander Beckett was a man of science but appearances were important to him. He wore a shirt every day to work despite telling his colleagues that he favoured an 'informal' atmosphere at the observatory.

'I could come back with you,' Elijah had followed them over to the door. 'I can keep you company, if you like.'

'You'll be needed here,' North threw him a sad smile. 'A new supernova is a big discovery. Alex will need everyone on it.' With a deep breath to steady herself, she looked at Alex, hoping her smile now seemed more confident than sad. 'So what caused its creation? A gravitational collapse or—'

'Whilst I admire your dedication to your work,' Alex leaned past her to open the door into the small corridor which led out of the demountable – a slender, temporary structure which would one day be replaced by something quite literally more concrete. The site consisted of three such buildings and the main telescope. 'You really shouldn't be here, North. Not so soon after what happened. Take all the time you need to heal, to process this.'

'But -' he was already walking away, the conversation, in his mind, concluded.

It was cold out in the corridor. Almost as cold as the interview room at the police station had been. The thin walls of the demountable did little to keep out the chill of a September afternoon.

Alex was gone. His voice drifted back to her as he continued addressing the others in the main office.

'I've been assigned to study what the supernova might become,' Elijah was still there, caught in the doorway between the meeting and the corridor.

'You have?'

'You've got the same assignment,' he tugged at the sleeves of his frayed woollen jumper which appeared to be several sizes too big. Elijah was small with large blue eyes which were constantly scrutinizing his surroundings and made him appear like a nervous bird. But when he smiled all the tension lifted and he had dimples in his cheeks. North had noticed his dimples before she'd even clocked the serene shade of his eyes. 'There will be a lot of hours of data collecting. Together.'

'She didn't kill herself.' It was the first time North had said those words without the presence of a police officer. It felt strangely liberating and also oddly forbidden, like she was breaking some law by vocally denouncing the police's assumptions about Kelly.

'They said she was found out in the woods.' Elijah looked down at his red Converse. 'Hanging from a tree.'

'She didn't do it,' North insisted. 'The police don't believe me but I know she didn't do it. I know that she wouldn't—' she bit down on her tongue. Her final thoughts were too predictable. And painful.

She wouldn't just leave me like that.

But she really wouldn't. Kelly was like North's parents. She yearned for adventure and loved to visit faraway places but she always came back, she never intended to leave permanently.

'No one believes me and…' a lump gathered in North's throat, choking her words. But there were no tears. Not yet.

'I believe you,' Elijah rested a hand on her forearm, his blue eyes staring into her own. They were like the ocean, bright and full of hidden depths. North was opening her mouth to express her gratitude when Alex's voice cut through the space between them.

'Eli, we need you in here.'

And he was gone. North was alone in the corridor but not alone in her belief. If Elijah agreed that Kelly didn't kill herself then there had to be some shred of truth to what North was feeling. Hope bloomed bright in her chest as she left the demountable and made for her little yellow VW beetle on the gravel car park.

There was ice on the wind, strewn across the town like dust. North turned up the heating in her car and drove through Millwater. It was the kind of town you could easily overlook on a map; it held nothing of distinction, no points of interest bar the observatory to the east. But even that tied itself to the next town over, Alston, more than Millwater. The knotted collection of Millwater's twisting roads was boarded by rolling green hills and if you journeyed far enough south you reached the coastline.

When they were eight, Kelly had insisted on cycling out of town until they reached the sea. It was dusk when they finally saw its sparkling surface over the crest of a hill and North's legs were numb from hours spent on her bike. Typically, Kelly had been keen to race away from the sleepy town, from the old-style pubs and the wearied supermarkets full of pinched faces. By the sea the world felt vast and wide, full of opportunity. As North stood astride her yellow bike, she had a fleeting sense of understanding for why her parents were always going away.

'There's a whole world beyond Millwater,' they'd say. But it was a world they never showed to their daughter, their adventures were reserved for just the two of them. And then together they left, never to return.

2

The flat was silent. Even the gentle hum of traffic passing by outside had ceased as North stepped inside. She dropped her collection of keys onto a nearby table. The sound of metal dropping against wood was almost deafening. North cringed. Why did her usually welcoming home suddenly feel like a morgue?

She checked her phone; no new messages.

Dust danced in a fragment of autumnal sunlight which filtered in through the large window in the living area. North remained standing beside her little kitchenette, the small dining table now bearing her keys to her left, the faded white units in her kitchen to her right.

Kelly was everywhere.

She was plastered across the fridge door, her smiling face held in place by brightly coloured magnets which had been trinkets from her many adventures. She was on the table, in a mosaic frame looking out across the flat as she smiled in her prom dress, arms clasped around North like a queen surveying her dominion. She was atop the mantelpiece which covered the electric fireplace. She was on every windowsill. In every frame, in every picture, Kelly was there. She was always smiling, as radiant as the sun.

'Fuck.'

North felt her knees buckle. She reached out and grabbed the table just before hitting the floor. She clung to it as if it were a life raft in a storm.

From every surface, every wall, Kelly smiled out at her. Her blue eyes shone and corn coloured hair glistened. If North closed her eyes she could hear the bubbles of laughter which usually accompanied such a bright smile. Kelly was always laughing. Always smiling. Always enjoying life. North was the morose shadow that stood beside her.

'You've eyes like ash,' North's grandmother had commented when she was just six years old. 'It means that death will always be drawn to you.'

Before, such comments had always felt like the rambled superstitions of an old woman. But now... North's hands found her chest. She pressed her palms against her beating heart and drew in long, steady breaths. Her parents were gone. Her grandparents too. And now Kelly. What if death *was* drawn to her?

'Dammit.' With a sudden surge of movement, North stood up. If Kelly could see her now, cowering beside the little table in her sad little kitchenette she'd be furious. She'd scold her friend for giving into fear. To despair. She'd tell North to go put on her most garish shade of lipstick and go outside and face the world with an impenetrable grin. Because that's what Kelly was always doing – painting on a smile, even when things got rough. She was the strongest person North knew.

'If you were going to leave you'd tell me.' North was addressing the pictures tacked to her fridge. She and Kelly were laughing on a beach in one, screaming on a rollercoaster in another, dressed up as witches for Halloween, sexy Santas for Christmas. In some pictures they looked impossibly fresh-faced. Had they ever been that young?

North tapped the image taken on the beach. She and Kelly had locked arms, doubling forward with spasms of laughter. Behind them the sky was vast and clear. 'You told me everything, Kel,' North kept staring at the picture, searching her friend's captured smile for answers. 'This isn't you. You wouldn't just leave me like this.'

The walls within the flat were starting to feel too close. Too tight. Unable to contain Kelly's lingering presence which was too overwhelming for such a small space. North had to get out.

*

It took less than ten minutes to drive over to the small terraced house Kelly had shared with her boyfriend, Dean Mason. It was a route North could drive with her eyes closed. So many times she'd sat in her car, clad in her pyjamas after being called out by Kelly on a whim.

'Bring ice cream.'

'Bring your Nsync CDs.'

'Bring your Labyrinth DVD.'

Whenever Kelly called, North answered.

She pulled up outside the familiar home and saw two cars were neatly stacked in the driveway. Dean's blue BMW and Kelly's mint green Fiat 500. North felt a physical pang of longing sweep through her as she turned off the engine. She and Kelly had once dressed up and made their own music video a la J-Lo in the little green car. It turned out to be as hilarious as it was awful.

'We should put it up on YouTube,' Kelly had gushed between bouts of laughter.

'No,' North had almost deleted the video in her haste to keep it hidden. The world of fun and make-believe they created belonged to her and Kelly alone. It was their little bubble. She didn't want to share it with the rest of the world.

'You can be so uptight,' Kelly had sighed but didn't push the topic further. She never did. She respected North's limited comfort zone.

Grey clouds had gathered along the narrow little street on which Kelly had lived. They blocked out the sun, dulled all bright colours into more sombre tones. North approached the ruby red front door and pressed the bell. Time stretched out in several long, awful moments.

Perhaps Dean didn't want to be disturbed. He was dealing with his own grief. After all, he'd lost Kelly too. But North had automatically headed over, needing to be around someone who would be as confused by Kelly's death as she was. Someone who knew her well enough to know that something was terribly wrong. That what the police and the news reporters were saying couldn't be true. A lock turned on the other side of the door and North released a held-in breath.

'Hey,' Dean squinted out at her as though the subdued light of the afternoon was glaringly bright. He wore joggers and a T-shirt. He had equalled Kelly in height, though he was much stockier than she was. North often considered that he was the human equivalent of a bulldog to Kelly's golden retriever. While Kelly had been spun from pure sunlight, long and lithe, he was squat and square with a thick neck and a round head.

'Hey, I don't mean to bother you, I just…' North looked down at her feet. Fiddled with her hands. The creeping sensation that she shouldn't be there danced along her skin. When Kelly had been at home she was always welcome at the little terraced house, no matter what time of day or night it was.

'Nah, I get it,' Dean dragged a hand down his face and stepped aside. 'Come in.'

It felt strange to enter Kelly's home and not find her in it. The place felt incomplete. Her touches were evident everywhere, from the large art print in the hallway to the cushions scattered on the sofa in the lounge in every shade of the rainbow. Kelly loved colour. She didn't pick favourites. The little kitchen at the back of the house was painted lime green with a kettle, tiles and toaster to match. The bathrooms were bright blue and the bedroom a deep purple. The spare room which North had regularly slept in had yellow wallpaper dotted with birdcages. The entire house was a spectacle of colour, an assault on the senses.

The silence was jarring too. Kelly loved music. Whenever she was home she'd put on a CD and sashay about. But now there was no music. Just the steady ticking of the cuckoo clock Kelly had bought in Switzerland. It hung above the fireplace and on the hour two little love birds would pop out and chirp sweetly.

'Can I get you a cup of tea or… something?' Dean hung in the doorway of the living room as North stiffly dropped down onto the sofa. He was trying to resume his regular role of host but Kelly's absence meant that they were both left playing parts in a play that had been cancelled.

'I…' North saw the despair behind his eyes. The pain that twisted within him. Despite his strong stature she had never seen him look so weak. He needed the distraction. Something to do. A way to feel useful. 'Sure. Thanks.'

The cuckoo clock ticked unevenly. It was slightly out of sync with the actual time.

'It makes it quirky,' Kelly had explained when North had noticed.

'But it doesn't keep the right time.'

'So it's not perfect,' Kelly had shrugged flippantly and turned up the music on the stereo to drown out the irregular ticking. 'Not everything has to be perfect, North.'

'Here you go,' Dean shuffled in carrying two cups of tea. He handed one to North in a mug marked *Drama Queen*. It was part of Kelly's collection and was half accurate. She was certainly royal and this house was most definitely her castle. But drama? No. Kelly didn't seek out drama. She sought out dreams and that was different.

'How are you doing?' North looked down at her tea, hating herself for asking such an obvious question, one which clearly neither of them could properly answer.

'I'm…' Dean lowered himself in to a nearby armchair and clenched his ceramic Chelsea mug with such force that North feared he'd break it. 'I just can't believe it,' the tension in his grip eased as his shoulders sank. 'She's gone and it makes no sense. She was just here and—'

'I don't believe that Kelly killed herself.' North let her truth escape, knowing she couldn't even hold it as long as a breath once she was in Kelly's home, in her friends' domain.

'What?' There were deep shadows beneath Dean's eyes. Perhaps he'd not slept since he'd heard the news. Neither had North.

'They said it was suicide. That they found her out on a jogging trail… by a tree.'

'Right,' Dean held her in a steady, wary gaze.

'But that's not Kelly. Did you ever know her to go jogging?'

He considered this for a moment and then shook his large head. 'No. She was always saying she was allergic to sweat.'

'Exactly!' North leaned forward excitedly. 'Kelly would never go jogging. It just wasn't her style. So why kill herself on a jogging route? It makes no sense!'

'Why kill herself at all?' Dean countered flatly. 'I thought she was happy. I thought we were…' his voice tightened and he stopped to clear his throat.

'That's the thing. I don't think she did kill herself.'

'North,' a sigh lifted from deep within Dean's soul. 'They showed me the pictures from when they found her. I had to identify her fucking body,' a sob broke from him, a strangled cry. He pressed one hand against his eyes. He was shaking. 'Her neck, it was red from the rope and she looked so… so different. Like her body was just a shell and the Kel I knew was… was gone.'

'They found her hanging in the woods,' North agreed, refusing to let the reality of her words gather enough weight in her mind to become a wrecking ball. 'But that doesn't mean that she hung herself.'

'Jesus, North, I know you're struggling with this as much as I am but—'

'Someone did it to her. Someone lured her out into the woods and ambushed her. Put a rope around her neck and tied her up. I bet the police didn't even bother to search for signs of a struggle, why bother when they think they've already found their answer?'

'I…' Dean looked like he was about to object but then his expression shifted from pained to curious. 'I mean we're talking about Millwater. People around here die from old age more than anything else. I doubt they were thorough at the crime scene.'

'This is what I'm talking about,' North took a quick sip from her mug. The tea was sweet, just as she liked it. She was touched that despite the chaos Dean could still remember how she took her tea. 'You and I know Kelly better than anyone else. We know that she wouldn't take off jogging first thing in the morning. Nor would she hang herself. Not without saying something to at least one of us.'

Tears glistened in Dean's eyes. 'She didn't,' he coughed and looked down at his mug. 'Not a word. Nothing. Didn't say a thing to me. Did she to… to you? I know how close you two were.'

'No, nothing,' North admitted. 'And that's not like her. If she'd intended to kill herself she'd leave us a note or… or *something*.'

'But there's nothing. I've checked everywhere.'

'Unless…' North chewed on her lip.

'Unless what?'

'Unless the jogging trail. That was the note.'

'What?'

'If she was in danger, then maybe she couldn't tell us anything, not really, not without endangering us too. Perhaps she suspected someone was after her so she lured them to the jogging trail so that if anything happened to her we'd know. We'd realise that something was wrong and look into it.'

'I want to believe that she wouldn't just leave me too. Knowing that she just left like she did is killing me but, North, you're reaching.'

'Dean, I'm not,' North was insistent. 'I've known Kelly since I was two years old, since our mums met at Mothers and Toddlers. We've been inseparable ever since. She's the one person I tell everything to and I know, I *feel* it, deep down in my gut, that something isn't right here.'

'I know it's hard to accept what happened but we need to. We need to just—'

'What was your instant reaction when the police gave you the news?' Dean had to believe her, had to feel the truth in his bones, After all, he'd loved Kelly too.

'Disbelief.'

'Because you didn't want to believe she was gone or because you knew she wouldn't leave this way?'

'North—'

'Just be honest, Dean. Your knee-jerk reaction.'

'She wouldn't leave this way,' Dean sighed and leaned back in the armchair. 'It's not Kel. She doesn't jog. She doesn't own any rope.'

'I get that I sound crazy,' North drank some more of her sweet tea. 'I get that everyone wants to tell me that I'm wrong but, Dean, I know there's more to this. I know that Kelly wouldn't just hang herself in the woods.'

'Well, if anyone is going to know it's you,' Dean stared absently into his mug. 'You two were like sisters. She adored you.'

North pushed down the sob which crept up her throat.

Sisters.

They'd always been bound by more than love, by a kinship which ran all the way down to their souls. And now –

North needed to stay focused, on point. She couldn't become untethered by her grief. Not when there were so many questions which demanded answers.

'I'm going to look into this. I'm going to uncover the truth of what happened to her.'

Dean gave a dry laugh.

'What?'

'You've never been afraid of going against people's expectations, North. Kelly loved that about you. How brave you were.'

'Brave?' North nearly spat out her tea. 'God, no. Kelly's the brave one of us. I'm just her sidekick.' North shuddered at her use of the present tense. When was she ever going to get used to placing Kelly in the past?

'Sure,' Dean's smile gave way to a more haunted expression.

'I won't give up on this,' she promised Dean as she began getting up, fearing she'd already taken up too much of his time.

'I'm going to find out what really happened to Kelly. Because she didn't do this. She wouldn't.'

'Well,' Dean got up to see her out. 'I hope you're right. But if Kel didn't do this, someone else did and I'm not sure which reality is easier to deal with.'

3

Kelly didn't kill herself.

It came again. Her phone had beeped in acknowledgement. The message had been there. North had read it, twice. But now it was gone, her inbox suspiciously devoid of it. Even the message she'd previously taken care to save was gone, it was like a slate had been wiped clean within the device. As she stared at her phone, North dared to wonder if exhaustion was playing its usual tricks on her, or worse, if she'd deleted the message herself in some half-asleep state. But surely she wasn't capable of that kind of self-sabotage? Someone was trying to connect with her, trying to get through and tell her that they believed in the same truth that she did.

Sleep.

The word was almost a mantra. North just needed to sleep and then everything would start making more sense, things would stop disappearing.

Kelly didn't have a cure for insomnia. But on the nights when North couldn't sleep they'd sit up together and watch *The Lord of the Rings* trilogy. Despite Kelly's best efforts, she'd usually drift off before the end of the first movie, leaving North to sit and watch the drama unfold across Middle Earth on her own. But listening to her friend's steady breathing just a few feet away comforted North.

Insomnia was a lonely affliction. It had first visited North when her parents failed to come home. As the police searched and her grandparents fretted, she lay wide-eyed on the single bed in her bedroom. When everyone else was overpowered by exhaustion, she sat at her window and watched the stars. Kelly couldn't sneak over back then, not during the night, not as teenagers. The next day at school she was always wrought with guilt over her friend's nightly plight.

'I'd have stayed up with you,' Kelly would insist. 'You shouldn't have to be alone, North.'

Back then there was only her namesake, her star, to keep her company. North would look up at it outshining the rest of its peers and wonder why her parents chose to name her after something so commanding when she herself was more darkness than light. A bringer of death, according to her grandmother.

On the television the gathered fellowship were daring to journey through dwarven mines which tunnelled deep into the ground. Too deep. North stirred on her sofa. She'd bought the duvet from her bedroom and snuggled beneath it but still sleep wouldn't come. Candlelight flickered around her but she wasn't even sure if it was night. The curtains were drawn. She'd banished any lingering daylight when she returned from Dean's flat. She couldn't return to work. Her grandparents' home had been sold several months ago. There was nowhere for her to go except to the hollowness of her flat. She was just drifting like an unsettled spirit. The DVD boxsets were stacked up beside the television, where they always were in case of such an occasion. Something to occupy the dead hours when everyone else was sleeping. North pulled her duvet up to her shoulders, wishing she could hear the soft breathing of her friend over the epic soundtrack.

Banging.

North twisted upon the sofa and blinked at the television. The characters looked afraid, backed into the corner of a stone room as a terrible sound echoed out from the depths.

More banging.

'What?' North rubbed at her eyes. Had she fallen asleep? Perhaps she'd slipped into a doze. The banging was coming from the television, wasn't it? She stared at the screen as the banging continued. It seemed to be coming from everywhere. 'Urgh,' she pressed the heel of her hands against her temples. First insomnia came for her sleep and then her sanity. Once, she spent an entire week believing that Leonardo DiCaprio had emailed her. She'd imagined the whole thing. Or even dreamt it. It was hard to know what was real and what wasn't when sleep failed to visit her. Of course Kelly had believed her. She'd kindly sat at North's side as she frantically trawled through her inbox trying to find the evidence and then, when it failed to materialise, agreed that it must be a malfunction within the computer.

North moved from rubbing her eyes. The banging didn't stop even though the scene on the television had moved on. With a groan, North reached for the remote and paused the action, freezing all of the characters mid-motion. The banging bounced around her little flat. Someone was at her front door and they were hammering on it with great force.

'I'm coming!' North shouted over the ruckus as she shed the duvet. She shivered away from its warm embrace. Hugging her arms around herself she scurried across her flat towards her door. She pulled it open without pausing to look through the peephole. 'Dean?'

He was standing in the corridor, one fist still held in the air ready to pound on her door again. His muscles twitched as though he was consumed with restless energy. His eyes were bloodshot and there was a wildness to him. A wildness which concerned North. She took a tentative step back and he immediately advanced towards her.

'Did you know?'

The question was a roar.

'Know?' North looked between him and the door. What was going on? Was she dreaming? She didn't even know what time it was. How many times had she watched the first movie in her favourite trilogy? Once? Twice? Four times? She'd been sat on the sofa staring at the television but had lost count of how much time had passed. 'Know, know what?'

'About Kelly!' Dean was in the middle of the flat. He looked so huge amid the small walls, like a giant invading a miniature village. His chest heaved as his eyes searched all the images of his deceased girlfriend that adorned the place. 'You knew! You had to know! You knew everything about each other! And to think you gave me hope!'

'Dean, look, I don't know—'

'Why come to me yesterday? Why suggest she didn't do it? Why? Did you want to hurt me? To *punish* me?'

'I – what? No!' North felt like she'd entered a race too late. Everyone else was sprinting towards the finish while she was still trying to find her pace.

'Kel and I had our ups and downs, sure. Every couple does. But to do this,' his eyes burned with resentment as he stared at North. 'To give me hope like that, is just cruel.'

'Dean, I,' North looked towards the sofa, the television, what on earth had she missed while she remained locked in her little bubble? 'I don't know what's going on. Truly. What are you talking about?'

'You don't know?' he narrowed his eyes, his thick eyebrows flattening.

'Know what?'

He inflated his chest but said nothing.

Keeping his words inside, she began to pace around the flat, inspecting all the pictures of Kelly.

'So you really didn't know?' he asked, his voice levelling out.

'Know *what*?'

'After you left yesterday the police came to see me.'

'They did?'

'They said that Kelly's autopsy had revealed something.'

'I told you she didn't do it!' North cried, jubilant at the vindication. 'I knew she'd never do that. Never kill herself. It's not Kelly. She would never do that she—'

'She was pregnant.' Dean's voice was oddly devoid of emotion. He was standing in front of the fireplace, staring at a framed picture of Kelly and North on a night out taken the previous summer. They both wore neon war paint and matching smiles.

'Pregnant?' The word pierced North and punched her deep in the gut. Kelly was pregnant? How could she not have known? Why hadn't Kelly said anything?

'Yeah, pregnant. Around ten weeks.'

'Oh my god, Dean, I—'

'It's not mine. She wasn't here ten weeks ago.'

'The police could have the dates wrong and—'

'I asked them to rush a DNA test for that very reason. It came back negative. It's not my baby.'

All the air withdrew from the flat as though they were suddenly standing in a vacuum. North made a sound, a splutter, but she had no words. Kelly was pregnant and the baby wasn't Dean's. It made no sense. It was ludicrous. There had to be some mistake, the police must have—

'So there's your answer,' Dean reached for the framed picture of Kelly and North and clasped it in his large hands. 'You wanted to know why she did it, why she killed herself, well now you do. Guilt. She did that to me and she couldn't live with herself.'

'She loved you,' North was whispering when she should have been shouting. She knew how much Kelly loved Dean. It was evident in the glow that flushed her cheeks whenever she spoke about him. They'd bought a house together, were building a life, a future. And Kelly Orton wouldn't do that with just anyone. She was picky about every aspect of her life, meticulously ensuring that she had the best of everything. She loved Dean. But then why would she cheat on him? For once North failed to find an answer. She hung her head with regret. 'I know how much she loved you,' she offered. 'If she did this, if she did sleep with someone else then there must have been good reason. She must have—'

'Stop defending her! Stop seeing her as this perfect person! She wasn't!' Dean threw the picture at the ground. The glass in the frame fractured with an audible crack.

North gasped and took a step back.

'Fuck,' turning away from her, Dean ran his hands over his head. 'Fuck, I'm sorry, North. I'll replace the frame I'm just…' he winced as he struggled to find the words.

'Please don't believe this,' North tentatively approached him. 'Don't believe that Kelly hurt you like this. That she killed herself due to guilt. That's not like her and you know it. She faced her problems head on. She'd have told you, she'd—'

'Isn't it exhausting?' Dean was looking over all the other pictures though his hands remained locked at his side as though he was restraining himself from tearing the rest of them down. 'Keeping her up on such a pedestal all the time. She was human, North. She made mistakes. We all do.'

'Not Kelly.' It was getting difficult to speak through her tears. North brushed some of them away and squared her shoulders.

'She didn't make mistakes. If she ever did, she owned them. She didn't shy away from things. She's the bravest person I know. Knew.' A sob caught in North's throat as she had to turn away from Dean.

'Well maybe you didn't know her as well as you think.' There was pity in his voice.

'What?'

He was talking about the pregnancy, he had to be. But that was a secret Kelly wouldn't have kept forever and she must have had her reasons for concealing it from North, mustn't she?

'When she went on that yacht this summer, she was running away. We were having some issues and she didn't face them. Did you know that? Me, you, we both let her down in our own way and rather than deal with that, rather than be an adult about it she just ran. Typical Kel, right? She took a three-month job on some bloody boat and just left.' He continued to search the collection of photographs around the flat and North sensed what he was looking for; something recent. But the newest picture on display had been taken nine months ago, back at the start of the year when the calendar was new and ripe with possibilities. Who could have known as they counted in the New Year that it would be the year that would be carved on Kelly's headstone.

'She said it would be an adventure.'

'She's not bloody Jack Sparrow,' Dean raged. 'She was thirty-two not twenty-three. Grown-ass women don't run off from their problems. But she did.'

'Kelly was a free spirit.'

'Did she tell you we were having problems? Before she left?'

Yes. But she had never stated it as her reason for leaving that summer. The truth was a knife in North's back. Kelly had been her usual bubbly self as North drove her to the airport. She gushed words like *adventure* and *excitement* between every other breath. Had she really been running away? That wasn't the Kelly North knew.

'You two haven't been as close this year, huh?' Dean made his conclusion and began advancing towards the door.

North was seething. She could feel the blood in her veins boiling with fury.

Alexander Beckett was to blame for her estrangement from Kelly. Kelly had stood by North through so much but not that. It was a step too far for her, which made the pregnancy even stranger.

'She never stopped being my best friend,' North confirmed resolutely. It was true. In the same way that someone could never stop being someone's sister or daughter. She and Kelly were bound together for life. And even though North was now tethered to a ghost, they remained bound to one another, a connection even death couldn't break.

'Did she know that? I know about the wedge between you two, how quick she was to judge you for being human. Kelly could be cruel, North, don't forget that. When she left she was looking to punish us both.'

'What? No, it's not -' He raised a hand to silence her. The shadows beneath his eyes seemed to have deepened during their conversation. With a weary sigh he turned away.

Dean left through the door and disappeared down the corridor, his heavy footsteps ringing out after him. When she was certain he was gone, North dropped to her knees and with trembling hands reached for her broken picture. The glass had not completely shattered. It remained in the frame, albeit cracked. And one long fissure cut along the picture, savagely cutting between North and Kelly, separating them.

From her pocket, North grabbed her phone. She needed to see the message from the unknown sender, to know that someone else still clung to the same truth that she did. But the message was gone. Frantically she searched through all her archives as her head throbbed. Exhaustion hung heavily behind her eyes but she ignored it.

*

'We're not ready for kids, not yet,' Kelly was nursing a Jack Daniels and Coke. North had copied her friend's order whilst at the bar but was struggling to cope with its pungent taste. Her drink sat in her hand, barely touched as its ice cubes melted.

Around them the music thumped like a heartbeat. It was Elijah's thirtieth birthday party and Kelly was North's plus-one.

'Why are you talking about kids?' North scrunched up her nose in protest. 'You and Dean have only been together, what, two years?'

'Almost,' Kelly agreed with a nod. 'But you know, we turn thirty this year too. It gets you thinking.'

'It does?'

North didn't feel like she was on the cusp of turning thirty. She felt more like thirteen, that being an adult was all just a charade.

'We want to believe that life is infinite but it isn't, it's fleeting.'

'So make the most of every moment, right?' North raised her glass in a toast though she had no intention of drinking it.

'Right.' Kelly flashed her a golden smile, her eyes twinkling. 'Speaking of which, why don't you go and dance with that slice of something fine over there?' she discreetly tossed her hair in the direction of the far corner of the club where Alexander stood, chatting to some of North's colleagues, his easy laugh carrying over the music. 'He keeps looking at you.' A mischievous edge crept into Kelly's voice.

'Kel, he's my boss.'

'Still fit.'

'And married.'

'Ah,' the ends of Kelly's mouth dipped momentarily. 'Well that does complicate things. What about Elijah then? He does remind me of Frodo and he definitely looks at you like you're *his precious*.' Kelly hissed the final words in a creepy way, reminiscent of their favourite movie franchise and North playfully hit her friend's arm.

'Urgh, stop, Elijah is a friend.'

'He *does* look like Frodo though.'

'True. But I'm not prepared to be his Samwise.'

'You'd be a hobbit though,' Kelly smiled shrewdly over her glass.

'Gee thanks.'

'And I of course would be an elf, off shagging Legolas.'

'I feel like I've got the raw end of the deal here.'

'Blame those short little legs of yours.'

'If my parents had hung around long enough I'd have blamed them,' North laughed and chanced a sip of her drink. It burned along her throat and laced her taste buds with fire. She didn't want to drink any more of it.

'Do you miss them?' Kelly was surveying the dance floor as she spoke, mentally assessing each of the men as a potential partner for North as she always did whenever they were at a social outing. Then she turned back to face her friend, her focus narrowing with laser-like precision. 'Do you think about them a lot?'

'No.' The truth didn't surprise North. It was a feeling she'd embraced long ago. 'Not when I have you.' She leaned against Kelly, a contented smile pulling on her lips. 'You're all the family I need.'

'Until I do eventually sprog up,' Kelly quipped. 'Or you and Frodo make lots of hobbit babies.'

'Eww, I don't want hobbit babies.'

'Then don't marry Frodo.'

'I'm not going to!'

'We'll see.' Kelly glided towards the dance floor without needing to look back, she already knew that North would follow.

4

The trees looked like they were on fire. Their bronzed leaves fluttered along slender branches like tiny flames. North tugged up the hood on her jumper. Autumn had grown teeth over the last few days. Soon the jaws of winter would bite down on them all.

It had been almost an hour since she'd left her flat. With just her keys and her phone in her pockets she'd started walking. Aimlessly she'd wandered through town. She'd passed the fish and chip shop outside of which Kelly had her first kiss. She'd walked by the Dog and Hare, the pub that religiously hosted a karaoke night every Thursday. During their student years she and Kelly had hijacked the event whenever they were home, hogging the microphone all night as they belted out the Spice Girls and Whitney Houston.

Now North was in the woods. Somehow her meandering route through Millwater and its twisting streets had led her here. Copper leaves that had already been discarded from their hosts were swept past her feet. There were conkers on the ground, smooth and shiny, ripe for selection. Stooping down, North grabbed one and rolled it against her palm.

'You leave them in vinegar to make them strong.' That had been her dad's advice when North was just a girl. After a prolonged acid bath he'd then bore a hole through the centre of the conker and fill it with string.

The plump conker in her hand was the colour of strong coffee. North added it to the contents of her pocket and kept walking. With each leaf that crunched underfoot she knew that she was making a mistake, like she was walking into Mordor. She was on the jogging trail. Here Kelly had died. It was the opposite of a pilgrimage, a descent into darkness. Or madness.

A dark-haired woman flanked by two springer spaniels hurried past, pausing to offer North the briefest of polite nods. Had there been anyone about when Kelly came down the track? Was North now walking in her friend's final steps?

'Hey, North.'

Was someone calling her? Had the voice come from outside of North's mind? Or were her own worried thoughts reaching out to her, demanding to be heard?

'North.'

A hand was on her shoulder and she was being turned around.

'I thought that was you.'

It was Angie, the officer from the police station. Only now she wore a garish neon yellow jacket over her regular uniform and her hair was squashed beneath her regulation hat.

'Are you following me?' North felt instantly hostile. She stepped away from Angie, heat creeping across her skin.

'What? No,' Angie's voice remained level and calm. 'We were called out to investigate reports of kids smoking weed in the woods.' She nodded in the direction of the treeline and North noticed a flash of yellow weaving between them. 'I thought I spotted you walking so I wanted to come over.'

'I'm fine.'

Angie cocked her head and looked unconvinced. Since her parents disappeared everyone handled North like she was a grenade. She pushed her hands deeper into her pockets, her mouth set in a hard line.

'Really, Angie, I'm fine. You don't need to follow me.'

'I'm not following you,' Angie reaffirmed. 'I saw you here and was... concerned. You really shouldn't be here.'

'Why not?' North stared heatedly at the officer.

'Because your best friend killed herself just up ahead. I figured it'd be too painful for you to visit the woods.'

North sunk into the depths of her hood. Angie was right. It was painful being in the woods. With each glance, she found herself wondering about Kelly, about what exactly had happened out here amongst the trees. Had there been a struggle? Or had Kelly willingly let someone wrap a noose around her neck? If only North could decipher the whisper of the leaves, maybe then she'd find some answers.

'Do you need a ride home or—' Angie was pointing back along the jogging trail when North interrupted her.

'I want to see it. I want to see where she died.'

'You sure?'

'Yes.'

Kelly had been born in the same maternity unit as North. Both of their mothers had pushed and sweated in the same NHS hospital just a few months apart. The aged St. Helen's Hospital just outside of town was where Kelly's life began. Here within the dense woods that bordered a jogging trail was where it ended. On foot you could journey between the two points in less than an hour. Such a small circuit for a girl who lived such a big life. North needed to see where it all ended, where her best friend's star had eventually burned out.

'Come on then,' Angie sighed but didn't object. She accompanied North further along the trail. Several more dog walkers passed by, only this time they didn't offer a polite nod, presumably because of North's police escort. She walked like she was in a dream, her legs carrying her there with no direction, as though she were merely following a set of pre-ordained steps in a play and was incapable of placing a foot wrong.

A giant oak was up ahead, dwarfing the other trees around it. Thick branches reached out like suspended snakes, twisting and powerful. At the base of the trunk were bunches of flowers, so many of them that it looked as though the grand tree were floating in an ocean of petals. There was no yellow police tape sealing off the crime scene.

'Why isn't it cornered off?' North pointed at the tree, the flowers. 'Angie, this is a *crime scene.* Where is the tape?' Her gaze dropped to the ground. Dozens of footprints were pressed into the soft mud and leaves. 'Fuck. Look at all this!'

'North, this isn't a crime scene.'

'Yes, yes it is. Have you swept the area for DNA? For any kind of evidence at all? Did you check for signs of a struggle? For—'

'Did you hear about the pregnancy?' Angie was maintaining a respectful distance from the tree. From North.

'Yes,' North lowered her hood to push her hands through her hair, feeling caught off guard. Dean had raged about the pregnancy. He'd been given all the reason he needed, now he felt like he understood why Kelly had killed herself. 'But it's not…' Pausing, North held a breath. No one was going to believe her, not now. 'Pregnant or not, Kelly wouldn't do this.'

'It's a pretty strong motive,' Angie gazed at the flowers. 'People handle guilt in different ways.'

'Kelly…' North steeled herself against the oncoming argument, one she was starting to struggle to win even with herself. The judgement in Kelly's eyes when North had told her about Alexander was like being hollowed out like one of her conkers. To Kelly it was all just one awful, huge mistake. She rebuffed any notion of love. Kelly Orton didn't believe in breaking hearts. She wouldn't cheat. She just wouldn't? 'No.'

North shook her head, 'This isn't Kelly. And I've been getting messages.'

'Messages?'

'Yes,' North reached for her phone and began scrolling through it. 'Someone else knows that Kelly didn't do this.' The message was gone. Again. North cursed and shoved her phone back into her pocket. 'It was there, I swear, but it keeps disappearing.'

Angie's voice became soft. 'Are you sleeping okay?'

'Fine, I'm fine.' North felt like she was fifteen years old again defending herself to her overly concerned grandparents.

'Because sometimes when someone is sleep-deprived they might see things that aren't there.'

North's blood froze in her veins. Had Angie been asking around about her, talking to people who might too quickly share unfavourable information? The messages were there, North had seen them, she wasn't hallucinating, not this time.

'I said I'm fine!' North's objection cracked like a whip through the cool air.

'Okay,' Angie raised her hands defensively. 'Like I said, I can show you the pictures from the scene if it'll help with closure.'

'She didn't do this,' North pointed an accusatory finger at the tree which loomed up behind her. It didn't seem possible, the tree so serene, so stoic. It was a creation of nature not a harbinger of death. Besides, it was all just so...wrong. Her friend's essence wasn't here, the air was earthy, scented by damp moss. 'Kelly would not go jogging. Would not hang herself. This isn't her.'

'I heard that you two had grown distant this past year.'

North bristled against the verbal slap Angie had just given her. 'What?'

'It happens. People grow up, they grow apart.'

'Yes, we were a *bit* more distant than usual but we were still close. I still know her. *Knew* her. Better than anyone else.'

'I'm not saying you didn't,' Angie always kept her voice soft, devoid of any threat. 'But, guilt, it can do strange things to people. Maybe you feel guilty that you didn't know that Kelly was suffering, that she was pregnant. Maybe that's why you can't allow yourself to believe that she killed herself.'

'No.' North's head ached with the growing pressure of tears gathering behind her eyes. She couldn't cry. Not here. Not now. To cry by the oak would be to admit that Kelly intentionally died there. Which she didn't. North grasped at her truth, wrapping it around herself, refusing to let it flutter away with the scattering of leaves.

'North, let's take you home and let you get some rest, you looked exhausted. Come on.'

'Why didn't you treat this as a crime scene?'

'Because,' Angie was glancing over her shoulder, probably searching for her colleague. 'Because it was obvious what had happened. We assessed the evidence and drew the most logical conclusion.'

'Were you here? Were you one of the first on scene?'

'No. Kelly had been discovered before my shift started.'

'So you don't know what they initially found?'

'There were pictures taken at the scene. Lots of them. All have been entered into evidence.'

'But a picture could be posed.'

'North—'

'Who made the decision to not protect this tree as a crime scene?'

'The on scene officers. They assess a situation and make that call. It was the right call to make, North. You don't need to be questioning anyone's judgement.'

'Maybe there was something here. Maybe there were signs of a struggle. Something. Only it was removed before the pictures were taken.' North wished she could see beyond the flowers, beyond the countless sets of footprints in the mud. She needed to strip it all back and see the oak tree as it had been that fateful morning when Kelly breathed her last breath.

'I think you've been watching too much TV.' Angie nodded at the jogging trail which led back out of the woods, 'Come on, let's get you home.'

'Is it normal to rule a suicide so quickly? To not bother to sweep a site for evidence?' North stubbornly remained by the tree, pleased that her questions seemed to have given Angie a reason to pause for thought. 'Now the site is tainted. Any clues it held have been trampled away, corrupted by all these flowers.'

'It's not normal,' Angie admitted, pursing her lips. 'I'll give you that. But I think the sensitive nature of the case, what with Kelly being so local and loved, meant that expediency was required. No one wanted what happened to her hanging over their heads. The department moved fast out of respect, that's all.'

'And the autopsy?'

Angie blinked but said nothing.

'That happened with *expediency*, wouldn't you agree? Quite the quick turnaround. You don't suppose someone is keen to have Kelly under the ground? All evidence buried away?'

'I think that the sort of thoughts you're having are only going to torture you.' Angie gave North a smile plump with pity. 'You need to let this go, North. For the sake of your own mental health.'

The branches of the tree creaked as though calling out to another potential victim. North petulantly stumbled over to Angie. Despite being thirty-two she hadn't forgotten how to play the part of a sullen teenager. 'I'm not making any of this up out of guilt,' she insisted as they walked back along the trail.

'You sure about that?' Angie kept her counter question light, breezy.

'Tell me that there's nothing here,' North needled the officer. 'Tell me that I'm completely off base, that there was nothing out of the ordinary about the discovery of Kelly's body.'

Angie stopped and turned to face the younger woman. 'Tell me that it's not impossible that Kelly did this. That you weren't stunned and hurt to discover she was pregnant and hadn't told you about it.'

North winced.

'So, we both have our doubts,' Angie concluded gently.

'But you think I should keep pursuing this? I should keep searching for the truth?'

'I'm not saying yes.' The police car that was parked up just beyond the woods came into view. 'And I'm not saying no. I suggest you do whatever it is that you need to do to help you heal.'

'Were you following me?' North started to slink away from Angie. She didn't want a ride home in a police car. Her neighbours already thought she was strange, so she didn't need to make it worse.

'No. It was merely a coincidence that our paths crossed this afternoon.'

'I like you, Angie. You seem… fair.'

'I knew your mother,' Angie was focused on the car, not on North. 'We were friends once.' There was an ache in her words.

'My mum? You did?'

North's parents had been wild and unpredictable. One week they'd be vegans, the next on a stringent seafood-only diet. They'd host theme nights at their house, making their little girl dress up along with them for vampire night, superhero Saturdays and even tarts and vicars poker club where North was always put in a little nun's habit.

'Get some sleep,' Angie advised. She sounded nothing like North's mother. If she was still around she'd be urging her daughter to follow her conspiracy theories, telling her that she could sleep when she's dead. Passion. It was part of her parents' genetic code, same as it had been with Kelly. It was a trait they'd failed to pass down to North.

'Yeah, I will.' The thought of sleep felt good. The reality would be far different though. Despite the exhaustion which turned her limbs to lead, North knew she'd struggle to close her eyes and drift off.

'You need to sleep,' Angie threw North one final, concerned glance before opening up the car and reaching inside for her radio.

'Sleep is for the weak,' Kelly would say back when they were at university, drunk on cheap alcopops and life. 'Who needs sleep? We're going to dance until dawn.' And they did. Whatever Kelly wanted, she got. She was the captain directing the ship that was North's life. Only instead of going down with the ship, the captain had jumped overboard, surrendered herself to the sea, leaving the ship rudderless and lost in the darkness.

5

It rained the day of Kelly's funeral. A constant drizzle coated Millwater in mist, softened the ground and chilled the air. There had been a service at the small local church. North had sat on the third pew in the little cobbled building with Elijah on one side and Kelly's Aunt Florence on the other. Words were said. Hymns were sung. None of them related to Kelly. The service was stuffy, formal, steeped in archaic traditions that Kelly resented. Where was the colour? The vibrant burst of individuality?

'Are you okay?' It felt like the millionth time Elijah had asked the question since picking North up from her flat. And she kept giving him the same answer.

'No.'

How could she be okay? Was this how people felt during a war, when bombs fell? One minute their life was perfect, all square little houses and ploughed fields. The next there was just chaos. And rubble. Everything had been destroyed. When North looked around, all she saw were the burning embers of her life taking all that was good.

Once the dour service concluded, people drifted out into the cemetery, gathering around the single open grave. The freshly dug earth looked like a sore against all the trimmed grass. Everyone wore black. Everyone looked down at their feet.

Someone was singing. As rain weakly splashed against Kelly's black coffin which had been wheeled out of the church, a raspy voice lifted over the muted sounds of sorrow that escaped through clenched tissues pressed against mouths.

'Bridge Over Troubled Water'. That was the song. And the singer was Kelly's mother. She stood in front of her daughter's grave as her gravelly voice belted out the familiar lyrics. In her moth-eaten blue shawl she was like Joni Mitchell, all cigarettes and sorrow. Her once bleached blonde hair had been frazzled by time and in her hands she waved an e-cigarette, a delayed response to saving her ailing lungs.

Irene Orton was from another time. A time when celebrities were lauded for indulging in sex and drugs along with their rock and roll. She claimed to have slept with Mick Jagger. Twice. Now her dimmed lustre and strained voice spoke of all the nights she'd spent partying, all the shots of whisky she'd thrown down the back of her throat. Irene was so much like North's mother that it hurt. They too had been best friends. North's mother was gone and Irene refused to believe that the party was over. She might as well have been on the boat that never returned for how present she was in Kelly's life. Even on this, the day of her only child's funeral, if you stood too close to her you'd smell the alcohol on her breath. You could excuse it, blame the day, but North knew it was a constant in Irene's life. Drink was a crutch which she regularly leaned on.

'Crap, has she been on the sauce?' Elijah whispered as they approached the collection of black dresses and suits. Long skirts blew softly in the breeze like pirate flags at half-mast.

North looked at Irene who continued with her one-woman concert oblivious to the mourners gathered around her. 'Probably.'

'She must be bereft.'

A howl broke out back towards the church, like someone stepping on a dog. North turned to glance back and saw the very epitome of bereavement. Dean was a broken man. He wasn't in a suit. He looked to be in the same clothes North had seen him in a few days ago. His mother held his elbow and was trying to guide him towards the others, towards the grave, but Dean refused. His face was red, his cheeks swollen and blotchy. He shook his head, gave another sorrowful wail and snatched his arm out of his mother's grasp. With all of his limbs reclaimed he hurried away from the church, in the direction of the waiting black cars which were neatly parked up along the street like dark dominoes.

'I guess it's too much for him.' Elijah's hand found North's elbow. 'Are you okay?'

'No.' She was tired of answering the same question, of being asked over and over if she was okay when surely it was completely obvious to everyone that she wasn't. How could she be?

'Do you want to leave? You got through the service okay. You don't have to stay any longer if it's too… if it's too hard.'

'No, I'll stay.'

Irene was reaching a crescendo in the song. Her arms were lifted at her sides, a note held in her throat. Then it was over and she dropped to her knees, hands sinking into the mud beneath her. She didn't cry. She just stared down into the grave.

'Maybe…' North took a step back. Leaving suddenly felt like an extremely good idea. There was too much emotion around the grave, fraught and sharp. If she wasn't careful she'd get shredded to pieces.

'Say the word and we go.' Elijah's hand remained on North's elbow. It had been so kind of him to offer to come. He knew Kelly, but not well. She was someone he'd exchange pleasantries with at the supermarket, nothing more. He'd put on a suit for the occasion. A slim-fitting black one with a skinny navy tie. He looked handsome, even with the rain soaking into his curls, making them springier than ever.

It had rained the day they held a funeral for North's parents too. Only the coffins wheeled out on that day were just for show. As they were lowered into the ground, few wept. Perhaps some still held on to the belief that the Stones would return. That one day they'd miraculously stumble back into Millwater, all long-haired and full of stories about their brutal survival against nature on a desert island. For North, the coffins might as well have contained her parents. She knew they weren't coming back. Whatever adventure they'd been on before, be it climbing Everest or trekking through the rainforest, they always came home. They would never abandon her indefinitely. Only death had prevented their final return.

'I'm…' North pulled away from Elijah, away from the group and drifted between the headstones, moving towards a place of painful familiarity.

'You'll always have me,' that's what Kelly had whispered the day of North's parents' faux funeral. The girls had held hands as they stood at the head of the dual graves, watching impassively as the empty caskets were lowered down.

'North, you okay?'

'I need you to stop asking me if I'm okay.' She kept her head bowed towards the headstone in front of her as she spoke formally, in a matter of fact way. Elijah held back a respectful distance.

'I'm sorry, I just—'

'They didn't mean to leave me,' North rested a hand on the wet granite stone which bore her parents' names and the date of their disappearance. 'They would have come back if they could. And Kelly wouldn't leave me either.' Her gaze flickered back over to the sea of black outfits. Now that Irene had ceased singing the priest was concluding his service, speaking about ashes and dust, which North figured sounded better than rot and decay which was actually the fate which awaited all who were buried.

'People were talking in the post office. I heard about the pregnancy.'

'News travels fast in our shit-tip town.'

'It wasn't Dean's.'

'Nice to see that the resident gossips in Millwater are staying classy. No, it wasn't Dean's,' North felt a storm growing within herself. 'But this isn't the 1950s. There's no shame attached to infidelity. Just because it wasn't Dean's bloody baby doesn't mean she's some scarlet woman. She didn't do what she did out of *guilt*.'

'Then why did she do it?' He needled gently.

'Someone did it to her! How can no one else see that?'

Elijah said nothing, his blue eyes continuing to hold North in a steady gaze. She listened to the gentle drumming of the rain falling against her leather jacket, her skinny jeans. She wore all black but she looked like she was headed for a rock concert instead of a funeral. Irene would approve. And Kelly would have too.

'Look, North—'

'You came!' Irene was weaving amongst the headstones, trampling over graves with careless abandon as she made her way towards North, arms outstretched. Her own skirt was stained with mud, as were her hands. 'Oh, dear North, I wasn't sure you'd make it.'

'I wanted to be here.'

Irene embraced her. Pulling her close and holding her against her ample bosom. North smelt the whisky, the smoke. The sorrow.

'This funeral was a fucking travesty.' Another thing about Irene – she spoke like a trucker. Something else she had in common with North's late mother. 'I mean, Kel wouldn't have wanted any of this. Bloody joke. She was an atheist for crying out loud!'

'So why the service?'

'Him,' Irene released North and tightened her damp shawl around her shoulders. 'He requested a burial. Said he couldn't bear the thought of her being cremated. Of her not *existing* anymore. Not that she exists now. Not really.' Reaching into her pocket, Irene retrieved her e-cigarette and took a long drag on it.

'Dean pushed for the burial?' North didn't try to conceal her surprise.

'I know, right? The bastard has been busy playing the victim since the whole pregnancy thing came out. Then he turns around and says he can't bear to have her cremated. Makes no bloody sense. But, you know,' Irene gave a weary shrug, 'Kelly was more his than mine in the end, I felt he should make the decision on how to deal with her...her body.'

'When did he decide this?'

'A few days ago.'

'Huh,' North chewed her lip.

'What's going on in there?' Leaning forward, Irene tapped her finger against North's forehead. 'You were always the smart one, the thinker. While Kel always acted on a whim you'd think everything through. Still waters definitely run deep with you, North.'

'I'm thinking it's good that he wanted her buried.'

'Really?' Irene's slim eyebrows shot up as her forehead crinkled. 'I was sure you'd be an ashes kind of girl. More pragmatic long-term and all that.'

'If Kelly is buried it means she still exists. That there's still evidence.'

'Evidence?' Irene's eyes narrowed and North feared she'd made a mistake. Irene was a volatile woman at the best of times and now she was a grieving mother, giving her the perfect stage for her random bouts of dramatics. But she was still a mother. And North couldn't help but be drawn to the echoes of her own lost parents that lingered in Irene, in her outlandish ways.

'I just… I don't think she killed herself. It's not Kelly. Dean isn't the father of her baby but someone is.'

'True,' Irene slowly turned back in the direction of the mourners still gathered in the far side of the cemetery. 'And Dean has quite a temper, doesn't he?'

'I…' North floundered, 'I mean…'

'Quite a stocky fellow. Could throw a fair punch if he wanted to.' Irene's gaze sharpened as she turned back to North. 'Did you ever get the impression that she feared him?'

'Feared… feared who? Dean?'

'Yes. Dean.'

North was shaking her head before any words came out of her mouth. 'What? No. Kelly didn't fear anyone. She was brave in the face of absolutely anything.'

'To commit suicide is a brave act, not a fearful one, don't you think?'

'But she didn't do this,' North was growing tired of being a record on repeat. 'You're her mother, you have to feel that way too!'

'I like how you think, North,' Irene's red-stained lips wilted into a sad smile. She blinked back tears as her eyes became as misted as the rain-soaked morning. 'You refuse to accept what's in front of you. You question things.'

'I was—'

'You are the only person who will feel her loss as deeply as I will.' Irene embraced her again, harder this time. 'I know that you'll keep her alive. In your thoughts. Your memories.'

'Yes. Yes of course.'

'And now we're both alone,' Irene stepped away, shoulder drooping. 'She meant so much to us both.'

'Irene!' A tear-streaked mourner was calling up the row of gravestones.

Irene turned with a swish of damp fabric and theatrically raced over to them.

'You know, you're not alone.' Elijah stepped closer to North, closer to her parents' grave.

'I…' Closing her eyes, she breathed in the damp earth. The world smelt rich and fertile. North felt the chill of the day settling beneath her clothes, pressing against her skin.

'You're shaking,' Elijah observed with concern as he hastily wrapped his arm around her shoulders. 'Come on, let's get you somewhere warm and dry.'

North let him guide her away from the grave, from all the other mourners. He took her along the street, towards his little vintage Morris Minor.

'Do you want to go to the Dog and Hare?' Placing the keys in the ignition, he turned to look at North.

She was staring down at her phone, willing the phantom message from the unknown sender back into existence. Each time she wanted to show it to someone, to discuss it, it was gone.

People would soon be gathering at the little pub. Bowls of crisps would be served alongside triangle cheese and ham sandwiches. Stories of Kelly would be passed around like a parcel at a kid's party. There would be tears. Laughter. As the drinks flowed, the crowd would thin until only the truly loyal were left standing, the ones who were lost without Kelly; North and Irene. In time everyone else would move on. Even Dean. But daughters and soul sisters are irreplaceable. You are fortunate if you get one during a lifetime. But North couldn't do it, couldn't let that little reality play out. Her heart wasn't strong enough to endure it. At the end of the night Irene would have to be propping up the bar alone.

'I'd like to go home,' North stared at the dashboard of the car. The engine chugged noisily as Elijah pulled away from the curb.

'Home it is.'

They drove through town, past all the sites which had become landmarks in North's life with Kelly. Almost every lamp post told a story.

'That was where we used the post as a wicket in cricket during the summer.'

'We tried to climb that lamp post and Kelly sprained her ankle when she fell.'

'I threw up behind there after trying absinthe for the first time.'

She wasn't sure if she was sharing her memories with Elijah or just herself. He didn't speak up, he just kept driving.

With the heat in the little car turned all the way up, the shaking stopped. North was still damp but no longer cold. It felt like a betrayal to find any sort of comfort these days. She wanted to be back in the graveyard, shivering and wet.

'It is weird,' Elijah commented as he turned into the car park for North's block of flats. 'About the burial thing.'

'You think?'

'Would Kelly have wanted to be buried? Do you know?'

'She used to say that if she died she wanted her ashes scattered on Robbie Williams' lawn. I'm not sure he'd approve though.'

'We could have done it at night, when no one was about.' Elijah smiled cheekily at her. She hadn't noticed before how mischievous he could look. It gave his youthful appearance a dangerous hint of manliness which really suited him. Not that she was about to say as much.

'Sounds like Dean called the shots on the whole thing. I imagine Irene's too distraught to fight him on anything.'

'Like you said though, evidence.'

North turned so quickly in her seat that she almost made herself dizzy. 'What?'

A blush crept up Elijah's freshly shaven cheeks. 'I mean, I was thinking about what you said. About Kelly not having killed herself. She was pregnant. We know that. But no one knows who the father was, and no one seems to want to find out.'

'And you think that's weird?'

'Don't you?'

North nodded eagerly. 'Yes, yes I do.'

'I reckon no one is looking into it because it would be seen as disrespectful. Better to let sleeping dogs lie and all that.'

'But there has to be a father.'

'Exactly.' Elijah's blue eyes glistened like two sapphire lined beacons of hope and North couldn't stop staring into them. 'The question is, who is he?'

6

The world at the end of the telescope was all darkness and light. It was beautiful. North peered up at the universe, at the black canvas of space speckled with diamonds. Each diamond a star burning distant and bright. Many of the stars she was looking out were long gone, burned out in a previous millennia.

Who is he?

Elijah's question tugged at North as she leaned back in her seat. She looked at the computer monitors around her. They were all humming a flat note as data danced across their screens. She scrutinised the nearest set of numbers and then with a click of her mouse pulled up a chart. Drawing in close to her desk, she watched how the flow of the chart rose like a wave. It had to mean that—

'I didn't expect to see you here.'

North blinked and turned away from the computers. Alexander's footsteps were harsh against the metal staircase as he approached the base of the vast telescope they all worked around. With the viewing roof open it was cold in the observatory. North was sat in her thickest coat, a threadbare blanket pulled up to her knees.

'This is my shift.' She took care when replying to him, making sure her voice remained level, her tone indifferent. It was an act she'd been working on for weeks, since the ground beneath them had shifted back to a professional base.

'I know but someone could have covered it for you.'

He was lingering around the data station, dressed in a long black wool coat and thick navy plaid scarf. In his hand he clutched a takeaway coffee from the twenty-four-hour service station down the road. No, two coffees. North clocked the second one as he drew closer. He extended it towards her, the drink held in his leather-gloved hand. An olive branch.

'I'm good, thanks.' Her jaw clenched as she returned her focus to the chart on the nearest screen. She could smell the coffee, its oaky aroma blending with the frigid evening air.

'It's a caramel latte with two sugars. Your favourite.'

'I thought you didn't expect to see me here?' The question sounded more like an accusation.

Alexander shrugged and gave her a wry smile as he placed one of the coffees on the desk beside her.

'I knew this was your shift,' he admitted, folding himself into the vacant chair to North's right. 'But I didn't expect to see you here. Like I said, someone would have covered for you.'

'I don't want anyone covering for me. I want to be here.'

'Drink your coffee.'

'No,' the word lashed from her lips like a whip. Then, softer, 'Thanks.'

'You having trouble sleeping again?' Alexander asked casually as he lifted his own drink to his mouth.

It was late. Midnight had ticked by a few hours ago. North was glad to be behind the telescope during this time. When everyone else was sleeping, she was observing the universe. Dreams were just dreams. She was spending her nights looking at something truly wondrous. It was within science that true magic existed. At least, that's how North felt.

'I know what Kelly meant to you.' Alexander was drawing closer, edging his seat towards hers. When his knee grazed North's she flinched.

'I'm sleeping just fine,' she snapped, raising a finger towards the computer screen. 'This is the data that has been collected over the last month, it seems to show that—'

'I'm worried about you.'

He was still so close. Too close. She could smell his cologne. The coffee on his breath. Why had he bothered to drive out to the service station? He hadn't done that for ages. Normally he just got her a coffee from the vending machine back in the demountable, same as he did for everyone else. Why was he suddenly showing her such kindness?

Because of Kelly.

North bit down on her lip and stared at the chart until all the numbers began to blur together. Alexander was being kind because she'd lost her best friend. And he could be kind. It wasn't so long ago that he'd—

'I can tell you're not sleeping.'

His words derailed North's train of thought. Jarred, she turned to look at him. 'Can we just focus on work, please?'

'I noticed you've taken all the night shifts for the rest of the month. Last time you did that we were—'

'Look, here,' North pointed at the peak in the flow chart. 'The supernova is getting brighter. If it continues to explode at its current rate it might be visible to the naked eye within the next ten years.'

'We need to determine if it's a gravitational shift that has caused it to collapse,' Alexander was finally playing along, looking at the chart with interest.

'It looks likely.'

'And we need to develop a theoretical future for the supernova. Will there be a black star there moving forwards or might some new stars be formed?'

'It's a big explosion.'

'Which will mean a big core.'

'A lot of displaced energy.'

It felt comfortable to talk with Alexander like this. About science. About the stars. It was like putting on one of your favourite old songs and remembering all the dance moves, remembering how good it used to feel to stand on sticky floors in sweaty night clubs thrashing them out.

'This is all really great work, North.'

His hand suddenly found her shoulder. Squeezed it. North wanted to scream. The nostalgic bubble that had formed around them burst. Why did he always have to keep pushing? Have to keep stepping over the lines she'd so clearly drawn around herself?

'It's been a team effort.' Could he feel how tense she was beneath his touch?

'I am seriously worried about you though, North.'

'Don't be.'

'Your best friend died and now you're not sleeping. You're not…. seeing things are you?'

'Alex, don't worry about it.'

'Because if you are then there're people who can help. Things we can do. Take some time off. Take as much as you need.'

'Do you not want me here or something?' North felt a lump rising in her throat. The observatory was her spiritual home. When she looked up at the stars she felt removed from herself, from all her troubles.

'Look, it's not that it's—'

'Is this about her? This is my job, Alex. I'm here to work. Nothing else.'

'North, yes, I know,' his hand didn't leave her shoulder as his voice became firmer. Deeper. 'And all this is about is my concern for you. I care about you. That will never change.

You've lost Kelly, I think you need to take some time to process that.'

'To say I lost her makes it sound like I misplaced her or something.'

'Words won't do justice to how you're feeling. Take some time to heal, North.'

'I want to work.'

'When your parents disappeared you never really grieved. Sometimes in the night you'd call out for them and then there were those times when you'd scream and swear blind that—'

'We made a promise to keep things professional.' North was growing cold. The blanket and her coat were no longer enough to fight off the ice in the air. Memories surrounded Alexander like a tainted aura.

'North.' He said her name so tenderly. So sweetly. As though she were the only star he saw in the night sky. But it wasn't real. She knew that now. Reaching forward, she snatched her gift of a coffee and drew it up towards her lips, needing its warmth, its sweetness. 'I can't switch off caring about you. Take some time off.'

'I don't need to.' The caramel coffee slid down her throat like liquid velvet. It was intoxicatingly delicious.

'I refuse to watch you spiral again. You need to sleep. To rest. To face your feelings on this.'

'I need to work.'

'Don't go beating yourself up about what happened. Kelly would have had her reasons for doing what she did.'

The coffee turned bitter in her mouth. It took some effort for North to swallow it down. Scowling, she put down her cup. 'You know nothing about what happened.'

'I know but—'

'And you know nothing about me.'

'Fine,' Alexander studied her face for a moment too long and then got up. 'Just promise me you'll try and get some sleep.'

'I'll do my job. I can promise that.'

'I'm here if you want to talk.'

'I won't.'

'I mean it, North. We can just talk, nothing else. I don't want you to shut me out completely.'

'I should never have let you in.'

She heard Alexander release a pained sigh as he walked back down the staircase, each step bouncing off the vast walls of the observatory, echoing back at North.

*

Someone was shouting. Something about their dad. About cigarettes. With a groan, North rolled onto her side and promptly fell off the sofa. Coarse carpet fibres dug into her cheek and hands.

'Dammit.' Slowly she used the sofa to claw herself back into a sitting position. The television was on. A film was playing. It took her a few seconds to register that it was *The Breakfast Club*. She gave a dry laugh. Her shift at the observatory was over. She'd come home and dropped on the sofa and put on a relevant movie. Everyone was having breakfast at this time and so her choice had felt easy to make.

Was the film on a loop? So often she set up her movies to just play over and over. The familiarity of the dialogue and music sometimes helped her drift off to sleep.

Who is he?

The question was present in all her waking moments.

With a grunt she stood up, stretching out the knots that had formed in her back. She really needed to think about trying to sleep in her bed.

On the TV the characters were still shouting. Trapped together on a Saturday morning, they were a group of mismatched teenagers with more in common than they thought. North regarded them with blurry eyes. She *was* tired. Exhaustion pulled on her wrists, her neck, making her feel cumbersome and heavy. Like living in shackles. Where did she fit amongst the stereotypes of the groups in the film?

'I'm the princess.' Kelly had said this with complete certainty after their first viewing of it almost twenty years ago. She delivered the statement as a fact, not an opinion. She was the princess. It was as obvious as saying that the sky was blue or that mountains are high.

'I'm…' North didn't know who she was with such clarity. She saw glimpses of herself in each of the characters. Even the princess. Though she knew better than to admit that to Kelly since only one of them could wear a crown.

'You're the basket case.' The statement was factual, like commenting that sugar was sweet.

'I am?'

'Yeah, totally. But it's a good thing, North. It makes you quirky. And the princess and the basket case are best friends by the end of the movie. That's us.'

North turned her back to the television as she wandered over to her little kitchenette.

'The basket case,' she muttered her label to herself. Did it fit?

Yawning North stretched her hands up over her head. She couldn't remember the last time she'd slept in her bed. The whole of Millwater thought she was crazy. What if they were right? Choosing to deflect from herself North's thoughts circled back around to the most pressing question, the paternity of Kelly's unborn baby.

Who is he?

Dean wasn't the father of Kelly's baby but someone was. An ex-boyfriend? A colleague? A neighbour? Who? If North hadn't known about the pregnancy what else did she not know about? Some affair? Some tryst?

North poured herself a bowl of cereal and thoughtfully tapped her spoon against the rim. She went back over to the sofa and sat cross-legged against the cushions.

Who is he?

Elijah seemed just as curious as she was about the identity of the baby's father. Kelly was in the ground now but the evidence from the autopsy, the DNA of her unborn child, that still existed, right?

Who is he?

New Year's Eve. It was the last time North and Kelly had truly laughed together. Had truly been themselves. The months that followed had been hard on them both. North had made a huge mistake and Kelly had fled for the summer, off on another one of her adventures.

'I'm taking a job on a yacht,' she'd casually told North over cocktails.

'For how long?'

'Three months.'

'Three months?' North almost choked on her mojito. 'Fuck, Kelly, that long?'

'Yeah.' Kelly squared her shoulders, a cool smile on her lips. The distance between them grew from a crevice to a canyon. How could North have disappointed her friend so savagely? And why couldn't she stop doing it?

'Three months? I can't be without you that long.'

'You'll manage.'

'Kelly, I'll—'

'Maybe you'll use the time to come to your senses. To stop being so bloody stupid. I can't stay around here and watch you hurt yourself like this all summer long. Besides, I need an adventure. Working on this yacht will be fabulous. Thrilling. And when I come back hopefully we'll both be a bit different.'

'Kel, I never meant to—'

'I don't want to hear about it. Remember?'

'So you going away, it's because of me?'

Kelly sighed dramatically. 'It's because of *me* , North. Because I need a goddamn adventure. Stop stressing over this. Don't overthink it. You always overthink things.'

'Yeah,' North winced against the pressure weighing down on her chest. She'd let down her best friend. She doubted if there were any greater pain. She needed to stop overthinking, to be more in the moment. To be more like Kelly. 'So the yacht,' the previous three mojitos in her system made it easier to turn off her negative emotions, to flip to a sunnier disposition. 'Tell me more about it.'

'It's owned by Spencer Daniels.'

'The playboy?'

'Uh-huh. His family are like a bloody dynasty because of all those diamonds they found when drilling for oil. But he's more than just a playboy, he's quite the philanthropist.' Kelly's eyes widened with admiration. 'He gave over a million pounds to cancer research last year and just last month he did a sponsored sky dive.'

'Will there be much travel involved?'

'So much,' Kelly gushed excitedly. 'I'll be like a pirate. Only glamorous. We'll sail around the Mediterranean and all I have to do is wait on some rich stiffs.'

'And Dean?'

'He won't be there.' Kelly downed the last of her cocktail.

'I mean, won't he miss you.'

'He's like you,' Kelly eyed her friend with disdain. 'He needs time to cool off and think about what he's done.'

'So you're mad at him too?'

'Yep.'

'What did he do?'

Kelly was silent.

'But you won't be mad at us forever, will you?'

'You, no,' Kelly's face softened as she smiled. 'Him,' she shrugged playfully, 'maybe.'

'I'm going to miss you so much.'

'I know. And I'll miss you too. But when I come back hopefully things will have played out. This…thing…you're entertaining you need to stop it on your own terms, I can't end it for you. I also can't stand around and watch you hurt yourself. You can't keep doing what you're doing forever you know.'

'I know.'

'Someone is going to get seriously hurt.'

'Kel, I *know*.'

'I just don't want it to be you, North. I never want to see you get hurt again.'

7

North had not invited the distance which crept between her and Kelly, kept them separate. Phone calls were shortened, text messages became blunt. All because of one thing. One thing that became many things and—

She slapped her empty cereal bowl down against the countertop with bone-jarring force. The ceramic held its shape. Barely. North had driven Kelly away. She'd lied to herself, cited again and again that it was Kelly's lust for adventure that had stolen her away that summer but North had to take some of the blame. She knew her friend disapproved of what was going on at work and still she acted, still she dared to defy her. Like Icarus, after Kelly had given her wings she flew too close to the sun. When she came crashing down to earth, Kelly wasn't there to protect her, to hold her as she wept. Kelly was off on some yacht, handing millionaires their martinis.

The last year was a gap in a previously perfect timeline, dragging everything down, tainting what surrounded it.

The last year.

North drummed her fingertips against the countertop, the cogs in her mind whirring furiously. She should have been heading to bed, trying to get some much-needed sleep, but how could she sleep when her mind was on fire?

The last year.

She became a whirling dervish as she swept around her small flat, throwing open drawers and hastily rummaging through their contents. She grabbed pens, Post-its, pictures, receipts, scraps of paper. Everything within her reach was dropped in the centre of the floor in front of the fireplace. Then she went to work.

An hour slipped by. Then another. North was focused on the one wall in her home, oblivious of everything else around it. She made frantic scribbles on Post-its, tacked up sun-kissed pictures of Kelly in rare moments of solitude when North had been the one behind the camera. It felt strange to see her friend alone when so often they were a duo.

The wall became a collage of dates, times, notes and pictures. North tacked everything up with tape, slapping more and more information against the beige paint of the wall. When she finally stepped back to admire her handiwork, she saw the year stretching out before her from New Year's Eve to the day of Kelly's death. Question marks upon Post-its were scars on the timeline. North gazed at them in turn.

Kelly and Dean were having trouble before her summer trip. *Why?*

Kelly was pregnant. There had to be a father. *Who?*

At some point Kelly must have known she was in danger. *When?*

Whoever had a hand in her death must still be out there. *Where?*

Exhausted, North collapsed onto her sofa. Her head throbbed. There were so many questions to which she had no answer. And she knew that it was within those answers she'd find the truth about what really happened to Kelly.

*

The door. There was someone at the door.

North stiffly lifted herself up off the sofa. It was dark in the flat. The sun was low in the sky and thick shadows gathered all around her.

'Urgh,' North rubbed her eyes, yawned, stretched out her arms. Had she been sleeping? She remembered being on the sofa, feeling tired, thinking about Kelly and then nothing after that. She must have managed to doze off. Already she could feel a tightness in her back. Her body wouldn't forgive her for forsaking her bed yet again. She did really need to snatch some decent rest when she could.

The knocking at the door persisted.

Was it Dean again banging on her flimsy front door, keen to engage in another shouting match?

'I'm coming.' There was more gravel in her voice than she'd expected.

After twisting open the latch, North pulled on her door and found Elijah standing on the other side of it, smiling sheepishly. His hands were hidden in the deep pockets of his Superdry jacket.

'Crap, sorry North, did I wake you?'

'What? No?' She staggered back into her flat and realised how dark it was compared to the garish neon brilliance of the main corridor. She flicked on a few lights and tugged her fingertips through her dark waves, hoping her hair wasn't gathered too wildly around her head.

'I just wondered if you wanted a lift to work. We're on the same shift tonight.' Elijah was following her inside. 'I did call but you didn't answer so I figured I'd just swing by and—' He stopped in front of the wall, eyes wide.

'Shit,' North winced and pushed a pained breath through her teeth.

'Wow. This is...'

North hugged her arms against herself and waited for his conclusion.

Mad.

Crazy.

Psychotic.

When he next looked at her would she see a glimmer of fear in his eyes?

'Thorough,' Elijah gave a thoughtful nod and stepped closer to the wall, sweeping his gaze along the length of the debris.

'It's… I was just…' North scratched at her lower arms. It felt good to rake her nails across her bare skin.

'Is this all for this year?'

'Uh-huh. Yeah.'

'Why this year?' He turned his body to look at her.

'I…' North gestured half-heartedly at the wall, feeling her shame burning upon her cheeks. 'Kel and I drifted a bit this year. Things… happened. I'm trying to piece things together. Trying to understand what happened when we weren't so close.'

'What happened between you two?'

Elijah sounded so genuinely concerned. North didn't want to lie to him but she also didn't want him to see her for what she was.

'I made a mistake.' Her voice was too small for such a grand admission. And mistake felt like she was devaluing what had happened, like she was calling a tsunami a slight wave.

'Oh?'

'Kel was…' North dug her nails deeper into the forearms. 'She was mad at me. At least for a while. She forgave me eventually.'

'Is that why she went away?' Elijah leaned forward to tap the point on the timeline when Kelly left for her summer job.

North's cheeks burned fiercer when she noticed how close Elijah was to the note about Dean. Would he judge her for delving into her late friend's business? If he saw it he, said nothing.

'She was gone for three months?' he moved on from his previous question.

'I think just over two in the end.'

'She came back early?' Elijah was gazing at the wall, assessing all the manically accumulated data. He could almost be at the observatory studying the luminosity of a star. Data was all they ever had to go on. They used it to track the past, present and future of the night sky.

'A bit early, yeah.'

'Do you know why?'

'No,' there was an ache in North's chest. Secrets. They were circling her like vultures, making ominous figures of eight overhead as they waited to pick her off completely. Where there had been none, it now felt like there were dozens of secrets, so much which Kelly had kept from her. But why? 'She never said why she came back early. She was... kind of distant when she returned.'

'Because of your... mistake?' Elijah suggested carefully.

'Partly.'

'How were things with her boyfriend when she left?'

'They were...' North paused. Kelly had always been so transparent about her relationship with Dean, about her suspicions, their arguments. It seemed tempestuous but nothing more. Yet Irene had asked if Kelly feared Dean and now North felt caught on a carousel of doubt. He *was* strong and quick to temper. But that didn't amount to him being able to—

'North, are you okay?' Abandoning the wall, Elijah strode over to her. 'All this, I mean, I get that you've got stuff on your mind and all but—'

'We're going to be late for work,' she dashed away from him, towards her bedroom. 'It's my fault, I'm sorry, I overslept,' she shouted through the thin door as she desperately searched the pile of clothes strewn atop her bed for something suitable, and clean, to wear.

'It's all right, I can just work this shift on my own if—'

'No.' North was panting, adjusting the emerald woollen jumper she'd just pulled on with a pair of pale denim skinny jeans. 'Honestly I'd rather be at work. Staying here on my own is driving me mad.'

She looked at her manic wall as she followed Elijah towards the front door. Her hand hovered over the light switch before she plunged her flat into darkness.

*

It was getting colder. With the roof open, the temperature within the observatory was sliding towards freezing. When winter came, the opportunities to survey the supernova would begin to dwindle. Automated sweeps of the night sky would replace humanly powered ones. It happened every year.

'I don't mind the cold,' North would tell Alexander. 'I want to keep up my night shifts.'

'I'm not having you catch pneumonia for the sake of stargazing.'

'I'll wrap up extra warm. I'll drink coffee constantly.'

'It's not up for discussion.'

Alexander shelved so many things that way, by removing them from being up for discussion.

'I remember the first time I looked through a telescope,' Elijah leaned back, a wistful smile on his face. A soft curtain of moonlight fell through the opening above them, bathing their workspace in a silvery glow.

'When was it? Your first time?' There was a cheekiness in North's question which she hadn't intended to include. She sank back in her chair, embarrassed.

Elijah's smile didn't dull.

'My granddad had a telescope out in his potting shed, at the end of his garden. I remember one night, I must have been about seven, he asked me if I'd like to see something amazing. Of course I said yes. He led me down between the rows of cabbages and snap peas towards this little shed. It was such a perfectly clear night, not a cloud in the sky. Anyway, he showed me his telescope, lowered the lens and told me to take a look.'

'And you liked what you saw?'

'I *loved* what I saw,' Elijah's smile was full of awe. 'It was the moon. Big and bright and beautiful and completely different to how I'd seen it before. I could see every crater, every mark on its surface. Over the years, it became as familiar to me as my granddad's face was. I couldn't get enough of it. This... this thing which had felt so far away, so unobtainable, was there for me to see. It was exquisite.'

'Magical,' North whispered with reverence.

'Yeah, magical.'

The computers hummed their flat melody as they churned through all the information being fed to them via the grand telescope.

'What about you?' Elijah's chair squeaked beneath him as he straightened and peered back up towards the lens. 'When was your first time?' he smirked to himself as he asked the question, which caused North to blush.

'I...' She felt a splinter in her heart. This was a story that had previously belonged only to Kelly, had been told to her ears and hers alone.

'You don't have to tell me.' Elijah's tone remained warm. 'First times are special. Secret.'

'I was six.' The memory floated up to the surface of North's mind untainted by time. She couldn't help but smile when she thought of the little flat she'd lived in with her parents, of all the chaotic parties which involved all the neighbours. It felt like living in a rainbow. 'It was my dad's thirtieth birthday party and our flat was rammed. Like, shoulder to shoulder packed, it was manic. I was like an imp at six and even I felt squashed. So I snuck out to the roof for some space. I found the guy from the flat above us there, his name was Arthur. He was peering through his telescope and asked if I'd like to take a look.'

'And it was love at first sight, right?'

'Actually, I was scared,' North admitted, feeling shy but enjoying how the embers from her memory warmed her. 'I looked through the lens and saw something burning. It was brilliant and vast and suspended in... nothing. I had tears in my eyes when I looked back at Arthur, but he told me not to be afraid. That we are all part of something bigger than ourselves and that the elements that make up me are the same elements that make up the stars. We're all connected.'

'That's a lot for a six-year-old to take in.'

'True,' North laughed.

'What happened to Arthur?'

'He died the following year.' Suddenly North's memory wasn't keeping her quite so warm. Arthur was her first adult friend, the first person in the flats who didn't look at her as a nuisance or a burden. He took the time to talk to her, to actually talk to her. He lent her books on astronomy and left his telescope up on the roof on clear nights so that she could wander up and look through it.

'That sucks.'

'He left me his telescope.'

'He did? That was kind of him.'

'I guess I have him to thank for my love of the stars.'

'What about your parents? Didn't they name you after a star?'

'They did,' North frowned. 'But… they liked the idea of the stars. They didn't really get them. My parents had a new obsession each week. There was a fondue phase which ended when my dad burnt himself on some cheese. There was an origami phase. Ooh, and for two whole months we were Buddhists. So I guess I'm lucky they named me after a star instead of calling me Edam or Cheddar.'

'Your parents sound like they were… eclectic.' Elijah was one of the few people who'd chosen Millwater as a destination. He came for the observatory, hadn't grown up hearing the stories of the infamous Stones. North found his ignorance about her past refreshing.

'More like crazy. They had a real passion for life. A thirst for adventure. Something I definitely didn't inherit from them.'

'Do you wish you had?' Elijah pushed himself away from the telescope lens so that North could look through it. She pulled her chair into the vacated spot and considered his question.

'No, I mean…' She looked at her hands, hidden in thick purple gloves that her grandmother had knitted for her the last winter that it snowed. 'The thing with going off on loads of adventures is that you always leave someone behind. That's what I didn't like about them.'

'Do you feel like Kelly left you behind? When she went away this summer?'

'Yeah,' a single tear slid down North's cheek. She quickly brushed it away before Elijah could see it glistening in the moonlight.

And she left me behind when she died.

The ultimate adventure. Kelly had finally gone where North couldn't follow.

'When someone has a thirst for adventure it just means that they want to experience things. It's nothing to do with you,' Elijah's hand gently rested atop her own as it idled on her knee. She didn't push him away.

'But each time my parents went away it made me feel like I wasn't enough. Like they wanted to get away from me.'

'North it wouldn't have—'

'And it's the same with Kelly. She made me feel left behind. She made me feel abandoned.'

8

'You're back early.'

It was the first few days of August. A dead heat had settled over Millwater, baking the brickwork of all the clustered houses. No breeze whispered through the trees and grass that had once been green curled into itself becoming shrivelled and brown. All nature's lustre and vibrancy in the town had been burnt away.

Kelly sat beside North on the park bench staring fixedly at the little playground in the distance. The metal of the children's slide sparkled as brightly as a sun. No one was playing. The slide was empty. As was the seesaw and the climbing frame. The swing set. Cautious parents were keeping their children out of the midday heat.

North was thankful for the large oak tree behind the bench which provided some much-needed shade. But even outside of the direct glare of the sun it was too hot. Sweat gathered behind her knees, along her neck.

The playground was empty and yet Kelly still kept staring at it as though she were waiting for a familiar face to step into the sunshine and greet her.

'I said you're back early,' North repeated.

'Um, yeah,' Kelly lowered her head a fraction, letting her chin dip towards her chest. 'A few weeks early, I guess.'

'How come?' North chewed on the words she wasn't saying. She wanted answers. Forgiveness. But this was the first time she'd seen Kelly in months; she wasn't about to behave like a bull in a china shop and risk scaring her off. The Kelly that met her in the park wasn't the one she'd been expecting. This Kelly wore a long sundress and thick black sunglasses. She seemed pale despite her time spent working in exotic locations, and rather than bursting at the seams to reveal all about her adventures she was subdued. Everything about home seemed to overwhelm her.

'Kel, you can tell me anything. You know that, right?'

'Right.' Kelly's response was nothing more than an exhaled breath.

'It's over, everything with—'

'I figured you'd see sense eventually.' Kelly turned and smiled but her eyes remained hidden behind her thick glasses. Looking at her friend, North saw only her own anxious reflection in the dual oval mirrors of the shades. 'I hope you didn't get too hurt.'

'I let you down,' North looked at her hands, at her bare arms which were reddened with the track marks of her nails. 'You expected more of me and—'

'You didn't let me down. It's okay.'

'But it's why you went away. Because I let you down.'

'North,' Kelly pushed her sunglasses up onto her head, pushing back her golden hair to reveal tired eyes. 'I didn't leave to… to punish you. I'd never do that. I just needed to get away. My time spent on the yacht this summer was more about me than you.'

'So you're not mad at me?'

'I was.'

Things between them were starting to feel easier, more familiar, like stepping back into a pair of old shoes which instantly fit in all the right places. North felt bold enough to be honest.

'I should have listened to you. These last few months without you here have been just awful. You barely called and—'

'Let's not talk about it,' Kelly clamped her hands down over North's.

'What?'

'This summer. What I did. What you did. I don't want to talk about it.'

'But,' North pulled her hands out from under her friend's grasp, 'you always talk about everything. You say that discussion is the cornerstone to reconciliation. You're forever forcing me to discuss my feelings.'

'Well, we don't need to about this.'

'You're still mad at me, aren't you? That's what this is about.' The premature sense of familiarity, of safety, began to sour.

'Jesus, North!' Kelly got up and began storming away from the bench, her long cotton dress sweeping out behind her.

North chased after her, refusing to abandon their conversation.

'This isn't you, Kel. You never walk away from me. What's going on?'

When Kelly spun around, the sunglasses were back in place, her eyes once again hidden. 'You're not the only one who makes mistakes. Let's just move on from this summer, okay?'

It might have been a trick of the light which was burning down overhead, causing North to squint, but she thought she saw the trace of a tear gliding down Kelly's cheek.

*

Kelly didn't kill herself.

Had she dreamt the message? She'd seen it in her line of vision but then all the letters blurred and faded to black.

'I know,' North whispered to the emptiness around her. 'I know she didn't kill herself.'

There was singing. Something about a babe and a magic dance. North sat up with an audible sigh and rubbed at her eyes until the images on the television came into focus. *Labyrinth*. She'd been watching *Labyrinth*. It had been one of Kelly's favourites, mainly for the infamous Bowie bulge. North had been drawn in by the magic of it all, the wonder.

Outside, the sun was shining brightly. A clear blue autumnal sky stretched away from her block of flats. The scene was deceiving. It looked as though the air would carry warmth but instead it was already bitter, a precursor of the winter that was to come.

North stretched, arched her back and shuffled over to the fireplace. To the wall. It was her own labyrinth. A maze of questions she was desperately trying to navigate her way through.

'Are you sure you're okay?' Elijah had fired off his favourite question at least six times during the drive home. North kept diverting the conversation.

When they reached her flats there was a longing in his eyes that she hadn't recalled seeing before. She was almost on the brink of asking him up for a cup of tea when she thought of her wall of notes, of the shame she'd felt when Elijah saw it the first time. She didn't want him looking over it again, realising the depth of her true despair.

'You're not the only one who makes mistakes.'

North muttered the words from her dream, her memory, as she stared at the wall. Kelly Orton was no angel. Growing up she'd made many mistakes, like the time she borrowed her mum's car before she had a licence and crashed it into a tree. Or at school when during PE she stole Lindsey Mortimer's uniform and shoved it down the toilet to punish her for bullying North.

Kelly had made mistakes but she always owned up to them, was always ready and willing to atone. If she'd cheated on Dean then as bad as that was there were worse things a person could do. The guilt over such a betrayal wouldn't have chewed her up inside, wouldn't have pushed her into doing something she couldn't take back. Especially since Dean had cheated first, North was certain of it.

*

Her hair was still damp from the shower as North pulled up outside Kelly's house. She didn't fully understand why she'd even gone there, but as she had scrubbed shampoo against her scalp she couldn't shake the sensation that something was dreadfully wrong. Everyone had made a mistake; the police, Dean. Even North. Kelly didn't kill herself. She'd been certain of that from the start, knew it, could taste the truth of it every time she opened her mouth. And if Kelly didn't do it then someone else did. But there was no proof of any foul play, at least not at her disposal. There had to be more at the house. Perhaps if Dean would let her on Kelly's laptop, let her check her friend's Facebook page, messages, then—

The front door opened while she was still in the car. Hastily she climbed out, tugging up the hood of her jumper to protect her wet hair.

'What the hell are you doing here?' Dean was striding down the small driveway, heading directly for her car. He'd shaved and the Metallica T-shirt he wore with jeans appeared to be clean and crease-free.

'Dean, hey,' North tried to sound cheery. 'I hope you don't mind me just dropping by but—'

'I said what are you doing here?'

All friendly formalities had been abandoned. With Kelly gone he clearly had no reason to go on tolerating North. Or had the revelation about the pregnancy worn away the goodness within him? Whatever it was she had been kicked down from friend, to acquaintance to annoyance in the space of a few days.

'I just…' She pushed her hands into her pockets and tried to think. She'd never been good under pressure, that was Kelly's forte. When they used to try and sneak into movies when they were underage, North would clam up when confronted by jobsworth ushers – but not Kelly. Kelly could wax lyrical about their lost birth certificates, and later when they tried to get into clubs, their lost driver's licenses. She could be charming and persuasive all at once. Few doors remained closed to Kelly.

'You can't be here, North. I'm trying to move on and you're just trying to stir shit up.'

'Her laptop,' North blurted.

'What?'

'Can I? Can I borrow it? I just want to see if there's anything that could—'

'Could what? Implicate me?' Dean's face was growing red as he approached her, his giant shoulders hunched up towards his thick neck. 'You're losing your grip, North. You think I knew about the pregnancy, you think I'm some psycho jealous boyfriend who hung my girlfriend from a tree?'

'No, Jesus, Dean. I don't think that at all, I only—'

He loved Kelly. He could never hurt her. Could he? Had the truth been under North's nose the entire time, overlooked by a sense of loyalty and trust which Dean clearly didn't share?

'You're trying to point the finger at someone when the guilty party is in the ground. *She* did this.' He jabbed a finger in North's direction. Thick creases lined his forehead as his gestured finger shook in the air. 'She left us, North. Both of us. Kelly could be a flake. You saw her as this wonder woman when she was just as fucked up by her boozy mother as you were by your missing parents. You were two peas in a mad little pod. Kelly killed herself. You need to accept that and move on.'

With a grunt he began doubling back towards the front door. North followed.

'She wouldn't. She couldn't.'

'Open your eyes,' he raged as he reached his threshold. 'Kelly killed herself and she's the only person who can tell us why. You're going to drive yourself mad looking for answers. Or should I say *madder*.'

North let the insult wash over her. He was hurting, lashing out. He didn't mean what he said. Did he? She swallowed down the question, letting it simmer in the pit of her stomach.

'This isn't Kelly. No matter what she did she wouldn't just leave me like this.'

'You're *obsessed* with her,' Dean loomed large in his doorway, forbidding further access. A troll guarding his treasures. 'You always were. I told Kel it was too much. That you were too much. She pitied you because you had no one else, because you two were emotional orphans.'

'That's not true. We were best friends.'

'If it'd been you found swinging from a tree do you think she'd refuse to believe it? Do you think she'd be harassing people looking for answers where there were none?'

'Yes,' North's chest felt hollow. She knew that Dean could be cruel but she'd never seen it first-hand before. Each word was a thorn, each look a dagger. He was flinging all he had at her, trying to bring her to her knees.

'Bullshit,' Dean threw up his hands in frustration. 'You were a burden to her. Why do you think she kept going off on all her fancy little adventures? To get some bloody space.'

'From *you*, not me,' North seethed. The tips of her nerves were fraying, she'd been pushed too far. 'You can play the grieving boyfriend all you want, but I know what you did. How you hurt Kelly so deeply that she couldn't talk about it, that she had to get away.'

'You don't know what you're talking about.'

'Her name was Liz, wasn't it? The girl from the gym?' North remembered all the times Kelly's eyes had glistened with tears when she spoke about her suspicions. There was no proof, but a heart didn't need proof to feel what was real. Dean had been cheating and Kelly knew it, just as North knew that her friend would never kill herself. Some certainties go beyond what we can see.

'North, get out of here.' His voice was cold, hostile.

'Did she fear you?' North's eyes glistened with the challenge of her question. 'Because I don't think she did but maybe she should have. Maybe you knew all along that she was pregnant, that it wasn't your baby.'

'We're done here,' Dean dipped inside his house, his voice booming like thunder. 'Don't you ever darken my doorway again, North. Next time you show up here I'm calling the police.'

He slammed the door. North winced as it snapped on its hinges, barring her way to further exploration, to further answers.

*

The bench hadn't changed since summer. It remained on a peak in the park, overlooking the playground. The tall oak behind it had shed most of its leaves. They gathered around the bench in coppery mounds.

North dropped onto the bench and rested her elbows on her knees, cradling her chin in her hands.

Going to visit Dean had been a mistake. He'd never liked North, not really. She should have known better than to be a strain on their crumbling relationship. Now he probably hated her.

'Dean can be hot-headed,' Kelly would say. 'But he's got a good heart.'

He had been so hostile. So angry.

You think I knew about the pregnancy, you think I'm some psycho jealous boyfriend who hung my girlfriend from a tree?

Was his accusation really so far-fetched? Had he shouted out what North was just starting to believe? Perhaps Kelly had come home early after an ill-fated fling. In true Kelly style she'd have done the right thing and confessed everything to Dean. And despite his own infidelities he wouldn't have taken the news well. He'd have been angry. Furious. But angry enough to kill?

North sat up and scratched at her arms through her sleeves. Her distrust of Dean's volatile nature wasn't enough to convict him. Evidence. That's what she desperately needed to reveal the truth to everyone.

Kelly's laptop was the key. It had to be. An old pink Sony Vaio covered in stickers and nail varnish. Together, North and Kelly would sit in front of the laptop and watch YouTube videos of all their favourite boy bands. LFO, NSYNC, Backstreet Boys, 98 Degrees. The laptop provided a virtual walk down memory lane. And now Dean was holding it, and its contents, hostage. Maybe he'd wipe whatever vital information the laptop held.

No.

North shot up to her feet. Dean wasn't smart enough to figure out how to wipe a laptop. He could delete stuff, sure, but he wouldn't know how to purge a hard drive. If North could get to the laptop before he had chance to reach out to someone with more knowledge than him, she might find something to prove what happened to Kelly. A message to an old flame, a threat. There had to be something on the laptop. North couldn't very well go back to Kelly's house and demand it though. Nor could she risk getting caught stealing it. She needed to do things right. By the book. She needed to get the police on her side. They had the means to take possession of the laptop, to take it into evidence.

Turning away from the bench, North was about to jog back to the car park. She felt bright with purpose when her gaze slid over the park one last time. No longer a field of green, the trees were all rusted, the playground empty. Kelly had chosen this place to meet back when she returned after the summer. The place where she and North used to play as children. They'd sit on the swings side by side and kick their legs out, trying to get ever higher, trying to touch the sky.

Had Kelly deliberately chosen such a nostalgic setting for their reunion? But then what if it hadn't been that at all, what if she had been trying to say goodbye and North just refused to hear it?

9

'I'm waiting on Angie,' North stood at the small reception desk. She saw in the uniformed officer's expression how dishevelled she looked. He raised his eyebrows but kept his plump face passive.

'Look, Miss—'

'I just need five minutes of her time. That's all.'

'Like I said,' the officer spoke slowly, deliberately, like he were speaking with a stubborn child, 'you can't just come in and—'

'It's urgent. Please.'

Perhaps North looked desperate enough to evoke some sympathy in the officer because instead of banishing her from the reception area he was waving a chubby hand towards the far corner.

'Okay, okay, take a damn seat and I'll see if she's about. But don't go making a habit of this.'

'Thanks.'

Ten minutes passed. Then twenty. North nursed a Styrofoam cup between her hands, filled with tea from the vending machine. Though to call it tea seemed overly charitable, it was more tainted tepid water.

The door that led into the bowels of the station opened every couple of minutes, creaking on ancient hinges. With each whine of the door, North's head snapped up and her body tensed with expectation. But Angie didn't appear. And time was growing short. Dean might have wiped the laptop by now, the hard drive burning as it spun in a microwave. He could easily follow a

YouTube video guiding him how to permanently erase all data from the computer. He was dumb, but North didn't want to make the mistake of underestimating him.

With a whimper the door opened and Angie strode through it. She scanned the reception area with a hard look which softened a fraction when she locked eyes with North.

'What are you doing here?' she asked as she came over.

North stood up, awkwardly holding her foul cup of tea like a chalice.

'I came to see you. We need to talk.'

'Are you all right?' Angie swept her gaze over North, taking in her crumpled clothes and frazzled hair. 'Are you still having trouble sleeping?'

'I'm...' North was almost sidelined into discussing her sleep, or rather lack of it. But she kept her focus. 'I need to talk about Kelly.'

'Let's get you out of here,' Angie started guiding North towards the main doors, the ones which led outside to the sun-soaked car park.

'Wait,' North twisted to look back towards the reception desk and the doors that whined whenever they granted anyone entry. 'Don't we need to go to an interview or something?'

'You need to go home,' Angie led her out through the doors. Sunlight danced atop the roofs of all the gathered cars, making them shine like jewels.

'No, I need your help.' North dropped her tea into a nearby bin. 'Kelly's laptop. You have to get access to it, bring it in for evidence.'

'I can't do that.'

'There has to be something on it. Some message, some email. Something which will say who the father of her baby was. Please, Angie, it could be the key to everything.'

'I can't claim the laptop as evidence because there is no case.' Angie looked at the parked cars, 'Which one is yours?'

North pointed at her yellow beetle as she kept talking. 'But there is a case. You agreed that it was strange that the site of her death wasn't preserved properly. And her burial was so swift. All to eliminate evidence. To remove suspicion from the real killer.'

'From your logic, wouldn't a cremation make more sense? You're not thinking rationally, North. Suicides are always sensitive.' Angie went over to the yellow car and rested her hand on its roof. 'With Kelly people wanted closure so that they could properly grieve. A swift response from the authorities enabled them to do that. There was no foul play, no ulterior motive.'

'She didn't do this. Something isn't right. Dean was weirdly aggressive when I went to see him, you need to bring him in for more questioning. He knows more than he's letting on. I just—'

'When did you last get some sleep?'

'Huh?' North felt jarred by the question.

'I don't mean a catnap, I mean a good night's sleep. Six hours, seven, unbroken rest.'

'I...'

'North, you look strung out. You need to rest. Lack of sleep will make you paranoid, prone to hallucinations—'

'I'm sleeping just fine.'

'I read your file.'

North went cold. Hugging her arms to her chest, she withdrew from Angie, eyes shining with tears. 'That... that's confidential. You shouldn't be able to see that.'

'Because you were a minor?'

'Y-yes.'

'Petty theft. Breaking and entering. Substance abuse. Wrapping a stolen car around a tree.'

'That was—'

'You spiralled after your parents' disappearance which is completely understandable. You were fourteen. It was why the judge showed such leniency and just gave you community service instead of a stint in juvenile detention.'

'It wasn't me, it was—'

'The arresting officer cited sleep deprivation as a motivating factor for your behaviour. And grief.'

'The laptop,' North struggled to speak as her chest tightened. 'You need to get the laptop, Angie. Forget all this stuff about me.'

'I'm telling you not to repeat your past mistakes.' Angie patted the yellow beetle, 'Go home. Sleep. Stop chasing rainbows. You need to grieve and then move on, as hard as that may be.'

'I can't let this go. I can't give up on Kelly.'

'Then at least sleep. It pains me to see you spiralling like this, exhausting yourself chasing ghosts.'

'Try and get the laptop, please.'

'This time if you get caught acting out there won't be a sympathetic judge to save you. You'll risk doing jail time, is that what you want?'

North shook her head as she reached forward and opened her car door with shaking hands.

'It wasn't me,' North got in her car and peered up at Angie. 'The crash, the petty thefts. It wasn't me.'

'So it was Kelly,' Angie shrugged, 'but you're the one with a record and it's your word against a dead girl's. You need to protect yourself, North. No one else will.'

'Get the laptop.'

Angie began walking away, back towards the station when she suddenly turned back. 'And stay away from Dean, okay?'

That was already a given considering his recent outburst.

'Focus on you,' Angie urged. 'Focus on getting some sleep, on getting your head straight.'

North watched the officer disappear into the station before slamming her car door shut. Why did everyone keep telling her to sleep? How bad did she look? Snapping down her visor, North looked up at her reflection in the small mirror in the back of it. She was a ghost. Her skin was so pale it was nearly translucent, threads of blue veins stretched across her cheeks, and beneath her eyes hung dark shadows. She looked gaunt, skeletal. Her silver eyes were flat, a heavy sky before a storm. Her sparkle was gone. Her body had become a vessel for darkness and regret.

Sleep.

Everyone was telling her to sleep, the advice coming in from all sides. If her grandmother were alive she'd prepare the guest bedroom, put hot-water bottles beneath the crisps sheets and draw the curtains. She'd place a steaming mug of hot chocolate in North's hands and tell her that everything was going to be okay. North would fall asleep to the sounds of her grandmother bustling around downstairs.

Sleep never came so easily when she was alone.

*

North had the night off. Her next shift began the following day at three. She was assigned to study the gathered data and assess the luminosity of the supernova. There were to be no more late nights. She figured that Alexander had taken her off them to spite her in his usual passive-aggressive style.

She was in her bedroom. It was a place in her flat that served as a walk-in closet rather than somewhere to rest. North had flung all of her clothes off the double bed, exposing the Star

Wars duvet cover beneath. All she had to do was peel back the sheets and climb in. Then sleep would surely find her. But North knew the routine, knew better than to trust her body to do the obvious.

Once she was in bed the thoughts would come. Like an army, they'd march towards her, relentless. And then a war would rage. She'd lie wide-eyed, staring at the cracks in her ceiling as she fought each wave of thoughts. The battle would become a cycle. She'd think about Kelly and thoughts of Kelly would lead back to her parents. Were they fish food at the bottom of the ocean or were they living a Robinson Crusoe style existence upon some island? The crueller children at school assumed it was the latter.

'Your parents deliberately fucked off because they didn't want you,' they'd spitefully taunt North. 'They're off on some island somewhere and they've just left you to rot.'

Over and over she told everyone that the Stones wouldn't return, that the sea had claimed them. But an acorn of hope had planted deep in her chest and other times it grew roots, grew to a shoot. Maybe one day her parents would return to Millwater, their skin golden and their hair matted. They'd embrace North and tell her how much they'd missed her, how they thought about her every day, how they couldn't sleep because of the torment of longing that haunted them.

Maybe.

The maybe of it all was a gift and a curse. It gave birth to childish fantasies of island life and loving parents when North needed to face reality – her parents had gone off on another wild adventure ill prepared for what lay ahead. As they idled across sapphire waters a storm had found them. Their final breaths had tasted of salt. The acorn in her chest turned to stone.

Kelly wasn't coming back.

North cautiously approached the bed. She was wearing a pair of flannel pyjamas which had been faded by time.

Night Nurse was in North's system. The guy at the chemist had assured her it was a reliable sleep aid.

'It'll send you right off,' he'd noted as he placed it in a plastic bag for her.

Sleep.

The sheets on the bed were smooth, untouched. North couldn't remember the last time she'd curled up beneath them. She only knew that she hadn't been alone. He had been there. He'd come over with flowers bought along with his petrol and somehow that was enough. Once he smiled, North was powerless to resist him. She'd lead him into her flat and she'd forget about Kelly, about the distance between them, forget about her parents and their ambiguous end. He was like a magician, able to place a sleeping curse upon the troops of thoughts that battled against North on a nightly basis. With just a smile he silenced them all.

North crawled into bed. The Night Nurse was living up to its declarations on the bottle. She felt tired and warm all over. When her head hit the pillow it felt like landing amongst the clouds – soft and inviting. North tugged her duvet up to her chin just as she dipped over the edge and left this world for another.

*

'Help me.'

Cold fingers were digging into North's shoulders. With a gasp, she sat up, opening her mouth wide as a scream died in her throat.

'Help me.'

Kelly was at her bedside, her skin blue and eyes hollowed. There was soil in her hair, on her clothes and a crude red band of skin circled her neck like a hideous choker.

'Help me, North, I didn't do this.'

Her fingers were icy splinters. She kept a hold of North, shaking her. She drew so close that North could smell the rot on her friend's breath.

'Kelly?'

'Help me. Help me, North. No one else can.'

'Please, Kel, what's happening? I thought you were—'

Kelly screamed. Her mouth opened unnaturally wide, like a snake about to devour its prey. As her jaw unhinged, the terror-filled sound spewed out. Like pigs being butchered, the scream was pitched and haunting, a shrill howl. Kelly kept screaming, kept shaking North.

'Please, Kel, stop.'

The sound was unbearable, it was tearing against North's eardrums, trying to punch through them. The scream seemed endless. It was full of so much pain. So much fear.

'Kelly, stop, stop screaming!'

The hands disappeared. The screaming stopped. North snapped open her eyes. She was in bed, on her back, hands clutching desperately at her duvet which was held against her chin. The sheets around her were soaked in her own sweat. Trembling, she looked to the side of the bed, to where Kelly had been. There was only darkness.

'Kel?' North called out uneasily, the word quivering as it travelled up her throat. 'Kel, are you there?'

Silence. There was no reassuring hum of voices coming from the television, just emptiness.

'Fuck,' North threw back the duvet and sat up, head in hands. Sleep had been a mistake. In closing her eyes she'd opened up a door to her nightmares. Her shoulders still carried the chill from her dead friend's touch. It had seemed so real. The scream, the smell. All of it. It felt like Kelly had truly *been* there.

Getting up, North flicked on her bedside lamp expecting to see a trail of dirt trod into her carpet, leading out of the room. But of course there was nothing. The lack of evidence mocked her, challenged her sanity.

'She was here,' North was certain of it as she drifted out of the bedroom and into the main body of her flat, flicking on lights as she want, bathing everywhere in a reassuring glow. 'She was here and she was asking for help.'

The bottle of Night Nurse was still on the countertop in the kitchen. North uncapped it and began tipping its remaining contents down the sink. The thick fluid glugged noisily as it disappeared down the plughole. North didn't need sleep. Sleep brought forth the demons from the dark. If Kelly had come tonight then her parents would surely come tomorrow, or at least one of them. North knew the tricks of the ghosts that haunted her of old. She was better off catnapping on her sofa when she could. At least then her rest was undisturbed.

Help me.

Kelly's plea had been a simple one. But help her how? She was already dead.

North turned on the tap and washing away any lingering remnants of the Night Nurse. How far away was the morning and daylight? She needed to get out of the flat, needed to feel the wind scrape against her cheeks. She needed to feel free.

Without bothering to shower, North pulled on jeans and an oversized hooded jumper. Kelly needed help and North wasn't about to ignore her friend's plea, even if she didn't yet understand what was required of her.

10

'This is where the dead live.'

That's what North's grandmother had said the first time they'd visited the cemetery to lay flowers on a distant great-aunt's grave. The jarring juxtaposition still troubled North.

It was early morning. The sky was bleeding as North meandered between the headstones, carefully picking her way around grass-topped graves. Her nightmare continued to linger on the fringes of her consciousness. Twice she thought she saw a flash of someone stalking her movements in her peripheral vision, but when she spun around she saw that she was completely alone.

Dew clung to grass and some wilting bouquets of carnations and roses that rested against ebony headstones. It was silent in the cemetery. The air was still. A melodic burst of birdsong was the only thing that broke the tranquillity, the last few cries of the dawn chorus.

Her parents, for remembrance, her grandparents and Kelly. This is where they all were, perhaps not all technically, some metaphorically, buried under six feet of dirt in polished wooden boxes.

North found her parents first. She stood at their shared grave, head bowed. A single line etched in gold against the dark stone was supposed to sum up their vast lives.

Forever sleeping amongst the stars.

It was more poetic than *rotting beneath the sea.*

In their final moments had they thought of their only daughter? As saltwater filled their lungs did they fear for her life as well as their own? Did they wonder what would become of her, orphaned at fourteen?

'Your mother always had itchy feet,' North's grandmother would state with an air of disdain. 'Couldn't stay in one place too long.'

Well now she was stuck. At least her name was. She was beholden to a tiny plot of land indefinitely.

Most of the graves nearby were clearly neglected. Flowers which had shrivelled and turned brown sagged in mouldy vases, weeds chewed at the corners of the once grand headstones. There were no flowers left on North's parents' grave. She'd never felt that floral offerings honoured the dead. Better to honour them through how you live. Yet here she was, drifting through a place she'd so fervently avoided as a teenager.

Her parents weren't actually *in* the cemetery so why go there to pay homage to them?

Kelly's grave was towards the back of the cemetery with all the fresher plots. There was no mistaking her final resting place – it looked as though a florist had displayed their entire wares atop of it. Flowers of every colour and description were mounted over the fresh dirt of the grave. They ran like a river into the surrounding grass. Roses, daffodils, carnations, lilies. North could smell their heady perfume when she was still a few rows away.

From the funeral remained some floral arrangements of words, included Kelly's name spelt out in pink roses. Little notecards barely protected by flimsy slips of plastic were wedged in with their individual bouquets, the ink of their messages damp and streaked. Some of the writing was still legible.

Kelly we will always love you.
Nothing will be the same without you.
We'll see you in heaven.

Shine bright, superstar.

North was drawn to the 'shine bright' card. It seemed like an oddly uplifting sentiment against all the declarations of grief. She pushed back several white roses to read the rest of the card but it carried just that one line of a neatly written message. There was no name, no signing off signature.

'Shine bright,' North straightened and instinctively lifted her chin to the sky. Clouds were drifting in, wisps of grey streaking away from the rising sun. Kelly had been a star. She was so impossibly bright, so strong, that everyone orbited around her, powerless to resist her gravitational pull.

None of the bouquets on the grave had come from North. To bring flowers to the funeral would have felt like acceptance, acknowledgement that Kelly truly had killed herself.

'Hey.'

North spun around so fast that she almost tripped in the slick grass. Elijah was walking towards her. When he got close he sunk into his shoulders and nervously pointed back in the direction of the cemetery.

'I was driving to work when I spotted your car. I wanted to stop and make sure you were okay. So, you know, are you okay?'

Always with the *are you okay?* North fought the urge to roll her eyes.

'I'm…' She shrugged self-consciously as she nodded towards the vast mound of flowers. 'Paying my respects, I guess. I don't know.'

'Want me to leave you to it?' Elijah offered a reluctant retreat.

'No. It's fine.'

So many flowers. All of them blooming bright but soon time would claim them. Their petals would wilt, their colour fade. No glory was permanent. Even the brightest stars cease to shine.

'Are you working today?'

'Later.' North kept looking at the flowers. She couldn't imagine that beneath them, beneath the dirt and the soil lay Kelly. 'I want to know who he was.'

'Who?'

'The father.' It felt strange to say it.

The father.

That would make Kelly the mother. Kelly was going to be a mum. What kind of a parent would she have been? Would she have been loving and kind or would she have been terminally flaky like their own mothers had been?

'You got any idea at all?'

'No. None.'

Elijah came and stood beside her. 'Maybe you just need to keep looking.'

'I've looked,' North heard the ache in her voice. 'I've gone over everything she said a thousand times in my mind. I tried to get access to her laptop but…' she exhaled sharply. 'That's a no-go. I bet Dean's wiped the bloody thing by now anyway.'

'What about your timeline?'

North felt fire in her cheeks. Not the timeline. She didn't want Elijah to bring that up, to dwell on her strange fixation with it all, her *obsession* as Dean had chosen to label it.

'Look, that was just—'

'Because I was thinking about it,' Elijah nervously glanced down at his feet, at the scuffed pair of Converse he was wearing. 'And from what I could see there's a gap, a glaring one.'

'There is?'

'We're all about data,' his mouth lifted in a half-smile. 'When we study a star, any gap in data represents an anomaly worth exploring.'

'Okay, so?'

'The yacht.'

'The yacht?' North felt the pull of intrigue within her chest.

'Kelly spent a considerable amount of time working on the yacht yet all you've got on the timeline is the dates she was there. She must have made friends on board. Maybe someone from the yacht crew knows who the father might be.'

'You think?' North wanted to slap herself for not reaching such an obvious conclusion sooner. Perhaps her lack of sleep really had dulled her mind.

'It's surely worth looking in to.'

'Yeah, it is,' North agreed, feeling rejuvenated at the prospect of a new direction to send her investigation in. 'Thanks, Elijah.'

'No problem.' He reached out and briefly touched her arm. 'I'll, um, leave you to it if you're sure you're okay? Need to get to work and all that.'

'It's all right, go, I'm fine.'

'I'll stay if you need me to.' And North could see in his eyes that he meant it.

'No, really, go, I'll see you there later.'

*

Work was the last place North wanted to be. She'd spent the rest of the morning staring at the timeline on the wall of her flat, trying to figure out what she was missing.

There were several things she needed to find out. They were all scribbled down in her notebook which was resting open beside her computer.

The name of the yacht
Other crew members
Where the yacht was now

At least one person had to know something about Kelly. She wasn't the kind of person who existed in the background like a wallflower. If you'd worked with Kelly you'd know about it.

Quiet chatter drifted through the office as North's computer groaned under the weight of all the data it was being fed. Night and day the team had been studying the supernova, trying to discern its secrets. She was supposed to be collating data, creating graphs, but she couldn't focus. Instead she scrolled through images captured by the telescope over the previous month.

Galaxies were floating halos. The moon a cratered face. She opened up a particularly clear picture of the moon. Its silver surface shone, each crater a story of its history like lines on an old face. The moon was reliable. You could chart its journey across the sky and it would never falter, would always show up exactly where it was supposed to be, showing the same face to the earth. The moon was a constant. North stared at her computer until the familiar feelings of contentment began to circulate through her veins.

Growing up she used the moon. Whenever she felt lost it was her anchor in the sky. She'd open her window in the guest bedroom at her grandparents' home and look up at it. Every clear night it was there, bright and welcoming. A beacon of something greater than herself. What North liked most about the moon was that when she stared at it, it was the same moon her parents would be staring at from their desert island. She imagined her mum and dad sat side by side on a white sandy beach, dark waves lapping at their bare toes as they both peered up at the silver orb. Its grey shades would remind them of their daughter, of her eyes, and together they'd both proclaim how terribly they missed her and how they hoped she was somewhere safe sat beneath that same moon. In the dark it was easy to give way to these flights of fancy, beneath the harsh light of day the truth was laid out like rotting meat, stark and unavoidable; her parents were dead. But at night, when sleep failed to come, North could allow herself childish fantasies, to play make believe until the sun rose again and burned through her lies.

'Pretty sure that one is all figured out,' Elijah's voice was in her ear, soft and teasing.

North quickly minimised the image of the moon and turned in her chair to look at it. 'I think the moon still holds a few mysteries.'

'If it does, no one's all that bothered.' He dropped into the vacant seat beside her. 'It's all about Mars these days. I hear it's where all the cool kids are going.'

'Didn't your cousin get selected for the Mars mission?'

'Marcus?' Elijah scratched at his chin. 'Yeah, yeah he did. It's all a way off in the future but he's already training for it.'

'It's intense,' North whispered with a shake of her head. 'To go on a mission like that, knowing you'll never come back, that you'll never see any of your loved ones, your friends, again.'

'Do you reckon your parents would have signed up?' Elijah looked between her and the computer screen.

'Yes,' North admitted with a bitter laugh. 'Absolutely. They were drawn to anything with a whiff of adventure.'

'But not you? If they were already going?'

'I like to play things a bit safer than they did.'

Zip lining. Bungee jumping. Parachuting out of a plane. These were all things that Kelly did while North watched from below and took pictures.

'It's weird,' North chewed her lip as she began scrolling through the collected data for the supernova. 'Some people go towards danger rather than avoid it.'

'It's seen as excitement though. Not danger. Like, no one would jump into a pit of fire.'

'I bet someone would.'

This made Elijah chuckle, a soft laugh that sounded like rain on leaves.

'My parents *loved* excitement,' she muttered as she began typing in commands for some of the data. 'They fought with each other just for the thrill of it. Just so they could make up,' she rolled her eyes. 'Some nights they'd be shouting at each other so furiously they sounded like a pair of screaming ravens.'

'I bet that was scary.'

'Sadly it was normal.'

'So have you looked into stuff about the yacht?' Elijah glanced at her open notebook.

'Not yet.'

'Well, let me know if you need any help.' He stood up and gave her shoulder a squeeze. 'I'm done for the day, off home to watch the new *Game of Thrones*.'

'Spoiler alert – someone dies.'

'Thanks for that.'

As Elijah left, North abandoned her work to look at the moon once more. Tonight it would show up again, ready to claim dominion over the sky in the sun's absence. It would never disappear without warning. It would always just be there. And North loved it for that.

*

It was dark when North returned to the cemetery. She had to use a torch from her glove compartment to guide her way through all the stones, hoping that the groundskeeper in the nearby cottage didn't spot her beam of light and call the police. North didn't want Angie showing up and concluding that North must be looking to add grave robber to her previous list of misdemeanours.

She wasn't even sure why she was there, just that as she was driving home from work she felt an ache in her chest that pulled her in the direction of the little church outside of town and its surrounding array of headstones.

The yacht was on her mind.

North knew she should be at her computer, furiously typing search terms in to Google in her ongoing search for her friend. But first she wanted to be near Kelly, or at least as near as she could be. The haunted face from her nightmare continued to plague her. Kelly's spirit wasn't at peace, North was sure of that. She half expected to see a ghostly spectre floating amid the headstones, wailing, seeking help.

'I'm going to find out who the father is,' North told the mound of flowers when she reached them, illuminating the nearest blooms in the beam of her torch. 'Maybe I won't like what I find, maybe that's why you never told me, but I'm going to go looking anyway. There's never been any secrets between us before, I don't see why that should change now just because you're... you know... here.'

The wind grew sharper, pulling at North.

'I know you need my help and I'm not going to stop until I've proved that you didn't do this. That you didn't kill yourself. Kel...' North sucked in a lungful of brisk evening air. It tasted of damp earth and roses. 'You'd never leave me. Not on purpose. I get that. You're my moon. My star. Despite what everyone is saying about closure and moving on, I won't give up on you. I swear.'

As North turned back to walk towards her waiting car, the wind scraped at her cheek and she thought it carried the whisper of a message along with its icy touch.

'Thank you.'

But then her sleep-deprived mind could just be playing tricks on her again. Quickening her pace, she didn't hang around to find out.

11

It was midnight. The digital clock on her laptop ticked over to read 00:00. A clean slate. A new day. North was slumped against the cushions on her sofa, her computer resting on her knees. Her eyes ached and the words on the screen were starting to blur together. But she'd done it. She'd found the yacht Kelly had worked on that summer.

The Orion. Almost 100 feet in length with six guest bedrooms. Owned by Spencer Daniels, available to accommodate up to twelve guests.

In the pictures The Orion looked more like a floating luxury home than a boat. There were chandeliers, bathrooms with a marble finish and a swimming pool on the upper deck. It was perfection. And Kelly had been there, had walked beneath the glittering chandeliers, served drinks from the opulent kitchen, maybe even swam in the glistening pool. She could have easily slotted in to such a life; she had already looked like a movie star, she was just missing the trappings of fame.

Finding the name of the yacht was easy. Learning about crew members was proving more tricky. It seemed as though The Orion hired its deckhands and crew through professional websites, websites which kept the identity of the people on their books confidential which wasn't really a surprise given the high profile status of their clients. The social media presence for the yacht was extremely limited. Only Spencer Daniels posted any pictures or information about his boat.

On Instagram he was often pictured leaning back in the hot tub up on the deck of his beloved yacht, champagne flute in hand, mouth held wide in a smile, revealing a set of flawless white teeth. None of the crew seemed to upload such images. In everything tagged with #theorion the image had come from Spencer and he was always front and centre, surrounded by beautiful women who were as flawless as he was.

The benefit of Spencer's love of social media meant that North could track the whereabouts of The Orion with relative ease. Two days ago he'd posted a picture of himself leaning against the railing wearing a captain's hat playfully cocked to one side. Beneath the image it read: *Almost time to be back on my beloved. Monaco bound in three days. S x*

North scrolled through his collection of pictures. It all looked like a photo shoot for couture clothes rather than the timeline of a life. She was looking for Kelly. In each image, she searched for her face, waited to see her suddenly hanging on Spencer's arm doubling over in laughter. He was clearly a popular guy, never short of female attention.

Each image contained fresh faces, new smiles. Spencer Daniels was handsome, in a polished sort of way. He had a strong jawline and thick brown hair which he overly moussed and pushed back. His eyes were blue but seemed to lack a twinkle, not that the bevy of beauties around him minded. He was in good shape, always wearing a tight-fitting shirt in either blue or white. Before extending her Google search on him, North assumed that he went to Eton. She was right. Spencer Daniels was everything an aristocratic millionaire playboy should be – groomed, confident and unthreatening. There was never even the slightest shadow of stubble upon his jawline.

Kelly would have loved Spencer. North knew it the second she saw him in his posed pictures. Kelly was always drawn to the cleanest cut members of a boy band while North was intrigued by the members who had tattoos and seemed to refuse to play by the rules. Of course they were all adhering to strictly laid out stereotypes, but as teenage girls they weren't to know that.

Thinking about Kelly led North to open up a file on her laptop that she'd told herself was strictly off limits. It contained ten short videos. She checked the time. 00.18. This was when a normal person would turn off their computer and slink off to bed. When they'd put their head down, close their eyes, and sleep.

Sleep.

North yawned but remained unconvinced of her need to sleep. She was keeping her time in her bedroom to a bare minimum. She'd run in, grab some clothes and dash back out. A cold lingered in the air as though Kelly's restless spirit had yet to leave.

She clicked on the first video. It was old, the image grainy and dull. Two years ago she and Kelly had gone through the stacks of VHS tapes that were stored in the attic of North's grandparents' house. Amongst all their favourite movies were the little home movies they used to make together on a camcorder. North's grandfather had bought himself a camcorder and he was kind enough to let the girls use it. In total there were five videos and eighteen cassette tapes. On the tapes North and Kelly used to create their own radio shows where they were the DJs. They'd chat about their favourite bands and play music, prattling on together for hours. The videos were different.

'Hi,' Kelly was in the centre of the screen, fifteen and fearless. She was standing in the doorway of her mum's terraced house, long hair loose down her back. She smiled boldly at the camera which wobbled slightly thanks to North's poor holding skills. 'I'm Kelly Orton. Welcome to my crib.'

North choked on a sob as her younger self followed Kelly into the little house, stalking her every step with the camcorder she was holding.

'This is the kitchen,' Kelly gestured grandly to the cramped space around her. She was so slender, so lithe in her denim pedal pushers and Kappa T-shirt. 'Want to see what we have in my fridge?' Her voice was playful and warm. Inviting. North awkwardly moved the camera towards the single off-white fridge which Kelly had just pulled open. Its contents made for sad viewing.

A half loaf of bread. A nearly empty bottle of ketchup, two eggs, an empty milk bottle and a two-litre bottle of vodka.

'This is for later,' Kelly hauled out the vodka with a smile, 'you always need to keep in a bottle of Cristal in case you have company come over.'

Of course, in the show the girls were mimicking, *MTV Cribs*, the celebrities kept expensive champagne in their vast refrigerators not store-brand vodka.

Kelly bounced her way through the rest of the small house. Always smiling, always playing up for the camera.

'This is where the magic happens,' she announced as she pushed open a door adorned with pictures of The Backstreet Boys, NSYNC and Take That.

North held a breath as she stared at her laptop. She watched Kelly and stepped back in time. She'd never forget the bedroom in which she spent so many hours. They'd sit on Kelly's single bed with their backs against the wall talking about boys, about school, concocting increasingly imaginative explanations for where North's parents might be. The faded purple curtains were drawn and posters haphazardly tacked over floral wallpaper. There were lots of Jared Leto, North had forgotten how Kelly used to put them up simply because North fancied him.

'He's too girly,' Kelly would scoff whenever they watched *Party of Five* together. But her room was basically North's too and so both girls influenced what went on the walls. There was a little dresser beneath the window, covered with half-empty bottles of Charlie perfumes and body sprays. A large mirror was bordered with passport-booth pictures of Kelly and North messing about, kissing the camera and inflating their cheeks. Even pretending to strangle each other. So much life in such a tiny room. A room no larger than a cupboard. Kelly used to keep her clothes under her bed because she didn't have a wardrobe.

'This is where I hang out when I'm not on set,' Kelly grandly told the camera as she went over to a stereo and slid in a CD from the nearby stack. North knew the song from the opening chords. Kelly began bouncing up and down on her bed, and in the video North abandoned her filming duties to join her.

'Stop that racket.' It didn't take long for Irene's slurred voice to come through the door.

North hopped off the bed and the video abruptly ended.

The flat was suddenly too quiet, the absence of Kelly's voice too stark. North quickly opened up another video. This time she was the host in their amateur episode of Cribs showing Kelly about her grandparents' house. She could barely get her words out for laughing.

Despite her parents' disappearance there had been so much joy in her childhood, thanks to Kelly.

North watched all the videos. She knew she shouldn't, that it was a bad idea but she needed to get absorbed in the past, let her memories embrace her. She watched her and Kelly act out their favourite scenes from movies, from music videos. They'd all been shot over one single summer. They giggled their way through a medley of skits. In each one they looked so wholesome, so happy. At least Kelly did.

When North scrutinised her own face she didn't like what she saw. There were too many shadows, too many signs of sleepless nights. The videos came after the misdemeanours, a year on from her parents' faux funeral. People thought she was settling down, that she was coping. But even then she had taken to sleeping on the sofa downstairs rather than in her bed. It would prove to be a habit she'd struggle to break.

In the final video, Kelly and North were lip-syncing to the Spice Girls singing 'Two Become One', dressed in matching denim dungarees. North could barely see the video through her tears. At 00.52 she shut her laptop already knowing that she wouldn't even bother to try and sleep.

*

Monaco was dubbed the playground of the rich and famous. A country in its own right, it bordered France and hosted the Grand Prix. North learnt all this the following morning when at four a.m. she awoke with a start. She'd been curled up in a ball on the sofa, one of the *Pirates of the Caribbean* movies playing on the television. Jack Sparrow was sauntering around on screen as North got up to make herself a much-needed coffee. Then she commenced her research.

Spencer Daniels and The Orion would soon be moored in Monaco. There wasn't an event on in the country at that time, he must simply be going for a holiday. This was in North's favour as there was no way she could afford to go there during the Grand Prix. If she flew out of Heathrow to Nice she could then get a hire car and drive to Monaco. She'd chosen The

Fairmount as her hotel. It had a central location and a reasonable price tag. Going there for a week would still deplete her savings, but how else was she going to learn more about Kelly's time on the boat?

North's finger hovered over her mouse, over the button on the screen which would confirm her holiday booking. One week. Just over one thousand pounds. Would that be enough to learn what happened to Kelly when she worked aboard The Orion? This would be North's first holiday alone. Not that it was even a holiday, more a fact-finding mission. But normally Kelly came too. They were a package deal. Girly spa weekends, trips to Disneyland Paris, together they'd done it all. Every minibreak a whirlwind of laughter and childish mischief. Kelly could make a paper bag seem fun. For most people when a flight was delayed it meant dismay, but not Kelly. She saw an opportunity to explore the airport. She'd assign quests to her and North. First to find a Starbucks. First to spot a 747. First to flirt with a captain. But such quests now seemed redundant.

What did North even hope to achieve by going to Monaco?

Chewing her lip, she looked between the laptop and her chaotic timeline on the wall. The gap in it was so glaring that even Elijah had noticed. She needed to go. Needed to ask questions, learn about the version of herself that Kelly had been when out there. But first there was a formality, a hoop to jump through. North needed to make sure she could have the time off from work. With a sigh she closed her laptop.

*

By six a.m. North was in the woods. Jogging. She'd had to pull on her Converse since she didn't own any proper running shoes.

It was still dark as she ran along the wooded trail, letting the dim light of the moon guide her. If Kelly could see her now she wouldn't believe her eyes. North could almost hear her voice in her head as she ran.

'Jogging. You're *jogging*, North. What the hell happened? Are you having some sort of breakdown?'

Maybe she was. Her flat had started to feel too small again, the walls steadily creeping towards her. She had to get out and she didn't want to visit the cemetery again, but she did want to be outside. She needed to feel the slap of cold air on her cheeks. More than that. She needed to think.

What did she want to ask Spencer Daniels? She needed to question him about Kelly, ask how she'd seemed when she worked aboard his yacht. Did she ever speak about Dean? Was she afraid of going home? Of him? North was confident that Spencer would answer all her questions. Online he appeared to be extremely posh but also approachable. He replied to fans who commented on his Instagram pictures, always thanking them and showing a surprising amount of humility for a playboy millionaire.

He was in the tabloids a lot. A quick search of him had brought up a stack of seedy stories about one-night stands with supermodels and television actresses. He had a love 'em and leave 'em reputation. A bit of a bad boy despite his clean-cut image. But so many celebrities were like that these days. And he was avidly involved with numerous charities; amongst the trashy stories, North found pictures of him reading to sick children in hospital, bringing them Christmas gifts. She couldn't help but be touched by the tenderness revealed in these more candid shots. North could see that he was more than just a playboy, and once upon a time Kelly had seen that too, it was one of the reasons she'd wanted to join the crew of The Orion.

Spencer Daniels was a celebrity. He'd probably never even spoken to Kelly directly. But then how could he not? Compared to the women he'd been linked to, she was a goddess, all natural beauty and charisma. Kelly Orton won over anyone she met with ease.

North was running faster, not caring for the dark, nor how it concealed the path at her feet. Then she tripped. Her foot caught beneath a tree root and she came crashing towards the leaf-strewn ground with heart-stopping force. She just had time to fling her hands forward to break her fall. She felt the force of the impact shudder through her bones. For a second she lay there, waiting to assess the damage.

'Fuck.' Slowly she got up and dusted the dirt from her grey joggers. Nothing appeared to be broken. She could still stand on her own two feet.

A trickle of something warm trickled down her chin. There was an injury after all.

Deflated, North abandoned her jog and dragged herself back along the trail, back towards her car, parked just beyond the woods. The sun was lifting in the sky. She could taste mud and the coppery undertones of her own blood. It was a new day.

12

There was a gash on North's chin which the plaster she'd put on struggled to conceal. She'd trodden leaves into her flat, souvenirs of her brief jog in the woods. Now she was at work, standing shoulder to shoulder with her peers as Alexander addressed them all. He was in front of a whiteboard, clicker pen in hand as he scrolled through data, but North felt like everyone was looking in her direction rather than forwards. She saw people staring out of the corner of their eyes, abandoning discretion as they took in her slashed chin, pale cheeks and shadowed eyes.

'I know we've all been working flat out since the discovery of the supernova,' Alexander was an expert orator. When he spoke you felt compelled to listen. His voice was a Gaelic folk song, lilting yet powerful.

Elijah was on the far side of the room, wedged between the Cooper twins.

'These are, of course, only preliminary findings.'

A new chart came up on the whiteboard. More interpreted data. North tried to listen only to Alexander's voice, not the stampeding of frantic thoughts creeping up on her. Her chin throbbed and she kept seeing flashes of The Orion in her mind. Of Spencer Daniels' perfect smile. She needed to be there. In Monaco. Instead, she was standing in a demountable attending a staff meeting. The pretence of normalcy was slipping. She couldn't be in Millwater anymore.

'We estimate that the supernova will burn out for at least a hundred years. It will be quite a spectacle.'

With a click of the pen in his hand, the screen changed, yet again replacing charts with a truly wondrous image. The supernova. The dying star.

It was a blast against the darkness. Light erupted out of it at all angles, fierce and bright. Debris streaked away, scattering to the far corners of the universe. A star never had a quick death. Instead it was always a slow, drawn-out process. At least compared to human perceptions of time. The star would burn as its core collapsed in on itself. Its destruction would forever change the face of its galaxy. And then—

'The theoretical prognosis is that a black hole will form.' Alexander clicked to another image.

North sagged against the table behind her.

A dying star would leave a black hole in its wake. She could have told him that.

The meeting concluded and North made for Alexander. She wove through her colleagues, keen to grab him before he disappeared. He had a flight that night to the Canary Islands where he'd be working with some of the most powerful telescopes in the world for the next three weeks. His working holiday was now general knowledge, but North had heard about it before anyone else, back in January when the seed of an idea grew roots. If things had turned out differently she might be heading there now instead of making plans to visit Monaco.

North cleared her throat and her mind and followed Alexander out of the meeting room.

'Hey.'

Someone caught her wrist and drew her back. Turning round, North saw Elijah in the doorway.

'What happened to you?' he looked directly at her chin.

'I fell.'

'You fell?'

'Yeah, I was out jogging and—'

'Wait. *You* were *jogging*?' she heard the disbelief in his voice and hung her head shyly.

'I know,' a soft sigh escaped through her lips. 'I don't know what I was doing either. Clearly I'm not very good at it, so it's not going to become a regular thing or anything.'

'What made you want to go jogging?'

'I needed to think.'

North froze. She examined what she'd just said.

I needed to think.

Did Kelly ever go jogging to clear her mind? No. That was impossible. She'd have told North.

Like how she told North she was pregnant.

'Dammit.' North picked at her fingernails, desperate to scratch at her arms.

'Doubt is the devil's handiwork,' her grandmother would say whenever North lamented that she couldn't do something, be it her GCSEs or a handstand.

'Hey, what's up?' Elijah shut the door and joined her in the corridor. They were alone. Alexander had disappeared into his own office at the far end of the demountable. 'You seem shaken up. Was it from the fall or—'

'I need to catch Alex before he leaves.' North stepped away from him and saw a shadow cross over his face. 'I need to book some leave,' she added, for fear of extinguishing the glimmer of hope that shone behind Elijah's blue eyes. She didn't want him to stop looking at her as he so often did, like she was the answer to a question he hadn't even realised he'd been asking.

'Oh. Right. Okay.'

'I'll be back in a minute.'

Outside Alexander's door, she knocked twice, a duo of brisk taps, and waited.

'Come in.'

Even through plywood he commanded authority.

'Hi,' North nervously shuffled into the small office. She wished she could burst into a room like Kelly used to, instantly filling it. 'Do you have a moment?'

'Actually I'm just about to leave.' Alexander was placing his silver MacBook into his laptop bag. He twisted his wrist to check the time on his Apple watch. 'My flight leaves in just over three hours.'

'I know. This won't take long.'

'Everything okay?' With his laptop stored away, he was able to really focus on North. His eyes narrowed as they swept over her wounded chin. 'What happened there?'

'A fall.'

'Are you sleeping?'

North ground her teeth together. She'd wanted to keep this professional. Efficient. Now they were diverting into dangerous territory. Alexander was a snake charmer when it came to the truth, always finding a way to draw it out of her.

'I'm...' she lightly tapped her chin. 'I'm clumsy, that's all. I fell in the woods.'

'In the woods?'

She was saying too much. She needed to make her answers more succinct so that Alexander couldn't read anything into them.

'I need to take some leave.' North decided to blindside him with the true nature of her impromptu visit.

'Oh?' For a man in a hurry Alexander suddenly looked awfully relaxed as he put down his laptop bag and leaned against his desk chair. 'Is this about Kelly?'

'I need a holiday.' Somehow she was managing to lie to him. Her request had everything to do with Kelly. 'I feel strung out and think a week in the sun will help me feel better. Help me move on.'

'Okay,' Alexander nodded and scratched at his chin. 'So which dates do you want off?'

'A week starting the day after tomorrow.'

'That's pretty sudden.' He flexed his hand into a fist and stared at her. 'You sure this is just about a holiday?'

'I need to heal. I need to stop dwelling on what happened to Kelly and find myself.' North was talking fast, trying to bounce her way around any verbal traps she might plant for herself. 'I know it's sudden but—'

Alexander held up a hand to silence her. 'Take the time, it's fine.'

'Really?' she felt light-headed with relief. She'd expected more questions. More resistance.

'You're right that you need to heal. Everything that has happened with Kelly has really taken a toll on you. Take the week. Take two if you need it. I just hope you'll be back when I return.'

'I…' North felt a heated flush gathered at her neck and start to creep up her cheeks.

'You could still come with me to the Canaries.' There was an intensity in Alexander's gaze which made North dizzy. She hugged her arms, squeezing her elbows and trying to anchor herself in place.

'I'm actually going to Monaco.'

'Monaco?'

She'd done it again, said too much and left room for Alexander to squeeze in a million questions which she didn't want to have to answer.

'It's… you know,' she shrugged, tried to sound flippant. 'All sunshine and superstars. I thought it'd be fun.'

'Off to chase a millionaire?' Did she detect a note of jealously in Alexander's voice.

'No. Course not.' She was going to chase Spencer Daniels and his yacht. Though not with a view to ensnare him for herself.

'Well, I want to hear all about it when you come back. Make sure you visit the Casino Royale.'

'I will.' North lied, certain she'd have little time for sightseeing.

'Though I've never had you pegged for much of a gambler.'

'I'm not.'

Alexander was making for the door now, but there was a reluctance in his stride. With his hand on the handle, he kept looking over at North instead of pressing down.

'Your flight?' she offered gently. 'It'll be leaving soon won't it?'

With a sad smile he turned his left wrist and checked his watch. 'All too soon I'm afraid.'

'Well, have fun out there.'

'You sure I can't tempt you with my giant telescope?'

North snorted with laughter. 'No, you cannot.'

'I miss that laugh.' He was staring at her. 'You don't laugh nearly enough.'

He had to be teasing. North laughed like a hyena, Kelly had told her as much.

'Take care in Monaco,' Alexander was finally going through the door. 'Make sure you come back. I'd be lost here without you.'

North refused to acknowledge his parting comment.

*

'What's this?' North opened the door to Kelly's uni room and found the small space dimly lit, her face cross-legged in the middle of the floor with a deck of cards fanned out around her.

'Sit,' Kelly urged with a grin. 'I'm teaching myself to play poker.'

'Been watching *Ocean's Eleven* again?' North flicked on the main light before joining her friend on the floor.

'And *21*,' Kelly's smile widened. 'I've decided that we are going to go to Vegas and make our fortune.'

'By card counting?'

'By card counting,' Kelly tapped the exposed deck.

'You know that card counting requires a photographic memory along with some decent mathematical ability?'

'Uh-huh.'

'Neither of which we have.'

Kelly scoffed. 'They make it look pretty easy in the movies. We just need to practise.'

'Kel—'

'I just need to train myself to see the cards. To feel the cards,' she ran her hands over the deck and hummed.

'Everyone is heading out to the union for indie band night.'

'Urgh,' Kelly's expression soured as though she'd just smelt raw fish. 'Let them. I don't want to have my hearing impaired by some sweaty boys with a Kurt Cobain complex who think smashing a set of drums and screaming into a microphone makes you a rock star.'

'You just want to sit here and try and card count instead?' North tried not to pout.

'Yep.'

North adjusted her position so that she was more comfortable on the floor. 'Okay then, let's do this.'

A month. That's how long Kelly's card counting phase lasted. At the end of those four weeks, North still didn't quite understand how to play poker but she had intimate knowledge of the various clubs and suits in a standard deck.

'One day we'll go to Vegas,' Kelly had promised as she put the deck away for the last time.

'Yeah, definitely.'

'And Monaco. We'll go there too. You can take pictures of me parading through the streets like I'm Grace Kelly. I'm already half there in name.'

'You do love your adventures.'

'The world is a big place. Your parents had the right idea; live frugally so that you can travel as much as possible.'

'I'm pretty sure my parents were just bad with money,' North sank onto the edge of Kelly's bed. There had been no money put away for her time at university. No life insurance policy that came into fruition after her parents disappeared.

'Maybe,' Kelly pursed her pink glossed lips. 'Maybe not. You got a lesson tomorrow?' She changed topic as she pulled a brush through her golden hair.

'Yeah. First thing. We're learning about supernovas.'

Kelly's expression remained flat. She was a drama student, the only stars she cared about were the ones on stage.

'When a star dies,' North quickly expanded on her answer.

'A star never truly dies,' Kelly declared with a theatrical wink. 'How early is your lesson?'

'Nine.'

'Good enough.' Putting down her brush, Kelly swept onto her feet and offered her hands out to her friend. 'You need hardly any sleep anyways. We're going out.'

'We are?' North queried as Kelly yanked her up off the bed.

'It's indie band night at the union.'

'I thought you hated that?'

'I did,' Kelly laughed. 'Until I heard that Tyler Bishop is in a band. He looks like just Robbie Williams.'

'I know.'

'He's bleached his hair.'

'I know.'

'And he's got that new tattoo that creeps up to his neck.'

'I know. You pointed it out when we were in the quad, remember? You kept looking at him and loudly commenting on his hair.'

'Well I wanted him to hear how I felt about it.'

'If you like him just ask him out.'

'I can't do that,' Kelly's voice dropped to a fearful whisper.

'Why not? It's not like he'd say no. No guy has ever turned you down.'

'Because I don't ask them,' Kelly stated primly. 'But you can ask for me.'

'Oh, Kel, not this again.'

'What?'

'Stop using me like your own personal Cilla Black.'

'I'm not.'

'Just ask him out yourself.' North was already cringing at what she was being asked to do.

'But it would sound so much better coming from you.' Kelly was ushering North out of her room. The corridor smelt like burnt toast.

'Kelly!'

'I'm just asking you to do this one teeny-tiny favour for me.'

'Fine. Whatever. Okay.'

'Yes,' Kelly clapped her hands together and gave a squeal of delight. 'I can't wait to hear what his band sounds like. I bet they're *amazing*.'

'Not just a bunch of guys with a Kurt Cobain complex?'
Kelly looked confused.
'I mean, he has dyed his hair blonde.'
'So what happens to a star when it dies?' Suddenly changing the subject, Kelly fell in step with North as they left their student halls behind and joined the throng of stragglers heading up towards the union. Music was already bleeding out into the night, shrill notes held for too long.
'I'll find out tomorrow.'
'Please,' Kelly nudged North in the ribs, 'you already know. You always read ahead. You're such a swot.'
'One – I'm not a swot, I'm organised. And two – maybe I do already have some sort of idea what happens. I'm committed to the course, Kel.'
'Well?'
'Okay, well, from what I've read, one of two things usually happen. Either the gravitational core at the heart of the star is so powerful that it binds everything to it creating a black hole.' Am I boring you yet?' She waited for Kelly to glaze over but her friend's gaze remained bright with interest.
'Or?'
'Or several new stars are born.'
'So a star dies to create new ones?'
'Uh-huh.'
'I like that,' Kelly gave a sincere nod. 'It's better than the black hole thing.'
'Agreed.'
'Why are they called black holes anyway? Isn't all space black?'
'Light can't escape from a black hole. The gravity within it is just so powerful, it absorbs absolutely everything.'
'That sounds... greedy.'

'Yeah,' North laughed. 'I guess it is.'

13

'So what was that about?'

North was back at her desk when Elijah came over.

'Everything okay?'

'Yeah, I…' Her mind was a spinning top. Thoughts whirled in a maelstrom but none were static for long enough for her to give them due attention.

She needed to book her flights. Her hotel. She needed to plan what she intended to say to Spencer Daniels when she encountered him and The Orion.

'North?' A deep crease had formed between Elijah's eyebrows as he dropped into a nearby empty seat and pulled it close to her desk. 'What's up?'

'I booked some leave, remember?'

'Oh, yeah.'

To anyone else she'd give them the spiel about needing time away from work, time to heal. But she knew that Elijah deserved the truth.

'I'm going to Monaco.'

'Seriously?'

'Uh-huh,' she kept her voice low as she typed on her keyboard and looked at her screen. 'I traced the location of the yacht Kelly worked on to there. It will be moored up in the harbour for the next couple of days.'

'And you intend to what? Board it and conduct some stealth investigation?' His tone was serious and non-judgemental. If anything he sounded concerned.

'I haven't figured it all out yet.'

'You're going on your own?' The question was pitched, and for a moment North could have been forgiven for thinking she was having a discussion with her late grandmother.

Both of her grandparents had exercised caution when it came to her. Every foray, every teenage jaunt was met with a barrage of questions.

You're going where?
With Kelly?
For how long?
How will you get back?
Do you know the train times?
Do you have enough money?

But they needn't have worried. North never acted on a whim. She wasn't her parents. When Kelly came to her with a wild idea, it was left to North to figure out the practicalities of it all. She was the plotter to Kelly's dreamer.

'I'm going on my own, yes.' North's voice turned to stone. She could do this. If she let her fears of the unknown, of adventure, hold her back then she'd be letting Kelly down. She had to go. She had to be brave.

'I think it's a bad idea.' Elijah sounded unusually stern.

'It's Monaco, hardly a place synonymous with danger.'

'I'll go with you.'

'What?' North squeaked in shock at the sudden offer.

'I've got some overdue leave I can take. When do we go?'

'Look, Elijah—'

His hand clasped hers and he looked deep into her eyes. 'This isn't up for negotiation, North. If you truly intend to do this then I'm going along too.'

Something fluttered in North's stomach which had been dormant for too long. Was it hope? The first flicker of a flame?

'Really, it's—'

'I get that you need answers about Kelly and I want to help.'

His eyes were so blue. So full of sparkle. Like sunlight dancing on a gentle ocean. He wanted to help. So many people kept slamming doors in North's face when it came to Kelly and here was someone willing to aid her as she desperately tried to pry them all back open.

'I'll be booking the next available flight,' she warned.

'Sounds good.'

'And there'll be no time for sightseeing. Once there it's all about The Orion.'

'Okay. Got it.'

'Then we're doing this.' A shiver of nervous excitement traced its way down North's spine.

'We're doing this.'

*

Kelly loved airports. She was always intrigued by the random collection of humanity you'd find there. People going on holidays, people going away for work. People returning to loved ones after a long absence. All these agendas collided in the departure lounges.

A day had passed. In that time North had bought the tickets to Nice, arranged a hire car and booked a room at The Fairmount with two double beds. She couldn't afford two rooms. Something she stressed to Elijah as they headed to the airport.

'I'm paying half anyway,' he told her resolutely.

'This is my trip, you shouldn't have to pay.'

'I'm a modern man, I believe in going Dutch.'

North smiled nervously. This wasn't some sort of elaborate date. This was a fact-finding expedition. She didn't want Elijah to get the wrong idea. Perhaps she'd been wrong to let him come along, but she'd been attracted to the idea of having company. She never travelled alone. Not like Kelly, who loved the thrill of a solo adventure.

'You make friends on the plane,' she'd explain.

To North that seemed impossible. She struggled to make small talk with strangers, let alone launch into a full-blown conversation which would result in friendship. It had taken her a lifetime to find just one person who truly understood her.

'At least it's not too busy,' Elijah commented as he pulled his suitcase towards the check-in desk.

He was right. There were bodies clustered around the large departure area but there weren't throngs of people. School was in session, most families wouldn't be taking their holidays at this time of year. The airport was vast and futuristic. It wouldn't look out of place in a science-fiction movie. Giant walls of glass revealed glimpses of planes, noses tipped towards the sky as they powered away from the runway making their ascent.

North closed her eyes and imagined Kelly's voice in her ear. 'Just think, every plane is a portal to adventure, to a new place. It's all so thrilling.'

'You got your passport ready?' Elijah was almost at the check-in desk looking back at her. To the people milling around them, did they look just like any other couple?

'You two are just adorable together,' she could almost hear Kelly teasing her from beyond the grave.

'Come on,' Elijah ushered her forward. 'Let's get checked in.'

*

The planes seemed to never stop. As one ascended up into the clouds, another appeared at the end of the runway, ready to sprint.

'It's one of the busiest airports in the world,' Elijah joined her at the window, hands full of newly bought cups of coffee. He handed one to North and smiled. 'I think there's less than a minute between each take-off.'

'Wow. That's... hectic.'

'Yep. It's up to the guys in that tower,' he pointed to a top-heavy structure in the centre of the network of runways, 'to make sure everything runs smoothly. There's a real science to it. If you get the timings between take-off and landing wrong you risk bedlam.'

'You sound awfully knowledgeable,' North noted with interest. She realised there was a lot she didn't know about him and she felt keen to learn more.

'I considered a career in air traffic control at one time,' Elijah confirmed with a nod. 'What can I say; I'm drawn to the skies.'

'I get that.' She looked at the thick cloud cover. An ocean of white that eagerly absorbed all approaching aircraft.

'We've got an hour before our flight.'

'Okay.'

'What do you want to do?'

North breathed against the ache in her chest. 'Kelly,' a bittersweet smile pulled on her lips. 'She used to like to play games to kill time in airports. Set challenges.'

'Right,' Elijah took a sip from his coffee and squared his shoulders. 'So what's my challenge?'

'You want to play?' North couldn't conceal her surprise. At work Elijah was so serious, so driven. It seemed surreal to now conduct Kelly's playful games with him.

'Sure.'

'We could just sit and read a book or something.'

'Where's the fun in that?' he smiled softly at her. 'Name the challenge.'

'Okay,' North tapped her cheek as she turned away from the glass wall to peer around the terminal. There was a cluster of duty-free shops, a wealth of vacant chairs and moving platforms which guided travellers deeper into the network of the airport towards their relevant gate. Soon the information on the digital departure boards would update and she too would stand on a platform and be taken ever closer to Monaco, to The Orion. First they just needed to kill some time.

It was always Kelly who set the challenges. She'd clap her hands together excitedly as she announced them, like she were auditioning for a *Challenge Anneka* revival show. North tried to think of some of their more memorable challenges.

Go and buy a hideous hat.

Find three newspapers with completely different headlines.

Order a really complicated coffee, slowly. Hold your ground when the barista gets annoyed. Then repeat it.

Use the men's toilet.

Sit next to a stranger, like right next to them. Then start humming to yourself. Loudly.

Kelly was forever trying to push North out of her comfort zone. She could complete any of the challenges without being fazed, but North struggled to engage with other people, especially when she knew she was annoying them. Her palms would go slick and her eyes would twitch and she'd yearn to scratch at her arms. But for Kelly she'd stick it out, for Kelly she'd be brave.

North decided upon the newspaper challenge now. That way she and Elijah could idle in the bookstore for a while. She fancied the idea of buying something new to read. She'd noticed a lot of chat online about a book where five friends get trapped in a cabin. People seemed to enjoy speculating on the truth behind it all since the author was in the cabin.

'That's a tall order,' Elijah noted of his challenge. 'A scandal broke only yesterday about the deputy prime minister and some former aide he was sleeping with.'

'The girl who died?'

'That's the one. I reckon it'll be all over all of the papers.'

North vaguely recalled reading about the story during her frantic yacht-based research. Most of the time she was blissfully blinkered to the rest of the world but occasionally something slipped through into her sphere of recognition.

'No one said the challenges were meant to be easy,' she playfully punched him in the arm before heading for the nearest book shop.

*

'You just sit there humming while the other person gets uncomfortable,' Kelly whispered, glancing towards her chosen target. He was a man in his mid to late fifties in an ill-fitting suit. He had thinning grey hair and an ample set of chins.

'I can't do this,' North wrung her hands together. She just wanted to sit and read her book not harass strangers.

'Come on,' Kelly urged, straining her voice. 'It'll be fun. We can't just sit here and wait for our flight like boring regulars.'

'Maybe I want to be a boring regular. Just this once.'

Kelly rolled her eyes with theatrical flair. 'Please, no one wants to be a regular. Ever. Go do it. Sit by him and hum the national anthem.'

'No.'

'Yes.' Kelly poked her in the ribs until she stood up. North wanted to throw up. She wasn't a peacock like her friend was, willing to strut around and draw attention to herself. North was more of a blue tit, timid and small. 'Go do it. Quick, before he leaves.'

There was no denying Kelly. North went and sat beside the man. She clasped her clammy hands together and hummed the national anthem. He regarded her warily out of the corner of his eye while he tried to read his newspaper. Finally, after three painful minutes, he coughed, got up, and went to sit elsewhere.

'That was amazing,' Kelly could barely speak over her laughter. 'Did you see his *face*? He looked *so* uncomfortable. That was awesome, North.'

'Can I read my book now?' North was already pulling the dog-eared novel out of her backpack.

'I suppose so. But I warn you – you're being a bore.'

'Then consider me a bore.'

'Sometimes it's good to push yourself,' Kelly leaned back in her seat and surveyed the people around them.

'I don't agree. If you push too hard you drift from who you really are.'

'If it wasn't for me you'd sit in your little bedroom at your grandparents' all day long reading your books and watching your films.'

'What's wrong with that?' she wondered innocently.

'There's a *world* out there, North. We've seen so many amazing things together. Paris, Rome, Thailand.'

'When I read I travel the world. This book,' she tapped the cover of her current read, 'is set in Russia during—'

'Not everyone who goes off on an adventure dies.'

North blanched as she realised where the conversation was going.

'Just because your parents never came home doesn't mean that you should never leave yours.'

'Look, Kel—'

'I'll keep making you brave, North. I'll keep dragging you out of your comfort zone, keep taking you to exciting places. And do you know why?'

'Because you're mean?' North teased.

'No,' Kelly countered with a laugh. 'Because I care about you. Because as much as you love looking up all the time at your bloody stars you miss seeing the wonders that are all around you. It's my job to keep you focused on what's here, on earth.'

'And you do a damn good job of it.'

'I know,' Kelly gave a falsely modest grin and batted her eyelashes. 'Like today we are Venice-bound. Because of me you'll get to visit the sinking city. Don't you just love me?'

'Thanks,' North slowly turned the page in her book.

'For what?'

'For forcing me to leave home now and then.'

'Don't mention it.'

*

'Well, I failed,' Elijah dropped a stack of newspapers on the chair beside North. 'Every paper has a headline about the same thing.'

'Ah, shame.'

'So what now? Do I have to do a forfeit or something?'

'Worse.'

'Oh?' Elijah looked more intrigued than scared.

'Whoever failed to complete their airport challenge forfeited their right to select music during road trips for the duration of the holiday.'

'So...'

'So it's all radio North once we reach Nice. Don't worry, I packed my iPod.'

'Sounds like you and Kelly used to have a lot of fun on your holidays.' He noted gently.

'We did,' North felt warmed by the nostalgia of it all. 'Kelly had a knack for finding the fun in every situation. She could be in hospital and she'd have the rest of the ward in stitches, so to speak.'

'How are you holding up now that she's... you know.'

'I think what she would do,' North admitted. 'She wouldn't sit around and mope. She'd be proactive. That was Kelly's style. Like after my parents didn't come back she refused to let me sit in my room and wallow. We went out. We went to see every movie going at the cinema, we went cycling, we went up to the town centre and sat beside the large green fountain gossiping until they pulled down the shutters on all the shops around us.'

'Sometimes it's important to take the time to process your grief.'

'No.' North picked up the paper on the top of the stack and began to riffle through it. 'Tears don't bring somebody back.'

'It's not always about bringing someone back. It's about trying to heal.'

'How do you *heal* a broken heart?' North thumbed through the large pages of the broadsheet. Kelly would have grabbed all the tabloid papers, drawn to their scandalous contents. 'Because the last time I checked there's no way to heal it, you just have to learn how to live with it.'

14

'Well, we're not in Kansas anymore,' Elijah remarked dryly as he pulled their little hire car up outside The Fairmount hotel. For hours they'd driven through wine country, rolling hills speckled green with twisting vines which baked in the French sunlight. Now they were at the coast in a tiny principality. She felt in a different galaxy to her sleepy little Millwater.

It was the cars which North noticed first. As they rounded a corner and began to descend into Monaco, she spotted Bentleys, Ferraris, Aston Martins. Every luxury vehicle imaginable was gliding down the same streets as her little hire car, sun glinting off their expensive roofs. The abundance of sunshine made the golden glow of Monaco even brighter. There was so much wealth about, from cars to couture, it was suffocating.

A suited doorman swiftly approached their modest hire car and popped the boot. He was grabbing her luggage with his gloved hands before she'd even opened her door.

'Hey,' she hurried around the back of the car. 'That's okay, thanks. I got it.'

With a baffled expression, the doorman straightened and glanced towards Elijah who was quickly climbing out of the passenger seat.

'Will you want valet parking?' the doorman enquired.

'Yeah, sure,' North nervously shoved her car keys into his outstretched hand. It felt strange to have people waiting on her, to be treated like she was worth something. Whenever she went on holiday with Kelly they opted for the cheap and cheerful route, hopping between hostels as they explored new cities. In

Monaco there was only luxury on offer. North had no choice but to opt for a grand hotel.

'This place is certainly...' As they pushed their way through the glass front doors, Elijah craned his neck to take in the lobby. It was huge, easily large enough to accommodate a number of double-decker buses. The footsteps of well-dressed ladies clipped against the marble floor.

Turning, North saw that an entire wall was made of glass and it boasted the most glorious views of the ocean.

'Come on, let's check in,' she grabbed Elijah's sleeve and tugged him towards a large mahogany desk.

A nautical theme ran through the hotel. The more North saw of it the more she realised that the entire structure had been built to feel like a cruise ship. Now, with room key in hand, she was meandering down a long corridor which snaked its way along the length of The Fairmount. The walls were crisp and white, the carpet a deep shade of blue.

Finally she reached her door.

408.

North slid the key card into place and as soon as the light turned green on the lock she pushed her way inside. The journey over from London was beginning to take its toll. Against all the pristine people sashaying around the hotel lobby she felt grimy with travel.

'Wow, not too shabby,' Elijah stepped in after her, eyes wide with awe.

It was the simplest room The Fairmount had on offer, but truly there was nothing simple about it. Two double beds were against the right wall, both immaculately made with white linen sheets. A flat-screen television was mounted opposite them, beneath that there was a sweeping whitewood sideboard. Further exploration of the drawers revealed a hairdryer and a mini bar.

Over by the marble bathroom which boasted a walk-in shower and claw-foot bathtub was a wardrobe equipped with a fold-out ironing board.

'Have you seen this view?' Elijah was over by the double doors which opened onto a sun-soaked balcony. There was a small table beside him adorned with complimentary tea and coffee-making facilities. He pushed open the doors and let the scent of the sea enter the room. North could hear the distant roar of the waves. 'This place is beautiful.'

'It's... lovely.' Exhausted, North sat on the end of the nearest bed. So far Monaco lived up to all the shine and stature it was synonymous with. Everything glistened like diamonds, even the people. But instead of feeling excited by all the grandeur, North felt nervous, like a human who had dared to climb up to the top of Mount Olympus and now risked facing the wrath of the Gods.

*

Sleep. The main requirement of being in a bedroom. Whilst North's bones ached, she doubted she'd actually be able to find respite in her soft bed. It felt good to shower, to change into clean clothes. Elijah was yawning in front of the television when she stepped back into the bedroom, the remains of their room service dinner order spread out around him.

'I'm beat,' he declared with another jaw stretching yawn. 'Shall we start our search for The Orion first thing tomorrow?'

'Um, yeah, sure.'

Beyond the balcony the sea had been claimed by darkness. The lights of Monaco sparkled against a canopy of stars. It was beautiful. It was paradise. North looked nervously at her bed.

Her stomach clenched as though it had been placed within a vice. Grinding her teeth, she quickly drew her nails along her forearms for some temporary relief.

'I cannot wait to sleep in this bed,' Elijah was folding back the sheets and tucking himself in. North envied his slow, sleepy movements. 'You can keep the TV on if you want,' he mumbled, 'and I'll try not to snore too much.'

The TV. North looked at it, grateful for its presence. She kept the news on as she sat on her own bed, tucking herself up against the pillows. Her body screamed for sleep, but she could already feel that her mind would forbid it. While every other muscle and organ relaxed against the softness of the bed, her thoughts continued to needle within her mind, sharp and relentless. If she dared to close her eyes would she wake to find Kelly at her bedside, haunted and afraid?

*

Three a.m.

North had watched midnight come and go, had listened to the steady rumble of Elijah's breath as he slept soundly in the next bed. She knew that the sandman had overlooked her this time. Resigned to her fate, she quietly slipped away from the room. Key card in hand she traced her way back down the vast corridor, towards the lifts and then down into the lobby. She expected solitude but she found life.

Despite the time, the lobby was pulsating with movement and sound. A band was playing, uniformed staff were bustling about and there were guests sauntering along the marble floors clutching champagne flutes and laughing loudly. North soon discovered the source of energy that fuelled the hotel through the night – its casino.

In a giant room she found a part of Las Vegas. Roulette, poker, blackjack. All were being played by guests dressed in ball gowns, suits, even Hawaiian shirts and cargo shorts. In the casino, all were welcome, everyone was a potential player.

North drifted amongst the crowds. It was reassuring to see so many other faces defying the body's desire to sleep when darkness fell. They laughed in the face of their naturally set rhythms, choosing to roll the dice, pick a card, make a bet, instead of closing their eyes.

Money. It didn't have a smell, it had a presence. When North sidled by a table, she'd glance down at the current wager being made. Some bets were modest – a hundred euros here, three hundred there. Some made her pulse quicken. At one table the minimum bet was ten thousand euros. North quickly shied away from that one. The winners would cry out with joy while the losers hastily made another bet, keen to experience the euphoria of their most successful counterparts. Everything was decided on the roll of the dice, on the suit of a card.

Sitting down on a vacant stool at a digital roulette machine, North pretended to play but really she was imagining how Kelly would have behaved in such a scene. She'd have swept in through the double doors, pushed back her shoulders, raised her chin and seamlessly fitted in with Monaco's finest. In a ball gown, she could easily be mistaken for a movie star or a princess. Kelly would have glided amongst the tables, flirted with the men making the largest bets. With eyes full of mischief she'd beckon North to follow her.

'Let's have some fun,' she'd whisper conspiratorially. Against the backdrop of dramatic wins and losses, Kelly would find the fun. She could turn any moment into an adventure.

'Are you going to play?' a grey-haired man with a handlebar moustache and a thick German accent pointed a wrinkled finger at the game North was currently neglecting.

'No,' she slid off her stool and gave him a polite smile. 'Not tonight.'

*

There was only one place The Orion could be and that was in the harbour. Luckily it was just a short walk from the hotel. They only had to navigate a few steep streets and sharp corners and they were there.

If Elijah had noticed North disappearing during the night, he didn't mention it. When he stirred at seven, she was back in the room staring dead-eyed at the television. She reckoned she might have sneaked in a catnap somewhere during the night but couldn't be sure.

They had breakfast up on the terrace by the pool. North nibbled on a croissant while she watched the early morning sun winking on the water of the sea. It was so serene that it was crazy to think that her previous breakfast had been eaten alone in her flat, a bowl of cereal hastily devoured while she stood in front of her wall of notes.

'What happens when we find the yacht?' Elijah asked as he walked in step with her. He wore a pale blue polo shirt and beige knee-length shorts along with boat shoes. He'd clearly packed with their destination in mind. North had lacked such foresight. She wore pale skinny jeans and an oversized Ramones T-shirt. Her hair was tugged back in a tight ponytail, but she had at least remembered to pack her wayfarer sunglasses.

'Let's find it first.' North walked with purpose. One thing she'd picked up from her time travelling with Kelly was to always look like she belonged. Kelly had taught her that it was about more than the clothes you were wearing, it was how you wore them.

'Shoulders back, chin up. Don't be sheepish, don't slouch,' Kelly would instruct sternly. 'If you act like you belong, people will just assume that you do. Don't give them any reason to doubt you.'

'What do you think of the place?' Elijah asked as they passed by a boutique Italian restaurant which was currently closed.

'It's nice.' North knew that Monaco deserved a more emphatic compliment. It was unblemished by pollution, graffiti, litter. Every street was freshly swept, meticulously maintained. There was an air of opulence but also of pride. Monaco was a beautiful place because it continued to strive for excellence, it did not let its reputation become its sole selling point, it worked to live up to the expectations of those who came to visit.

'Christ.' They'd reached the harbour. Elijah stopped abruptly as the path beneath their feet turned to decking. 'Damn, honey, I can't remember where we parked ours,' he joked.

The harbour was a sight to behold. North had seen it on television where grand yachts bobbed up and down in the current like bathtub toys. But seeing it in person was something else. The scale of the yachts was just staggering. They were huge. Mini mansions on water. Some even had smaller boats moored on their lower decks. Looking around, North saw yachts with hot tubs, helicopter pads, through open double doors chandeliers and the distant sheen of giant cinema-sized plasma televisions. It was all around her, an abundance of insane wealth crammed into a tiny harbour.

Because whilst the boats were big, the harbour wasn't. North could walk the length of it in less than thirty minutes, which would hopefully aide their search for The Orion.

'Okay,' Elijah placed his hand on the small of her back. It sent a pulse of excitement up her spine. 'Let's get looking.'

So many boats were named after women. North saw the bow of the Diana, the Gail, the Stacie, the Emily. Some names were more grand; the Goliath, Titan, Trident. Every yacht had a gangway up towards its main deck sectioned off by a sliver of silver rope. It seemed a flimsy barrier to separate the rich from everyone else. North wondered what would happen if she just lifted a leg over the slim length of rope and boarded a yacht. Kelly would have risked it. In a heartbeat she'd have been climbing aboard the biggest yacht she could fine. But North sensed that such playful behaviour wouldn't be tolerated. There was a dignified air around, not just the harbour, but all of Monaco. People here *behaved.* Those who didn't surely didn't get to visit a second time.

'North, over there,' Elijah was nodding discreetly at the yacht just up ahead. It was dwarfed by the ebony boat which flanked it but was still grand in its own right. A trio of wooden decks rose up out of the body of the yacht. It was white with a silver trim. And in ornate silver writing along its side it read *The Orion*.

'Shit, that's it,' North bent forward, for a moment struggling to breathe. The boat was here, overwhelmingly real. If she reached out, she could touch its smooth outer surface. It was on this boat that Kelly had sailed. The air dipped in temperature, sending goose bumps racing up North's bare arms as the past collided with the present. Kelly had waltzed on the deck, trays of champagne in her hands. Had she leaned over the railing to watch the rush of the waves as the yacht powered out to sea?

'What now?' Elijah was looking up and down the decked area of the harbour. There were tourists mingling around them, pausing to smile in front of the grandest yachts and take smiling selfies on their phones.

'I…' North eyed the slip of silver rope barring entrance to the boat. She peered up at the deck and wondered if anyone was currently on board. They had to be. Despite this being Monaco who would leave such a prized asset unattended? 'We need to find someone to talk to,' she quickly formulated a plan in her mind as she approached the gangway.

'Okay, but how?' Elijah drew her back by the elbow. 'All I see around here are more tourists. There has to be a harbour master or something. Let me go and—'

North surged forward. Lifting one foot, she stepped over the silver rope. No alarms started screaming. The harbour remained tranquil and quiet.

'Shit, North,' Elijah's face turned pink with panic. 'You can't just… go aboard. What if someone finds you? You might get arrested for… for trespassing!'

She was channelling Kelly. She was being bold, brave. Reckless. But what did it matter? That step over the rope brought her one step to the answers she sought.

'I'm only going to see if there's someone around I can speak to.' She dared to proceed across the main deck. 'I'm not looking to cause any trouble.'

Elijah was at her back, his chest rising with every frantic breath he drew in. 'Fine. But you're not doing this alone.'

15

'You can't be here.'

Kelly boldly met the uniformed security guard's stern gaze. 'We're here to see Nick,' she flicked her kohl-laced eyes briefly in North's direction, 'and AJ.'

'Girls,' the guard approached them, spreading his thick arms wide like he was trying to herd a flock of sheep out of the corridor. 'This part of the venue is *off limits*. You need to leave.'

The screams from within the arena vibrated through the surrounding walls. The high-pitched pluck of an electric guitar indicated that the support act had just started their set on stage.

'Girls, come on, you're missing the show.' He kept trying to usher them out, but Kelly stood firm. She folded her arms over her Backstreet Boys concert T-shirt and pouted her glittery purple lips.

'We showed real ingenuity by finding our way back here.'

'You fans are always persistent,' the guard agreed with a weary sigh.

'All we want is an autograph to take home.'

'Girls, the meet and greet is over. The guys are getting ready for the show and you should be doing the same. Go and take your seats now and stop giving me trouble.'

'It's scribble on a piece of paper that would make our day. Our year.' Kelly wasn't budging. Even though she was several inches shorter than the guard and considerably less stout, she managed to be just as intimidating. 'We took three trains to get here.'

'Look, girls, I appreciate that you came a long way to be here but—'

'Last summer her parents disappeared off a boat,' Kelly nodded at North. 'People keep telling her they won't come back. I bought her here to cheer her up. I promised her that I'd get an autograph from AJ for her.'

'Girls,' the guard held a thick hand against his forehead as he ceased trying to herd them back up the corridor. 'I'm sorry about your parents.' He looked at North and she knew what to do. All over the country people had heard about the couple who were lost at sea, at the poor little girl they'd left behind. She started to cry. Thanks to Kelly they had been dining out on her parents' disappearance for weeks now.

'Play the hand you get dealt,' Kelly had explained. 'Right now your parents are a hot topic, everyone has heard about what happened. We need to use this.'

'But why?'

'Something majorly shitty happened to you,' Kelly had stated with uncharacteristic sincerity. 'The only way you survive something shitty is to use it to your advantage. Remember that.'

Tears were sliding down North's cheeks and the security guard looked very uncomfortable. He kept shifting his gaze back along the corridor, at the parts of the venue which were supposedly forbidden to those who didn't have a coveted backstage pass.

'An autograph, that's it,' Kelly stated simply as they reached the end of their negotiations. 'AJ and Nick. It will take them less than a minute tops.'

'Fine,' the guard grumbled as his walls of authority came tumbling down. 'This way, but make sure you're quick.'

*

'You can't be here.'

North had barely crossed the deck when a slim ginger-haired man slipped out of the main body of the boat wearing a white polo shirt with the logo of the yacht emblazoned in the upper corner.

'I'm...' North looked about. She was standing beside long beige sofas that were fitted into the sides of the deck. The crew member barred the way into the rest of the yacht. Behind him she could make out the twinkle of a chandelier.

'Seriously, you can't be here,' he repeated in a sharp Irish accent. It made North think of Alexander. She clenched her hands into fists and tried to remain in the moment. 'If you get caught here, they'll call the police. This is private property – you need to leave.'

'I just wanted to ask some questions about my friend. She used to work here.'

'Any questions should come in via the website, not be asked in person.' The ginger guy advanced towards her, his green eyes glazed in a menacing stare.

'Kelly Orton. Did you know her?'

He instantly softened. North could see a mixture of emotions swirling behind his eyes.

'If you're Kelly's friend then you'll know she doesn't work here anymore. You need to go.'

'Hey man, come on,' Elijah was at North's side, 'it's just a few questions. Can't you just hear her out?'

'You've been asked to leave.' A new voice entered the conversation, one which made the ginger guy jump and spin around.

'I was just telling them, Mr Daniels, that they needed to go.'

Spencer Daniels stepped out onto the deck. He looked just as quaffed as he did in his social media photos. He was dressed in all white. White shirt, white trousers, white loafers. The only shock of colour came from his bouffant hair, into which he'd pushed a pair of designer sunglasses. His skin was golden, his tan accentuated by the white of his outfit. In his online pictures he was handsome but in person he was stunning, like a god who'd just stepped down off Mount Olympus to charitably spend time with mere mortals. He was awe inspiring in looks alone, just as Kelly had been. Beauty that was blinding.

'You've been politely informed that we can't answer questions in person. Please, send any in via email.' He sounded charming with his private school accent, but his mouth was held in a firm, unwelcoming line.

'Mr Daniels, I—'

Spencer clicked his fingers but didn't turn back in the crew member's direction. 'Go check on lunch.'

The ginger guy almost ran back towards the chandelier.

North locked her feet in position, squared her shoulders and pushed out her chest as she stared Spencer Daniels straight in the eye. Kelly wouldn't be dismissed so easily so nor would North. 'We're not here to cause trouble, we just have a few questions.'

'No.'

'What?'

'No pictures. No autographs. Not today. I'm sorry but these sort of encounters need to be pre-planned, especially when you choose to just board my yacht. I'm not at the public's beck and call, you know.'

'I'm not here for a picture, I'm—'

'Enough pleasantries. Get off my yacht before I call the authorities,' he overly gestured towards the gangway and the harbour beyond it.

'I'm here to ask about Kelly Orton.'

The hand which had been extended promptly dropped against Spencer's side. 'Who?'

'My friend, Kelly. She worked on this boat last summer.'

'A great many people work upon my *yacht*,' he dragged out the final word through clenched teeth.

'Yes but you'd remember Kelly.'

'And why's that?'

'Because she's beautiful, she stands out.'

'Sweetheart,' Spencer was laughing as he ran his fingers along his lean jawline, 'I'm surrounded by beautiful women every day. Beauty is commonplace to me.'

'Please,' North stepped forward, wanting to appeal to the philanthropist not the playboy as Spencer flinched in disgust. 'I just need to talk to someone who worked with her. Maybe you don't remember her but someone has to.'

'We're done here. Get off my yacht. I won't ask again.'

'She's dead,' the words blurted from North before she'd even considered the consequences of revealing that much. She was just playing the hand she'd been dealt, just as Kelly would have done.

Spencer said nothing. North boldly carried on, assuming his silence was a mark of stunned grief.

'She died recently and I wanted to ask her crewmates if they noticed anything strange about her behaviour this summer. It won't take long, I promise.'

'My condolences about your friend.' Spencer was again pointing at the gangway, his expression blank.

'Kelly,' North sternly corrected him. 'Her name was Kelly. Kelly Orton. She worked on your *boat* and recently died in suspicious circumstances.'

'Suspicious?' Spencer's nostrils flared. North wished she could see his eyes but they were hidden behind the flat sheen of his sunglasses.

'Yes, suspicious,' Elijah confirmed. 'Hence the questions.'

'Are you police officers?'

'No.'

'Private investigators?'

'No,' North shook her head. 'But—'

'Then you can't talk to my staff. I'm not going to risk one of them accidentally implicating themselves in these...' he paused and clicked his fingers in the direction of the main area of the yacht, 'suspicious circumstances. People have an abhorrent way of twisting the truth for their own means.'

Two security guards appeared out of the glass double doors. They had tree trunks for arms and wore matching black uniforms. Considering their size, they moved with relative stealth. North watched as they flanked Spencer. His lips lifted into a celebratory grin as he nodded again at the gangway.

'As I said before, we're done here.'

'Please,' North pleaded. 'I only want to know who she was friends with. Who she hung out with while she worked here.' She stepped forward and was met with the palm of the nearest guard. It was pressed squarely in her face, forbidding further access to Spencer. Not that it mattered. He was leaving. His footsteps bounced off the wooden planks of the deck as he disappeared back into his luxurious bolt hole.

'You need to leave.' The guard had a voice as deep as the Mariana Trench. North shuddered fearfully when she heard it.

'Show a little compassion,' Elijah urged the large man. 'She lost her best friend in the whole world and just has a few questions, that's all.'

'It wasn't a request.'

Five minutes later and they were back in the main harbour after being unceremoniously hustled off The Orion. The guards lingered on the deck like a pair of prowling panthers.

'Well,' Elijah smoothed his hands down his shorts. 'That could have gone better.'

'We pissed him off,' North scratched her nails against her lower arms. 'Now we'll never find out anything.'

*

Kelly didn't kill herself.

The message didn't return. It seemed now to exist only in North's mind. But she so desperately needed to see it on her phone's screen, to know that she wasn't alone in her conviction. Someone was directing her towards the truth, but who? If only the message would stop disappearing.

Or was it ever there?

North swiftly pushed the thought out of her mind. It was there. She'd seen it. She wasn't hallucinating, it had been real. It had to be.

*

'Did you see Emily's new car?' North asked as she walked straight into Kelly's uni room and dramatically threw herself onto the bed. 'A KA. *Brand new.*'

'Bought by Mummy and Daddy of course,' Kelly rolled her eyes from where she sat at her desk, focused on her reflection in her propped-up make-up mirror as she expertly traced her eyes with liquid liner.

'I'd kill for a car.'

'No you wouldn't.'

'Yes, I would,' North challenged petulantly. 'Depending on who I had to kill.' She rolled onto her side and reached for the book on Kelly's bedside table. She absently flicked through the pages as her friend kept carefully applying her eyeliner.

'Emily will be the loser in the end,' Kelly stated as she capped her eyeliner with a flourish and returned it to her neon make-up bag.

'How so?' North grumbled, unconvinced.

'Her parents buy her *everything*. Did you see those Chanel shoes she was parading around last week?'

'Yes, I saw. How does having designer shoes make her a loser?'

'She's privileged.' Kelly pursed her lips as she slicked red gloss over them.

'So?'

'So there's no hunger, no drive. If you already have it all what motivates you to succeed?'

'Wanting to keep it all?'

Kelly smacked her lips together and then blew a kiss at her reflection. 'Not always. If you grew up spoilt you become entitled.'

'Having money does make things easier.'

'True,' Kelly rummaged through her make-up bag for her blusher. 'But someone like Emily is always going to look to buy her way out of trouble. If she fails on a test she tries to bribe the examiner, which in the end only cheats herself.'

'This is starting to sound like an awfully noble stance for you to take.'

'I can be noble,' Kelly spun around in her chair to face her friend. 'Like, we get good grades because we work hard. We study. One day we'll own a car that we bought with our own money. Money we earned. And it will feel good.'

'Will it?' North wondered sourly. 'Even if my parents were still around, they could never afford to get me a car. And while we'll be squashed by the weight of student debt, Emily will be all carefree driving around in her fancy ride in her designer shoes.'

'Jeez, could you be more morose about it all?'

'I'm just stating the facts.'

'And dwelling on your situation in the process.'

North rolled onto her stomach. She didn't like to face Kelly's judgement, especially when her friend was right.

'It's not money that makes the world go round it's the gravitational pull of the sun. You taught me that.'

'Don't make this about existentialism.' North grumbled.

'From our humble beginnings we will rise up, North.' Kelly landed on the bed with a bounce. 'One day we'll have a wardrobe full of fancy shoes. And furs.'

'No furs,' North objected. 'Absolutely no furs.'

'Fine, no furs,' Kelly shrugged the suggestion away. 'But we'll make it and it will be on our terms. It won't be because our parents paid for fancy schools and cars. It will be because we worked for it. Because we worked our asses off for it.'

'And if we're not successful?'

'Define success,' Kelly challenged. 'If I'm loved back by the people who I love I'd consider that pretty successful.'

'I know but—'

'Stop trying to measure it by shoes and cars or anything else. Someone's worth shouldn't have a price. If it does, avoid them. You're better off without people like that.'

'Since when were you so zen about the elite?'

'Since Thursday,' Kelly turned back towards her mirror to check her reflection. 'Aiden is vegan. I'm trying to be all... you know... liberal and shit.'

'But you want a wardrobe full of furs?'

'That's *wearing* an animal, not eating it.'

'Still killing it.'

'Don't let the bad stuff drag you down,' Kelly slid off the bed and then leaned back to give North's shoulders a squeeze. 'You've been through a lot; don't let it hold you back.'

'It doesn't.'

'Because I won't let it.'

'And I love you for that. See – you're successful. Hallelujah.'

'So what if you don't have a brand new car?'

'I'd take any car at this point. Think Emily would consider selling me her cast-off at a discount?'

'Being rich doesn't make you a better person. It just makes you... rich.'

'It's everything it can buy,' North lamented. 'Beyond the cars and the shoes, the backstage passes, the things off limits to everyone else. We're just the little guys, we risk getting squashed beneath some designer boot.'

'Stay strong and play your hand.'

'Kel—'

'Because that's all you can do. Don't back down, North. Keep fighting. The flashier the opponent, the bigger the punch you need to knock out some of their oh-so-perfect teeth.'

'Remind me to never get into a scrap with you,' North laughed.

'I don't need to.'

'Why's that?'

'Because I know you'll only ever be fighting on my side.'

16

'The guy was a dick,' Elijah slung his arm around North's shoulders as he drew her in for a consolatory hug. 'He was never going to tell us anything, no matter how nicely you asked. Shame, he comes across okay in the media.'

'I know,' North leaned against Elijah. He smelt of limes. 'But I was at least hoping he'd tell us *something.*'

'Guys like that learn from an early age to keep their cards close to their chest.'

They'd rejoined the tourists gathered around the harbour and were slowly ambling away from The Orion. Excited chatter filled the air as people gazed in awe at the moored floating masterpieces gently resting on the still sapphire waters of the bay.

'I don't know how Kelly tolerated working for him.' North angrily kicked her shoe against the decking beneath her feet.

'He was just being protective of his crew. Besides, maybe she barely had to deal with him.'

'She hates guys like that. People who are rude and entitled.'

'Looked like an impressive boat though. Maybe the perks outweighed having an arrogant boss.'

'Hmm.'

'Did she ask you to go?'

'On the boat?'

'Yeah. It sounds like you two were often a package deal when it came to holidays.'

'I…' North let her fingertips graze along the skin of her arm without applying any pressure. Deep red rivets looked visibly sore from where she'd given in to the desire to scratch. 'Boats aren't my thing. Besides, she didn't ask. I was working, I couldn't have got the time off. The Orion was her adventure. She wanted some time away, a chance to explore exotic places. A chance to avoid…certain people.'

'Do you wish you'd gone with her?'

North looked at Elijah, at the double-edged sword he had just presented her with. If she'd gone with Kelly then perhaps she'd already know the identity of her friend's unborn baby's father. Perhaps Kelly wouldn't even have got pregnant had North been there to act as a constant chaperone. No invitation had been extended in her direction, not that it mattered.

But boats were an issue. Static in harbour they were fine, approachable even. Like visiting a wild animal in the zoo. You knew that despite its ferocious nature there was glass between you, protecting you from the predator's base instincts to tear you apart. Out in the wild it was different. The animals of the zoo could be lethal out in a savannah with speed and savagery on their side. A boat out on the open water was constantly being hunted by the sea. One rogue wave, one brutal storm, that's all it would take for the ocean to claim another victim. The Titanic was proof that unsinkable didn't exist.

There had been reports of rogue waves on the night her parents disappeared off the coast of Gibraltar. They were over ten miles out according to the last sighting of them. In their hired sailing boat they were merrily navigating the waters together. A rogue wave could be up to twenty feet in height. A roaring wall of water. North often wondered if her parents saw it coming, knew that they could never outrun it. Were they holding onto one another as they were dragged down to the depths?

'I'm not good with open water.' North desperately wanted to scratch her arms until there was no skin left on them.

'Jeez, yeah, your folks. I get it. I'm sorry I asked.' Elijah's arm was still around her shoulders, still holding her close. North was grateful for the proximity. With him there she had to be strong, had to keep walking, couldn't dwell on her fears.

Every night Kelly had spent on The Orion, North lay awake in her little flat because whenever she dared to close her eyes she saw giant walls of water coming for her as she lost hours of sleep fearing that her friend would meet the same fate as her parents.

'Wait up.' Quick footsteps bounced along the decking, coming from behind. North and Elijah turned in unison to see a girl in an Orion polo shirt and beige skinny jeans hurrying over to them. Her black hair was cut in a sleek bob and she had a thick fringe above her hazel eyes.

'You were asking about Kelly Orton, right?' As the girl caught her breath she glanced between North and Elijah. 'I was below deck before. I heard you talking with Spencer.'

'Yeah, he wasn't exactly helpful.' There was a challenge in Elijah's voice. Was this girl friend or foe?

'I knew Kelly.' The girl gave a sad smile. 'Is she really dead?'

'Yes,' North confirmed as her heart tried to sink down into her stomach. 'She is.'

'Fuck, what happened?' the girl sensed the unease in the couple. 'Shit, sorry, I'm Cassie,' she held out her hand which Elijah and North shook in turn. 'I've been working on The Orion for three years now, ever since I left uni.'

'So you were friends with Kelly?' North queried dubiously.

She certainly looked like the kind of girl Kelly would be friends with. The hint of a tattoo peeked out from the capped sleeves of her polo shirt and her pretty eyes were adorned with thick eyeliner. Her lipstick was purple and though her skin was golden she was still pale against the more sun-kissed bodies that meandered along the harbour.

Cassie looked over her shoulder in the direction of The Orion. When she turned back towards North there was a glimmer of fear in her eyes. 'We probably shouldn't talk here. It's frowned upon to fraternise with non-guests. Are you staying close by? I can pop and see you when my shift finishes.'

'We're at The Fairmount.'

'Great,' Cassie nodded. 'I can meet you at the bar there at, say, eight? That good?'

'Yeah, that's good,' North confirmed.

Cassie bid them farewell and disappeared towards Spencer's yacht.

'You sure we can trust her?' Elijah wondered when she was gone from sight.

'What choice do we have? She's our only lead.'

*

A band was playing. The suited quartet put a classic spin on a number of popular contemporary songs. North was getting swept along with the music, helped by the fact that she was on her third mojito. It was eight thirty and it was starting to look like Cassie wasn't going to show.

'I knew we shouldn't have trusted her,' Elijah stated tersely as he nursed his gin and tonic.

'I'm sure she'd be here if she could. She didn't have to chase after us like she did.' North crossed and then uncrossed her legs beneath the small table they were sat around. She was wearing a dress, the only one she'd packed for the holiday. It was a black lace skater dress and left too much of her legs exposed for her liking. Even in her Converse she felt overdressed. Her hair was down and she'd put on a slick of eyeliner to try and blend in with the made-up perfection that permeated throughout Monaco.

'Just don't pin all your hopes on her,' Elijah advised. 'There are still other avenues of enquiry we can pursue.' He was wearing a white shirt and dark jeans, managing to appear just as polished as all the other suited men in the bar. When North had entered the lobby with him she'd felt a swell of pride bloom in her chest. Elijah looked good and it was confirmed by the sideways glances he kept receiving from the women in the bar. 'North, just—'

'She's here,' North stood up and waved Cassie over. She was out of her uniform and wearing a black jumpsuit with heels. She quickly came and joined them at their table.

'I am so, so sorry,' she said through ruby red lips. 'Things were crazy on the boat because of this charity thing Spencer is throwing later this week so it was harder to get away than I thought it would be. And I can't stay long. I can't risk anyone noticing that I've gone.'

'You said you knew Kelly?' Since time was not on their side, North knew she had to be direct.

'Yes,' Cassie nodded. 'I'm so sorry to hear that she died.' She bowed her head and cleared her throat. 'Kelly was so much fun. So full of life. I adored working with her.'

'Were you two close?' North wondered hopefully. She needed a lead.

'Reasonably,' Cassie clasped her hands in her lap. 'She spoke about you a lot.' She stared directly at North. 'You're the best friend with a quirky thing for stars, right?'

'Yeah, that's me.' Knowing that Kelly had spoken fondly of North during their summer estrangement was like walking into a room with no air. Her lungs tightened, clenching against what little oxygen they already held. She couldn't breathe. Couldn't focus. In her mind she heard Kelly saying the words with her trademark smile and vivacious attitude.

'North has this real quirky thing for stars.' Did she get a lump in her throat when she talked about home? Did she miss North each time she stood out on the deck at night and looked up at an endless diamond sky?

'And you're well now, right?' Cassie asked the question so lightly, her voice full of only concern, but North was struggling to swallow. What else had Kelly said about her? What other secrets had she divulged to the strangers amongst the crew she'd so quickly began to call friends?

'Was Kelly close to anyone else in the crew?' Elijah stepped in when North clammed up. He leaned across the table, keeping his voice low.

'Look,' Cassie dipped her head and glanced at them both heatedly. 'I shouldn't be here. It's more than my job's worth to be caught talking to you two, it's basically as bad as talking with the press but…' she breathed in deeply. 'I liked Kelly. A lot. She was a good person with a huge heart and…' Cassie pressed her fingertips to her temple and sighed. 'Shit. I can't believe she's dead. She…' With another deep breath, she composed herself. 'She was meant to be signed on for a three-month shift.'

'But she left early?' Elijah prompted.

'Yes, she left early. I mean she always had this restless vibe but…' Cassie paused to chew her lip. 'The thing is, on board The Orion, it's not unusual for a pretty girl like Kelly to just suddenly leave. We were in port in Marbella. One day she was there, all smiles, everything was fine. The next she was gone. No explanation, nothing. She emptied out her stuff overnight and disappeared. And, like I said, it's not the first time I've seen that happen during my three years on board.'

'Why do you think she suddenly left?' Elijah's eyes were wide with intrigue.

'I…' Cassie's lips twisted with regret. 'I wish I knew. Truly. But something went on. Something the rest of the crew knew about. I suggest you keep digging. Someone has to know the truth. As for me – I was never here, okay? I need this job. It pays better than anything else out there and Spencer's connections are invaluable. I know someone who went on to work for the Royal Family because of his recommendation.'

'Who else was Kelly close to on board?' North found her voice and quickly fired off her question.

'Me mainly. We shared a room. I really missed her when she left.' Her hand found North's shoulder. 'I'm so sorry to hear that she's gone. What happened?'

'Suicide,' Elijah said softly.

Cassie stiffened, her nails digging into North's shoulder. 'Seriously?'

North could only nod numbly.

'That's…' Cassie seemed speechless. 'She didn't seem troubled. I mean, restless, sure. Most people on a yacht tend to be. She had all these plans for the future. She wanted to walk the Great Wall of China and she was trying to book tickets to go and see *Hamilton* in London next year, with you,' she stared at North. 'Kelly was lightning in a bottle, all spark and intensity.'

'I'm trying to understand why she did it,' North looked down at own hands, fighting against the tears that were hammering against her eyes like an internal wall of water.

Lightning in a bottle. That was Kelly alright.

'Well I can't help you there. She was one of the happiest people I've ever met. But she left so suddenly, without a goodbye or anything.'

'You said there were others,' Elijah pressed. 'Other girls who left suddenly. Can you tell us their names?'

'Ha,' Cassie gave a dry laugh. 'Yeah, and I'll also go and sign on to the dole.'

North and Elijah exchanged a confused look.

'You two are seriously in over your heads.' Cassie swept her gaze around the bar one final time and seemed satisfied that she didn't recognise anyone. 'When girls go disappearing, there's usually something strange going on. Something dangerous. I like my job. I like working, if I start saying too much I risk never finding work again, you get me? I also like life in general which is why I can't tell you anything else. I was never even here, remember.'

Elijah frowned. 'Okay, but why stay working on the Orion if it's so potentially dangerous to do so?'

'You deaf?' Cassie sighed wearily and stood up. 'It pays well. Really well. And fine, judge me all you like, but everyone has a price. Including me. I need the money more than I care to admit.' Her gaze drifted back to North. 'We all have baggage we're dealing with. I'm truly sorry about Kelly.' She moved away from the bar, towards the breadth of the lobby.

North followed her as she strode across the marble floor.

'Please, just one name would really help.'

'You have a name,' Cassie spun around just as she approached the glass doors which led outside. 'Kelly Orton. If she's already dead you don't risk putting her in danger. But don't go after the living,' she pleaded. 'Don't put a target on anyone's back. They were all nice girls, none of them deserve that.'

'What now?' Elijah joined North and together they watched Cassie disappear down the street, an elegant silhouette in her all black outfit.

'Right now I need another drink,' North sighed as she turned back towards the bar.

*

'They're missing.'

North curled herself against the banister on her grandparents' landing as she listened to the police officer downstairs in the living room. He was holding a freshly made tea in a china cup and saucer which her grandmother had insisted on giving him. Company was company even when the news they were bringing was bad. The old woman had even laid out a plate of Rich Tea biscuits. The second officer in the room was sat silently nibbling on one.

'Missing?' North's grandfather sounded more annoyed than alarmed. This wasn't the first time his wayward daughter had failed to come home. Even a child couldn't tether her wandering spirit to one place.

'They were to return their sailing boat four days ago. They've since missed their flight home.'

'So are you looking for them?' North's grandmother asked as the cup and saucer in her own hands shook.

'It's difficult as it happened beyond British borders,' the police officer responded carefully, each word having been pre-selected before his arrival on her grandparents' doorstep. 'The coast guard are conducting a thorough search, but given the timelines they are inclined to rule them as missing indefinitely. Or lost at sea.'

North heard her grandmother's breath catch in her throat like a mouse in a fatal trap. A pitched, desperate squeak.

'Lost at sea?' her grandfather repeated in his deep, resonate tone. 'So they could still return?'

'We don't believe that they will. I'm so sorry.'

All eyes suddenly lifted skyward.

'They have a daughter,' North's grandmother's voice was as brittle as the china of her cup. 'North. She needs her parents. What will she do without her parents?'

'Maybe it's a good thing they left her behind when they went, else she'd be lost too,' the officer who'd been eating his biscuit offered as a silver lining.

'Don't you see,' North heard the fury building in her grandfather, 'the poor girl is lost either way.'

17

'Something is going on here.'

The only light in the hotel room came from the television on which a stern-faced news presenter was repeating the day's main headlines. North was sat on her bed, a pillow clutched against her chest. She turned to look at Elijah, his face illuminated by the blue glow that filled the room.

'Cassie was afraid.'

'Of losing her job,' Elijah yawned and stretched his hands up over his head. 'I imagine Spencer Daniels isn't an easy guy to work for and he'd be especially pissed if he knew she was talking to us.'

'But she mentioned other girls. Girls who had left abruptly like Kelly did.'

'Maybe they just grew tired of treading on eggshells around him,' Elijah countered. 'Or maybe they moved on to bigger, fancier promotions like Cassie hinted at and didn't want to make anyone else jealous?' He raised his hands. 'I'm just trying to cover all our bases here.'

'Or maybe there's something going on here,' North hugged the pillow tighter, pressed it hard against her chest in the hope of easing the tension in her lungs. She was on edge. Her arms were slashed by her own anxiety. Elijah had noticed.

'Maybe wear gloves when you sleep,' he'd suggested gently.

Sleep.

North wanted to laugh at the suggestion. She couldn't sleep, not when she was in the midst of searching for answers about her dead friend.

'Try not to get too hung up on the other girls,' Elijah urged as he lay down and turned away from her. 'We came here looking for the father. Let's focus on that.'

'But the other girls have to mean something,' North edged to the end of her bed, getting closer to Elijah. 'We can't just dismiss them.'

'Try and get some sleep. We'll both have fresher heads in the morning.'

*

The hours slid by like treacle – slow and sticky. North sat on her bed, bunched up against all her pillows watching the television through waxy eyes. She knew the headlines of the day by heart. She whispered along with the presenter, never missing a cue.

At three a.m. she curled up onto her side, still hugging a pillow. Missing Kelly felt like carrying around a ball and chain. North was always weighted down by her grief and she was tired. So very tired. But she couldn't risk closing her eyes. Couldn't risk falling asleep…

'Help me.'

The words darted around the room like a trapped bird.

'Help me. Please, help me.' The voice – feather-light and fearful. A desperate whisper. *'Help me.'*

North woke up. The television was off. The silver glow of the moon drifted in through the balcony doors which were ajar. Long curtains swayed in an idle waltz as a breeze came in off the sea to dance with them. North could taste salt.

'Help me.'

Elijah was still sleeping. She could make out the outline of his body beneath the white sheets in the other bed. But there was someone else in the room, North could sense them. Backing up against the headboard, her eyes darted around the darkened corners. At the foot of her bed stood a figure.

'Help me. Please.'

The figure was pale and wore a thick black cloak that was wrapped around their shoulders. Their head was bowed.

'Kelly?' North had to force the word out of her. 'Kel? Is th-that you?'

The figure raised their head. Kelly's blue eyes held an icy fury. The flesh on her cheeks had started to rot and corrode, revealing the unsettling whiteness of bone. *'Help me.'* Her lips were too thin, her teeth too exposed. North whimpered as she gripped her pillow with increased fervour. *'Help me.'*

'Kel, I'm trying. I'm here. I'm trying.'

Something fluttered within the cloak. A wing. One became many. Dozens of jet-black wings flapped as ravens began to break free from Kelly, cawing and shrieking. The birds took flight and in unison descended on North's head. She screamed as the wave of black feathers bore down on her.

*

'North… North. It's okay, calm down.'

She was thrashing on her bed, twisting to get away from the beaks of the ravens.

'North!'

Her eyes flew open. Panting, she looked at Elijah. His hands were on her shoulders and he looked stricken with worry.

'You were having a nightmare and you just started screaming,' he explained as he helped her sit up.

As the image of the birds receded, North looked around. The television was still on, the balcony doors firmly closed.

'I…' she fought to find her voice. It felt raw within her throat.

'It's okay, I'm here. You're safe. It was just a nightmare,' Elijah was rubbing her back in sweeping, soothing circular motions. North leaned against him, exhausted.

'I should never have done it,' she rasped. 'I should never have closed my eyes.'

*

'Talk to me about what happens at night,' the psychiatrist peered at North through her red plastic glasses which matched her lipstick.

'What do you want to know?' North was sat in the centre of a sleek grey couch sucking on an aniseed ball which she'd plucked from the glass bowl on the receptionist's desk when she'd been waiting for her appointment.

'Your grandparents report that you are having night terrors,' the psychiatrist briefly released North from her intense gaze to glance at her notes. 'That's why you've been sent to see me.'

Dr Lockhart. That was the name on the door. Dr Lockhart had dark hair streaked with blonde styled in a classic sweeping bob. She wore a black dress with stiletto heels and there was a gentle cadence to her voice which instantly put North at ease.

'I'm…' North rolled the aniseed ball around in her mouth, relishing its sharp taste. Everyone else was currently having to endure double science. But not North. Since her parents disappeared it seemed there was no end to the special treatment she was being afforded at school. 'I'm sleeping okay.'

'Your grandparents reported,' Dr Lockhart again checked her notes, 'screaming, hysteria. They apparently found you filling up the bathtub one night claiming you wanted to join your parents. Do you have no memory of these incidents?'

'No. None.'

North was learning to adapt to the new routine. She'd fall asleep and the next day have to face her grandparents' fearful expressions over breakfast when they told her what she'd done the previous night. She had to pretend she couldn't remember. If she told them the truth they'd send her somewhere much more permanent than a psychiatrist's office.

'It's common to have problems sleeping after a traumatic event. It's been three months since your parents were officially declared as lost at sea.'

'Uh-huh.' The last of the ball slid down the back of North's throat. She instantly yearned for another.

'You must miss them terribly.'

'Yes. Of course.'

And North did miss them. They were her parents. But living with her grandparents was a welcome change. There was structure in their home, actual mealtimes. There were bowls of fruit in the kitchen and the milk in the fridge was always in date.

'It might help to talk about how you feel about them. Do you miss seeing them?'

I see them when I close my eyes.

North shuddered. When sleep came so did her parents. They'd float up from their watery graves and leave puddles upon her carpet as they beseeched her to never forget them. To remember them. To join them.

'Let's try something else,' Dr Lockhart regarded North with a kind smile when she didn't immediately offer an answer. 'Your grandparents mentioned how you've stopped sleeping over the last few weeks. Obviously, this isn't a solution. We need to find a way for you to get over this bout of insomnia. Are you not sleeping because you're afraid of having nightmares or sleepwalking?'

'Uh-huh.'

'If we talk about things here, during our sessions, it should stop the nightmares and help you sleep. Would you like that?'

'Uh-huh.'

Her grandparents had promised that the doctor could help but it felt like she was declaring that she could perform miracles. Sleep never came for North, no matter what she did.

'So, tell me about your parents. Let's start there. What were they like?' Dr Lockhart seemed genuinely interested.

'They were dreamers,' North shrugged. 'Adventurers. They were always chasing something.'

'And how did that make you feel?'

Left behind.

Jealous.

'Alone.'

'Rather than feeling part of their adventures did you feel like more of a spectator?'

'Yes.'

'I'm told that your parents loved each other very much. Did you ever fear that there wasn't enough love left for you?'

'I didn't fear it. That's the way it was. The way it always had been.'

'Your parents loved you, North.'

'The idea of me, maybe,' she shrugged.

'Do you resent them for leaving? For not loving you enough?'

'No,' North shook her head. 'They were always going to leave one day. My grandmother says that death is drawn to me.'

Dr Lockhart's eyebrows flew up her forehead. 'And why would she say that?'

'My eyes,' North vaguely gestured at her face. 'Can I get another aniseed ball please? They're really nice.'

*

'North, you're not making any sense,' Elijah kept rubbing her back, remaining by her side. 'You have to close your eyes. You have to sleep.'

'She was here,' North realised she was shaking as she looked at the spot where Kelly had been. If she checked the floor would there be a trail of dirt leading over to the balcony?

'Who was?'

'Kelly.'

He didn't flinch. He didn't loosen his grip or edge away from her. He was undeterred by her admission.

'She was here and she needs my help.' North buried her face in his shoulder and wept. 'I have to help her.'

'I know,' Elijah whispered soothingly as he kept rubbing her back. 'I know.'

*

'She sounds like a quack,' Kelly scoffed before crunching down on a stack of Pringles.

'She's actually really nice.'

They were sat in North's bedroom, cross-legged on her bed as they watched a movie on her little television. *The Neverending Story.* The VHS case for the film showing a boy and his lucky dragon lay discarded on the floor.

'Did you tell her about your parents?' Kelly mumbled as she chewed on her savoury snack.

'What about them?'

Kelly swallowed and swept the back of her hand across her mouth. 'That they haunt you.'

'No!' North was appalled at the suggestion. 'She'd think I'm crazy.'

'I don't think you're crazy.'

'Yeah but you're... you. You'd never think anyone was crazy.'

'I'd never think *you* were crazy,' Kelly clarified. 'You chose me as your best friend which makes you the sanest person I know.'

'I'm scared to tell her too much in case she... I don't know... medicates me or something.'

'Has she given you anything yet?'

'Other than aniseed balls? No.'

'How long do you have to keep seeing her?'

'Until I stop freaking my grandparents out.'

'So forever then,' Kelly playfully elbowed North in the ribs.

'You sure you don't mind me keeping the TV on all night?' North glanced sheepishly at the television.

'Course not. Especially if it keeps your parents away.'

'I miss sleep,' North leaned against her Care Bears cushion and sighed. 'I wish I could just close my eyes and forget about everything.'

'You'll be able to. In time.'

'Yeah, but when?'

Existing on the edge of exhaustion was dangerous. North often felt her focus drifting in school, during class. An hour could pass and feel like a minute. She was losing her grip on time.

'When your parents grow tired of haunting you.'

'And if they don't?'

'They will.' Kelly sounded so confident. She reached for another pile of Pringles and gleefully shoved them into her mouth, smirking at North.

'How can you be so sure?'

'Because,' Kelly raised a hand while she chewed furiously. She swallowed and then cleared her throat. 'Because even ghosts get tired.'

'Why do you even believe me? No one else would.'

'I'd believe anything you told me. You're my best friend.'

18

'I can't let this go.'

The air was warm out on the balcony. North sat on a sun lounger with her legs curled up beneath her, head lowered to stare at the iPad she was holding. She kept furiously scrolling through Spencer Daniels' Twitter feed.

'I think you have to.' Elijah was leaning against the balcony railing looking out to sea. 'Cassie isn't going to say anything else and I doubt the rest of the crew will be any more talkative.'

'He knows something,' North angrily jabbed a finger against Spencer Daniels' smarmy smile which beamed up at her from her tablet. 'I know he does.'

'Cassie seemed genuinely scared of him. We need to let this go.'

'I thought she was just scared of losing her job,' North looked up to squint at the railing, at Elijah silhouetted against the sun. 'You changing your tune?'

'I'm just concerned.' With a slump of his shoulders, he turned to face her. 'Concerned about you. Last night—'

'I have night terrors,' North stared at her iPad, clutching it with unnecessary force. Her nightmares had followed her out to Monaco. Would they haunt her to the ends of the earth? She'd always assumed that at some point she'd outrun them.

'I'm not trying to—'

'I need one more shot at him,' she held up the iPad which had focused in on a flattering image of Spencer. He was smiling as he raised a glass of champagne, dressed head to toe in white like a saint. 'Let me ask him again about Kelly. I'll be more direct this time. I'll be able to tell if he's holding something back.'

'North—'

'One more shot. That's it. Then we're done, we can go home and I'll stop fixating on Kelly's missing summer. Okay?'

Elijah sighed but nodded his head. 'Okay.'

*

She'd been ordered to sleep. Elijah had gone out to get lunch and left North with strict instructions to stay in bed and try to nap.

'You need to rest,' he told her before slipping out through the door.

On her back, North pressed her spine against the firm mattress of the bed and examined the painted ceiling of the hotel room. Sleep would not come. She wouldn't let it. She felt it grab at her ankles, try to work its way up her body, making all her muscles feel warm and comfortable. Just when sleep had her in its grip she flung herself onto her side, forcing her eyes wide.

This went on for over an hour. North was sat up and staring at the television when the door opened and Elijah returned. He looked flustered.

'Are you okay?' she asked as he placed some store-bought sandwiches down on the sideboard.

'I'm...' He ran his hands through his hair, chewing his lip.

'Elijah?'

'You wanted one more shot at Spencer Daniels?'

'Yes,' North agreed slowly.

Elijah clicked his fingers. 'You got it.'

'What are you talking about?'

'That dress, your black lace one, you can wear that but not with your Converse.' He hurried over to the wardrobe, swept along in the tornado of his own harassed thoughts.

'Elijah!'

'Oh.' With one hand on her dress, he looked over his shoulder at her. 'We're going to a party.'

'A party?' North jumped off the bed, surprised and suspicious.

'On my way to lunch I did a bit of social media stalking of my own. Tonight all of Monaco's elite will be at a gala event out in the harbour aboard the largest yacht, The Meridian. Spencer will of course want to be seen there. So I got us an invite.'

'An invite? *How?*'

Elijah wasn't a man with connections. He was cut from the same modest cloth as North.

'Simple really,' he smiled proudly and pushed back his shoulders, 'I pretended that I want to buy a yacht.'

'You *what?*' North was shocked, and also mildly impressed. It was the kind of lie that Kelly would have told.

'I made like I was some tech millionaire from the UK. The organisers practically bit my hand off when I said I was in the market for a boat. It was hilarious. You'd have loved it.'

Kelly would have loved it.

The thought rang through North like a bell. It was exactly the kind of scam Kelly would have masterminded.

'Let's pretend to be millionaires,' she'd have gushed as she put on her cheapest clothes and her richest smile.

'So tonight we board The Meridian, sip on champagne and make vague small talk while you look for Spencer Daniels.'

'You…' North tentatively approached the wardrobe. 'You didn't have to do this.'

'Yes, I did,' Elijah smiled as he handed her the hanger holding her black skater dress. 'This is important to you, North. I wanted to help.'

'Well then,' she eyed the garment with a critical eye. 'We'll need to go shoe shopping.'

*

'I feel like I was born to wear heels.'

Like many of Kelly's boasts it had been one she more than lived up to. Her feet seemed to have been formed with the crucial arch to allow her to wear towering heels with ease. She'd strut around in stilettos, peep-toes, courts, all with eye-watering heels that elevated her from merely tall to goddess status. In her heels Kelly glided like a catwalk model as though the ground beneath her had been replaced with air.

'I don't know about this.' North looked down at the dress, the shoes. She'd played it safe and opted for mid-height patent Mary Janes in black. Kelly would have approved. She'd state that they were *quirky but feminine* or something similar. 'We're not going to blend in.'

Elijah smoothed down the front of his freshly ironed shirt and adjusted his tie. 'We'll be fine.'

'I just don't…' North stepped out of the bathroom, away from her tortured reflection. Her eyes were framed with liquid eyeliner and her lips were ruby red thanks to a generous coating of lipstick. 'I don't feel comfortable,' she tugged on the hem of her dress, noticing the sore lines that streaked up her arms. She'd covered them in concealer, but if you looked hard enough they were still more than visible.

'You look…' Elijah's blue eyes widened and he sucked in a breath. 'Stunning. B-beautiful.'

North smiled shyly. Words were just words. She'd learned that the hard way. A man might say you're his everything, his world, but that didn't mean that you actually *were*.

'It matters more what he does than what he says.' Another slice of wisdom from the Kelly's cake of knowledge.

But Elijah acted more than he spoke. He'd come to Monaco for her, pretended to be some British millionaire. His actions were screaming louder than any words ever could, but North was in no mind to hear them. This wasn't the time. Things were about Kelly, not North.

'I'm just worried people will tell that we're,' she shrugged and bit her lip, 'not super rich.'

'Worse case, they kick us off the boat. Best case, you find Spencer and needle some more answers out of him.' Elijah was being so confident. He could be so quiet at the observatory, so focused on his work. North would never have guessed that a lion hid beneath his gentle demeanour. 'Come on,' he held out his arm to her the way gentlemen did in old-time movies. With a laugh, North hooked on to it and together they left their hotel room.

*

The Meridian could have been a warship. Its sides were jet-black and swept up out of the harbour. It was moored as far away from Monaco as possible, right at the end of the jetty. If it were any bigger it couldn't come in to port, at least that's what people were saying between mouthfuls of canapés and champagne.

A string quartet was assembled on deck. They played a combination of classic and contemporary tunes beneath the fairy lights which were strung along the railing and up the impressive main body of the yacht. Though in scale it felt more like a ship.

'Twelve bedrooms,' someone whispered reverently.

'A bowling alley,' said another.

'A cinema room.'

'*Eight* bathrooms.'

So The Meridian was basically a floating boutique hotel.

As they'd approached the gangway, North and Elijah had been greeted as equals. A suited waiter had nodded courteously at them and offered them each a flute of champagne. Elijah accepted but North declined. She was nervous enough without the added pressure of amber bubbles rising up within her.

'See, this is fine,' Elijah led her around the deck, around the sea of strangers who all wore couture and smelt like all the seasons had collided. There were oaky perfumes and fresh ones, notes of fruit and some of cinnamon. North was grateful when a breeze blew in off the water and knocked most of it away, filling her lungs with crisp, salt-laced air. 'Let's do a lap,' Elijah skilfully wove them through the crowd. All the while North kept looking, her head flicking back and forth like a bird.

Spencer Daniels would surely show up. The event reeked of him. There was caviar in the canapés. People said the word 'bolly' without any irony as they downed their drinks. Here were the rich, the elite of Monaco. Spencer would be drawn to them, powerless to resist an Instagram opportunity.

'See him there?' Elijah leaned in close to whisper in North's ear, his warm breath tickling her neck. 'He owns Chelsea football club. And the guy he's talking to, he owned PayPal before he sold it for millions.'

'Wow, you're very knowledgeable. I don't recognise anyone.'

'I scrolled through the Forbes list from last year as research,' Elijah admitted.

North stifled a laugh as she pressed her fingers to her lips. 'That's impressive. Want me to quiz you later?'

'Please don't.'

How would Spencer fit in with these self-made millionaires? He was part of the Daniels dynasty and hadn't earned any of his wealth himself.

'Ooh, and her,' Elijah nodded in the direction of a tall woman with lilac hair. She was laughing uproariously as the short guy beside her with spiky hair made a joke. 'She owns the company Diowater.'

'Diowater?'

'Designer water,' Elijah lowered his voice as he rolled his eyes. 'Apparently it's going to be the next big thing. She was on the Forbes to watch list.'

'But we're not on any list,' North nervously drew closer to Elijah's side. 'People must be looking at us wondering who the hell we are.'

'Don't worry about it.' Elijah was remaining so calm, so measured. 'There's too much ego at play here. No one would want to know if someone else had more money than them. Being at the party is evidence enough that you're loaded.'

'She'd have loved this,' North glanced around at all the faces plumped with Botox, at the abundance of red-soled shoes.

'Kelly?'

'Yeah. The danger and drama of it all. She'd have made me pretend we were in a Bond movie or something.'

'Hi,' a man with skin the colour of aged varnish cornered them, holding out a manicured hand. 'And who might you be?'

While North's heart stopped, Elijah's kept beating. He smiled confidently and shook the varnished man's hand. 'I'm Eli and this is my beautiful girlfriend, North.'

'And what a beauty she is,' the man exclaimed.

'Though my real eye is on the beauty gathered around us,' Elijah was gesturing to the boats. Beyond the deck of The Meridian, they sat in port, bobbing upon idle waves adorned with swatches of fairy lights.

'In the market for one are you?' the man's eyes twinkled as though they'd captured the light of the surrounding yachts.

'Always.'

This is my beautiful girlfriend, North.

Had that all been part of the act or something else? North wished there was some way to decipher between their little game and reality. In her thirty-two years she'd rarely been a girlfriend. Most guys wanted to stick around and spend the night together, to sleep side by side in a loving little bundle. North couldn't have that. She'd steal away from their bed and return home under the cover of darkness. The next day they'd say she was cold. Over time they'd call her heartless. No one understood that her lack of desire to snuggle didn't represent a lack of desire completely. But so many people placed such great importance on actually sleeping together.

'One day you'll find a guy who understands you,' Kelly would promise. 'Until then don't you dare settle. He's coming, don't sweat it, but don't wait around either. Have fun. Life's a game remember, make sure you're playing.'

So often Kelly sounded like she was quoting words from a stitched cushion or kitchen plaque. Positive affirmations. They rolled off her tongue on a daily basis. She loved life. She loved it so fiercely that she spent most of her time trying to grab it with both hands.

She'd never just leave it all behind.

'I need to find the restroom.' North politely excused herself and drifted away from Elijah's side. She could feel the presence of the stars overhead but couldn't bring herself to look up at them. She missed Kelly with every beat of her heart. And she knew, right down to her core, that her friend wouldn't have left without a goodbye.

North leaned against the railing of the upper deck and looked down at the dark waters. A breeze tugged through her hair and North opened her mouth to draw it in, to let it fill her lungs to bursting.

She didn't know when he'd arrived. The glittering crowd hadn't parted like the red sea when he climbed aboard. In fact, no one seemed at all concerned by his presence. He drifted amongst the waiters and guests just as she and Elijah had done. And just like North, he made for the quiet places of the yacht, for the outer railing on the upper deck.

The smoke of an e-cigarette obscured her vision, fragranced yet clotting. North turned and saw him. He was in a casual stance, head tipped in her direction. This time the suit he wore was a navy so dark it was almost as black as the boat on which he stood. His back was against the railing, shoulders slumped as he lazily inhaled, a small blue light glowing at the end of his cigarette like a false star.

'Fancy meeting you here,' Spencer Daniels coolly greeted her. 'I think we need to talk.'

19

'Then let's talk,' North clenched her jaw and gave Spencer what she hoped was a confident yet menacing gaze. She refused to be intimidated by him.

'Not here,' he pulled his e-cigarette away from his pale lips and glanced furtively at the party unfolding just a few feet away from them. 'Too many eyes. Ears. Let's go to my yacht.'

'No,' North stood firm. 'I'm perfectly fine talking here. So talk.'

'You want answers, don't you?' Spencer narrowed his eyes as he stared at her. 'Then come with me. We can't talk here.'

Elijah was still detained by the varnished man who was gesturing grandly with his hands, becoming quite animated. North gripped at the railing of The Meridian and searched her feelings.

What would Kelly do?

She'd go. Without a doubt. She'd fall in step with Spencer and glide off the grand yacht with him, never looking back, never doubting her decision.

North did want answers.

Drinking in a deep breath of sea air, she steeled herself for what was to come next. Then she did exactly what Kelly would have done.

*

'He's an iron fist in a velvet glove,' Kelly was leaning against the bonnet of North's Beetle, regarding the demountable on the other side of the car park.

'What?' North peered around the car from the boot where she'd been stacking away box files she was taking home for the weekend to study.

'That new boss of yours,' Kelly nodded at the long building, a scowl settling within her pretty features. 'I don't like him. He's too polished for a stargazer.'

'You don't even know him,' North slammed her boot closed and came around to the front of the little yellow car.

'I have eyes.'

'If you're going to meet me after work the least you can do is not bitch about my boss.'

'He watches you, do you know that?'

'He watches everyone.' North was tired. It was her second week at her new job and every day was an exhausting exercise in trying to fit in, to make friends and also adapt to the environment.

'Why would a stargazer wear a suit?'

'We prefer the term astronomers. Or cosmologists.' It was everything North had worked for, a dream come true to finally get paid to stare up at the stars.

'Pfft.' Kelly climbed into the car and sat down with a heavy sigh. 'There's just something about him, he's all posture.'

'He's just well dressed,' North argued as she climbed in behind the wheel and jangled her keys in the ignition. But he was more than just well dressed. He was charismatic, handsome. But North kept those feelings to herself.

'You go to work in jeans and a hoody,' Kelly pointed at her friend, raising her eyebrows.

'I'm not the boss.'

The Beetle came to life with a low grumble. North pulled out of the car park and glanced back at the only demountable where the lights were still on through her rear-view mirror. Alexander was just stepping out of sight. Had he been watching her?

'He's peacocking. And peacocks are dangerous.'

'What are you on about?' North was driving through the familiar streets of Millwater. Normally by now Kelly would have turned on the radio and fiddled with the dial until she found a station she was happy with. Today, however, she was opting for silence.

'Peacocks can peck and they have this mega-scary scream. I was at this place once where they sold roses and they had one and—'

'No,' North interrupted as she came to a halt at a red light. 'How is my boss peacocking?'

'You know, showing his worth, hauling his designer threads out of his rickety old wardrobe. Always being suited and booted.'

'Maybe he just likes looking nice. What's wrong with that?'

'Iron fist. Velvet glove.'

'You talking in riddles again?'

'It's something my mum says.' Kelly leaned forward to drum her fingers against the dashboard. 'Guys who are too dressed up are trying to hide something. He wants you to see the velvet, to admire it, touch it even, so that it's easier for him to land you with an iron punch.'

'And you deduce all this from a guy wearing a suit?'

'If the situation doesn't warrant it. The rest of you guys at the observatory look like a right ragtag bunch. He's the Fagin to your street rats.'

'Nice.'

'Just be wary of him, okay?'

'Okay.' The lights turned green and North pressed down on the accelerator, wanting to distance herself from her Kelly's concerns.

'You made many other friends there? Who was the guy who helped put that box in your car last week?'

'You mean Elijah?'

'Yeah, the little one in the big green jumper. He seems nice.'

'Why does he seem nice? Because he dresses in a grunge-esque style like I do?'

'Exactly,' Kelly clicked her long fingers. 'He's not trying to hide anything. To deceive you. He's... real.'

'He's also mega shy.'

'I like him,' Kelly leaned back in the passenger seat.

'So are you done assessing my new colleagues?'

'Almost,' Kelly smirked. 'Let's go through the girls there.'

*

It was eerily still on board The Orion. North had followed Spencer up his roped off gangway, along the pristine outer deck and was now on a small balcony at the bow of the yacht. It offered a serene view of the flat, calm waters which stretched away from Monaco. There were plush corner sofas fitted around the balcony, but both Spencer and North remained standing.

'You keep asking questions about Kelly.' He was looking out at the ocean, his hands in his trouser pockets.

'That's right. She was my best friend and I think something happened to her while she was working on your yacht.'

'You the crazy friend?'

North tensed. 'W-what?'

'The one who didn't sleep and saw things that weren't there?'

'I…' The sting of betrayal burned through North.

Kelly had told him about that. But why?

The truth burned more than the betrayal.

To impress him.

Just like at university North was once again the support act to Kelly's grand performance, even when she wasn't even there.

Spencer released a slow smile of satisfaction. 'Yes, that's you. Kelly and I talked. Often at length. We were friends for a time. She could be… amusing.'

'You claimed not to know her.'

'In front of others, yes,' Spencer coolly confirmed. 'It doesn't aid my reputation to have people know I have a tendency to bond with my staff. Better they see me as cool and aloof.'

'Something happened to her on your boat,' North found her voice, squeezed her hands into fists and forced out her line of interrogation.

'Something like what?'

'Something like…' North bit down on her tongue. She had no concrete ideas about what had happened to Kelly the previous summer, at least none she was willing to share. 'I don't know. That's why I'm here, looking for answers. If you could tell me who she hung out with, who she was close to then—'

'I told you,' Spencer cocked his head to look at her, 'Kelly was a member of staff, at a push a friend. There's nothing to be discovered here so you can stop prying into my business. First you rudely board my yacht and then you lie your way into a party under false pretences. Are you and that little boyfriend of yours con artists? Are you after money? Is that what this is about?'

'No! I'm here about Kelly. She was meant to work for you for three months but left early. Do you know why?'

'Look, staff on yachts can be spirited and often leave early. I don't know why Kelly didn't finish out her contract. She didn't say.'

'What about the other girls who left early? Do you know why they did so? Why so many girls are leaving your employment before their contracts have concluded?'

'Look,' he marched over to her and when he reached her he didn't stop. He grabbed her shoulders and pushed her back, her feet tottering across the deck towards the railing. She felt its thick bars digging in to her lower back. Still he pushed, causing her to lean precariously over the water. 'Stop with your questions. I have the terrible sense that you're trying to paint me as some sort of villain and you're wrong. I liked Kelly. Everyone did.'

'You know why Kelly left early, don't you?' Despite the tremors in her body, North kept her voice level. She looked directly into Spencer's eyes as his own contorted face hovered just inches above her own, cheeks red and nostrils flared. He blew a hot, alcohol-laced breath against her.

'Do you know what?' He shoved her so hard the railing met her spine with a crunch. Then he was stepping back, allowing North to straighten up and catch her breath. 'Ask all the questions you want. Dig a hole so deep for yourself you'll never be able to climb back out of it.'

'What happened to Kelly?'

'The thing with dead girls is they can't lie. Every fantasy you concoct in your twisted little mind about what happened here on my yacht will forever remain just that – a fantasy. You have no one to corroborate your delusions. Let your dead friend rest, be a good girl and go home and commence grieving.'

'I'm going to find out what you did to Kelly.'

'Good luck with that,' Spencer laughed dryly at her. 'You don't have the strongest track record. Petty theft, a car accident. Yes, I did my homework. You're hardly a reliable source of any sort of information, and if you stay in Monaco one more day I'll have you arrested for trespassing. Twice you've been on my yacht.'

'You invited me!'

'My word against *yours*,' Spencer gestured between them and then tapped a finger against his chin. '*Who* would they believe? The upstanding gentleman who regularly contributes six-figure sums to local charitable events or the depressed stray who is rumoured to be crazy that came in with the tide. Kelly is dead. If you've any sense in that head of yours you'll accept the finality of that and move on with your sad little life.'

'You don't scare me.' North wanted to conquer the fear swelling within her.

'No?' Spencer gazed at her in mock surprise, pressing a hand to his chest. 'Then you're dumber than I thought. I don't make idle threats, so get the hell out of town before I run you out.'

'I'm going to find out the truth.' The air tingled with the proximity to it. North was close, so close.

'Say one inflammatory thing about me and I'll bury you in years of legal papers for defamation. Now get the fuck off my yacht.'

'Gladly,' North stormed past him. 'I wouldn't want to spend another second on your bloody boat.'

*

'Where were you?' Elijah found her in the harbour as she made her way back to The Meridian. His cheeks were flushed. 'I turned around from chatting with that crazy chap and you were gone! You said you were just going to the bathroom but you'd disappeared.'

'I went off the yacht.'

'Why?'

'To chat to Spencer Daniels.'

She saw a shadow settle in the blue depths of Elijah's eyes. He clenched his jaw and rested his hands on her shoulders. 'Why the hell would you do that? You shouldn't be disappearing off alone like that.'

'He said he was willing to talk. That he had answers about Kelly.'

'And did he?'

North looked down at her pretty patent shoes. They were pinching at her toes and rubbing against her ankles. She couldn't wait to take them off. 'No. He didn't. All he did was threaten me.'

'Threaten you?' Elijah stepped in closer, breaking through the space that lingered between them. He kept his hands firmly on North's shoulders as he regarded everyone else within the harbour with suspicion. 'What did he say? Do we need to go to the police?'

'I'm pretty sure the police are in his pocket,' North rolled her eyes. 'He just told me to leave in not so nice terms.'

The ache at the base of her back told her otherwise. She was certain that when she took off her dress she'd find a red bar-shaped mark that would darken to a bruise over the coming days. Could she show that to the police? But Spencer was right – when all she had was her word, they'd believe him because he was what Kelly had always feared; an iron fist in a velvet glove.

'Then we leave.' To Elijah the solution was simple.

'No,' North shrugged him off and began to storm along the harbour, in the direction of the hill which led up to their hotel. 'Don't you see, we're close. He wouldn't lash out unless he was afraid.'

'He's a man protecting his reputation. To the elite your reputation can be worth more than your accumulated wealth' Elijah hurried to keep up with her. 'I say we count our losses and leave. This isn't worth making powerful enemies over.'

'This is all for Kelly,' North heard the fire in her voice, felt the sting of heat in her eyes. 'This is about discovering what really happened to her. Of course it's worth making some enemies over.'

'But...' Elijah dropped his head, his voice pinched with regret. 'But it won't bring her back. None of this will.'

'I'm not trying to bring her back,' North sped up, shouldering her way past him as she reached the steep climb of the street.

I'm trying to bring her peace.

There was forever a question mark besides the names of North's parents. The Stones were presumed dead, but the how, the when, the why, that would remain a mystery. People could speculate but no one would ever know. North couldn't handle another ambiguous death. Kelly didn't deserve a question mark, she deserved resolution.

*

'What's your biggest fear?' Kelly asked from her bed as North lay snuggled on the floor in a faded blue sleeping bag.

'Huh?' North groggily replied to the voice in the darkness.

The movie had ended. With their stomachs full of junk food, the girls had gone to bed on the eve of their first ever sleepover. North imagined her mum and dad already knocking back shots in the small lounge of their flat, excited for a night off from their parental duties.

'Your biggest fear,' Kelly repeated. North heard her friend roll onto her side. 'What is it?'

'Um,' North chewed her lip. She was tired. All the sugar in her system had sent her crashing. She wanted to curl up on her side and sleep. Tomorrow was Sunday and the day that Kelly officially became a teenager. Irene had bought a tray-bake cake from Asda and they were going to the cinema in the afternoon to watch a movie of their choice. North already knew that it was going to be a perfect day, rounded off by a roast dinner at her grandparents' house.

'Fire. Spiders. Ghosts,' Kelly began reeling off potential fears.

'I don't know, why?'

'Well, once we figure out our greatest fears we can help each other overcome them.'

'Why would we do that?'

'To ensure we are fearless. Duh.'

'Okay, then what's your greatest fear?' North sent the question back up to the bed.

'Ah,' she heard more shifting above her head. 'See, I've given this great thought. My biggest fear is to be forgotten. And so, I need to ensure that me, and my life, are memorable.'

'Okay...'

'So what's your greatest fear? Search your mind for that one thing that if it happened you'd be truly lost. Landing in a snake pit or... or being trapped in the boot of a car.'

'Losing you.'

'What?'

'Losing you,' North repeated. 'You're my best friend in the whole world. If something happened to you I'd be truly lost. See – you're already memorable.'

'Good to know, but your fear,' Kelly's voice sounded closer as she rolled up against the edge of her bed, 'I don't have to help you get over that one.'

'Why not? Isn't the whole point of this exercise to be fearless?'

'Because I'm not going anywhere. Soul sisters are bound for life. It's in the friendship by-laws, look it up.'

'Ha, I will.'

'I mean it.' In the darkness, Kelly lowered her hand and reached for North's. 'I'm not going anywhere, so start thinking about picking another greatest fear, one we can actually work on overcoming.'

'Roger that.'

They stayed holding hands until they both fell asleep.

20

North's footsteps tapped out an erratic melody as she hurried across the marble lobby. A brass band was playing over by the far wall. In Monaco classical music was as prominent as the salt in the sea air. Everything felt so civilised, so safe. But despite all the lavish trimmings, North's heart continued to beat out a rhythm as manic as her steps.

On the deck of The Orion, Spencer's mask had completely slipped to reveal the cruel, snarling monster beneath.

Her hand pressed against her throbbing back as she reached the lifts and pounded the call button.

'I'm not trying to make you mad,' Elijah implored as he caught up with her.

'I'm not mad.' Lifting her head, North focused on the descending digital numbers above the sealed metal doors of the lifts. 'I'm just wound up.'

'I'm only thinking of you.' He reached for her arm as a gentle chime signalled the arrival of the lift. North slipped from his grip and stepped inside. 'You said that he threatened you. We can't take that lightly.'

'He's all hot air and hair mousse.'

'North—'

'He *knows* something. About Kelly. About the other girls. And if he won't talk, Cassie will.'

'No, she won't. She's too afraid, and rightly so by the sounds of it.'

The walls of the lift creaked and shuddered as it climbed ever closer to their floor.

'I don't care who talks. I just want answers.'

With her feet feeling swollen and burning hot, the walk back to their room felt long. Each corridor dragged, an inch becoming a mile. It took only three minutes for North to sigh loudly and kick off her shoes.

'Damn things.' The sudden freedom was welcomed by her aching toes. She pushed her feet against the soft fibres of the carpet, savouring the sensation. Then she ran. Quick, fluid steps all the way to their door. After presenting her key card, the little security light turned green and she stepped inside with Elijah following close behind. She flicked on the main lights and froze.

'Christ,' the word was a squeak in Elijah's throat.

North's hand was still raised, resting beside the switch as she took in the devastation. It looked as though their room had been hit by a tornado. The balcony doors were thrown open, bringing in a tepid breeze that rustled through the debris on the floor. Both beds were completely overturned. The sheets had been pulled free and one of the mattresses was now stacked haphazardly against the sideboard. Every drawer had been pulled out. North saw her own familiar garments strewn alongside the sheets. The minibar hung open, all of its miniature contents shattered close by. Alcohol was seeping into the carpet.

'What the—' North stepped forward as she turned her head to look into the bathroom. More chaos greeted her. The shower curtain was pulled down, all of her toiletries scattered across the tiled floor. Her shampoo had split open.

Elijah roughly tugged her back before she could take another step.

'Look,' he pointed at the carpet, at the shards of glass which glistened upon it.

'Jesus,' North pulled her shoes back on. 'What is this? Has someone broken in?'

Her throat tightened, closing around the breath she'd just pulled in. A question spun in her mind, making her dizzy.

Did I do this?

She tried to mentally map the evening. She'd left Elijah, left the party, to talk with Spencer. But they'd been alone. There were no witnesses to their exchange. What if instead of meeting with Spencer she'd come back to the room, had tossed everything like that time at her grandparents' house and—

'No,' North pressed a hand to her temple and tried to breathe. This wasn't her doing. Her insomnia was back, sure. But she wasn't sleepwalking, hallucinating... was she? Panic was an ice pick down her spine. Kelly, her grandmother, they knew the signs to look for and they were gone. North looked at Elijah, her eyes wide and fearful. Was this all just an escalation from the messages she was deleting, more self-sabotage? Did he see her guilt written across her face? Did Elijah share her terrible suspicions about herself?

'Who do you think did this?' She asked the question directly, braced to hear her own name given in reply.

'I think we know who,' Elijah dragged his hand down his face, growing paler by the second.

'Anyone could have broken in.' She declared, trying to sound rational. 'Anyone at all. A total stranger. Maybe we should call reception. Is anything missing? Let's check,' North tiptoed her way through the carnage, thankful that she'd kept the passports in her handbag for safekeeping. The book she'd been reading was face down beside the bare bed. Some of the pages had been torn out.

'We need to leave,' Elijah remained by the door. 'Whoever did this was sending a message and they can consider it received loud and clear.'

'No,' North batted a hand in his direction. 'We can't leave, because that's what he wants. All this,' she gestured around the damaged room, 'all this means that he really does know something, that he's fighting to keep me from the truth. And I won't be afraid, Elijah. Kelly would be fearless and so I'm fearless too.'

Or am I telling myself to leave?

It had to be Spencer. Had to be. She couldn't slip towards madness again. Not like before. This needed to be Spencer's doing, felt compelled to convince herself of that.

North felt desperate to start cleaning up, to hide the mess she might have created. She needed time to sit down and run through her thoughts, to check her back and see if the bruise was still there. It was caused by Spencer pushing her, wasn't it? Or had she hurt herself as she thrust a mattress up off the bed and got knocked against the wall? Nothing was making sense.

Who had done this? Was it truly Spencer? It had to be, didn't it?

'You don't need to keep trying to measure up to her. North, shit just got very real for us here. We have to go.'

'Measure up to her?' she scoffed at the suggestion. 'No one *measures up* to Kelly Orton. All I can do is try to honour her legacy. I thought you understood that.' Her words snapped like her frayed nerves.

'I do but—'

'Are you going to help me or what?' North was hauling the mattress back onto the divan.

'Leave that, we need to call reception.'

'That's what he wants us to do' Blinking back tears, North focused on straightening up the mattress. Her arms ached beneath its weight. 'I'll bet he reported a commotion coming from our room. He's going to try to pin this on us – a drunken ransacking of our own room.'

'We weren't even here!'

What if one of us was? North didn't dare breathe life into her question. If her sanity was falling apart, piece by piece, she wanted to keep it from Elijah for as long as possible.

'In Monaco money is king. It won't matter what we say, what we can prove. Spencer has everyone in his pocket. We need to clean this up as best we can and pay for whatever damage is left.' She glanced at the empty mini bar. 'Fucking bastard.'

'Then… fine,' Elijah pushed up his sleeves. 'I'll help. But you need to promise me that we're done here, North. If Spencer does know something about Kelly, did have a hand in her death, then you're in greater danger than I thought.'

*

Two hours. That's how long it took to pick up all the glass, to straighten the bed, to scrub away the worst of the stains with just water and soap. Thankfully the television hadn't been damaged, North wasn't sure her bank balance would stretch to replacing a large plasma flat screen. The minibar would be the greatest cost. A doll-sized bottle of vodka cost eight euros and almost twenty little bottles had been unceremoniously smashed.

When North finally collapsed against her freshly made bed her body ached with gratitude. It had been a long night. She lay on her back and waited to hear the tell-tale deepening of Elijah's breath but it never came. Sleep, it seemed, was evading him too.

*

'Do you even realise what you've done?'

North had faced her grandmother's wrath so many times that she no longer bothered with the protective armour of tears. Instead she just stared blankly at the old woman who sat across the small kitchen table from her, wrinkled hands clasped in a basket.

'The car is *beyond repair*. That means that Mrs Orton will need to buy another one. Do you think that money grows on trees, North? What were you thinking?'

'I…' North opened her mouth and then promptly closed it again. She shook her head, knowing that nothing she said could diminish her grandmother's anger. North had brought shame in through the front door. The damage, the danger, all of that paled against the social burden of having a wayward granddaughter.

'What will I say to the people at church?' Her grandmother unclasped her hands to let them flutter up to the sagging skin that gathered around her neck. 'You used to be such a *good* girl. Is this about your parents? Do you need to see that psychologist again?'

'No,' North braced herself against her chair. She didn't want more doctors. Didn't want someone else trying to navigate around the darker recesses of her mind. There were some things that no one should have to see. North thought of the watermarks in her little bedroom and shuddered.

'Did Kelly put you up to this?' her grandmother pursed her thin lips. 'Hmm? You were both in the car when it crashed. Was this another adventure of hers, another way for you two to go gallivanting off?'

'Don't blame Kelly.'

'The *police*, North. They were here. In *my* home.'

So, now that North was misbehaving, it was no longer her home too. Looking up at the ceiling, she mentally calculated how many months needed to pass before she could leave for university. Her conclusion – too many.

'They said they will be lenient, given the circumstances. But North, dear North, don't let this be the start of some dreadful pattern. Don't make the mistakes that your mother did.'

'My mother?' The elephant in the room had just been acknowledged to North's surprise. Usually her parents existed only in photographs, not conversations.

'She was as wild as the four winds. Your father couldn't tame her, could only bend to her whim. But you're not like her. You're a good girl, you like structure, you work hard in school.'

'I'm dull?' North raised an eyebrow.

'Not dull,' her grandmother instantly insisted. 'Smart. There's a difference. You're a bright girl with a good future. Don't ruin all that now. Think of all your dreams, of university. Don't spoil those well laid plans with a childish act of defiance.'

'I know. I don't mean to ruin everything.'

'You were both lucky to walk away from the accident with your lives.'

'Urgh,' North shook her arms out dramatically. 'It wasn't that bad. We were hardly in danger of dying. Don't be so maudlin, Gran.'

Her grandmother held her in a steady stare.

'Oh, I get it,' North slapped her hands against the table and stood up. 'It's not about the accident it's about my eyes, right? I should be more careful because I invite death or some crap like that?'

'Don't speak to your grandmother like that.' On cue her grandfather was emerging from the living room, pipe in hand. The side of his face was crinkled as though he'd previously been sleeping in his armchair, pressed up against his favourite cushion.

'Come on,' North was striding out of the kitchen, away from them both. 'As if my eyes attract *death*. Besides, haven't you heard what all the cool kids are saying? Don't fear the reaper. You both might want to try that sometime.'

Upstairs in her room North heard her grandparents dissecting her outburst.

'She's becoming more and more like her,' her grandfather lamented.

'She's becoming a woman. It's mood swings, that's all.'

'And the car? Was that a mood swing?'

A sigh so loud it carried up to North's ears. 'I don't know. She's going through such a lot, we need to try to understand that.'

'Our North has never been wild. She's always been good, kind. Polite.'

'She lost her parents.'

'She still has us.'

'Yes,' North's grandmother agreed. 'But are we enough?'

The doubt in the old woman's voice tore through North like a machete. Upstairs on her bed she writhed against the pain of it as she wept. They were enough. She wanted to scream it until her lungs started to bleed. They had always been enough. It was her parents who had continually failed to measure up.

At first light the next day North found Kelly. They were both in the same uniform only somehow Kelly managed to make hers look fashionable. She wore her regulation tie short and squat, hitched her skirt up a few inches too short and made sure her sweater was always several sizes too big so that it hung off her shoulders.

'I can't mess up again,' North sternly told her friend as they commenced their walk to school together.

'It happened. Let's move on.'

'My grandparents are really upset.'

'They'll get over it.'

'No, they won't,' North insisted, emotion clotting up her throat. She coughed the worst of it away. 'I hurt them, Kel. This, what we did, what we told the police, it hurt them. They think I'm acting out.'

'Then let them think that. Besides, once word gets out it'll make you seem edgy.'

'I don't want to seem edgy.'

'So, what, you want to seem normal all your life?' Kelly stopped and wedged a hand against her hip, tapping her foot impatiently.

'I—'

'You played your orphan card and I appreciate that. Really, I do. But every time you decide to bend the rules you can't wind up regretting it. You need to own everything you do, even your mistakes.'

'Aren't you supposed to learn from your mistakes?'

'Whilst owning them.' Kelly sounded so sure. Like always, she peppered her conversation with wisdom. Was she an old soul trapped in a teenage body? Is that why she was always so restless? Had North's mother been afflicted in the same way?

'Do you wish things had turned out differently?' Kelly asked, suddenly becoming serious. 'Because if they had I'd be sat in some cell right now awaiting sentencing. Is that what you want?'

'No, of course not.'

'Your grandparents are just trying to guilt you. It's what grandparents do, a way to keep you from acting out again.'

'Well, it's worked,' North kicked at a stone on the ground.

'No,' Kelly grabbed her shoulder and looked her square in the eye. 'Never stop making mistakes, North. It's our mistakes that make us interesting. Every mistake is a sign that we took a chance, that we tried to do something different.'

'Don't you worry about being reckless?'

'I worry about not being remembered.'

It had started to rain. A soft drizzle fell from pewter clouds that loomed low and heavy in the sky. North welcomed the bite in the air, the dampness that was settling upon her sweater. Kelly was staring absently ahead, hadn't yet reached into her bag for her polka dot umbrella which she normally did the second she felt the faintest drop touch her fair skin.

'My hair,' she'd shriek as she popped the umbrella up. 'I refuse to frizz.'

'Kel—'

'Life is short. We need to live it that way. Now stop moping and be prepared to milk the hell out of this little adventure of ours. Danger is about to become your middle name.'

*

North had to turn on the TV. She needed to hear the murmur of voices, to know she wasn't alone. After settling on the twenty-four-hour news channel she snuggled against her pillows. Neither bed had been pristinely remade but she and Elijah had done their best. The putrid stench of raw alcohol persisted even though they'd kept the balcony doors ajar to let in a free flow of fresh air.

'The TV,' Elijah rolled onto his side to face her, his voice thick and drowsy. 'Do you put that on to help you sleep?'

'Uh-huh.'

'Does it help? Does it stop the nightmares?'

In the glow from the television she saw his eyelids getting heavy. It took less than a minute for them to completely close clearly unable to fight off the exhaustion which gnawed at him, but he kept speaking though he began to sound more distant, as though he was speaking within a dream.

'Keep the TV on. Keep the nightmares away,' he urged. 'Try and get some sleep.'

North knew that if she got a stolen nap she'd be lucky. Sleep never came for her. Not properly. Because the nightmares never left. They were just waiting for her to close her eyes.

21

The sun bleached away the sins from the night before. Baked in a golden glow, Monaco looked more welcoming than ever. As North sat outside on the hotel's upper terrace eating breakfast it was easy to forget what had happened, how Spencer had threatened her, how her room had been ransacked, though by whom she still wasn't certain. Light danced across the placid ocean and the warmth from the sun sunk into North's bones.

'We need to leave. Today.' Elijah's words brought a sliver of darkness to the table. With his fearful gaze he managed to weaken the rejuvenating embrace of the morning sun.

'And we will,' North looked down at her plate as she split a croissant in half and then smothered it in jam.

'I'm serious. You insisted on coming to eat breakfast like nothing was wrong and I agreed, but we have to think about leaving. If we went now we could be in Nice for—'

'There's one more thing I have to do.' The jam didn't bring the expected burst of sweetness as North shoved her croissant into her mouth. The pastry was ashen and tasteless. Her insomnia was eroding everything, even her enjoyment of food. She knew that she needed to sleep and it would come eventually, it had to.

'What? No!' Elijah's hands were on the table and they balled into clenched fists. 'We need to leave. You're in danger. I – I won't let you stay.'

'We can leave for Nice at noon.'

The whiteness in his knuckles eased. 'Noon?'

'Like I said, there's one more thing I have to do. Just one. Then we're gone.'

'You promise?'

North swallowed down the last of her breakfast. 'I promise.'

*

The harbour was off limits. North knew better than to return there, to let Spencer clock her face amid the crowds of tourists. Instead she angled herself away from the gleaming yachts, away from the air of indulgence that lingered in port and followed the route that the map on her phone had marked out for her. Elijah was back at the hotel loading their luggage into their hire car. He'd wanted to go with her. Insisted.

'I need to do this alone.' It was all she could say. If he knew where she was really going he wouldn't let her leave, would beg her to decide against it. A feeling squirmed in North's gut, a feeling that told her she needed to pursue this avenue one final time, else she'd regret it.

So now she was stood outside a French supermarket watching the ebb and flow of people pushing their trolleys across the large car park. She was waiting on one particular individual in the hope that this was where they would come on a Saturday morning. North had tracked social media feeds, had studied the whereabouts of other crew members. It seemed that most of them used their Saturday mornings to do mainland chores – she had to hope that Cassie was doing the same. This was her last chance, her last opportunity to push for the truth.

People meandered across the car park behind trolleys laden with goods. North felt her skin begin to prickle in the heat as a minute became five and then an hour. She was running out of time.

The shadow behind North was long when Cassie finally emerged through the glass-fronted doors of the store, paper bags stuffed with goods in each hand. She strode with purpose, head high and shoulders pushed back, but her swift steps told of the fear that shadowed her every movement. Her eyes were hidden behind thick glasses and she darted her gaze around the parked cars as though she were looking for something. Or someone. North cornered her a few feet away from the store.

'You.' The second Cassie saw her she physically flinched and stepped back as though North were poisonous. 'You shouldn't be here. You can't be here. Don't talk to me. No.' Keeping her head down, Cassie cut a quick route across the car park.

North chased after her.

'Please, Cassie, I just need a moment.'

'No. I've told you enough already.'

'Cassie, please.' North reached for her shoulder but the other woman shrugged her off and quickened her pace so that she was almost sprinting. Defeated, North let her hand fall to her side. 'He threatened me,' she called out to the rapidly departing figure.

Cassie kept walking, kept powering across the car park, but then she stopped. Her chin dipped to her chest and slowly she turned around and retraced her steps until she was at North's side.

'I can't say that I'm surprised. How bad was it?'

'He pushed me against the railing of his boat. Pretty much told me to get the hell out of Monaco and when I went back to my hotel room it had been trashed.'

She'd checked the bruise in the mirror that morning. Her reflection told her the frightening truth, that she hadn't been behind the destruction of her hotel room and she feared the charismatic millionaire more than she did herself.

'Yep,' Cassie pursed her purple lips as she nodded. 'Classic Spencer.'

'Why would he threaten me? What doesn't he want me to find out about Kelly? About the other girls?'

'Jesus.' Placing down one of her bags, Cassie freed a hand to furiously massage her furrowed brow. 'I told you, the other girls they are off limits. Do you understand? Chase down the truth about your friend all you want but leave them out of it.'

'Why? Maybe they know something? Maybe they know what happened to Kelly!'

'And maybe they'd rather swallow their own tongues than tell you what they know.' There was gravel in Cassie's voice. With a sigh she seemed to re-evaluate her tone as she pushed her sunglasses up and held North in a pitying gaze. 'You've seen first-hand, Spencer is volatile. He's also richer than God. And charitable. And with friends in very high places. He makes people…' She paused as she glanced at the empty cars around them, studying each one for someone hiding behind the wheel. 'He makes them disappear.'

'Disappear? How?'

Cassie shrugged. 'I've no idea. But girls go missing. One day they're working on The Orion and it's all smiles and then they're not. They've gone home. At least that's the line fed to the rest of us. But they sever all ties with the crew – delete us off Facebook, won't answer our calls. They ghost the hell out of us and no one knows why.'

'You think Spencer is the reason they leave? The reason they disappear?' North pressed, needing more information.

'I think,' Cassie leaned in close, 'that rich men wield a lot of power. Spencer can *incentivise* someone to leave. But to make someone disappear entirely, Kelly is the first I've heard of that, and honestly, it's scared the shit out of me.'

'You think he had something to do with Kelly's death?' North searched Cassie's expression for more answers.

'I think I've said too much. Again. Dammit.' Leaning down, Cassie grabbed her bags and began hurrying across the remainder of the car park.

North wouldn't give up. She chased after Cassie, fell into step with her. 'I need your help. I need to find out what happened to Kelly. Please.'

'I liked Kelly. And she loved you. So I'm going to do the right thing and honour what she'd want me to do for you. Get out.'

'Cassie, just—'

'Get the hell out of Monaco. Do not test Spencer. Do not think that turning over your room was just a message, it wasn't. It was just the beginning. He's as cruel as he is rich and he's very, very rich.'

'Then why keep working for him? Why not quit The Orion and go to the police, tell them what you know? I'll go with you. Together we can—'

'Have you not been listening?' Cassie demanded through clenched teeth. 'I'm not going to disappear for this cause of yours. Risking our own lives won't bring Kelly back. From the bottom of my heart I'm sorry she's gone, but I urge you to end this campaign, don't set yourself on a path that had a dead end.'

'I—'

'This is where we part ways. For good. Follow me and I blow my rape whistle. Understand?'

'Look, Cassie—'

'She said you were the nicest person she knew. That you were like a sister to her. I get why you're here but go back. There's no answers for you here. Leave while you can. Leave while I still have a job.'

North watched Cassie disappear from the car park, taking all her secrets with her.

*

'You okay?' Elijah was in the driver's seat, the boot full of their luggage. Monaco was in the rear-view mirror, disappearing into the horizon with every inch of road the little hire car chewed up. North was slumped in the passenger seat. 'Our flight is at five so we're going to make good time.' He rounded a sharp corner. A Ferrari sped past them, a flash of fiery red. 'Luckily we were only charged for the minibar. It could have been much worse.'

'I went to see Cassie,' North squirmed and angled herself to peer out of the window, catching the last few glimpses of the sea. Since returning to the hotel she'd been withdrawn and Elijah seemed to sense that she needed space. He didn't pounce on her for answers, just calmly waited as they checked out.

'You did?' He rounded another corner and the sea disappeared entirely. 'Why?'

'She knows more than she's telling us. If Spencer threatened me then he's trying to hide something.'

'So what did she say?'

North picked at the fabric of her seat belt. There were fresh red marks down her arms. 'Nothing. She basically said nothing. She fears him and seems scared to say anything.'

'Maybe you shouldn't be so quick to underestimate him.' Elijah accelerated along a clear stretch of road. 'If everyone fears him maybe they have good reason to.'

'Or maybe he's just a bully.'

'A bully with a lot of money. That makes him dangerous.'

'I know he's connected to Kelly's death. I just know it.' North ground her teeth together. All she had to show for her trip to Monaco was a depleted bank account. She'd found no definitive answers just speculation and a tyrant millionaire.

'But maybe it's time to drop it and move on, as hard as that is.'

Drop it and move on. As though Kelly were a thing, an unsolvable equation rather than a person, a part of North's soul.

'I can't.'

'You want to find out the truth. I get that. You've come all the way out here to do it and, I mean…' Elijah put one hand against his chest, over his heart, 'I don't know anyone who would do that for me. You're one hell of a friend. Kelly was lucky to have you.'

'It was the other way around.' The words rolled so quickly off her tongue. The sparking core at the centre of their friendship which North knew everyone could see but they were always too polite to acknowledge it. 'I was lucky to have her,' she clarified. 'She taught me to be a better person. To be brave.'

'You're braver than you think, North. You need to give yourself more credit.'

'Can we just…' Leaning forward, she turned up the volume on the stereo. 'Just drive,' she ordered over the music. 'I don't want to think anymore. I just want to sit.'

*

The plane touched down with a thump. North bounced in her seat as the landing gear connected with the runway, brakes screeching and the smell of burning rubber finding a way in from outside. It was getting dark at Heathrow. Lights twinkled beyond her little window of the plane and North could almost find comfort in them. As a child she used to try and create constellations out of street lights.

'We're here,' Elijah covered her hand with his own. 'We're home.'

North felt impaled by her sorrow. This was the first time she'd returned from a holiday without Kelly by her side. Giddy with exhaustion they'd head home and then collapse on the couch together and sleep away their jet lag. The next day Kelly would host a fashion show of all the items she'd bought while away. Now all North had returned with was more questions, each more pressing than the last.

Numbly she followed Elijah off the plane, through customs and towards the baggage collection, wondering with each step how Kelly had felt when she returned prematurely from Monaco. When her plane landed at Heathrow was she running from something? From someone? And all the other girls who'd suddenly left their posts upon The Orion, where were they?

'Here,' Elijah wheeled her suitcase to her, cheeks glistening with a sheen of sweat from having wrestled it off the conveyer belt. 'You okay?'

'No.' She was too tired to be anything other than honest.

He squeezed her shoulders before heading back to find his own luggage. Around her people were sleepily chatting with one another, making plans for what they'd do when they got home.

'We could order takeaway.'

'I should call Diane.'

'We need to pick up Mr McIver before anything else. The kennels aren't far from here.'

North zoned in and out, their words mingling together in a ribbon of conversation. Their voices became warped as though her head was being held underwater.

'So what's the plan?' Kelly's question was always the same as they pulled their suitcases out of the arrivals gate. 'We need a plan, North. In life, you've always got to have a plan.'

'Let's go home.' It was a simple suggestion but one Kelly readily welcomed.

'Yes,' she'd smile, bringing back the sunshine from their exotic getaway. 'Let's go home.'

But going home wasn't always a given. Sometimes they'd dawdle in arrivals, waiting to watch couples get reunited and loved ones returned.

'That's the best part about leaving,' Kelly would whisper as they watched a family fiercely embrace, 'coming home.'

When North was sixteen, she and Kelly had hitch-hiked their way to Heathrow and stood in arrivals for nine long hours in the feeble hope that North's parents might suddenly walk through the gate. They didn't. They were found by the police and sent back to North's irate grandparents and Kelly's understanding mother.

'I get it, kid,' she whispered to North as she tenderly stroked her head. 'You figured if you stand there long enough they'll just come back. And who knows,' she's shrugged, the scent of whisky radiating out of her, 'maybe they will.'

'You ready?' Elijah was pulling both their cases towards the main doors, out of the arrivals lounge.

North twisted to look back at the corridor through which humanity kept flowing. People fell into one another's arms as though their legs had suddenly stopped working. There were tears. Whoops of joy.

'Actually,' she turned to fully look back at where they'd just walked through, 'could we just stand a while and watch people arriving back home?'

The suitcases hissed along the polished floor as Elijah angled them back towards North. 'Okay, sure. Is everything all right?'

She kept staring at the new arrivals. 'I just need to see some compassion. Some love.'

Elijah stood solemnly at her side. 'We can stay as long as you like.'

'I came here once and waited for my parents. I sneaked away from my grandparents and me and Kelly bundled our way to Heathrow. I stood here until my legs ached and my back burned. They never arrived.'

'But they were lost at sea, they were never going to come back.'

'I know,' North agreed with a sad smile. 'But I never gave up hoping that they would.'

22

It was raining in Millwater. A powerful downfall that bounced on the pavements and ran in rivers along gutters. It made the small town feel even greyer and more oppressive than usual. North stood at the window in her flat, her unopened suitcase by her feet.

'I'll stay,' Elijah had offered as he lingered in her corridor, glancing longingly at her front door.

'It's fine, really. I need to shower and unpack.'

'I don't want to leave you alone.'

North had sent him away with assurances that she truly was fine. That she'd see him at work the following day. That the disappointments she faced in Monaco hadn't settled deep within her and grown roots like a decaying rot.

The rain slapped against the window, landing on the glass with force and then meandering down towards the brickwork, all previous fury drained out of it. North pulled in a long breath. Everything about her little flat was the same. It still smelt of vanilla and burnt toast, still creaked like an old man's bones when she turned on the heating.

'What did he do to you?' She turned away from the window and delivered her question to her wall of notations, staring fixedly at the empty space which marked Kelly's summer upon The Orion. 'He did something, Kel. I can feel it.'

Although the red mark on her back had faded, North could recall with complete clarity how it felt to have Spencer Daniels push her, threaten her, his eyes wild and his cheeks burning red. He was a man to be feared.

'Did he hurt you?' She kept staring at the wall, ignoring the lead in her bones. Travel had made her weary. She could easily drop onto her sofa, turn on a movie and gaze at the television until she spaced out. But she felt bound to the wall. To her questions. 'I know that he did something.' Tentatively she touched the spot on the wall that was Kelly's summer. She pressed her hand against the cool paintwork as her mind raced through all the details she'd amassed in Monaco. 'I'll make him pay,' she whispered to the emptiness around her. 'Whatever he did to you, I'll make him pay.'

*

There was so much data. North's eyes ached as she scanned her computer screen, trying to take it all in. A day had passed and the rain had not left. It had whispered against her window all through the night as she fitfully tossed and turned on her sofa. As Baz Luhrmann's *Romeo and Juliet* played on a loop, North sat in darkness beneath a blanket and waited for her eyelids to slide south.

'Aye me, sad hours seem long.' It was Kelly's favourite line from the movie, one she loved to quote with a theatrical sigh whenever she was feeling blue. But Shakespeare was right. Sad hours *were* long. They dragged in a way that happy ones never did. North felt every minute grate by as she wished for rest and found only restlessness.

'You're back.' A hand was on her shoulder and without spinning around North knew it belonged to Alexander. He smelt of coffee and cologne as she slowly turned to look up at him, pulling her lips into a welcoming smile like she was putting on a mask.

'Hi, yeah, I'm back.'

'How was Monaco?'

'It was…'

Disappointing.

Dangerous.

'Good. It was good. What about your trip?'

'Productive.'

Something was off. Each time Alexander smiled it failed to reach his eyes and he looked at her like she was a star he'd previously categorised which had started to behave erratically, like he was trying to figure her out.

'Everything okay?' North felt uncomfortably small in her chair as he stood over her.

'Yeah, everything's great,' he massaged his jaw and didn't meet her gaze. 'When you have a minute can I see you in my office?'

'Sure.'

He strode away and North looked back at her screen, at the mass of numbers which were now merging together. She knew that she should get straight up and follow Alexander out to his office but he could wait. He wasn't a patient man but she didn't care about getting on his bad side. After discreetly glancing around, North expanded the window she kept furtively checking when no one was around. The Twitter page for Spencer Daniels.

The millionaire playboy was still in Monaco. Still on board his beloved yacht. He'd updated his feed twice since she'd last checked. First he'd tagged some friends as they enjoyed lunch at an exclusive eatery and then he'd posted a picture of himself on a sun lounger, golden chest exposed as he wore nothing but a pair of designer swimming trunks. His world still glistened, was bathed in perpetual sunshine. With a scowl North looked up from her computer at the nearest window where the rain relentlessly lashed against it.

She looked again at the sun-kissed image on her computer screen. Spencer Daniels looked as though he were on another planet not just in another country. But no matter where you were the sun would always set, Spencer couldn't remain in its warm glow forever.

*

'You took your time,' Alexander commented abruptly as North closed the door behind her.

'I am working. I've got a lot of catching up to do.' She sat in the chair across from his desk and folded her arms against her chest.

He arched an eyebrow in surprise and then ran his long fingers down the stubble on his cheeks. 'I just wanted to have a little chat.'

'Okay,' North leaned back expectantly. And then something strange happened. Alexander Beckett actually squirmed in his seat. He awkwardly shifted from side to side and North had to bite down on her tongue to stop herself from laughing or saying something like, 'hey, you're stealing my bit.' She was the one who was meant to feel uncomfortable in her own skin whenever she was around him.

'So, Monaco, you enjoyed it?' his voice tightened and he settled upon a position, leaning forward and clasping his hands together upon his desk.

'It was… an adventure.'

'You went alone?'

North tilted her head to the side. 'Does that matter?'

'Did you?'

'Again, does it matter?'

'Because I heard that you went with Elijah.'

'Did you now?' North kept her tone cordial which she knew would infuriate him.

'And...' Alexander cleared his throat as his knuckles turned white. 'And if you two are an *item* then I feel like I should be informed as there may be implications on the working environment and—'

'*If* Elijah and I are an *item* then it's nobody's business but ours.' North watched a deep flush creep up from her boss's collar and spread across his cheeks like a hungry fire.

'Actually it's—'

'Who I sleep with won't impact my work here or anyone else's.' She began to stand up, her body elegantly releasing itself from the plastic chair. 'It never has before,' she added darkly. 'So you needn't worry.'

North didn't wait for him to respond. She reached for the door handle and stepped out into the corridor of the demountable. When she dropped down at her desk, the moment had settled and she gasped when she realised how much she'd sounded like Kelly when she'd been sat in Alexander's office.

*

According to Facebook, Twitter and Instagram, Spencer Daniels was living his best life. He was constantly drinking designer champagne, flanked by beautiful women in skimpy bikinis who were either pouting or laughing uproariously at some joke he must have made. Every shot looked as though it were out of a beer or aftershave advert. How could perfection like that be real?

When North looked at his face, at his chiselled smile she saw only that he was dead behind the eyes. She could still hear the malice in his voice, feel the pressure of his touch against her shoulders.

Cassie feared him. Had Kelly too? Or had Kelly challenged him – refusing to laugh at his juvenile jokes, calling him out on his hideous nature? Such resistance from a beautiful women would be like showing a bull a red flag. Had Spencer charged? Had he hurt her? Pushed her against the railing so hard she thought her spine might snap?

North kept trying to remember the Kelly who had returned that summer. Her friend had been subdued but North had attributed that to the space which had crept between them, the space which North had created. Hate simmered on her cheeks, causing her skin to burn. North should never have upset Kelly like she did. She should have listened, she should have—

'What are you doing?' Elijah was drawing a chair up close to her computer screen. 'What are you looking at him for? I thought we were moving on from what happened in Monaco?'

She quickly minimised Spencer's Twitter page but the damage had been done. Elijah had seen what still gnawed away at her. She felt ghastly and exposed. 'I was just…'

Obsessing.

North wanted to know where he was. What he was doing. Every new post gave her hope that somehow Spencer would slip up and reveal some crucial detail which would tie him to Kelly, to that summer.

'Stop,' Elijah urged. 'Just stop. You went over there, you did everything you could.'

'I know he's hiding something,' North couldn't stop herself from admitting the haunting truth. 'I know he knows more about Kelly than he's letting on. If only Cassie had been willing to talk more then—'

'Look around,' Elijah gestured to the office around them. Their co-workers were gazing at their computer screens, their pale faces lit up like the moon by the electrical glow. Fingers were pounding on keyboards, hard drives were whirring as they chewed up data and spat out theories. 'We're at work. We're back in the real world now. You need to let go of Monaco. Of Spencer. Okay?'

'Alexander thinks we're dating.' North tried to change the subject. It worked.

Elijah brightened, his mouth twisting up into a surprised smile. 'He does?'

'Yeah, he called me into his office to ask about it. I assured him it wouldn't affect my work.' She sounded so brazen as she playfully referred to their non-existent relationship. So confident. So like Kelly. It was unsettling how regularly she was slipping in to her late friend's persona. North shook off the cloak of confidence and shrunk in her seat. 'I'm sorry.' She couldn't meet Elijah's gaze. 'He was just asking if we were an item. He heard we went away together.'

'I mean...' Elijah raised a hand to scratch at the back of his head. 'If we *were* an item, it wouldn't be such a bad thing, would it?' The hope in his voice almost strangled the sentence.

'I—'

The door to the office was thrust open and Alexander came in, instantly filling any empty space in the room. 'Team meeting,' he declared with a clap of his hands. 'I want you all assembled in five minutes.'

North felt the string of her response snap on her tongue. The moment had been broken. Shyly she tucked a strand of loose hair behind her ear. 'We'd better get ready for the meeting.'

'Yeah,' Elijah agreed stiffly. 'Let's go.'

*

Spencer Daniels is the eldest son of Ernest and Maureen Daniels and an Eton graduate.

North discreetly scrolled through Spencer's Wikipedia page as Alexander conducted the meeting.

'Thanks everyone, I just want to relay some of the work that I was doing over in the Canaries.'

Zoning out, North focused only on her phone. She was searching for anything suspicious, but there was nothing. Spencer didn't have a police record. There wasn't so much as a rumour about him being anything other than an entitled rich boy. He was labelled arrogant, cocky, sometimes brash, but none of the insults rose to anything more concrete, anything more damning. It seemed to be a perpetual loop of parties and showbiz events, wearing a different suit for every occasion. He was a public figure, a star.

There had to be something. North searched with more ferocity. Cassie mentioned other girls. What had he done to them? To Kelly? If he'd pushed North against the railing of his boat when he barely knew her, she dreaded to think what he'd be capable of doing to someone who really pissed him off, who took the time to get under his thick pig skin.

The internet seemed to be complicit with all Spencer's lies. Every site painted him out to be a Lothario, a party boy, but harmless.

Alexander was still talking, discussing his recent findings. North knew that what he was saying was fascinating but she couldn't listen, couldn't focus on his voice, not when the pressure of all her unanswered questions kept building up inside her. If she didn't learn something useful soon she was going to explode.

'As I've reiterated it's still early days and we can't risk jumping to any conclusions yet.' The meeting was coming to an end. North slid her phone back into the front pocket of her hoodie and rolled her shoulders, trying to shake off her overwhelming disappointment.

She was back at her desk when her computer pinged with an incoming instant message from Elijah. It simply said 'read this' followed by a link. North clicked the link. It was a chat site forum which appeared dated in format but some of the entries were as recent as several months ago. North clicked through them.

He abused my sister.

There was an out of court settlement with my cousin and a gag order. It was for around £40k.

He's a pig. If it weren't for the legal fortress he surrounds himself with then everyone would know.

Seems money can buy forgiveness. Prick.

At least fifty entries but no names were ever given. Were they all talking about the same guy?

'I think it's him,' Elijah sat next to her and looked only at her computer screen. 'So much seems to be linked to his estate in Kent, to his yacht. I can't be sure though. It's on a strange proxy on a closed server so relatively discreet but still accessible. I guess no one can risk saying anything that would implicate both him and themselves. There're never any dates, just suggestions of things that have happened.'

'You think this is Spencer?' North turned to face Elijah but he remained transfixed by the screen.

'Maybe,' he shrugged. 'But there's no way of knowing. It could be anyone. The point is that you need to drop this. All of it. You'll drive yourself mad if you don't.'

'If this is him then he keeps getting away with harming women.' North scrolled through some more of the posts. Many mentioned out of court settlements and gag orders. Was the man they were discussing truly Spencer Daniels? North felt her conviction growing with her curiosity.

'All this, it's dangerous.' Elijah gestured at the screen.

'I just *know* he did something to her.'

'I sent you this as a warning,' Elijah sternly informed her. 'I don't want you to end up like one of the names on this screen, bitter and resentful. Let it go. Move on. For your sake.'

'Okay, thanks.'

He got up and was about to leave.

'I'll let it go,' she agreed as he stepped away from her desk. 'And it definitely wouldn't be such a bad thing.' North smiled, confident in the knowledge that at least half of what she'd just told him was true.

23

North sat on the crooked arm of the tree. Around her the woods gently stirred. An owl hooted as soft steps trampled across the ground. The flowers at the base of the grand oak had all wilted, battered by rain and time. The tips of their petals had begun to droop and curl. No fresh bouquets had been laid out. But in the darkness North couldn't see the flowers, could only smell their pungent presence. She'd used the light of her phone to guide her along the jogging trail, towards the tree.

An hour earlier she'd been sat on her sofa gazing at her television as *Legally Blonde* played for the third time that night. Sleep would not come for her. North knew that before the title character in the movie, Elle, had been dumped for the first time. But she played along, sat and listened to the familiar dialogue, recalled how Kelly would recite it all with a smile. North's eyes remained wide, her spine rigid. And slowly, the walls of her flat began to creep in on her. She scratched her nails deep into her arms, ground her teeth, chewed her hair, but there was no escaping the feeling of claustrophobia. She had to get out.

Millwater was not New York, it was a town that did most definitely sleep. The observatory and the twenty-four-hour petrol station were the only businesses that operated late into the night. There had been talk about the local supermarket adopting extended hours, but so far those discussions had yet to morph into anything more than mutterings.

Everything was closed. Quiet. North drifted through town like a ghost. She looked longingly at windows with the curtains drawn and the lights out, imagining the occupants inside tucked up safely in bed lost to the depths of a dream. She hadn't intended to visit the jogging trail but she'd found herself there just after two. The night held a damp cold and North shuddered inside her thick coat.

Once she found the tree she climbed it. Eventually she rested her back against the trunk and let her legs hang astride a thick branch, trying not to think about how much weight it could support, how easily a rope could fit around it. North breathed in the damp earth, the moss, the gentle decay of the floral carpet beneath her.

This was where Kelly had taken her final breath. Before she jumped – or was pushed – had she looked up at the sky one last time? Had she thought of her best friend? Her unborn baby?

It was a clear night. North saw the shine of the moon through the network of branches overhead. It's imperfect face always a beacon to her. She kept staring at it, imagining her parents adrift on some raft, trying to get home to her. The water bobbed beneath them as arm in arm the Stones looked up at the silvery moon and thought of their lost little daughter. With a sigh North closed her eyes.

*

The dawn chorus was shrill, sharp. Birds hopped on branches eagerly screeching to the rising sun. With a groan North shifted against the tree and opened her eyes. The morning was bright, all darkness drained from the sky which was now a pale blue.

'Crap.' Night had passed and during some of it she'd dozed up in the tree, her limbs already aching from being held in an uncomfortable position for so long.

With some effort North climbed down from the tree, landing amid the dying flowers. Her body felt as stiff and gnarled as the branch which had supported her.

'Crap,' she repeated as she checked the time on her phone. Almost seven. The cold was a cloak that hugged her tight. North shuddered against its embrace. She needed to get home. To get warm. But once again her legs led her astray. Instead of walking back towards her little flat she began to tread the familiar route to Kelly's home and by half seven she was stood at the base of the tidy little drive, peering up at the front door.

It didn't take long for the door to open. Dean came out, dressed for work in the gas company's polo shirt and a pair of worn-out jeans and thick lace-up boots. He locked up and then froze when he turned and saw North, his tired face alighting with surprise.

'What the hell?' He gathered himself and promptly marched over to her. 'North, what is this? Why are you here? I told you to stay away from here. Did I not make myself clear?'

'He did something to her,' North whispered the words which powered around her mind in a closed loop. 'He did something to her. I know it.'

'What? Kelly?' Dean was keeping her at arm's length but he leaned forward to peer at her face. North waited for the tidal wave of anger to wash over her. He was going to lash out, to shout at her, to turn the air around him as blue as his shirt. Instead he pressed his thick hand against her forehead. 'Jesus, you look terrible. Did you sleep rough last night? And you're freezing! North – what's going on with you?'

'He did something. I know it.'

'Look,' Dean dragged a hand down his face and looked between North and his car, weighing up what he should do, 'let me give you a lift home, okay? Clearly you're not yourself right now.'

'He hurt her.' She couldn't risk rambling, she needed to be direct but she could see in his face the lack of understanding there.

'Kelly did it to herself, remember?' Dean gripped her shoulders and directed her up the drive towards his car. 'You really need to stop dwelling on all this stuff. It's making you sick.'

In the car North shook. Her body felt as though all her organs had been replaced with blocks of ice. Her teeth noisily clattered together and when she glimpsed at her reflection in the wing mirror she saw that her lips were the same colour as the early morning sky.

'Maybe I should take you to the hospital,' Dean considered as he pulled out of the drive.

'Home,' North assured him. 'Home is fine. T-thanks.'

'What are you doing?' he asked as he paused to turn at the end of the road. 'Where did you even sleep last night?'

'In a tree.' She was too tired to lie.

'In a tree?'

'I don't know. She keeps asking me to help her.'

'Who does?'

North pulled her lips into a tight line, awake enough to know that she'd already said too much.

'I'm worried that you're losing it,' Dean admitted as he turned in the direction of her flat. 'I mean, I know that Kelly's death hit you hard, I get that. But have you thought about talking to someone? Like a professional?'

'Have you?'

'I'm not sleeping in trees,' he responded gruffly. 'And I have my own way of dealing with things.'

As the car went over a speed bump North heard the metal bottles knocking together in the boot.

'I know things didn't go well last time we spoke,' Dean grunted and cleared his throat. 'We were both vulnerable and hurting but...' another grunt. 'I'm here if... you know. You need to talk about Kel. Don't... don't go sleeping in trees, okay? Don't do anything to hurt yourself. That's not what Kelly would have wanted. She thought the world of you, you know that, right?'

The ice in her body was swiftly turning to fire. North turned in her seat, struggling to feel comfortable.

'You're trying to make sense of everything, I get it.' The car slowed as Dean reached her block of flats. He pulled up outside and turned off the engine. 'This isn't the way to deal with her death.' He gave North a long, sad look as she unclipped her seat belt and struggled to open her door.

'Thanks for the l-lift.'

'Wait.' She had one foot out when Dean grabbed her arm and tugged her back. 'You don't need to suffer alone, okay? If you don't want to talk to me then at least talk to someone. Accept what happened and move on.'

'Uh-huh.' North climbed out. She hugged her arms around herself as she looked back into the car. 'Thank you.'

Dean turned on the engine and glanced at her. 'Let's not be enemies, okay? We were friends once. And we both loved Kelly, that won't change.'

'Not enemies,' North smiled against her trembling teeth. 'Got it.' She waved as Dean drove off. Stiff and exhausted she headed towards her flat.

*

Showering helped. North stood beneath the stream of hot water and let it slide down her back, across her shoulders, over her arms and legs. She let it wash away the cold, the damp, the rot. She stood in her bath as the shower purged her skin until she turned pink. Then she bundled herself in her thickest towel and trotted out of the bathroom. The heating puffed and buckled within the walls, making her little flat feel marginally cosy. North hugged the towel tight and went to peer at her wall. She focused on the main gap and then doubled back to her kitchenette to grab a fresh Post-it note and a marker pen. She made a furious scribble and then slapped the neon note within the centre of the gap with force. On it were two words;

Spencer Daniels.

He was the beating heart at the centre of Kelly's death. North knew it. She just had to prove it.

*

The star was still dying. North logged her most recent stream of data and sipped on the cup of tea she'd made herself. Its warm sugary sweetness was a welcome respite against the chill which had settled in her bones.

It was warm in the office. The demountable could retain a surprising amount of heat given enough direct sunlight. Glorious light fell in through the western wall, scalding tables and desks. From inside it looked like a beautiful summer's day. It was only when you looked closer that you realised it was just a façade, that the leaves on the trees were amber and gold, and come the morning, instead of dew, there would be frost upon blades of grass.

'Hey,' Elijah looked as bright as the sun as he came in to start his shift. His hair seemed tidier than usual, more styled. And he was freshly shaven, emphasising his boyish looks. He regarded North with a slightly nervous smile as he sat down at the desk next to hers. 'You okay?'

Had Dean told anyone what he'd found at the end of his drive that morning? North tensed at the thought. Had he mentioned to her co-workers that strange little North Stone had taken to sleeping in trees? Gossip spread faster than the plague in Millwater. From the postal worker's ears to a hairdresser's lips it grew wings as it carried from place to place and became wild and fast, always gaining momentum and power.

North tried to read Elijah's open expression. Was he asking how she'd slept? *Where* she'd slept?

'I'm a bit tired.' She thought of the moon, thought of how despite her aches it had felt good to sleep beneath it, to feel connected to the stars. Her stars. Their constellations were woven into her DNA.

'Look, about what we were discussing yesterday,' Elijah leaned in, looking eager. 'I was thinking maybe we could, I don't know, go to the cinema or something. There's a new Star Wars movie coming out, how about we go and...' he shrugged and his cheeks began to turn pink, 'you know, go together. Like... a date.'

'Sure.'

This was normal, right? A normal request. A guy asking a girl out on a date. North's fingers twitched with the impulse to call Kelly. If this were a year ago she'd have grabbed her phone and dashed out to the toilet to type out a frantic message. And Kelly would have called back. Instantly. No matter where she was or who she was with, her response would arrive in the next heartbeat.

North tried to imagine the elation that Kelly's voice would hold. 'He asked you out? *Finally.* That's so awesome! Now we just need to plan out your outfit.'

But there was no one to call. Not Kelly. Not her mother. Not her grandparents. All of the people who North cared about were in the graveyard.

*

'Nothing lasts forever.' That's what North's grandmother had said the day they'd lost her grandfather. The old woman had knitted her wrinkled hands together and blinked back tears as she sat in the stiff plastic chair in the hospital waiting room. 'Although,' her thin lips had twisted with despair, 'I thought it would. Does that make me foolish? I thought he and I would see an eternity together.'

North embraced her grandmother, held her as she wept and shuddered. She kept telling herself that soon she'd be able to call Kelly and receive a much-needed cuddle of her own.

'I just hope that wherever he's gone, he'll wait for me there.' With a brittle sigh North's grandmother straightened and fished a tissue from her sleeve which she then dabbed against her red eyes.

'I didn't do this? Did I?' North fretted.

'What?'

'You've said that death is drawn to me. Because of my eyes.' Guilt made North's words feel too thick in her throat and she had to fight to get them out.

'Sweet child,' her grandmother cupped North's chin with her cold hands, 'in the end, death is drawn to us all.'

'So he's gone?' Kelly was waiting on the doorstep of North's grandparents' home, a bag of liquorice in one hand and a tub of ice cream in the other.

'Yeah,' North agreed sadly as she helped her grandmother up to the front door. 'He's gone.'

Kelly followed them inside, not deterred by their grief. She helped North sit her grandmother down in the living room with a cup of hot tea.

'You're such good girls,' the old woman kept saying. 'Such good girls.'

'I'm sorry,' Kelly declared when they were finally alone in the kitchen. 'You've lost your granddad. That sucks.'

North fell against her. She cried until there was nothing left and all the while Kelly kept holding her, kept promising that everything would be okay.

'Death eventually comes for us all,' North whimpered as she stepped back, cheeks blotchy and eyes sore.

'True,' Kelly agreed. 'But that doesn't mean that we have to hang around and wait for it.'

'I don't want to lose anyone else.'

This was the part where Kelly was supposed to promise that she wouldn't, that everything would be fine. Instead, her friend regarded her with a solemn stare. 'You will lose other people, North. But together we'll get through it. Together we can get through anything.'

24

What film shall we go and see?

The question from Elijah went unanswered on her phone. North was sat on her sofa, laptop open and gaze transfixed. She'd been that way for almost an hour, searching a digital haystack for the whisper of a needle.

Night came on swift wings lately as it squeezed down the hours of daylight. Once again North was in her flat and the clock was approaching midnight. Most people would now be in their beds, nestled beneath their duvets, exhausted but content.

'Come on,' she punched the refresh button on the page she was searching and scowled at the digital screen.

Spencer's Twitter page updated. He was no longer in Monaco. He was in—

'London.' North stated the name of the city with breathy reverence. He was so close. Within touching distance. In his latest post he was sprawled out in the leather booth of an expensive bar surrounded by champagne, girls and sparklers. The caption read;

Great to be back in my home town in time for tomorrow night's launch of @Diowater_UK's limited edition bottle at the Savoy. S x

North read the caption over and over. He was giving away so much; his location, his plans. Was he goading her to come find him? Or was he simply so arrogant that he didn't care who read his posts, just wanted the whole world to know his itinerary?

'The Savoy. London.' North stated the facts to herself as she started searching for more information about the launch of Diowater's new limited-edition bottle. It was apparently going to be pink. North didn't go to London often. She went to use the airports occasionally, sometimes for a concert. She found the pace of the city exciting, invigorating. And Kelly would feed off it like a vampire fed off blood. In London Kelly came alive. She lit up amongst the crowds, relished the hurried bustle of tourists moving along congested streets. She'd have read Spencer's Twitter post as a personal invitation to go to London, to attend the launch party at the Savoy. And so North decided to do the same.

*

'I love the glamour,' Kelly giggled as she strode arm in arm with North, strutting through Covent Garden. 'Look, there's a Chanel store. Ooh and Kurt Geiger. *So* exclusive.'

'Uh-huh.'

For North it was the history. She was pretty sure she'd clocked a pub named after Nell Gwyn while they were walking around but she resisted the urge to suggest going in for a drink, already knowing that once Kelly saw the dark décor and understated frontage she'd turn her nose up at it and drag them over to a brightly lit champagne bar instead.

'Can you imagine being able to go in there and *buy* something?' Kelly was gazing adoringly at the display in the Chanel window, pawing her gloved hand at the glass. 'Chanel *is* sophistication. One day I'm going to own something by them. Even if it's just a pair of pants or a shoe.'

'Just the one shoe?'

'Two might prove too expensive,' Kelly scrunched up her nose. 'But one, maybe I could stretch to that. How much do you think a pair are?'

'Couple of hundred pounds. More maybe.'

'Urgh. That's basically the rent. Not sure Dean would approve.' With a roll of her eyes Kelly backed away from the window and steered them further along the historic cobbled street. It was busy. Street lights shone almost as bright as all the store frontages, and glittering snowflakes were threaded between the buildings like ice laced cobwebs. Christmas was coming. The entire city seemed to sparkle in anticipation.

'Maybe he'd be okay about the one shoe,' North reasoned. 'And next year you could buy the other one.'

'Enough about Dean and his penny-pinching nature,' Kelly pulled her friend close. 'Tonight is about us. Girls' night. And…' they tottered around a corner together, 'here we are.'

North held a breath as she looked up at the Royal Opera House. It looked just as impressive as it did on TV and tonight she and Kelly weren't just there to walk past and look in with wistful admiration, they were actually going to attend a show. The tickets were in North's bag – they were going to sit in the highest, cheapest seats and watch *The Nutcracker*, a dream both girls had harboured since childhood. It was all so wonderful that North could almost taste the magic in the air.

'Now we just have to act like we belong.' Kelly slowed her pace, pushed back her shoulders and tilted her chin up towards the vaulted glass ceiling as they walked inside. 'I'm going to pretend that my shoes are more Chanel less Primark.'

North giggled.

'For one night only we are ladies,' Kelly continued grandly. 'Ladies who belong in the most luxurious parts of London. And damn anyone who suggests otherwise.'

Kelly was a chameleon. Wherever she was, she had a gift at being able to adapt. If everyone seemed rich and expensive, then so would she. If everyone seemed bohemian and well-travelled, Kelly did too. She would be whatever she needed to be. All the while she'd stand out as the best of what was on offer. Sometimes North wondered if the Kelly she knew and loved was also part of this grand act but it couldn't be. They were best friends. They knew each other inside out. There were no secrets between them, no play-acting for one another's benefit.

*

North stood on the platform, feet nervously tapping against the ground. She wanted to run. She wanted to turn around and sprint back towards her little yellow car and just drive away. Instead she was outside shivering despite the protection of her thick coat as she waited for the train to take her from Millwater to Euston, a journey which would last almost an hour. She was once again wearing her black skater dress since it was her only outfit that was even remotely party appropriate. It was coupled with the shoes she'd bought in Monaco. Looking at them made her stomach churn with guilt.

She should have told Elijah what she was doing. Instead he thought she was home with a cold and they'd rescheduled their plans to go to the cinema. Because the cinema could wait, there would be other weekends, other showings. Spencer, however, would not. There was no telling how long it would be before he left London on a private jet and disappeared across the globe to a place North couldn't afford to follow him to.

A train thundered through the station but didn't stop. Warm air rushed against North, causing her to cautiously back away from the yellow line painted on the platform.

There wasn't even a plan in place. She was going to go to London, make her way to the Savoy and then what? Try and blag her way into a high-end party?

It's what Kelly would do.

Kelly would have co-ordinated her outfit, ensuring she was just as glittering and pink as the limited edition Diowater bottles. She'd paint on her brightest smile and walk with a swing in her step, like her hip bones had been replaced with a highly flexible snake. Kelly would just fit right in. If there were doormen, they'd grant her access as a reflex. Beauty opened doors. Kelly was living proof of that.

North hugged her arms against herself and quivered in the cold. Again she asked herself what she was doing and failed to provide an answer. She just needed to get close to him, to Spencer Daniels. He was the key to it all.

What will I even ask him?

If only her arms weren't covered, she'd be able to scratch at them, to enjoy the momentary release from her panicked thoughts.

Ask him for the truth.

Because he had it, locked away in his privileged little mind. He knew what had happened to Kelly and others like her. The truth was there. North just needed to find a way to take it from him.

*

'This party is *insane*.'

North looked past Kelly, at the beach which had changed when the sun set. It was no longer a stretch of pure white sand, it was a mass of writhing bodies, all twisting and turning in time to the music being blasted from loudspeakers.

'This is amazing.' Kelly pulled North by the hand, leading her deeper into the swell of movement. All the swaying, jumping, shaking was making North nauseous. Her stomach hadn't settled since they'd arrived in Thailand. She blamed the storefront curry she'd had on their first day. 'Come on,' Kelly hauled her up to a bamboo bar and bought them both a beer. North eyed the green glass bottle, unsure if she could force even a sip down. 'This is what I call a party.' Kelly had to shout to be heard over the bass which pounded through them like a heartbeat.

There were so many people. So many limbs surging together, co-existing in a moment. It was dizzyingly hedonistic and North felt wretchedly out of place. Everyone was bronzed and glistening while she was pale and green-tinged.

Kelly was already waving her arms about and whooping, effortlessly sliding into place. North spotted guys almost snapping their necks in their desperate attempt to get a look at her.

Kelly shone. She was a star that everyone gravitated around. Soon she was the centre of the beach party and everyone else was dancing around her. Everyone except North.

The water was refreshingly cool as it slid over North's feet. She savoured the sensation before dropping to her knees and retching. She felt like she could taste everything she'd ever eaten, from her first banana to that final curry.

'There are you.' Kelly had broken away from the mass, from her adoring crowd. She knelt in the sand beside North and rubbed her friend's back. 'You still sick?'

'Uh-huh.'

North doubled over and wretched again.

'It'll pass,' Kelly promised as she kept rubbing.

'I shouldn't have come here,' North wiped at her mouth.

'To the party?'

'To Thailand.'

'What?' Kelly sounded genuinely stunned as North dropped onto her back, defeated. She tried to focus on the stars overhead as a maelstrom continued to angrily swirl in her stomach. 'Why would you say that?' Kelly was lying beside her, threading her fingers through North's.

'Because.'

'That's not an answer.'

'Because I'm not built for adventure. I'm not like you.'

'No one is *built* for adventure. Like no one is built for greatness. You seek it out.'

'We ate the same curry,' North kicked at the sand in frustration, 'and you're fine, while I'm…' she limply raised her free hand and sighed. 'I'm a sickly mess. I've been like this for days. Because I'm not built for adventure.'

'You've just got a dodgy tummy. It'll pass.'

'What if my parents didn't pass the adventurous gene onto me?'

'You're being crazy.'

'They lived for adventure. They were like you.'

'Do you know what makes you special?'

North turned her head to look at her friend. Kelly's eyebrows were raised, her expression serious.

'No,' North mumbled. 'Because I'm not special.'

'You're special because you never once hated them.'

'My parents?' Intrigued, North completely rolled onto her side.

'Yeah,' Kelly nodded. 'Some people in your situation would be pissed that they left you behind. Or pissed that they went at all. Their main focus in life should have been their parental duties to you, right?'

North was silent.

'But you understood their impulse, their desire to break free, to see the world. And maybe you don't spread your wings as fully as they did, maybe you still like to keep one foot at home when you step out the door, but there's an adventurous spirit in you, North Stone. That's how you can forgive your parents, because the energy that beat in them, that kept them moving, it beats in you too.'

'Have you ever considered being a TV therapist? Like a passionate American one like Ricki Lake or something? You'd be great,' North teased as Kelly flicked sand over her.

*

North's train arrived. It sidled up to the platform at a slow and deliberate pace. With a hiss the doors opened and only one person got off. This was it. No opportunity to dawdle. North got on and made a sharp right, sitting down in the first vacant seat that she saw. Thankfully it was warm on the train. Glancing around, she noticed that her carriage was relatively empty.

There was another hiss and then a toot of a horn before the train pulled away from the platform and resumed its journey. The steady vibrations held North in a rocking motion. It didn't help her growing nerves.

With her phone out, she checked the multicoloured network of Tube lines, plotting her route to the Savoy. It wouldn't do to disembark and then mill about looking lost. North needed to move with purpose right from the moment she arrived at Euston. She needed to embody the spirit of an adventurer, of someone who belonged. She couldn't shuffle about nervously like she desperately wanted to.

Belong, she told herself as she checked the Tube. *Act like you belong.*

A quick look at Spencer's Twitter page confirmed that he was most definitely in London and shortly heading to the Savoy. He'd posted a selfie of himself in a pure white tuxedo. A grin that others might deem charming looked devilish to North. She saw the predatory hunger behind his eyes, the sinister smirk in his smile.

Are you feeling any better? X

Elijah's new message blinked on her screen and North instantly pushed it aside with a scroll of her finger, unable to deal with the guilt. He was so good. So kind. And he cared about her. If he knew where she was, what she was intending to do he'd be furious. Which was exactly why she hadn't told him. This plan was solely North's.

Leaning back in her seat, she tried to adjust to the rocking of the train. Across the aisle there was a balding man reading a copy of *The Guardian*. He coughed every time he turned the page. North watched him with passive interest, wondering where he was going. He wore a suit and had a black briefcase stowed by his feet. Perhaps he was heading home after a long day. She considered who might be waiting for him – someone he loved? Children? A devoted dog who'd wag their tail so hard at the sight of their master that it risked falling off?

When someone looked at North she wondered what they saw. Did they imagine someone waiting for her? Or when they saw her sunken eyes and flat skin did they somehow know that her flat was empty, that when she walked through the door no one came to greet her because there was no one left. They'd all deserted her.

North scratched at her arms through the thick fabric of her coat, willing her sorrow not to show. It chaffed. It burned. It did not fit her like a glove. She longed to discard it, to finally be able to walk effortlessly through life just as Kelly had always done.

25

North kept muttering her new mantra to herself as she ascended up from the Tube station.

Belong. Belong. Belong.

It felt as though the entire world was in London. The pavements were tightly packed with people walking with purpose and the streets were crammed with cars sitting bumper to bumper as they wove their way through the congested streets. Music pounded out of a Lamborghini, a throbbing beat that North felt all the way down to the soles of her feet. Her nerves had become thorns.

But she wouldn't give in. North thrust her shoulders back, her chest forward and raised her chin, clenching her hands into fists. She kept walking, kept striding along as though she belonged on the busy streets.

A crowd had gathered around the entrance to The Savoy. Paparazzi were being held at the curb, their heavy cameras constantly exploding in a savage display of light. North looked ahead at the flashlights, at the crowd. Each time a bulb lit up it reminded her of a star. The lights were frenzied, manic, disorientating. And in their own way hypnotic, and North was mesmerised.

North stared as women in long metallic dresses that fit them like a second skin sashayed into the hotel. Men in suits and polyester smiles followed after them. Everyone looked so expensive, so polished. Only the most prized gemstones were allowed to enter The Savoy.

Somehow North kept walking. In her mind she rehearsed what was going to happen. She was going to approach the entrance to the hotel without pausing. She'd just keep walking, keep moving, in the feeble hope that no one would stop her.

North didn't breathe as she walked up the steps.

Be like Kelly.

She told herself. *Act like you belong.*

The heat of a dozen different gazes briefly singed her skin but then they moved on. Her face was not familiar, an image of her worth nothing to the gossip magazines and the tabloid papers. North kept walking, kept holding her head high.

Eventually she was past the paparazzi. Their constellation of stars didn't light up for her. It mattered not. She kept walking, gliding through the main doors as though she were one of the polished princesses that had proceeded her. And then she was in. North paused to push out the breath she'd been holding in her lungs.

The madness from outside on the street had crept into the hotel. There were people everywhere. They darted about, flitted across the lobby like birds. North tried to figure out what came next. She hadn't expected to get this far and wasn't prepared. Glancing around, she saw a pink sign that sparkled, it was directing her down a long corridor towards the Diowater event. Adding a spring to her step to help preserve her cover, North hurried off in the direction the sign was pointing.

She heard the party before she saw it. The walls trembled with the power of the music from inside. She reached a pair of oak double doors that were propped open and looked inside.

A vast ballroom had been transformed into a jewelled pink grotto. The chandelier in the centre of the ceiling was fitted with rose-hued bulbs, draped from its edges were pink fairy lights which tethered out to the four corners of the epic space. There were high tables against which people were leaning as they sipped pink champagne from flutes made to look like the warped plastic of the Diowater bottles.

She scurried back to the coat check near the double oak doors and pasted on her brightest smile as she handed over the garment and accepted a typed ticket number, all the while reminding herself to keep acting, to keep pretending to fit in.

As she tentatively moved into the main room, North saw the scattered jewels atop the tables, chips of pink plastic made to look like real diamonds. And in the centre of the room was an ice sculpture of a bottle of Diowater. It was all so beautiful. So surreal.

North couldn't give in to the assault on her senses. She wanted to gape, to gawp, to take in the wonderment all around her but she couldn't.

Belong.

With a look of mild disinterest she drifted amid the tables, no longer a spectator but a hunter and she was determined to find her prey. Would she be drawn by his false laughter or the brash baritone of his voice? Either way, she was going to find him and when she did—

Someone was watching her. Every hair on her body prickled with the knowledge of it. North wrung her hands together and glanced about. She wished she hadn't bothered with the coat check near the door. If she wanted to make a hasty retreat she'd need to grab it first else she'd risk freezing before she reached the Tube station. North spun around and locked eyes with a man on the fringes of the party. A man she had seen before. He was heavyset and wore all black. In his ear there was the spiral of a communication device dangling down. It was Spencer's bodyguard. North felt sick.

Though his face was stern she knew she'd witnessed a flicker of recognition dance across it. She'd been discovered. He'd know she didn't belong there, that she was at the party for Spencer not the designer water brand. And where was Spencer? Glancing just beyond the guard, she saw him stood beside a high table, a blonde on each arm, both of whom were laughing heartily at something he'd just said. North took a step in his direction and in her peripheral vision saw the bodyguard move, his body twisting in her direction. She'd made a mistake. She needed to leave.

Turning, she moved back through the party goers, back through the glittering pink spectacle. There was a queue at the coat check booth. Really she needed to stand in it, to nervously tap her feet until it was her turn to be served. But there wasn't time for manners. North pushed to the front of the queue.

'I'm so sorry,' she said to the angered woman behind her who looked to be holding a fur coat. North baulked at the sight of it, no longer feeling guilty for cutting in. Only animals wore fur. 'Please,' she slipped her ticket to the assistant, 'I need my coat urgently. I've been called away on an emergency.' There was no resistance on the other side of the booth, no request for additional information. With a curt nod the assistant took her ticket and then returned with her coat. 'Thank you,' North tore it from her hands and hurried away from the queue. As she thrust her arms into the sleeves she looked back and saw the bodyguard advancing towards her, calmly navigating his way through the mass of bodies at the party. North pulled up her zip and ran.

Running in heels was a skill she'd not managed to acquire in her thirty-two years. Her steps were clumpy and clumsy. Twice she almost skidded across the slick floor in the hotel. But she couldn't stop. She needed to keep moving. If the guard caught up with her there would be questions, maybe even threats. She tottered across the lobby and was then out through the front doors. Again the paparazzi ignored her. Pulling up her hood, North powered down the street, not daring to spare a second to glance back.

*

'We're of age, I swear.' Kelly was having her weekly argument with the bouncer on the door at Dreams. Sadly her speech was already slurred by the vodka she'd sipped on at home before heading out.

'Then let's see some ID,' the burly bouncer demanded, extending his thick hand in anticipation.

'I told you,' Kelly draped a hand against her waist and gave him a sultry smile, 'I losht it last week when I was at the gym.'

So many lies in one sentence; Kelly had never even set foot in a gym. North had to admire her friend's brazenness. She stood awkwardly behind her, wishing the sign on the door to Dreams would just stay still. It kept tilting one way and then another as though they were on some fairground ride.

'You don't get in without ID,' the bouncer briskly informed her. 'You girls know the rules.'

'Please,' Kelly batted her eyelashes and ran her fingers along his forearm. 'Pretty please.'

'I wish…' North pointed at the door. 'I wish the sign would stop… spinning.'

'You two are out of here,' the bouncer nodded at the next in line. 'Try coming back when you're of age.'

'But we are,' Kelly bleated, but it was too late. She and North were being elbowed aside by the next eager set of clubbers who were more prepared than them, standing, IDs extended, ready to gain entry into Dreams. 'Fuck him,' Kelly stormed away from the doors, maintaining perfect balance in her high heels despite her drunken state. 'He's a fucking jobsworth.'

'Why…' North followed after her friend and swallowed against the sickly feeling rising up inside her. 'Why did you say you los-lost it in the gym?'

Kelly gave a flippant shrug. 'Sounds mature, I guess.'

'Hmm.' North leaned against a wall. The brickwork felt surprisingly soft against her back. She could easily just curl up in a ball at its base and just fall asleep.

'I'd never go in one.' Kelly joined her at the wall. 'A gym,' she added for clarification. 'It's not… me. I don't sweat unless it's for pleasure.'

'True.'

'If I ever wind up dead out jogging like women in those police dramas on TV just know that I've been murdered, that the whole damn thing has been,' she paused to hiccup, 'staged. If I'm found by some bloody dog walker it's all a lie.'

'I'll…' North pressed her hands against the wall to steady herself as the floor begin to tip upon some invisible axis. 'I'll remember.'

'We should disappear at sea like your parents.'

'Huh?'

'There's something glorious to that,' Kelly gazed wistfully ahead. 'Never found, forever missing. It's poetic. It's elegant.'

'They're fish food.'

'They're lost souls.'

'They're not lost,' North sagged to her knees and leaned forward. She needed to throw up. 'They found their way back to me.' Whenever she closed her eyes they were there, dripping and desperate.

'I know,' Kelly dropped down to join her.

'He's just doing his job,' North nodded in the direction of the door to Dreams where the bouncer was granting entry to more suitable club goers.

'He's being a tyrant.'

'Noo,' North sleepily drew out the word.

'He thinks he's a gatekeeper. He thinks he's important, when he's just some heavy guy being used.'

'Aren't we all being used?'

'We should be getting in,' Kelly pouted in dismay.

'Maybe we don't belong in… in there,' North focused on the floor at her feet. At any moment she was going to cover it in vomit. She could taste bile and vodka.

'We belong everywhere,' Kelly insisted as North bent over and retched. 'I don't care who he is or what his job is, we're getting in that club. Once you're finished here we'll try the back door.'

'I don't feel so good.'

'I'll get you some water when we're inside. Because we're getting in. We came here with a mission and we're going to complete it.' Kelly helped North back onto her feet and held her as she wobbled unsteadily. 'Come on, we're not done yet.'

*

'Hey.'

A heavy hand landed on North's shoulder. She wanted to scream. Her body clenched with the impulse to run, her muscles contracting ready for a burst of release.

'Hey, stop running.'

Swallowing down her fear, North turned and looked into the eyes of Spencer Daniels' bodyguard. He must have followed her out of the hotel and down the street and now he'd caught up with her with ease. Around them were wheelie bins and old newspapers. North had somehow stumbled down a side street, away from potential witnesses. How could she have been so stupid?

'Look, please, I'm leaving,' she stepped back from the guard and raised both hands in a show of submission. 'I'm not going to talk to him. I'm just going to leave. Quietly. I didn't come here to cause trouble.'

'But you came here to talk to him, right?' the guard's voice was deep, as though every word was conjured up from the very pit of his stomach.

'I...'

'I recognise you. From Monaco.'

'Look—' North felt her nervous thorns constricting around her, breaking the skin as they dug in deep. She'd been caught in a web of her own making and was now within the spider's grasp.

'Come with me.'

'Please, I didn't mean to cause any trouble. Just let me go home and you'll never see or hear from me again. I promise.'

'You were asking about Kelly. Kelly Orton?'

'Yes,' she's...' a pained sigh fell from North's lips. 'She was my best friend. She worked on The Orion the summer just gone.'

'I remember.'

For someone who was about to bring about some form of punishment, the guard seemed more morose than mad. He raised a hand and disconnected the device in his ear. 'Come with me,' he repeated his initial command.

'Look, I said I'm sorry. Please, just let me leave.'

'Don't you want to talk?' he levelled the question so calmly at her that North felt crazed to be behaving so fearfully.

'I—'

'That's why you came here, because you have questions about Kelly, right?'

The guard walked off but North didn't follow, uncertain if she could trust the situation.

'Come on,' he turned and gestured towards her when she didn't move. 'We're going to talk, that's it. I knew Kelly.'

I knew Kelly.

Something twisted deep inside North. To know Kelly was to love her. If this guard knew Kelly then he had to have liked her. Not everyone on board The Orion could be as wicked as its master, could they?

It was a chance. North just wasn't sure if it was worth taking. She closed her eyes and released a breath.

What would Kelly do?

She'd already be marching along confidently with the guard, informing him that she wanted to know everything. 'I'm here for answers,' she'd boldly announce. 'And I'm not leaving without them.'

North was stunned to find that those same words had just flown from her lips as she followed the guard with measured, confident strides. She left the fearful girl pricked with thorns over by the wheelie bins as she let the guard guide her to a waiting car. A car that must be Spencer's. Was the guard the driver? She was willingly stepping into the hornet's nest. She hoped that whatever she learned would be worth the stings she was risking.

26

North saw the tree just before they hit it. Her stomach lurched for a second and the air was forced out of her lungs as her body snapped forward against her seat belt with the impact.

Kelly was screaming over the sound of breaking glass and twisting metal. The branches from the tree had reached in through the smashed windscreen. North drew in swift, panicked breaths as she looked ahead at the chaos. Smoke was rising in plumes from beneath the condensed bonnet.

'Fuck,' Kelly's hands remained glued to the steering wheel, held rigidly at ten and two. 'Fuck.'

'You took that corner too fast.'

'You *think*?' Fear made Kelly furious. With a grunt she released the wheel and then smacked the centre of it, setting off the old car's horn. 'Fuck, fuck, fuck. My mum is going to kill me. Like, actually *kill* me. She's had this car longer than she's had me.'

With shaking hands, North unbuckled her seat belt, noticing the droplets of red blood that were pooling on her knuckles. 'We need…' She was waiting for her pulse to slow, but it kept racing as though still carried along by the previous momentum of the car. 'We need to get out.'

'The police,' Kelly punched the wheel again, letting the horn bleat. 'Someone is going to call them. They're going to show up. I'm fucked. Truly fucked. Mum won't let this slide, she'll say I stole the car. She'll think she's teaching me a bloody lesson.'

The tree was still standing even though the bark on its trunk had been badly splintered by the crash. North admired its fortitude.

'Say it was you.'

She twisted in her seat to stare at Kelly.

'Say it was you,' her friend repeated, her voice steady, calculating. 'Say you were driving. Say you hit the tree on purpose.'

'*What?*'

'Play the orphan card for me, please.'

'Kel, I—'

But wouldn't that hurt her grandparents who'd taken her in? Who'd done so much to try and shield her from the pain of her parents' disappearance?

'North, people pity you. When they'd give anyone else an inch, you get a whole freaking mile. And I get it – your situation makes them uncomfortable. Sad. Use it. Use it to get us out of this hellish mess I made.'

'I'll still get in trouble.'

'Yeah,' Kelly admitted quietly. 'But not as much as me. My mum will crucify me for this. You know I'm right.'

North looked down at her bloody hands. She didn't have parents to disappoint, just her grandparents. And that wasn't the same, was it? Kelly was right, people did treat her differently. Since her parents disappeared, everyone treated her like a feral cat, not bothering to try and tame her just keen to keep their distance. She was different and different was dangerous, something to be feared.

'Fine.' Groaning, North dragged herself out of the car and began fumbling her way round to the driver's side. Her neck burned and her back ached. She considered the unseen damage that had been caused by the crash as she reached Kelly and pulled open the door.

'You're really willing to do this?' Kelly was peering up at her, pale with shock and fear.

'Yes. You know I'd do anything for you. Now hurry up and get out.'

Kelly scrambled out and hurried over to the vacated passenger seat. 'I really appreciate this.'

'Uh-huh, whatever.'

In the distance they heard the squeal of sirens. Soon the crash site would be circled by blue lights. The police were coming.

'I'm serious,' Kelly reached over the glass and branches to grab North's hand, carefully squeezing it. 'Doing this for me, it's huge.'

'It's what best friends do.'

'No,' Kelly whispered as a police car tore around the same corner she had previously overshot. 'It's what *you* do. You're special, North.'

Before North could respond, the glare of a flashlight was shining in her eyes, blinding her as an officer asked if she needed medical assistance.

*

'You okay back there?'

North fidgeted in the back seat of the silver Bentley. The windows were blacked out which was why the guard had suggested she sit back there. 'Away from prying eyes,' he'd said. The car had a leather interior which made North slide around. She squirmed and tried to get comfortable whilst leaning forward to speak to the guard who was sat in the driver's seat, staring ahead as though he didn't have a passenger in the static vehicle.

'I'm fine.'

'So you're Kelly's friend?'

'We grew up together.'

'I met her on The Orion,' the guard rested his hands upon the wheel, making it seem miniature. 'She was always so happy. So full of life.'

'Do you have any idea what happened to her?' Her fingertips scratched against the arms of her coat, longing to reach skin. At any moment Spencer could appear, could haul her out of the car and call the police. She had to be quick.

The guard gave a grumble of resistance.

'Well?'

'There have been others like her,' he said in his deep baritone. 'Other pretty girls who caught Spencer's eye and disappeared into thin air.'

'So she caught Spencer's eye?' This was something, confirmation, North clutched the headrest of the driver's seat as she pulled herself forwards, trying to read the guard's expression.

'No,' he firmly scolded her. 'Stay back. I can't be seen talking with you. If Spencer knew you were here he'd be livid.'

'So why are you talking to me?'

'Because...' he sighed and shook his head. 'Because I liked Kelly. She was like sunshine, always warm, always welcoming. She'd ask me about my wife and my twins. She cared about people, connected with them. When she suddenly left I knew he'd got to her and it twisted me up inside.'

North nodded with understanding.

'Spencer got to her how?'

Another sigh. Larger than the first. 'Like I said, she caught his eye. Most pretty girls do.'

'Meaning what?'

'Meaning they'd ignore his advances at their peril.'

North could feel herself going cold. She leaned against the soft leather of the Bentley, needing to relax her racing pulse. Riddles were one thing but she needed words, no matter how terrifying it might be to hear them..

'The other girls, where are they?'

'Gone,' he confirmed stiffly. 'Hidden. You won't find them.'

'Hidden? Or hiding?'

'Both.'

'You make it sound like they're in danger. Are they? Do you think Spencer had a hand in Kelly's death?'

'I think…' the guard drummed his hands against the wheel. '*Maybe*,' He concluded. 'I mean, yes, definitely maybe. I've…' he massaged his neck. 'I've seen things. I've worked for Spencer Daniels for five years and in that time I've seen him do terrible things to women.'

'What things?' North couldn't help it – she surged forward, keen not to miss a word of the guard's confession.

'Stay back,' he ordered, his voice thickening with fear. 'If he catches you in this car we're both as good as dead, you hear me?'

'I…' North sunk back. 'I'm sorry.'

'I've seen enough that I can see no more,' the guard admitted. 'I handed in my notice last month and I'm leaving.'

'Then you can hand him in,' North urged. 'We can go to the police, together, you can tell them what you saw, what you know and—'

'No, no, no. Absolutely not. Little lady you need to realise that what I'm saying to you right now is strictly between us. Between the *two* of us and I'm only talking because I liked Kelly.

Because I can't keep on turning a blind eye to all of Spencer's shit. He's a rich man which means he's very protected. He could destroy you. And me. Against him we're no one.'

'But we have the truth. If we can provide evidence that the police can't refute then—'

'Maybe you didn't hear me when I mentioned my wife and my twins. I'm sorry, but I need to protect them. This conversation can't go any further than this car.'

'Then what are you actually telling me?' North demanded, her muscles tightening with frustration. 'So far all you've done is confirmed my suspicions about Spencer, that he's a monster. But what can I do with hearsay?'

'Money.'

'What?'

'You need to look for money.'

'Money?' North threw her hands up in defeat. 'I have no money. I can't afford some fancy lawyer to help me go after him.'

'No,' the guard gently shook his head. 'Look for money in connection with Kelly. If Spencer was involved with her early departure from The Orion there will be money, a lot of it.'

'Like he… paid her off?'

'Exactly.'

'For what?'

The guard caught her gaze in the rear view mirror. 'What do you think?'

'Wait, you're saying—'

'I'm saying look for the *money*. If Spencer was connected to Kelly leaving The Orion it will be there.'

'And what then?'

'You just keep going down this rabbit hole, don't you?' the guard gave a sad shake of his head. 'I'd suggest you stop, else you risk your loved ones getting hurt.'

'All my loved ones are dead.'

'Oh.' He tipped his chin towards her chest. 'I'm sorry.'

'So I've nothing to lose. What would you advise someone with nothing to lose to do?'

'Honestly?'

'Honestly.'

'I'd say keep digging until you have enough evidence to hang the bastard. He's a wolf in couture clothing. Now get out of the car before someone sees you.'

Back in the cold evening air, North reeled against the slap of reality that greeted her. She had *something*. A lead. And she intended to follow it. But she sensed that she might not like where it took her.

*

The grey-haired nurse wound the bandages around North's hand.

'You and your friend were very lucky you know.'

'I know,' North agreed as she kicked her legs against the bed. The hours had slowly slid by after they'd arrived at A and E. There had been doctors, police, and many, many questions.

'If you'd been going any faster than you were the both of you could have been flung through the windscreen.'

'I know.'

'It was a foolish and reckless thing to do.'

'I *know.*' The bandages were reassuringly tight against North's knuckles, pushing against the pressure of her numerous cuts.

'Your parents must be sick with worry,' the nurse began tidying away her equipment.

'My parents are at the bottom of the ocean,' North retorted dryly. 'The only sickness they suffer from is sea sickness.'

'Of the ocean?' the nurse's tired eyes widened and her mouth fell open in horror. 'Oh, forgive me. North Stone. Stone. Yes of course. Oh, your poor parents and you, you poor, poor child.'

It was like flicking a switch. One moment the nurse had been judgemental and borderline cruel and now she couldn't gush over North enough.

'No wonder you were out driving like. Things must not make much sense these days. But you need to be strong. These things… they are sent to try us, aren't they?'

'I guess.'

The nurse hugged her. Actually leaned in and embraced her, before pulling back the stiff blue curtain and vacating North's cubicle. The hospital stank. North cringed with every lungful of its odorous air that she had to breathe in.

'Piss and bleach,' that's how Kelly had described it when they were brought in together. 'With a vomity undertone.'

And she was right.

Where was Kelly now? North dropped off her bed and peered around the edge of the cubicle, searching for her friend. They'd been admitted at the same time and then separated. In their individual cubicles they had to answers questions from good-intentioned doctors and police and now North was waiting on the arrival of her grandparents. What a glorious conclusion to an eventful evening. Had Irene arrived to take Kelly home? How had she taken the news that her beloved banger of a car had been completely totalled?

North didn't have to wait long to find out. Heels clipped against the linoleum floor as Irene Orton strode her way with Kelly reluctantly in tow.

'What should I call you?' Irene coolly levelled the question at North as she entered the cubicle.

'Sorry, what?'

'Because I hear you're going by Mad Max these days.' It was a joke, but Irene wasn't smiling. Her face remained as smooth and hard as polished steel.

'Mum, come on, let's get out of here,' Kelly tugged on her mother's sleeve whilst mouthing the words 'sorry' to North.

'I told her grandparents I'd drop her off,' Irene shook off her daughter's grip. 'They want to buy me a new car.'

North shamefully drooped her head. Her grandparents didn't have the money for a car, even a decrepit old one with hundreds of miles on the clock.

'I told them not to bother,' Irene extended a hand to North. 'It's fine. I get it.' Behind her mother Kelly shrugged. 'You're lashing out.' As they walked out of the A and E department Irene looped her arms around North's shoulders. 'I did it all the time at your age, although I didn't have a good reason like you do.'

As they waited for a taxi, Kelly whispered 'currency'. North's trauma truly was currency and it seemed they could use it to buy anything – even their way out of trouble.

'Who knows how far this can go?' A week later and Kelly was still keen to exploit North's orphan status. 'Maybe you can get caught shoplifting next. Something truly epic like a Chanel handbag, one of the quilted logo ones. God, I'd *kill* for one of them.'

'No, I'm done.'

'But just think,' Kelly playfully nudged her shoulder as they sat side by side on her little bed, 'you could rule our shitty school, our shitty town. You could be the untouchable North Stone.' She held up her hands as though she were reading the writing in neon lights. 'Car crash today, drug run tomorrow.'

'I'm not running drugs.'

'I'm just saying that—'

'I don't like buying my way out of trouble.'

'*Our* way.' Kelly corrected her. 'There are two beneficiaries to your heartbreaking situation; me and thee.'

'Yeah, well I don't like doing it. It feels like cheating.'

'People do it all the time,' Kelly dramatically sagged back against her pillows. 'Money, power, sex, people trade it all to get out of trouble. It's the way the world works.'

'I refuse to work like that.'

'Then you're a fool,' Kelly stated haughtily. 'Because that's how it's done. Notice how trouble never finds the rich.'

'I'm pretty sure trouble finds everyone.'

Like death.

The dark thought sent a shiver down North's spine. She did her best to shake off the feeling.

'I'm just saying that morality is overrated,' Kelly turned onto her back and stretched her long legs up the length of her wall. 'Your situation is currency, make sure you spend it all.'

'What if someone wronged you and then used money, or sex, or power, to get out of trouble over it?'

'I wouldn't sweat it.'

'You wouldn't?'

'No.' With a grunt Kelly dropped her legs and rolled back onto her front. 'Because I know you – you won't spend all your orphan currency now, you'll save some for a rainy day. And when someone has the gall to wrong me, you'll show up and outbid them in the trouble stakes.'

'You sound very sure of that.'

Kelly smirked and then twisted onto her back and kicked her legs back up. 'I am.'

27

'North?' Dean flinched with surprise when he opened his front door.

'Hi.' North nervously played with the tips of her fingers. It was a new day. She'd returned from London, showered, pulled on some clean clothes and then waited for the darkness outside to recede. Now the sky was pink-hued and the chill in the air had weakened.

'What…' Dean clenched the edge of her door and cleared his throat. 'What are you doing here? It's not even seven. Are you all right? Do you need help?'

'Yes,' she replied pragmatically. 'Although, I mean, it's about Kelly. I'm… I'm okay. But yes, I need your help.'

With a sigh, Dean stepped aside granting access into his home. 'I suppose you'd better come in then.'

It still felt strange to walk into Kelly's house. Her presence lingered there in more than just framed photographs. Her laughter still echoed along the hallway, her footsteps still seemed to pound down the stairs with her infectious energy.

'Just… sit down,' Dean pointed into the lounge, 'I'll go fix you a cup of tea.'

North sat on the sofa and threaded her fingers together, clenching her hands into a ball as they rested in her lap. She wasn't sure if Dean would welcome her investigation into Kelly's finances but she had to ask. Spencer's guard had turned her compass of enquiry towards money, something which she and Kelly had never had much of.

The clock ticked and around it the house was strangely still. If Kelly were still there, music would be floating down the stairs, interrupted by the blast of a hairdryer. She'd bounce into the living room, cheeks still flushed from her shower, and greet North with the warmest of hugs. She wouldn't even ask why her friend was there. The invitation into her home was always an open-ended one.

'So what is this about?' Dean came in with a tea for North and one for himself. He sat down in his own chair but didn't lean back.

'I need to look at something.'

'What?' His eyes narrowed and his shoulders lifted.

'Not the laptop,' North hastily assured him. 'It's... um...' She pressed her palms against her mug of tea and bit her lip.

'What the hell is it you need to see?'

'Her bank statements.'

Dean blinked in surprise and gave a slow shake of his head. 'Look, North—'

'I'm following a line of investigation. I can't say more than that, but I've been instructed to look for money. A chunk of it. Did Kelly receive any strange payments over the last couple of months? Anything unexplained?'

The clock ticked and Dean took a long drink from his tea. Finally he lowered it from his mouth and pointed his free hand at North. 'I'll... Wait. Just wait. I'll go and get them.'

So North waited, surprised by Dean's swift compliance. She had been braced for more arguments and barbed words.

The staircase creaked as he returned from upstairs carrying a metal biscuit tin which depicted a plump panda eating a pink treat. He popped the lid and began riffling through its contents. North could see that it was full of paper bank statements.

'I did see... something,' he mumbled to himself as he grabbed a piece of paper, scrutinised it for details and then dropped it to the ground. 'But, I don't know, I wanted to ignore it. Wanted it to not be real.'

'What did you see?' North left the sofa to kneel at his side.

'A couple months back there was a big payment made to Kel. Really big. I even mentioned it to the police but they explained it as...' He quickly scanned more statements. 'Ah!' Triumphantly he waved the paper and then poked at the critical detail with a stubby finger. 'Here,' he offered the document to North.

She looked it over. It was a bank statement. Kelly's bank statement. For the month of August. She'd left the employ of The Orion by this time. On the eighteenth, £35,000 had been deposited into her back account by The Daniels Corporation. Spencer. The transaction was labelled "salary". I mean that's a hell of a salary for a few months' worth of work, right?

'Right.'

North coughed as bile raced up her throat. Here it was, in her hand, the evidence the guard had told her to find. Why hadn't she made the connection to money sooner? Why did she need the guard to point out the obvious; that where there was a millionaire there was money. Tainted money.

'The police just dismissed it, said it was just payment for her time on the yacht.'

'Thirty five grand for two months' work! That's insane.'

'I know,' Dean scratched at his cheek, at skin which was as thin and stretched as aged parchment. The shadows beneath his eyes were deepening. 'I thought it was weird, but when the police dismissed it, I...' he gave a sad shrug, 'I figured it was nothing. What's this lead that you're chasing?'

She was still staring at the statement, at the trio of zeros. It was such a lot of money. A payout. Or a payoff. But for what?

North felt like she was gathering the pieces but that the puzzle still refused to come together in a coherent image. Or maybe it was just too painful to accept the seemingly obvious truth.

'This,' she traced the line of the suspicious transaction with the tip of her finger, 'this is really helpful. Thank you for showing it to me.'

'I get it.' Dean began stuffing the discarded statements back into the tin. 'Why you're chasing this. Why you don't want to believe that she killed herself. I get it. I wish she'd said goodbye to me too.'

'There's more to her death,' North folded up the piece of paper she was holding. 'I just know it. Can I keep this?'

'I guess, yeah.'

'Thanks.' She jumped up to her feet.

'Wait.' North was almost at the door when Dean called her back. 'I have a right to know what's going on here. Who told you to look for that money? Was Kelly in some kind of trouble?'

'I…' She had nothing concrete, not yet. Was it cruel to once again plant the seed of hope within Dean? 'I don't know anything for certain. But it looks like something went on last summer, on the yacht.'

Dean said nothing but his eyes glistened with pent-up tears.

'Once I know more I'll come straight to you. I promise. You deserve answers as much as I do.'

'She wasn't the same,' he pushed his hands deep into the pockets of his jogging bottoms and stared solemnly at North. 'When she came back, she was so distant, like she was punishing me for something, only I didn't know what.'

'She was different with me too.'

The gap in the wall on North's timeline back in her flat, she'd thought it was just for the summer, but what if it extended further than that? A fissure had opened up in their friendship and it kept spreading. Why hadn't North noticed sooner? If she'd made better choices there wouldn't have been a gap at all.

'Let me know what you find out.'

North nodded and advanced towards the front door, pleased to have the statement in her possession, it felt as weighted as a smoking gun.

'And North.' Her hand was on the door handle about to apply pressure when she turned back to him. 'Look after yourself. If Kelly were here, she'd tell you to make sure you're sleeping right and so, you know,' he shrugged awkwardly, 'make sure you're sleeping right.'

'Thanks. I will.'

*

Thirty five thousand pounds. It was such a lot of money. North stared at the bank statement which she'd laid out on her kitchen counter. The oaky aroma of the coffee she'd just made filled her flat, but she didn't even need its caffeine to enter her system, she was alert enough from the discovery of the money. And it had come from Spencer.

Her phone buzzed in her pocket. Placing down her mug, North grabbed it.

Are you in work today? X

A message from Elijah. It was her day off. A day that had crept up on her. Lately she didn't even check her calendar just drifted through an endless day. Without sleep to break things up, every day blended together. A week became a stream of long hours, a weekend just a respite from work. Somehow her body clock had sensed it was Monday. Her day off. It was just after nine. She had a free day and in the bank statement a crucial document. She needed to figure out a way to make the most of both of them.

No. Day off. But can I meet you later? I need your help with something x

Her phone buzzed with his reply after less than five minutes.

Of course. I'll come round after work x

An idea was forming in North's mind. Like a snowball, it kept rolling, gathering in size and speed.

Spencer.

The money.

The summer.

The other girls.

It was all adding up to something.

North drifted over to her sofa and opened up her laptop, fingertips tapping on keys as her body didn't wait for her mind to execute the order; she was already making the connection, jumping ahead.

So much money to pay for what? Silence? What could Kelly have said? What had happened between her and Spencer?

On her laptop she found what she was looking for. Grabbing her phone, she punched in the relevant number and waited out the three long rings.

'Millwater Coroner's Office.' The person who picked up sounded alarmingly chipper considering their chosen line of work.

'Hi,' North took a deep breath. 'I was wondering if I could come by today to look at some files regarding a recent case.'

Kelly's death wasn't being treated as suspicious. Her files were not sealed as part of a crime investigation. North just had to hope that—

'If you come for ten someone should be around to assist you.' Then they hung up.

North panted with relief and then fear. The coroner was about to help her answer a very difficult question.

*

'If I won the lottery…' Kelly dragged out her answer.

The sun was shining brightly as they sat in the park. North scratched against the stiff blades of grass grazing her bare legs. Bubbles of laughter lifted up from the playground and the distant chimes of an ice cream van made North's heart flutter with excitement. They were in the middle of a long, hot, summer. The kind of summer which felt like it would never end.

'I'd buy an island,' Kelly declared as she plucked a nearby daisy and began admiring its delicate white petals.

'An island?'

'Uh-huh. I'd buy myself my very own island and make myself queen of it.'

'How much do you think an island goes for? I doubt you could buy one with a lottery win.'

'All right then, killjoy,' Kelly scrunched up her nose, 'what would you buy?'

'A state of the art telescope like the Sonic 6000,' North smiled as she thought of the piece of equipment she'd secretly been coveting for months after seeing it in an astronomy magazine. 'Apparently when you use it you can see the moon in so much detail that you can see every crater.'

'Can you see the flag?'

'Huh?'

'The flag,' Kelly picked another daisy and began to make a chain. 'You know, from when the Americans landed on the moon and had a walk on. They planted a flag. Could you see that with the Sonic 6000?'

'Well, no,' North admitted. 'But that's because no telescope is powerful enough to reveal that level of tiny detail. I mean, if you think about the size of the flag and the distance then—'

'It sounds like your telescope 6000 would be a waste of money. Better to buy an island.'

'You wouldn't be able to buy an island.' North leaned back on her elbows and let the sun warm her face. Freckles had already appeared on Kelly's nose, softening her features. North hoped for some too.

'How do you know?' Kelly kept making her chain. 'It's not like you've ever tried to buy one before.'

'And how do you know my telescope would be a waste of money?' North thought of the one she currently used, sat atop her block of flats. It showed her stars like balls of fire instead of distant diamonds. It was a portal to another world.

'You could come visit my island with your parents,' Kelly offered. 'So long as it didn't interfere with my royal obligations.'

'They didn't call last night.'

'They forgot again?'

North opened her eyes and for one moment stared directly at the sun. Her irises burned and she was instantly dazzled by the brightness. Blinking, she kept seeing its fiery face even though she was now looking away. 'I don't know. They keep missing the times when they're supposed to call and check in with me.'

'They are on a boat,' Kelly's chain was now eight daisies long. 'Must be pretty tough to get signal out in the ocean.'

'Before they left the harbour they promised to buy a satellite phone so that they could call me from wherever they were.'

But North hadn't believed her mother's promise even as she'd said it. They were always promising her the stars and failing to deliver.

'Well, if you win the lottery you can buy them one. That way you can always be in touch.'

'Yeah,' North sat up and rubbed at her eyes, scrubbing away the lingering image of the sun. 'I doubt they'd use it even if I bought it them.'

'They'll be back soon.' Kelly wove another daisy into her chain. 'And then school will start and life will suck. Let's enjoy the summer while it's here.'

'Would you only buy an island?'

'Well,' Kelly tilted her head as she considered the question. 'Depending how much money I had left I'd maybe get a penthouse in New York, a townhouse in London and a mansion somewhere rural. Like Bath.'

'You're hoping for a big win then.'

'That or some rich idiot who I can marry for all his cash. If he won't marry me, I'll sleep with him and then blackmail him for all he has. Say I'm pregnant or something. I saw a woman do it in this BBC drama I watched with my mum. This woman and her boyfriend were scamming this old millionaire. It was really juicy. Did you see it?'

'My grandparents wouldn't let me watch it.'

'Urgh, living with them must suck. I bet you can't wait to go home when your parents are back.'

'It's really not so bad. At least they're always home, always there to ask me about my day.'

Kelly delicately held out her completed daisy chain, where both ends had been tied together to create an endless floral circuit. 'When I'm queen of my island,' she draped the flowers atop North's head like a crown, 'you can be princess. Together we'll rule the land.'

'What will this island be called?' North gently touched the edge of her crown and smiled.

Kelly shrugged and began searching for more daisies, keen to create a crown of her own. 'Who knows? We can call it whatever we want. When we're dirty rich we'll answer to no one. You and I, we'll live out our greatest life. We just need that lottery win.'

'Or your rich idiot?'

'Yep,' Kelly agreed. 'Whichever comes first.'

28

'I know you.' The guy in the white lab coat was tall and lean and wore black plastic rimmed glasses which he was now peering at North intently through. 'You're North Stone. You were the year above me at school. I'm Jake Rogers.'

No bell of recognition chimed in North's head but she smiled sweetly and nodded. 'Oh yeah, of course.'

'And you're here to,' he frowned as he repeated her initial request, 'view the coroner's report for the Kelly Orton autopsy?'

'Yes, that's right.'

'Why?' Jake rested his elbows on his desk and leaned forward with interest. 'I mean, I remember you always hanging on Kelly's coat-tails but to want to look at her autopsy report. That's kind of dark, don't you think?'

North managed to hold her sweet smile. 'It's...' she shrugged. 'Closure. I guess I need closure.'

'She's dead,' the wheels of Jake's chair squeaked sharply against the linoleum floor as he stood up. 'How much closure do you need?'

Kelly would have known Jake Rogers. Would have remembered him. She remembered everyone, collecting names like currency she could use later. So often on a night out she'd saunter up to a complete stranger only to inform North that they all actually went to school together. Time didn't dull Kelly's recollection, she could always see beneath the gained inches and laughter lines at the child who had once existed within the adult.

'I guess you're not holding up too well, since her death?' Jake was guiding North deeper into the morgue. It felt like descending into a bunker. All the walls were tiled and the air was dry, lifeless. North could feel death seeping out from beneath closed doors. It was bitterly cold. Despite keeping her coat on she felt the icy extension of the chill reached down to her bare flesh. 'It takes some getting used to.' She wondered if Jake was talking about Kelly's death or the cold.

Their dual footsteps rang out along the long corridor. Double doors with high windows were closed and North didn't dare peek in and glimpse a pale pair of feet sticking out on a gurney. With each step she regretted her decision to come. She hadn't prepared herself for what she might see. What she might feel. She—

'Here,' Jake opened a door and they entered a room full of filing cabinets. It was marginally warmer than in the corridor. 'You know,' he leant against the nearest one and stared at North, 'it's not common practice to let Joe Public just come in here and ask to view a report.'

'Right, I appreciate that.'

'But,' Jake dragged the word out from between his teeth, 'I remember Kelly. And you. Going around school like a little pair of conjoined twins. I guess you maybe count as family in this instance. Which means you can view the report.' He turned to open a nearby cabinet and then swung back to face her, eyes wide and abnormally big behind the thick lenses of his glasses. 'It doesn't make for easy reading,' he clicked his fingers at her. 'Consider yourself forewarned. I often forget that a layman won't be as comfortable with certain terms as I am. I'm sure you remember at school that I was somewhat of a prodigy when it came to science.'

'Mmm,' North watched him pick his way through the cardboard files in the third drawer.

'Orton,' he muttered to himself. 'Oscars, Orson, Orton.' Jake closed his fingers around the file and pulled it free. 'Right,' he led North over to a desk at the back of the room and flicked on a reading light before placing down the file and flipping it open. Its contents consisted of a single page. On it was the crude outline of the human form covered in scribbled annotations. 'Like I said,' Jake clasped a hand on North's shoulder, 'these things can make for tough reading to outsiders, but lucky for you I'm here.'

North slid her hand forwards, trying to grasp the file.

'Nope.' Jake swatted her away. 'You can't *touch* the file. You can view it. That's what we're doing here. Have a good read but nothing more, no snaps on your phone or anything.'

'Right, thanks.' North tried to hide the tightness from her voice as he stepped close to the desk and looked down. The notes were written in small, rushed strokes and difficult to decipher.

'Okay,' Jake tapped the neck on the diagram and then the accompanying note. 'This here references that cause of death was self-inflicted asphyxiation. To the guy on the street that means she strangled herself. There's a reference to rope burns, which is to be expected, time of death estimated to be between three and four a.m.'

'Any scratches on the rest of her body? Her hands? That kind of thing?'

Clearing his throat, Jake traced his finger down the rest of the document. 'Nothing unexpected. I mean she was found outside, so there's some general marks that would be associated with that. Dirt under fingernails, so on and so forth.'

'And she was pregnant?' North focused on the arrow that came from the diagram's stomach and went over to a lengthy side note.

'She was.' Stooping closer to the document Jake thoughtfully stroked his chin. 'Yes, she was definitely pregnant. Both the blood work and the autopsy revealed that.'

'Anything else in her bloods? Any drugs, sedatives?'

Jake paused and then shook his head. 'Nope.'

'The pregnancy,' North pulled his attention back to the centre of the sheet. 'How far along was she?'

'How far along?'

'I mean, the coroner would be able to deduce that, right?'

'Right,' Jake tapped the relevant note. 'Okay, so it says here that she was around eight weeks.'

'Which would put the time of conception around when?'

North needed to hear it.

'End of July. Give or take a week or so.'

Even with the week or so, it meant that Kelly's unborn baby was conceived when she was on board The Orion. North's knees went weak and she sagged against the desk.

'Hey,' Jake grabbed her shoulders and helped steady her. 'I know this can be overwhelming. We get family members in here more than you think, asking questions, wanting answers. I remember Kelly being as bright as her blonde hair. She lit everywhere up.'

'Yeah,' North's throat felt so dry, as though she'd just swallowed a hive of bees. Her nerves swarmed within her as she fought against a crippling sense of unease. 'The... um...' she coughed, trying to make her voice more viable, 'the baby. It's DNA was taken, right?'

'Right, that's standard procedure.'

'And it'll be kept on file?'

'Sure. Why?'

'I'm just curious.' North coughed again, trying to force out some of the bees. She heard the rattle in her own throat and Jake kindly patted her back. 'I mean, hypothetically speaking, if someone had an assumption about the identity of the father, the DNA could be checked against the baby's?'

'Yeah, why. You got someone in mind?'

'Like I said, it's hypothetical.'

'Trying to find out all her secrets?' Jake raised an eyebrow at her. 'Sadly she's taken those with her. All we can do is speculate.'

'Right, yes.'

'I'm sorry for what I said.'

North blinked, afraid she'd spaced out for some of their conversation.

'Earlier,' Jake awkwardly nodded towards the door, 'I said about you were always riding on Kelly's coat-tails. That was harsh. But you were always, you know, aloof. Kelly engaged with everyone, remembered everyone, you were never present. Like you always knew you were meant for something better than our shitty school before anyone else did. It was kind of intimidating.'

'Seriously?' North almost choked on her own surprise. She was Kelly's shadow not her detached companion. People always failed to see North because they were so blinded by Kelly's halo. But Jake was saying that he saw, and what was worse was that she never saw him. She never saw anyone. The fringes of her existence ended with Kelly.

'I mean,' Jake shrugged and shyly lowered his head, 'you were going through such a lot back then, with your parents. I remember people talking about it at school. That must have been rough.'

'Yes, it was.'

'But you overcame it,' he patted her on the back. 'And you'll overcome this,' Jake tapped Kelly's autopsy report. 'I used to look at you and think how strong you were, to lose both parents and still rock up to school. Most people they'd just fall apart, but you held yourself together.'

Barely.

North wanted to tell him the truth. Wanted to tell him about the endless sleepless nights, the red marks on her arms, the ghosts that came to her whenever she dared to close her eyes. But if he thought she was coping, maybe she wasn't falling apart as hopelessly as she'd previously feared.

'Thanks,' she gestured at the file. 'This has been really helpful.'

'It has?'

'Yes. I genuinely feel closer to getting some closure now.'

'Well, I'm glad I could help.' Jake looked and sounded elated. 'And you remember me winning that chemistry award in year eight, right?' he asked as he walked her to the door.

'Oh yeah, of course. You did really great.' Her voice was sweet and her smile sincere. It was easy to pretend, to act as though that memory still lingered in her mind. It was almost too easy.

Out on the car park North paused. Had it been that easy for Kelly too? Did she not really memorise every name, every face, did she just perfect the act of pretending?

A cold wind swept a plastic bag across the tarmac as large raindrops began to land at North's feet. The weather had turned from sweet to sour. It was time to go.

*

JULY.

North wrote the month in big, bold letters and then slammed her newest Post-it note against her wall. Towards the end of July

Kelly had sex with someone. Got pregnant. And that someone wasn't Dean. It had to have been someone on The Orion.

It had to have been Spencer.

The thought of Kelly sleeping with the slimy millionaire turned North's stomach. All thoughts of eating lunch quickly died. He wasn't Kelly's taste at all. He was cocky, arrogant and completely lacking in charm. No, Kelly would never willingly have sex with him.

Willingly.

The word became a rope that tied all North's thoughts together. She grabbed a fresh Post-it and slowly wrote four more letters followed by a question mark and pressed it against her wall, the gap in the centre of her map now looking markedly fuller. She stared at the new note until she could no longer see through her tears. It was such a potent suggestion that it was sapping the air out of her flat, her lungs.

RAPE?

Is that what had happened? Had Spencer taken a liking to Kelly but when she spurned his advances did he become violent? Proprietary? Had he taken her out to the back of his boat and done something far worse than just bruise her spine? The other girls, had it been the same for them too?

'You should have told me,' North addressed the wall as she shook with grief. 'Kelly, you should have told me. Together…' Her knees buckled and she dropped to the ground, leaning forward to bury her head in her hands. 'We could have done something. You should have told me.' Her shoulders heaved as tears poured out of her. 'Why didn't you tell me?'

*

'He touched me.'

'What?' North had to keep her voice to just below a whisper because they were sat in double maths. Outside, snow fell like sleet across the sports field, blanketing their view with a white haze.

'Bobby Stevens. At lunch.' Kelly glanced furtively at the other students who were too absorbed in their own afternoon gossip to pay her any mind.

'What happened?' North asked, already appalled. Bobby Stevens was a brat. He wore too much cologne and hair gel and called all girls 'skirt'. He'd say it with a sneer, like being female made them somehow beneath him. North failed to understand his arrogant bravado since his test scores were always much lower than hers. He was dumb, but he was tall and good with a football. These dual attributes were enough to get most girls to forgive him for calling them not by their name but by an item of clothing. But not Kelly.

Kelly hated Bobby Stevens and those cut from a similar cloth. She was forever telling him that he didn't stand a chance with her, and she wasn't just playing up for his attention, she meant it.

'He touched my bum,' Kelly whispered, face hardening with anger. 'I walked by his table with my lunch tray and he pinched my bloody bum. If my hands hadn't been full I'd have slapped him.'

'The pig!'

North must have spoken too loudly because Mrs Albright was turning around from the blackboard, her lip simmering with rage. The teacher was as mean-spirited as she was old and always smelt like OXO cubes.

'Girls, will you quieten down! I'll bet you've not even solved the first half of these equations.'

'Mrs Albright we were discussing the sexual degradation of females in this school. I'm sure that, as a woman, you'll agree it's a most apt topic.' Kelly raised her chin to confidently stare down the withered old teacher.

'Maths,' Mrs Albright pawed at the board behind her. 'In my classroom you discuss maths, nothing else.'

'But Mrs Albright,' Kelly gave a loud gasp and clasped a hand against her chest, 'these discussions concern all us females. It is about our unjust treatment and—'

'Learn to keep your mouth shut or I'll be issuing a detention.'

Kelly was silenced but her rage still burned.

'I'm going to get him back,' she whispered once Mrs Albright's back was turned to them.

'Bobby?'

'I'm going to get him back. He can't go around grabbing bums as and when he pleases. It's sexual harassment.'

'I agree. But how will you get him back?'

To half of the student body Boddy Stevens was a demigod.

'I don't know,' Kelly's shoulders sagged with indecision. 'But I need to do something. Maybe… maybe I'll kick him so hard in the balls that they shrivel up and fall off.'

'You could risk expulsion for that.'

'True.' Kelly tapped the rubbery end of her pencil against her pink glossed lips. 'I have to do *something* though. Bobby can't just get away with it.'

'You're right,' North nodded. 'He can't.'

29

'So,' Elijah stepped into her flat and shook off the raindrops that clung to his jacket. 'Everything alright? What do you need?'

North had torn down her wall of notes. She couldn't risk Elijah spotting her central conclusion. Now the pieces of paper lay crumpled on the floor like forgotten confetti.

'It's something… technical.'

'Technical?' He looked between North and the now bare wall. 'Is everything okay?'

'Everything is good. Great even. But like I said, I need your help with something.'

He extended his hands towards her, palms up. 'Whatever you need.'

'First there are some conditions.'

Elijah dropped his hands to his sides and bristled.

'You can't ask me what it's for,' North informed him, 'and you can't try and intervene with my plan in any way. I just need you to help with me this one task and be there for me. Can you do that?'

Raising a hand, Elijah massaged his temple with the tips of his fingers. He looked at the scrunched up notes, at the vacant wall. 'Is that about Kelly?'

'You can't ask me what it's for. Remember?'

'North—'

'I need to do this one thing and then it's all done. All of it. I swear.'

'This one thing,' slowly he drifted towards the little kitchenette and leaned against the counter, 'is it dangerous?'

'No.'

Define dangerous.

North knew there was danger involved. Getting close to Spencer one more time was a risk in itself, but she had to do it. She had to ask him one final time what he'd done to Kelly because in her heart she already knew the answer, she just had to hear him say it.

'I mean,' Elijah stared at the pattern in the countertop. 'I'll always want to help you. Of course I will. And if you say this isn't dangerous then... I want to believe you. But if you're lying to me...' he swallowed as though something was lodged against his Adam's apple.

'This one thing,' North assured him with as much brightness as she could muster. 'Then that's it, I'm done. Back to being regular North. But,' she glanced at the backpack he'd bought in with him, 'I'm not sure you'll have the equipment I need on you.'

'What do you need?'

North's eyes shone with excitement. 'Something very particular.'

*

Once again she was at the little train station in Millwater, waiting for her ride into Euston. Elijah's words of warning echoed in her mind.

Be careful. Be quick. Stay safe.

She hugged her arms against herself.

'It has a long battery life,' he'd assured her. 'But still, be quick. I'll meet you at the station when you get back.'

Elijah had wanted to come to London but North knew it was too great a risk. She needed to go alone. That way it was easier to slip in and out, easier to attempt to go unseen.

Dried up leaves rattled along the platform as they danced in a stiff breeze. Reaching into her pocket, North grabbed her phone and checked her Wi-Fi. Then she found him again. Spencer's Twitter page was forever being updated. That morning he'd been shopping for a new suit on Savile Row and now he was preparing for an evening at the theatre, off to see *42nd Street* with his mother and two step-sisters. He presented the image of the perfect gentleman. North felt herself fill with hate as she looked at the mask he wore for the public.

Spencer was staying at the Mandarin Hotel. He'd booked out one of their grandest suites for himself and his family. They were, according to his Twitter feed, 'making an evening of it'. North could imagine the expensive bottles of champagne being uncorked at his behest, the caviar he'd wolf down like it were supermarket brand baked beans.

She would find him. At the Mandarin she would wait, and once Spencer returned from the theatre, tipsy and in high spirits, she'd pounce. She'd end him. His habitual torment of women, his legacy of payouts were the rope around his neck. North just needed to kick out the stool from under him. It would feel good to see him hang, to let him gasp for that final breath just as Kelly had done.

Kelly.

North forced her phone back into her pocket as a tear stole down her cheek. Her plan wouldn't bring Kelly back. Nothing would. Like her parents, Kelly Orton was gone, her body slowly turning to dust.

But this wasn't about bringing anyone back. This was about justice. About doing the right thing. North's train pulled up to the station and she boarded it with purpose. This was the night that Spencer Daniels would fall and North couldn't wait to see it.

*

The Mandarin Hotel was over by Hyde Park, away from the theatre district and surrounded by luxurious townhouses with white walls and glossy black front doors. Clearly Spencer and his family didn't mind a chauffeur-driven ride through London to get to their show. It was comical to imagine them getting the Tube. North guessed that Spencer had never ridden on a train his entire life.

It was a little after eight and North was starting to fear that her plan wasn't so clever after all. She'd need to linger in the lobby until the show in Covent Garden concluded and then wait for Spencer to return. It could be as late as midnight when he resurfaced at The Mandarin and then North risked missing her own train home.

'Dammit,' she chewed on her lip as she paced past the front steps of the hotel for the third time in twenty minutes. In her haste to get to London, to Spencer, she'd failed to figure out the finer points of her timings. It was something Elijah would have done. It was something North would definitely have done if she were in her right state of mind. She was usually such a stickler for plans, for punctuality.

Now she was helplessly drifting back and forth outside a five-star hotel, risking security moving her on for vagrancy. The web she'd been trying to create was already unravelling around her. Turning on her heel and marching past The Mandarin once more, she fought the urge to burst into tears and drop to her knees.

*

'A schedule?' Kelly looked first at the piece of paper she'd been handed and then at North.

'Yep.'

'Seriously North, *a schedule?* Who goes on holiday with a bloody schedule? We're supposed to just go where our mood takes us.' Kelly studied the paper with increased scrutiny. 'My God there are *times* on here. 'Eight a.m., breakfast,' she recited. 'Nine a.m. leave hostel to explore the city. Christ, North, it's all a bit rigid don't you think?'

'We need to be prepared,' North snatched the schedule back from her friend. 'If we don't go in with a plan we risk not seeing everything.'

'But there's a plan and then there's a *plan,*' Kelly pointed at the paper in North's hand. 'Don't you think there's something exciting about just winging it?'

'No.'

'Don't you ever just want to exist in the moment?'

'No.'

'Okay, okay,' Kelly gently reached out for the schedule and read it again with renewed interest. 'I mean, you've been thorough, I'll give you that.'

'I just…' North sat down on the beanbag in the corner of Kelly's uni room. 'I want to take advantage of our time together. This is our first big holiday and I want it to be perfect.'

'And it will be.'

'I know but…' Dropping her head, North thought of the copy of the schedule which was already tacked up on her grandparents' fridge. She wanted them to know her whereabouts every second of every day. She didn't want them to wonder why she'd missed a call, to fret that she was stranded somewhere, or worse, that she was—

'We can be flexible around it, right?' Kelly cocked her head at her as she remained standing, schedule held out in her hands like she was making a speech. 'I mean, breakfast doesn't *have* to be at eight every morning. Some days we could live dangerously and eat at say, I don't know, eight fifteen.'

North laughed.

'I love that you're so organised,' Kelly joined her on the beanbag and looped an arm around North's shoulders. 'You give me some much-needed direction. I'd be lost without the study schedule you made for me this semester.'

'It has all your deadlines on there too.'

'In red, I know,' Kelly laughed. 'You take care of me. I know that because of you we won't miss a single sight on our holiday, it will be amazing. But…'

'But?'

'Sometimes you have to let go and let life just happen. It might surprise you, things might just fall into place without militant precision.'

'I doubt that.'

'And you know,' Kelly pulled her close, 'boats sink even when manned by the most prepared crew. Shit happens. That's something you can't prepare for.'

*

North feared she was on the brink of looking extremely suspect to the doorman at The Mandarin when a grey Bentley slid up in front of the hotel with the stealth and speed of a panther. Her heart raced with recognition. It was Spencer's car, she just knew it. She staggered further down the street, away from the hotel and hopefully just out of sight.

The red-coated doorman approached the Bentley and neatly leaned down to open the door. A man in a blue striped suit stepped out. He clasped the doorman on the shoulder and thrust a banknote into his hand before striding up the stone steps towards the lobby. North moved fast. She hurried in the man's wake, hoping her instincts were right, that it was Spencer.

Dressed in jeans and a woollen jumper, she looked casual yet discreet. Her red ankle boots made for much more appropriate espionage footwear then her heeled shoes had. She could move swiftly and silently across the tiled floor of the lobby. The walls were lined with dark wooden panels and the air smelt of oranges and freshly washed linens. Perhaps someone had noticed her, was currently stalking her every movement but she was too focused to notice, or care.

The man in the blue suit was making for the lifts. A dual set of silver doors stood closed at the far end of the lobby. North kept moving, knowing she had to be in that lift. There was no one else around, if it stayed that way then the lift would provide the perfect venue for interrogation.

She was almost beside him as the man leaned forward to press the call button for the lift. He didn't look at her. His attention was held by the phone in his hand. North tried to discreetly steal a glimpse at the screen. Was Spencer updating his Twitter page yet again? He seemed to live off the attention he gained online. And it was him, wasn't it? North hadn't yet dared to fully look at him, to risk seeing his face and revealing her own. Currently they were just two people in a hotel lobby waiting on a lift but all that could change. If it was Spencer then—

With the gentle tinkle of a bell the lift arrived and the steel doors effortlessly parted to reveal a mirrored interior. Clenching her fists at her sides, North followed the suited man as he stepped forwards.

*

North sat cross-legged on the grass which had grown over the façade that was her parents' gravesite. The sun beat down on the back of her neck, causing beads of sweat to gather along her skin.

'It's nice here.' Kelly was beside her, legs stretched out and eyes hidden behind heart-shaped sunglasses. 'It's peaceful, quiet.'

'We're not supposed to be sunbathing,' North noted with a sideways glance at her friend.

'True,' Kelly was leaning back on her elbows, chewing on bubble gum. 'We're supposed to be letting you grieve.'

'I don't need to grieve,' North bristled, feeling self-conscious.

'Well you asked to come here. If not to grieve, then why?'

'I…' North shifted awkwardly upon the grass. Why had she come there? It had been her idea. They were out on a bike ride. They'd already ridden through the woods and stopped at the corner shop for ice creams. There weren't many destinations left. And North didn't want to go to the park. Everyone would be at the park and she wanted to keep Kelly just to herself for a little bit longer. 'I don't know,' she picked at some blades of grass and threw them at the headstone which bore her parent's names. 'They don't exist anywhere, not really. It's weird.'

'You think about them a lot?' Kelly wondered cautiously.

'I guess,' North shrugged and threw more picked grass at the stone. 'More than I should. More than they ever thought about me.'

'Don't say that.'

'I always wonder what happened to their boat. Is it just at the bottom of the ocean somewhere? If someone went deep- sea diving would they find it?'

'Well, let's go and see,' Kelly sat up straight, her eyes bright and full of mischief as an idea formed in her teenage mind.

'What?'

'One day let's go and dive where they were last seen. Like you say, there has to be something.'

'I know but…' North threw a final handful of grass. 'What would finding it prove?'

'It might make you feel better,' Kelly offered gently. 'Like you said, they're not here,' she gestured at the headstone. 'If you found the wreck, maybe you'd feel like they are there.'

'But they wouldn't be.'

'It's worth a shot.'

North twisted to glance back at her friend. 'Why don't you think I'm crazy?'

'Huh?'

'My grandparents tell me I dwell on stuff too much. When I can't sleep they send me to a bloody psychiatrist. You're the only person who takes me seriously.'

'Maybe I'm just really nice,' Kelly smiled as she lay back against the grass, 'or maybe I'm just as crazy as you are. I guess we'll never know.'

'Ha,' North laughed as she dropped down to lie beside her, the sun burning against her face. 'I guess we won't.'

*

The doors to the lift closed and elegant piano music drifted down from the ceiling. North's hands were still in fists. She had to remind herself to breathe.

In the mirrored wall the man in the suit caught her eye. He turned sharply, his snakeskin shoes squeaking against the polished floor.

'What the fuck are you doing here?' Spencer Daniels snarled at her.

North took a breath and unclenched her hands. Her moment had arrived.

30

'Oh, great,' Spencer's lips curled with resentment, revealing his immaculate teeth. 'So you're stalking me now. Another weirdo to add to the list.'

They were supposed to be having a verbal fight. North should have been throwing questions like punches but instead she was being backed into a corner.

'Am I going to have to get a restraining order against you, because this is fucking pathetic? What do you even want? You know what, it doesn't matter I'll call my lawyer now and—'

'I know what you did.'

Spencer's phone was out, his finger scrolling down the screen as he found the relevant contact. 'Right,' he laughed wickedly to himself. 'Now you're ranting like a lunatic too. Fucking wonderful. If only I wasn't on the top floor I wouldn't have to suffer your company for so long.'

North threw a sucker punch. 'I know you raped Kelly.'

Spencer stepped back from her. He slid his phone back into his pocket and pressed the red emergency stop button in the lift. The metal box holding them grated to a premature halt.

'Is that what you think you know?' He advanced towards her. She could smell the whisky on his breath. 'You want to be careful what you're saying.' He planted both hands on the mirrored wall behind her, holding her in place between his thick arms. 'People have lost their tongues over much less.' Spencer drew in close, eyes wild.

'I know that you raped Kelly and that she wasn't the first.' She met his manic gaze, kept her spine straight against the wall, ignoring every instinct which was telling her to tread carefully, to not poke the bear too sharply

'Is that so?'

'You paid her off. I saw the transaction in her account.'

'Well,' Spencer laughed in her face. It sounded more like a bark as he withdrew, letting his arms fall to his sides. 'Then you'll already know that you've reached a dead end. Kelly and all the other little fuckwits from my boat aren't going to talk, aren't going to corroborate your little story.'

'Because you paid them off too?'

'Because silence, like anything else, can be bought.'

'So you admit to raping Kelly?'

'Rape?' Spencer's grin widened so that he resembled a Cheshire cat. 'Such an ugly fucking word. You bitches call it rape. You swan around, throw flirtatious smiles about the place like confetti, hitch up your skirts, unbutton your blouses and then when a guy gives you what you've been *begging* for you go from a whore to saint and cry rape. It's utterly ridiculous.'

'You're aware that rape is sex without consent?'

'You sound like a fucking feminist,' Spencer seethed. 'The short skirt is the consent. The coy laughter, the sexy eyes. Sex isn't about words it's about gestures. Every guy knows that.'

'So you raped Kelly. Did you know she was pregnant?'

'Yes.' Spencer's face turned to stone as it settled in a flat expression. 'I knew. She realised early on, so I bumped up my usual offer. To cover, you know, expenses.'

'Expenses?'

'Do I need to spell it out for you?' He threw up his hands mockingly. 'I wanted the bitch and the brat gone. God. You're fucking naïve, you know that?'

'So you wanted Kelly to have an abortion?'

'The payment came with strings, like all money does.'

'But Kelly didn't get an abortion.'

'No,' Spencer advanced so that he was just inches away from North and smacked his hands against the wall either side of her face, drawing her into the corner. He loomed large over her. She noticed the muscles beneath his jacket, the thickness of his neck. Spencer Daniels was powerful. Her back still showed what that power could do.

Fear pricked her skin. Her arms sung with despair at their desperation to be scratched but North ignored all the feelings swirling within her. She remained calm, glacial, serene.

'She didn't get the fucking abortion,' Spencer recalled, tone darkening. 'She took the money, promised to do the right thing and then, I don't know, grew a conscience overnight. She threatened to report me. The gall of it. The damn right stupidity of the bitch. As if she could ever pin anything on me. I'm Spencer fucking Daniels.'

'You killed her? To silence her?'

'I see what you're doing,' he leaned so close that she felt the heat of his breath against her neck. 'You want me to confess to killing your little friend, but as if I did it. Whores are only good for being handled in one way. I wouldn't dirty myself with murder you ignorant bitch.'

'You bought everyone else, but when Kelly refused to be bought you had to find another way to silence her,' North wanted to spit in his face but she remained composed, stringing her words together as though they'd existed within her for decades.

'I think she got what she deserved,' he raised a hand to stroke a finger down North's cheek. 'The only person who could truly lobby blame in my direction is dead, found hanging from a tree. And ghosts don't talk. Kelly got what was coming to her for doubting me, for not believing that I'd make good on my word.

And if I ever see you again you'll meet a similar end. I can promise you that. No one would miss a little busybody from some backwater town. I bet no one even misses your precious Kelly. No one other than you. Maybe they'd even think that the pair of you had some sad little suicide pact going.'

He was goading her. North's nostrils flared as she faced the red flag but she wouldn't charge.

Spencer grunted with dismay and then smacked the wall behind North's head. She felt the vibrations rippling through her skull.

'Stay the fuck out of London and my life.' He straightened, adjusted his jacket and then returned to the red button on the wall and promptly pressed it. The lift creaked and groaned as it came back to life.

They rode the rest of the way in silence. At the top floor the bell chimed and the doors opened. Spencer stepped out and disappeared into the corridor. He didn't glance back at her.

North waited for the doors to completely shut before she let her knees finally buckle. She remained on the floor in a heap until the lift reached the lobby. Then she clambered to her feet and dusted herself off. It was only when she walked out into the brisk evening air that she realised she was shaking.

*

North walked through London like a ghost. She drifted along the streets feeling directionless. There was so much she had to take in. So much she had to process. Like when she was at the observatory so much data would come in via the vast telescope but it took time to decipher what it all meant, to understand what they were truly looking at.

Kelly had been raped. However Spencer dressed it up the words had been there, hidden beneath his bolster and bravado. The truth of it made North's steps sluggish. Her vibrant, beautiful friend had been assaulted by a man in the worst way. And then she'd come home and not told North about it. That was the salt in the wound. Why had she not spoken out? Was she afraid? Was she all too aware of how real Spencer's threats could be?

But had he killed her? North kicked the question around as she meandered along the streets. He'd confessed to rape but not murder. Did it matter? The police would now have motive. Evidence. North dropped down onto a vacant bench and pressed her hands against her chest. Her heart was pounding, her breath coming in rushed, anxious gasps. Kelly had suffered. She had returned home from her summer on the yacht heavy with the knowledge of what had happened, with the terrible secret that she carried inside her.

'You should have told me,' North whispered as she pressed the heels of her hands against her eyes. She couldn't cry, not here. The streets were still thick with people. She needed to get back to Millwater, to safety.

Spencer had proved himself to be a vile, detestable pig. Now North needed to finish it. She needed to butcher and roast him.

*

'Kelly?' North awoke from a fitful catnap and saw her friend sat over at her bedroom window. The curtains were drawn and Kelly's gaze was lifted up towards the ethereal light of the moon. North climbed off her bed and went to sit beside her friend, surprised to find her resuming a position that was usually reserved just for her. 'Kelly, everything okay?'

'I couldn't sleep,' Kelly smiled shyly as she tucked a long strand of golden hair behind her ear. 'I guess that's usually your line, right?'

'What's up?' North folded her legs underneath her and joined Kelly in her vigil at the window.

'I was just thinking about my dad.' Kelly was tracing shapes upon the glass with the tip of her finger.

'Your dad?'

'She never talks about him,' she bowed her head and dropped her hand. 'My mum. She never even mentions him.'

'Why's that?'

'I don't know.' Kelly turned her back to the moon and drew her knees up to her chin as she sat upon the floor. 'I found my birth certificate yesterday.'

'You did?'

'Mum fell asleep just after four after enjoying one too many glasses of wine. I went up to her room and found an old ice cream tub under her bed full of all these important documents like bank statements and stuff.'

'And your birth certificate was there?'

'Yup. Right at the bottom. All dog-eared and crumpled. She's taken mighty fine care of it these last sixteen years.'

'Well, what did it say about your dad?'

'Take a look,' Kelly pointed to her rolled out sleeping bag and beside it her school backpack which was adorned with slogans written in Tippex.

'It's in your bag?'

'Uh-huh.'

North scrambled across the floor of her bedroom and grabbed the bag. When she unzipped it the smell of nail varnish and Impulse body spray greeted her. Inside there were a few textbooks, a tin pencil case with NSYNC on the front and several loose tampons. And nestled beneath an old copy of William Shakespeare's *Romeo and Juliet* was a folded piece of paper which felt thicker than their standard-issue school paper. North fished it out and carefully opened it up.

Back over by her friend North used the light of the moon to take a closer look at the document. Within the boxes someone had neatly scrawled all the crucial information; Kelly's full name, her date and place of birth. Her mother's name. Her—

'You see,' Kelly slumped against the window, looking morose.

North tapped the empty box. 'There's nothing here.'

'Exactly.'

'How could that be?' North held the certificate up to the light, searching for the faintest outline of a name. 'They can't just leave it blank, can they?'

'They can if they don't know.'

'What?' North's head twisted in Kelly's direction as she brought the document to rest in her lap.

'If they don't know who the father is, they can leave the name blank.'

'How can they not know?'

Kelly groaned and in the faint light she suddenly looked so much older than her sixteen years. Lines gathered across her brow and her eyes became shadowed, haunted. 'Think about it,' she urged flatly.

'I…' North looked down at the vacant space. On her own birth certificate her father's name was neatly written there in permanent ink. There had never been any question of her connection to him, though his connection to her always seemed more transient.

'She must have been raped.' Kelly pressed her hand and cheek against the window and resumed looking at the moon.

'What? No,' North stared at the telling document. 'She might have wanted to keep his identity secret because he's actually a millionaire. Like, ooh, maybe Rod Stewart or Mick Jagger are your dad! Didn't your mum used to follow them around when she was younger?'

'It's like she drinks to block it out,' Kelly concluded with dismay. 'All of it.'

'Kel, I'm—'

'Don't say you're sorry.'

'But I am and—'

'I don't want you to be sorry,' Kelly clasped North's hands within her own. 'Because don't you see how this brings us closer together?'

Looking between her friend at the certificate, North failed to find the connection. 'No, Kel, I don't.'

'Look,' Kelly urged, shaking off her gloom as she stabbed the thick paper with her finger. 'North, look. This proves that neither you are I were ever truly wanted. We both know what it feels like to be forsaken by our parents. It's why we're connected. It's why we're soul sisters.'

North started to cry. The pain, the ache she constantly felt because of her parents' abandonment was something she never wanted anyone else to feel. Especially not her best friend.

'We'll be each other's family,' Kelly wrapped North up in her arms. 'It's okay. We'll be mother and father to each other. Nothing will ever come between us. I won't let it.'

*

North stood up and left the bench. Her make-up was smeared by her tears but she didn't care. It was time to return to Millwater. Time to finish what she'd started. But her steps weren't as swift as she'd hoped. She kept thinking about the birth certificate. Irene never explained why the name of Kelly's father was absent, which allowed the girls to jump to their own conclusions.

Kelly had always been fiercely against men taking advantage of women. She respected the sanctity of marriage with an intensity that scared North. To North it was just words on a piece of paper but in Kelly's eyes it was an eternal binding union.

It was why Alexander should have never happened. To potentially hurt his family was one thing but to hurt Kelly – that was something North could never forgive herself for. So many times she tried to apologise, tried to promise that it was all over, forgotten about. But by that time Kelly had returned from a summer away closed off and consumed by her own terrible secrets.

How had North not known? How could she have confused Kelly's sorrow for resentment? It wasn't through madness that she'd stayed away but from sadness. Spencer had taken so much from Kelly. He'd taken her light, her life.

Crowds surged at Euston station and North cut her way through them all. Little did they know that she was now a missile. There was a countdown within her, a secret that had to be told, and when it did, everything would catch fire. The world around Spencer Daniels would burn.

North boarded the train and watched her reflection in the grimy window as she pulled out of the station. Her eyes were rimmed red, her skin sallow and pale. She looked like she'd just been through hell and in many ways she had.

31

Beyond the window there was just darkness which was occasionally punctured by the lights of a passing town. North wilted against her seat. She felt so awfully heavy, so used up. Slowly she let her hand drift to her stomach, to press against the soft fabric of her jumper. Beneath it she felt the bump of the wire she had taped to her bare skin. It came up to her throat and then descended to the little battery pack at the base of her spin. She hoped it had worked. If it had, then every hateful word that Spencer had uttered at her in the lift had been recorded. The file would have simultaneously streamed to Elijah's laptop. He should have heard everything.

A soft smile spread across North's tired face.

*

Elijah was waiting at the train station. North saw him as soon as she stepped onto the platform. A surge of energy swept her towards him and she fell into his arms. He held her as she shook, as the last of her tears fell.

'I heard,' he whispered against her hair. 'It recorded everything. You got him.'

North hugged Elijah tighter. She yearned for the safety in his embrace.

'Okay, come on,' he soothingly rubbed her back and began to guide her away from the platform. With a hiss the train released its brakes and continued on with its journey. 'You must be exhausted. Let's get you home.'

The moon was bright and brilliant above the car park. A silver face in an ebony sea. North tilted her head to gaze at it as she wiped at her cheeks. The warmth from her tears still lingered as did their salty taste. But the time for crying had passed. She had the recording. The evidence. All that remained was to kick out the stool from under him.

'It's on your laptop, the recording?' she glanced at Elijah as he continued to guide her towards his car.

'Yeah, it's all there. Every awful word. I'll send it to your phone.'

'Thanks.'

'I can't believe that he…' Elijah's voice broke off as he sniffed loudly and ruffled his hands through his hair. 'It's just so wicked. So wrong.'

'I know,' North opened the passenger door of the car and froze.

It *was* wicked. It *was* wrong. She couldn't just go back to her flat and indulge in a long hot bath knowing what she did. Where was Spencer? He was probably wedged between his mother and sisters enjoying the high-kicking crescendo at the end of the show, having finally shown up after intermission. His money made him feel safe. Untouchable.

North traced the line of the wire she was wearing beneath her jumper. 'I can't go home. Not yet.'

On the other side of the car Elijah straightened to peer at her over the curved roof. 'It's late. You're exhausted.'

'Please take me to the police station.'

'What, now?'

'Yes,' North confirmed. 'Now.'

*

Millwater at night was an uneventful place. There were the occasional drunken tussles outside the busier pubs but for the most part the little town was as still and quiet as the rolling green fields that surrounded it.

North looked out at the familiar buildings as Elijah drove her towards the police station. How many times had she walked the street past the library housed in an old church? A thousand? More? And for so many of those times Kelly had been beside her. Arm in arm they'd walk together, perfectly in sync despite their differences in height. Every step was a collaboration between their two bodies.

Kelly was gone and now North knew why. When she closed her eyes she saw Spencer looming over her on his boat, in the lift. His strong arms could easily hold a woman in a vice-like grip. Had he clamped a manicured hand against Kelly's mouth as he violated her so that she wouldn't scream out?

The car bounced over a speed bump and North snapped back into the moment. 'Hey,' she frowned as she looked beyond the windscreen. 'You're taking us to the wrong side of town.' Twisting in her seat, she looked back at the small roundabout that was always covered with tulips during the spring. Elijah had gone straight over instead of left. 'Turn around,' North sternly instructed him. 'I want to go to the police station.'

'We're not going there.' The car began to twist down a narrow country lane. Even in the dark, North sensed where they were going.

'Turn around,' she pleaded. 'Please. I need to go to the police station.'

'Just… just trust me.' Behind the wheel Elijah was growing flustered.

Panic rose within North. It climbed up her throat and sat in her mouth. 'Please,' she kept begging, 'turn around, take me to the station.'

'No.'

Another sharp turn. The shadows of stooped trees crept up beside the trimmed hedges that lined the road. They were almost at the woods. North struggled to breathe. Why was he taking her there?

'Elijah, please,' she needed him to see sense, to at least return her to the lights of Millwater. Out here on the fringes of town there was only darkness and farmland. 'Turn around. Take me home. Yes, I want to go home.'

'We're almost there.'

'Just take me back,' North was on the precipice of sobbing. Tears gathered behind her eyes, she could feel their hot pressure building. 'I don't want to go to the woods. It's dark. Take me home. Elijah, *please*.'

'Just trust me,' he instructed. But she didn't.

*

North knew that her grandmother was dying. The old woman's skin was like paper and when she sat in her favourite armchair in the sunlight you could see how it was stretched too thin over brittle bones. The blue lines of her veins were a patchwork across her bare arms.

For two weeks the old woman had spoken to the shadows in the far corner, greeted them like friends.

'There you are,' she'd gasp with delight, her watery eyes slowly widening. 'Oh, but you're dripping all over my nice carpet. Do be careful.'

Glancing towards the corner, North saw only shadows. 'Gran, you all right?' she'd asked as she handed the woman a fresh drink of tea, no longer in her favourite bone-china cup and saucer set but instead in a plastic sippy cup more often used by children. The china had shattered a week earlier when it fell from the old woman's shaking hands. Yet still she asked for it each time North brought her a drink.

'Where's my good china?' Parts of her mind remained shrewd as she examined her drink.

'It broke, remember?' North offered kindly. 'So you're using this, to avoid breaking any more of your china.'

'We have guests,' her grandmother pointed a shrivelled finger at the corner. 'I can't take my tea in… in *this* when we have guests.'

'Gran, we don't have guests. It's just you and me here, although Kelly might pop by later.'

'Of course we do,' the old woman kept pointing. 'They've come for me. They've come to take me with them.'

Sorrow clotted in North's throat, a lump around which she had to swallow. Who did her grandmother see? Was it the ghostly spectres of her parents? Had they finally forsaken haunting her for her grandmother?

'They want me to go with them.' The old woman sounded excited by the prospect. And she had every right to be. Wherever her imaginary guests wanted to take her it had to be better than sitting beside a window day after day watching the world unfold outside but being unable to be a part of it.

'Is it…' North hated that she needed to ask but she couldn't ignore her curiosity. 'Is it my parents, Gran? Mum and Dad, are they here for you?'

'You wouldn't go,' the old woman's voice darkened as her pupils widened. 'They came for you and you denied them. They won't come again. You'll have to fight your own way to the other side.'

'Fight?' North peered at the gathered shadows in the corner. Wasn't death supposed to be the blissful end of a struggle rather than the start of one?

'I should go now,' her grandmother tried to get up but her legs wouldn't obey her. They kept her held in her armchair and she wailed like a baby. 'They're calling for me; I must go.'

'Gran, just calm down.'

'You brought them here,' the old woman's hand closed around North's wrist and she squeezed with surprising strength. Her touch was like ice. With a gasp North tried to twist out of her grandmother's grasp.

'Gran, let go.'

'You bring death,' the old woman hissed between her false teeth. 'You brought it for them and now they bring it for me.'

'Gran, enough,' North reclaimed her wrist and staggered back from the armchair. For a moment she thought she heard whispers behind her, in the vacant corner. She spun around, heart racing. But there was no one there, only shadows.

'Oh, my good china,' her grandmother once again sounded meek and childlike as she looked at the sippy cup in her hand. 'Where is my good china. North, have you seen it?'

'It broke,' North shook off the moment with a shudder and returned to the old woman. 'Remember, Gran?'

'So many things break,' her grandmother replied shrewdly. 'It's hard to keep track of them all.'

*

Elijah stopped the car and got out. They were at the woods. In the glow of his headlights he waited for North to vacate the car and do the same. Discreetly she slipped her phone from her pocket to check if he'd sent her the file of her recorded conversation with Spencer as he'd promised at the station. But she had no signal.

'Shit,' North seethed as she slipped the phone away and used the following few seconds to gather herself. Whatever reason Elijah had for bringing her to the woods where Kelly had died it couldn't be good.

32

'What are we doing here?' there was a snap of a twig underfoot as North climbed out into the bitter night and stormed around to the front of the car. 'You've brought me to the woods where Kelly *died*? What the fuck, Elijah? Are you trying to intimidate me or something? Did he get to you? Did Spencer get to you? Are you in his fucking pocket?'

Where there should have been fear there was only anger. It tore through her like a furious fire. They were wasting time. She should have been at the police station, presenting her evidence, implicating Spencer Daniels in the death of Kelly Orton. Instead they were outside in the dark, lingering on the edge of the woodlands.

'Spencer didn't get to me,' Elijah pressed his hands against the bonnet of his car and shook his head. '*You* did.'

'What?' North was beside him now. She jabbed at his shoulder, forcing him to straighten and face her directly. Tears gathered in his eyelashes like dew drops.

'*You* are the one who got to me,' he raised his hands towards her. 'When you were in the lift with that... that monster I heard everything. Everything! North, he threatened you and I can't...' he stepped in close. 'I can't let him hurt you.'

'He's the one who is going to get hurt,' North raged. 'I have it, the evidence; it's strapped to me right now. It's enough to launch an investigation into him, into the other girls and what he did to them. Once this gets out, the tabloids will destroy him. He'll be ruined.'

'Do you know why I brought you here?' Elijah stepped forward, destroying what space remained between them, and took North's face in his hands.

'Because you're a psycho and you want to kill me,' North deadpanned. Because this was Elijah. He wouldn't hurt her. He was gentle, kind, considerate. When he went out for lunch into town he always brought her back either a doughnut from Greggs or a slice of Victoria sponge from M & S. He didn't spoil anyone else like that. Just North. He made her feel special, valued, safe.

He cared about her.

The thought made North tremble. She'd felt so alone since Kelly died, when in truth she hadn't been, not completely. There was still someone in her life who saw her as something other than strange, who was willing to stand by even when she faced dangerous obstacles. He wasn't a threat, threats didn't care about you, just subdued you.

'I want you to feel how real this is,' his hands were warm against her face. 'I heard Spencer threaten you,' Elijah continued. 'I've no doubt in my mind that he had a hand in Kelly's death. The things he said were ugly, hateful. He's dangerous. Don't you see that? If you take what you have to the police he'll come after you. I can't let that happen.'

'The police need to know. Kelly deserves justice.'

'But she's gone,' Elijah pressed his forehead against hers. North closed her eyes and tried to steady her breathing. There were too many emotions trapped within her – fear, impatience, despair, even love. They raged against one another, fighting for prominence. 'I brought you here to make you see that no matter what you say to the police, no matter what happens to Spencer, it won't change what happened in these woods. And North,' he stroked his thumb across her cheek, 'I don't want to lose you to these woods. To Spencer's wickedness. He could easily come for you, string you up from a tree and have the world believe that you killed yourself out of grief.'

'But you'd know,' North looked deep into his blue eyes, 'you'd know that I hadn't done it. That even though I miss Kelly with every beat of my heart I wasn't willing to join her.'

She was crying. Hot tears landed in Elijah's hands. She'd always been so willing to follow Kelly anywhere. But this final departure was one North just couldn't do. Growing up believing that death was biting at her heels, stealing her loved ones from her, made North value life, want to fight for it.

'You know the truth,' Elijah kept stroking her cheek, wiping away her tears. 'You know what happened to Kelly last summer, who the father of her baby was. You have closure, North. Why not just leave it at that?'

There had been other girls. And North knew in her heart that Kelly wouldn't be the last woman Spencer would molest. Men like him didn't change. With each acceptance of a payout and a promise of silence his victims were enabling him to go on. North recalled the fairy tales from her youth, how the only way to truly vanquish a beast was to behead it.

'I have to do this. I have to make Spencer pay for what he's done. It's not about Kelly anymore. It's about the other girls and the ones he has yet to hurt. I want to stop him for good. This is about more than closure.'

'I'm scared he'll hurt you.' His voice was soft with tenderness and concern.

'Kelly was always telling me not to let fear become a cage. I need to listen to her now more than ever.'

'I just want to keep you safe.'

North knew the feeling well. She so often wanted to shy away from a challenge, an adventure, for fear of what could go wrong. It was Kelly who hauled her out of her comfort zone, who taught her that life was for living and that living in fear didn't count. Kelly made her bold. Brave.

'I have to do this.'

It's what Kelly would have done.

'I have to do the right thing.'

Elijah kissed her. His lips pressed against hers, soft and sure. And North kissed him back. She let go of everything – her regrets, her fears. She folded into the kiss, the moment. Her heart ceased aching, instead beating only with excitement, as though she had been atop a cliff for so long and had finally decided to jump, to embrace the bliss of oblivion. Only Elijah was there to catch her, his hands pressed against the small of her back and then lifting to tangle up in her hair.

The boy with the blue eyes was embracing her, holding her tight and in his arms North was floating amongst the stars. She was home.

If Kelly were looking on from deep within the woods she'd have been smiling with pride.

*

'You're sure I can't talk you out of this?' Elijah was back in the car, turning the key in the ignition to bring the engine spluttering back to life.

'Sure.' North's lips pulsed with a delicious, aching throb. She'd kissed Elijah until she was breathless, until she had nothing left to give. And then she'd kissed him again. But she couldn't linger with him in the woods forever no matter how blissful it was. There was something they had to finish.

Slowly he reversed away from the woods and began to steer the car back along the twisting lanes that bordered Millwater.

'So we're heading for the police station?'

'Uh-huh.' North nodded. She was ready. She had the evidence.

'To tell them about Spencer?'

'Yep.'

'Look,' Elijah slowed as they approached a set of traffic lights, 'I know I can't stop you doing this but, let me play devil's advocate for a moment.'

'Okay...'

'You're going to tell the police about Spencer. About him being the father of Kelly's unborn baby.'

'Right.'

'You've got the recording, the bank statement.'

'All on me. I'm good to go.'

'Is there someone you should maybe call on first?'

The question hung in the air as the lights turned green and Elijah drove the car forwards.

'Dean,' North felt like someone had punched her in the gut when she said his name. She knew that Elijah was right. Dean deserved to know the truth about what had happened to the woman he loved and he deserved to hear it from North, not from some local gossip who'd heard about it at the police station.

'Besides,' Elijah briefly turned to look at her, 'you want to wait until morning to visit the station, make sure all the best officers are around rather than the skeleton night staff who might be dismissive.'

North had been hoping to speak to Angie. When would she be in? Did she work nights? What if she wasn't at the station? What then? Would another officer hear her out? She sincerely doubted it.

'What time is it?' she checked her phone. It was approaching midnight. 'We can't very well call on Dean now.'

'He won't be home anyway.'

'How do you know?'

'People talk.'

'Then where is he?'

'Apparently,' Elijah twisted the car around a tight roundabout, 'he has trouble sleeping. At night he likes to head to the cemetery.'

'The cemetery?' North couldn't hide the shock from her voice. People thought she was strange and bordering on disturbed but she wasn't wandering around headstones at night.

'My brother knows the groundskeeper,' Elijah explained. 'They leave their outside lights on for him and let him drift around.'

'I didn't…' North picked at the sleeves of her coat. 'I didn't realise he was hurting so badly.'

'Not many people do. Dean likes to keep to himself. I guess you guys have that in common.'

'I didn't know you had a brother.' Guilt fluttered through North. Elijah knew so much about her and was always keen to learn more. Yet she'd failed to determine even basic information about him, like how many siblings he had. She'd been so distracted for so long. First by Alexander and then Kelly.

'I have a brother,' Elijah confirmed with a smile. 'And two sisters.'

'And a busy set of parents by the sound of it,' North joked but her shoulders sagged with regret. 'I've been a shit friend to you. I'm sorry. Especially when you've been so good to me.'

'I was kind of hoping you'd see me as more than that,' he glanced at her out of the corner of his eye.

'Yeah, I mean,' North blushed and ran her fingers through her hair. She could almost hear Kelly chiding her from the back seat.

'Way to go, North. Good job making the guy you like feel like he's still being friend zoned. Have I taught you nothing?'

North twisted in her seat to glance behind at the worn upholstery. Kelly wasn't there. Of course she wasn't. But each time she accepted she was gone, North's heart broke all over again. She choked back more tears as Elijah parked up outside the cemetery, pressing his car against the curb.

'Well, we're here.' He killed the engine.

'And you're sure that Dean is here too?' North wondered with playful dubiousness. 'This isn't just another trick to lure me somewhere dark and creepy at night to kill me?'

Elijah's face dropped with sadness. 'Look, North, I'd never—'

She leaned over the gearstick to plant a kiss on his lips before he could conclude his sentence.

'Let's go,' she whispered when she eventually drew away from him. 'Let's try and help Dean find some much-needed closure of his own.'

33

'A moonlit graveyard,' Kelly spread her hands wide as she spoke in a majestic tone. 'It's the perfect setting for some ghostly storytelling.'

'No,' North scratched at her Lycra-clad legs, regretting deciding to dress up as Catwoman. Her leggings chafed, so did the leotard which was two sizes too small and stretched painfully over her ribcage, accentuating the flatness of her chest. 'We're not going to the cemetery.'

'But it's Halloween,' Kelly pulled her lips into a pout. They were painted black. She was dressed as a witch, but her hat was worn at a jaunty angle and she'd opted to look more sexy than sinister. There were holes in her fishnet tights and she stood even taller than usual in the stilettos heels she'd borrowed from her mum's wardrobe.

'Not the cemetery. Pick somewhere else to go.'

'Come on.' With a whiny plea, Kelly grabbed North's hand and began to pull her along the street. 'Other people will be there. It'll be fun.'

'Exactly,' North snapped her hand free. 'Other people will be there. It won't be spooky. Or fun. It'll be crowded and then things will get rowdy and we'll all get discovered and kicked out.'

'All bar one.'

North didn't like the way Kelly's eyes shone. Her black lips lifted into a smile as she continued guiding North down a path towards a destination only she could see.

'No.' North dug in her heels and refused to move. She knew what Kelly was getting at.

'But you have a reason. They won't kick you out. Not when you're visiting your parents' faux grave.'

'No.'

'This will be fun. Let's go the cemetery to have fun not to mope about. It'll be good for you.'

'No. It won't be.'

'Let's mix things up,' Kelly wasn't backing down. She kept pulling on North's wrists, edging her further along the street, and despite her verbal protests, North found herself following along like a reluctant dog being taken on a walk. 'Instead of going to the cemetery to grieve we are going to tell stories, to scare each other silly. We're taking a sad place and making it, you know, better.'

'It's a sad place for a reason. I try to avoid it.'

'I promise you'll have fun. Have I ever failed you before?'

'No.'

That was the truth of it. Whenever Kelly promised fun she always delivered. And only Kelly could take a morose destination and make it somewhere appealing, make it about more than remembering the lost.

'We'll tell stories and scare everyone senseless. Our goal is to make them all want to leave before midnight.'

'My grandparents want me back by eleven.'

'Are they staying up?' There was mischief in Kelly's eyes. Like the witch she was pretending to be, she was casting a spell as she spoke.

'No,' North admitted. They never did. They'd fall asleep to the closing credits of *Heartbeat*, jerk themselves awake a half hour later and then make the short journey up the stairs to bed.

'Well then, there you go. You've a perfect opportunity to stay out. To have fun.'

'Won't your mum be waiting up for you?'

'By midnight she won't even know what day it is. Come on, let us own the night. Let us be wild and adventurous.'

'These leggings itch,' North ran her long plastic nails that were supposed to resemble cat claws along the glossy fabric.

'But you look great,' Kelly gushed. 'A cat and her witch, we're the perfect partnership.'

'Fine, let's go.'

'You won't regret this.' Kelly looped her arm through North's since she no longer had to drag her along. 'After tonight you'll never look at the cemetery in the same way again.'

*

The black iron gate which led into the cemetery whined as North pushed it open. The darkness around her was thick and viscous, like wading through treacle. Slowly her eyes began to adjust to the absence of light as she drifted up the main path in the direction of the freshest grave in the lot, the one which belonged to Kelly.

'Well, it's confirmed,' Elijah hung close to her side.

'What is?'

'This place is just as creepy at night as it is in the day.'

'Ha,' North smiled. 'Kelly liked to come here at night and tell ghost stories, especially on Halloween. She liked the eeriness of it all.'

And it certainly was eerie. Silver light threaded between the headstones weak and feeble, unable to push back the mass of shadows. All the cemetery was missing was a light fog on the ground and then it would truly be the perfect setting for a horror movie.

There was a small church and a house within the grounds of the cemetery. Both had outside lights which burned bright as North drew closer to them. A large moth fluttered around the outside light of the church, each time it met the glass it sprang back with shock only to perform a tight circle of flight and try again.

'Are you sure he'll be here?' North wondered. It didn't feel like the kind of place where you'd find a man like Dean. He drank beer by the pint not the bottle. He enjoyed going to the gym and working with his hands and had once listed Jason Statham as his idol. Men like Dean didn't wander around cemeteries after dark. At least not usually.

'He's here.' Elijah was looking ahead, at the figure barely visible against the sea of shadows that gathered at the far end of the cemetery.

North squinted and saw him, head bowed as he stood at Kelly's grave. Was he speaking to her? What was he saying?

Why did you leave?

Why didn't you say goodbye?

North made her steps loud and clumsy against the gravel of the path as she approached Kelly's grave.

With a grunt of surprise Dean turned around.

'What the—' He looked between North and Elijah. 'What's going on? What are you doing here?' Dean gestured at the grave. 'I'm not doing anything wrong I just… I just—'

'I'm just here to talk,' North calmly assured.

'I don't come here every night,' Dean dragged the back of his hand across his eyes and sniffed loudly.

'I know.'

'Just sometimes when I… you know… can't sleep.'

'I know.' North felt the fibres of their friendship thickening, renewing.

'I think its best I wait in the car,' Elijah whispered in her ear and then moved away. His footsteps disappeared into the darkness.

'So, what's this about?' Dean's voice was hoarse. He sounded tired, as though he'd been shouting at Kelly's grave instead of reverently whispering his thoughts.

'I found something out, about Kelly.'

'Is this to do with the money?'

'Yes.'

'Do I want to know?'

Dean was a man mountain of muscle but beside Kelly's grave he seemed so feeble, so weak.

'Yes, you'll want to know.'

'Because I'm not sure I can take it,' he admitted, clenching and releasing his thick hands. 'I thought I knew Kel. I thought that we had our differences but that we loved each other and I come here and find myself asking all these questions, asking her why she left, but it's like asking questions in a bloody letter, I'll never get an answer.'

'She didn't cheat.'

Dean's posture changed. His shoulders pulled up and he took a step in North's direction. Kelly was now directly below them both, trapped in an eternal sleep.

'What?'

'That's why I'm here. I'm going to the police first thing, but I felt that, I knew that, you had a right to know the truth.'

'The truth?'

'Kelly didn't cheat on you. When she was working away in the summer, she was…' North winced at the knowledge she was about to impart. 'She was raped. By Spencer Daniels. That's why she came home early, he tried to pay her off. That's what the money was for. He paid for her silence and for an abortion, but when Kelly refused to do the latter he came after her.'

'How do you... how do you know this?'

'Because I recorded him confessing to everything.'

Dean pinched the bridge of his nose and shook his head. 'Wait... what... you're saying—'

'I'm saying she never cheated. I'm saying she never intended to hurt you. Or anyone. I'm saying someone did this to her.'

With a whimper Dean dropped to his knees. He pushed his fingers into the mound of dirt which covered Kelly's grave. Her floral tributes were gone, resigned to the bottom of a bin when they started to turn from fragrant to rotten.

'Kelly,' he kept saying her name as he grabbed handfuls of dirt, his shoulders shaking. 'Kelly, oh Kel, why didn't you tell me?'

'I'm going to make him pay. I won't let Spencer Daniels get away with hurting her.'

'I just...' Dean was sinking deeper into the ground, his words punctuated by sobs. 'I didn't... she didn't... say... and...' He was weeping. North tentatively crouched beside him and placed her hand on his back. 'I believed it,' he said through his tears. 'I believed that she cheated. What does that make me?'

'Human.'

Arching his back, Dean raised his gaze up to the moon and brushed his hands against his cheeks, leaving muddy streaks. 'I should have listened to you.'

'It's fine, don't think about it.'

'I should have,' he turned in the dirt to grab North's shoulders. 'I dismissed you. Belittled you. I was cruel.'

'You were hurting. We both were. We both are.'

'You and Kel, you were like one heart in two bodies. You *got* each other. She adored you, North. Truly. She never once uttered a word against you.'

'Not even when I let her down?' North's lips quivered as she tried to speak. She could still see the look of disappointment in Kelly's eyes when she learned about Alexander. No amount of baths and showers could remove the stench of failure which North had felt cloaked in ever since.

'I called you a homewrecker,' Dean admitted with a sad smile. 'And do you know what Kelly called you?'

North shook her head.

'Human.'

The tears came. Thick and fast and soaked North's cheeks, her hands, as she buried her face in them.

'She felt he wasn't good enough for you. That his whole situation wasn't good enough. That you could do better.'

'I drove her away,' North whispered through her damp fingers. 'She left because of me. I did this.'

'Whatever part we each played, Kel got on that boat because she wanted to. No one ever made her do anything. She was master of her own destiny. It's what I loved about her.'

North couldn't stop crying. There were so many things she wished she'd been able to say to Kelly and now they were all in her throat, trying to choke her. She felt branded by every unspoken apology, every held in declaration of love.

'Thank you.' The pressure of Dean's hands on her shoulders helped North climb out of her well of sorrow. She blinked at him, her vision blurry. 'Thank you,' he repeated. 'For telling me the truth. For telling me before I had to hear it at the petrol station or the post office.'

'You deserved to know,' North sniffed. 'And you deserved to be set free. Now you know it was all real, your relationship. She never stopped loving you.'

'Am I a fool to say that this pours salt in my wounds? It was easier to think she didn't love me.'

'No, you're not a fool,' North shook her head in understanding. It was easier to miss someone who had knowingly wronged you. To miss someone who never stopped loving you, never stopped caring, that was a bittersweet agony.

'Make him pay,' Dean's grip on North's shoulders tightened. 'This bastard, Spencer Daniels, make him pay. You say you have evidence?'

'Yes. More than enough.'

'Good. Because if he doesn't end up behind bars, I'll go after the fucker and snap his neck myself. He took Kel from us.'

'I think that he took her from herself. She wasn't the same when she came home over the summer.'

'And now we know why.'

*

'He's married.' Kelly said it so simply, so flatly, that North could already feel her heart breaking.

'I know but - '

'He's married.'

'Yes, Kel. If you just - '

'And you slept with him.'

'Yeah,' North shamefully looked down at her hands as she sat on Kelly's sofa, her mind blurred with thoughts of Alexander.

'North, this is your *job*, your *life*. Don't be the cliché that sleeps with your boss.'

'Kel, I - '

'You're looking for a father figure but you won't find one in him. Start looking for someone real, someone you can actually legitimately love.'

'I love him.' She blurted the words before she'd even had chance to truly think about them, to search her heart for its truth.

'No, you don't.'

'Kel, I do.'

'Trust me, you don't.'

'What do you know?' North felt brittle with shame as she jumped to her feet, the walls around her beginning to feel like bars on a cage. She thought that Kelly would understand, would even be happy for her perhaps. Instead there was just judgement on her face, cold and hard. 'I love him and you're, you're just jealous!'

'North!'

'I did something you told me not to and you don't like it! You don't like me not being your puppet!' North was storming out of the room, making for the front door. Never before had she left Kelly's house, Kelly's side, in such a way. Her friend was hurrying after her, looking stricken.

'You're not my puppet. But this, with him, it's a mistake.'

'No!' North pushed away tears with the back of her hand and flung open the door. The warmth of a balmy spring evening greeted her. 'Kel, you were supposed to *understand*.'

'No, I'm supposed to tell you the truth.'

'Whatever.' North was drunk on Alexander's touch, on the words he told her as they lay side by side in his sumptuous double bed. She climbed in the car and gunned the engine then drove away. She didn't look back at the house, didn't see the sadness etched into Kelly's pretty face. With each turn of a corner she let the distance between her and her friend grow, all because she'd been blinded, blinded by a man who could never be hers.

*

North felt numb as she walked back to Elijah's car. She wasn't sure if it was cold that had settled in her bones or the aftermath of releasing Dean from his own demons. He'd chosen to linger at Kelly's grave.

'I owe her an apology,' he explained. 'When I thought she'd cheated, I said some unkind things. I just want her to hear me.'

'And she will.' North had gently touched his arm and then left.

Exhaustion shadowed her every move. To sleep would be a blessing. As she wandered through the darkness, North imagined how it would feel to lie down in a warm bed nestled between soft sheets. If she closed her eyes would there just be more darkness, inviting and delicious? Or would Kelly still be there, wide-eyed and desperate?

Help me.

That had been her ghostly plea. Had North helped enough?

When she reached Elijah's car, she realised she'd been scratching at her arms through her coat. With a jerk she snapped her hands into fists.

'Hey,' he smiled cautiously at her as she climbed in. 'How did it go? Is he okay?'

'He's okay.'

'Good. That's good. So you ready to go to the station?'

North looked at the glittering street lights. It was still so dark out. 'We need to wait for a new day first.'

'Okay. So what shall we do until then? Do you want me to take you back to your flat so that you can try and get some sleep?'

She could curl up on her sofa and put on a movie. Something gothic like *The Craft* or *Crimson Peak* would be appropriate. Films which Kelly had loved in life. Against the sounds of spells and secrets, could North find some rest? Kelly might still be there, waiting for her eyes to close to make one final desperate plea.

No. She couldn't sleep. Not yet.

'Could we just drive around town for a bit? I don't think I'll be able to sleep.'

'Sure,' Elijah started up the engine.

'I mean, that's if you don't mind,' North quickly added. 'If you want to go home and sleep I totally get it. I know that most normal people like to do that at night.'

'It's okay,' Elijah pulled away from the curb. 'I used to suffer from insomnia growing up too. I guess it's how I came to fall in love with the stars. We can drive around together. I don't mind.'

'You sure?'

'Totally. I'm not about to leave you alone. Not now.'

34

Dawn arrived. It spread across the lightening sky like a bloodstain. North stretched out her legs as she sat atop the bonnet of Elijah's car.

'Are you ready?' he sat beside her, a cardboard cup of coffee in hand. Its rich smell was inviting and induced memories of crowded airport lounges. North breathed it in. They were parked on the side of the street. To their left the local park spread down a steep incline before bottoming out in a medley of trees, benches and swing sets. Ice-tipped blades of grass stood stiffly against the morning breeze that tried to stroke against them.

'What time is it?' North raised her arms as she yawned. The night had been an endless ribbon of conversation and road. She had talked and Elijah had listened. She'd mostly talked about Kelly. And her parents. After unburdening all her feelings of loss, she felt oddly hollow, like all her organs were marbles rolling around an oversized barrel. But the hollowness subsided each time she glanced over at Elijah, each time she was reassured that he was by her side.

Elijah checked his phone. 'Just after seven.'

It was a new day. At Millwater police station officers would be swapping shifts. Fresh faces would come in to replace the weary ones who'd presided over the small establishment during the night.

Was Spencer Daniels awake or was he still dreaming? And Dean, had sleep found him once he'd finally left the cemetery?

'Okay,' North dropped down off the car. 'Let's go. It's now or never, I guess.'

On the short drive over to the station she ran through everything she needed to say.

The rape.

The money.

The tape.

A trinity of accusations and evidence.

It was enough.

North promised this to herself as Elijah drove through streets which were gradually swelling with more and more cars as people commenced their daily commute.

It had to be enough.

Police cars sat idle in parking bays outside the station like gaudy peacocks. Their neon shades an assault to the eyes. North could feel her muscles tightening, a flower closing its petals in preparation of the coming storm.

'You can do this,' Elijah assured her after he'd parked up. He leaned over to rest his hand on hers. 'Want me to go in with you?'

'No. It's fine.'

This was her journey, one she'd gone on for Kelly and now she needed to take the final steps.

'I've got this.' North got out and eyed the entrance to the station with purpose. The last time she'd walked in stating that Kelly hadn't committed suicide she'd been cast aside as crazy. But that was weeks ago. Kelly was now in the ground and in North's pocket was a recorded confession of the man who'd put her there. The deck had been shuffled and the hand she'd now been dealt was much stronger than her original one.

'Okay,' North drank in the cold morning air and squared her shoulders. 'I can do this.'

It was busy in the reception area. People who still stank like last night's beers sat slumped in plastic chairs with red eyes and sour expressions. North strode towards the desk, keeping her steps brisk, efficient.

'Hi,' she greeted the officer behind it with a smile as bright as any Kelly had ever worn. 'I'm here to see Angie. Is she in yet?'

'You got an appointment?' the officer scrutinised her, his green eyes narrowing as he glanced over her windswept hair and crumpled clothes.

'Yes.'

The lie was out in the air before she could stop it.

It's what Kelly would have done.

North took a moment to breathe.

'Okay, fine,' the officer nodded, oblivious to the deception. 'She'll be here in a moment. Just wait over there.'

'Thank you.' North had barely dropped down into a vacant blue chair when the front doors opened and Angie swept in along with a frigid breeze. Her uniform was stiffly starched, her eyes bright. Fatigue didn't hang over her like it did the officer behind the front desk.

'Hey,' he pointed in North's direction when Angie drew closer. 'Your morning appointment is here.'

'My what?' Angie spun round and locked eyes with North. 'Hey,' her expression remained hard although her voice softened. 'What's this about? We don't have an appointment.'

'Actually,' North sprung up and hurried to Angie's side. 'We do.' She lowered her voice. 'There's something I urgently need to show you. Hear me out. Please.'

Surprise and suspicion raged behind Angie's eyes but she kept her expression level. Her red lips pouted as she edged towards a conclusion. 'Fine,' her response was blunt. 'You've got ten minutes and not a second more, got it?'

'Got it.'

North followed Angie into the main area of the station, towards the interview room she'd previously sat in.

'In here,' Angie held open the door and then followed her inside. 'I don't have time for niceties so I can't offer you a tea or coffee. What's this about, North?'

'This,' North bundled two items out of her pockets. She placed them out on the worn table that sat in the centre of the room. A sheet of paper and a USB stick.

'What are these?' Angie was slowly sitting down, looking at the items with interest.

'This,' North tapped the piece of paper, 'is evidence of a payment Spencer Daniels made to Kelly after she'd abruptly left the employment of working on his boat, The Orion, last summer.'

'It was a standard payment for services provided. We've already looked into it so—'

'And this,' North moved her finger to touch her second piece of evidence, her ace. 'This is a recording of Spencer Daniels admitting to not only raping Kelly Orton during her time on board The Orion but also paying her off to ensure not just her silence, but the abortion of her unborn baby.'

Angie's eyes widened.

'The DNA from Kelly's baby will match his. I guarantee it. It's all in the recording. He did this. He had a hand in her death. And Kelly wasn't the first girl he's assaulted and bought off. There have been many.'

'You…' Angie drew the items close, to her side of the table. 'You uncovered all this yourself?'

'I've been investigating Kelly's death. I went to Monaco, I found Spencer, spoke to some of the crew from The Orion and slowly it all started to fit together. The confession was recorded yesterday in London. His admission of guilt is very clear.'

'He raped her?' Angie grasped the USB stick and turned it over.

'It's there, all of it,' North gestured at the items. 'The payment. The confession. The DNA. It's enough to convict him, right?' Panic began to scratch at the base of her spine, a creature fighting to get loose. 'Right?'

She'd come so far. Since losing Kelly, her sole mission had been to understand what had happened to her friend. And now she did. It was all here, out on the table, the cold, hard truth about what occurred during the summer.

'This is—'

'Please don't say this is inadmissible evidence. He has to pay.' Tears of frustration gathered in North's grey eyes like a brewing storm. 'He hurt Kelly. He's hurt others. He can't keep buying people off, he can't keep—'

Angie reached towards North and clasped her hand. 'I was going to say that this is extraordinary. If the recording is as you say it is then along with the DNA from the unborn baby we're looking at what we'd consider to be a wealth of evidence.'

'You can convict him?'

'With this we can certainly try. You may need to testify in future court proceedings.'

'Absolutely.' For Kelly she could do anything.

'You did a very brave thing.' Angie kept her hand over North's. 'I imagine that none of this information was easy to come by. And yet you persevered, even when no one believed you. Kelly would be proud.'

'No,' North sniffed back some of her tears. 'I only did what Kelly would have done if it were the other way around.'

'But it's not,' Angie said, her voice warm with admiration. 'You did this. It was all you. You kept fighting, kept searching. You never stopped being a friend to Kelly, even when others would have given up.'

'She was… the…' North's lips trembled and it was a battle to get her words out. 'The best person I knew.'

'And if your roles were reversed,' Angie squeezed North's hand, 'I've no doubt that she'd be sat here saying exactly the same thing of you. You've done yourself proud, North Stone. You can trust that I'm going to look into this. Spencer Daniels will be brought to justice for all he has done.'

'Thank you,' North raised the heel of her hand to her eyes and applied pressure. 'Thank you so much. I just… I want…'

I want her back.

But no amount of brave investigations could achieve that. North heard the scraping of a chair's metal legs against the hard floor and then the embrace of Angie's arms as the officer came around the other side of the table to hold North tight. She held her as she cried, not caring about the tears which were soaking into her freshly cleaned uniform.

35

'Are you okay?'

North blinked. Elijah's hand was on her arm, his head tilted to look deep into her eyes.

'I'm okay,' she nodded slowly.

It was late afternoon. Branches heavy with damp leaves scratched against the windows of the demountable as a fierce wind shook through them. North's computer whirred and groaned as it chewed through fresh streams of data.

'So, I was thinking,' Elijah dropped his hand as his expression brightened, 'about the cinema tomorrow night. What time shall I pick you up?'

Time.

The one commodity that could not be claimed. When Kelly faded away beneath the thick branch of an oak tree clocks did not stop. Everything continued as it always had, as it always would. And North had been forced to continue along with it.

She had done all she could. The implicating information was now with Angie and the rest of the Millwater police force. They could now move forwards, could arrest and interrogate Spencer Daniels. North hoped his vast wealth wouldn't slicken his sides, making it easy for him to slide out of the law's grasp. There was a backup plan. In her mind North had allocated Angie a month. If after that time Spencer still walked free she'd upload her recording to YouTube, let the public become judge and jury for his sins. Until then she was willing to have faith in the legal system. In its ability to prosecute those who did wrong.

'North?' Elijah's hand found her arm again as he pressed his question. 'I was asking about time, for tomorrow.'

'Huh?' She was still a zombie. Lack of sleep and surplus worries had drained her dry. Her skin felt paper thin, her eyes burned with the effort of staying awake. North had tried to rest. Had spent the rest of her morning balled up in the corner of her sofa as the final movie in her Lord of the Rings trilogy played. When Frodo thanked Sam for being with him 'here, at the end of all things', she had been on the cusp of sleep. But the motion of the movie had picked her up, swept her back towards consciousness.

'North?'

'The messages,' she whispered something she'd been keeping close, contemplating in the darkest moments when sleep evaded her.

'Messages?'

'After she died someone was messaging me, someone anonymous, saying that Kelly didn't kill herself.'

'Okay,' Elijah eyebrows drew together. 'What about them? Who do you think sent them?'

'No one.'

She watched him look stunned and then confused.

'I mean,' North chewed her lip, wishing she'd managed to keep her thoughts to herself. 'Sometimes, when I'm not sleeping, when I'm stressed I can see things which aren't there.' Her chest ached with the relief of trusting in someone again, of having someone worthy by her side with an attentive ear and an open heart.

Elijah said nothing, just kept patiently watching her, waiting for her to go on.

'Like years ago I was convinced that my parents sent me a postcard. There was an image of this idyllic beach and on the back in my mum's chicken-scratch handwriting was the message "we're coming back." I utterly believed that I'd seen it, I had my poor grandparents turn their house over, looking for it.'

'So you didn't see it?'

'No,' North's voice was soft. This was an admission she'd only previously ever made to Kelly. 'I think I thought I saw it because I needed to see it, because I needed to believe they were coming back. Does that make sense?'

His regarded her with a look of deep caring, untainted by pity or concern. 'Kind of.'

'And the messages about Kelly, they must have been that too because each time I looked for them, wanted to show them to someone, they were gone.'

'You think you needed to see them?'

'I think I needed to believe that I wasn't alone in my conviction. That someone else was concerned about Kelly, concerned about finding the truth.'

'North,' here was only tenderness in Elijah's eyes, 'you've never been alone in this, in any of it. I hope you know that.'

She smiled at him, at what was developing between them. It made the sun shine brighter each morning, made the loss of Kelly feel fractionally less monumental. Kelly was still gone but at least North was no longer alone. There was someone who cared, who she cared about in return. Someone who Kelly would have deemed worthy.

'I do now.'

'Everyone,' Alexander came in, voice booming. The sleeves of his shirt were rolled up to his elbows. 'I have an announcement if you could all give me a moment of your time.'

Was he leaving? Were they hiring some new? Was his role changing? Had something happened during his trip?

The questions slid around North's empty insides like rotten apple cores. Whether he stayed or left it mattered not. Alexander was now just her boss, she just his employee. All hearts involved in what had transpired were relatively intact.

'It doesn't make what you did okay,' North could hear Kelly's judgemental words in her mind, bouncing around like an echo of what might have been.

'First, I want to thank everyone for all your hard work over these past few weeks. I know you've all really pulled out all the stops to focus on our studies of this new supernova.'

People were abandoning spreadsheets and complex formulas to peer up at Alexander over their computer screens. His skin still glowed from his time spent in the Canaries. As he spoke his gaze drifted across the faces of his staff, never dwelling on anyone for longer than a heartbeat, not even North.

'Our preliminary research indicated that a black hole would ultimately form once the star had died.'

North fought to remain engaged. She was so very tired. Every muscle in her body throbbed with the desire to rest. The weeks since Kelly's death had been so long, so ripe with uncertainty and now it was all over. North felt herself slipping into her own black hole. There was just darkness. Never-ending darkness.

'However,' now Alexander's eyes found hers and they bored deep, calling out to her flagging soul, 'extensive analysis has shown that these initial theories were incorrect. We actually anticipate that once the supernova has fully collapsed that a new star will be formed from its residual mass. Possibly two.'

A new star.

Slowly a gentle smile pulled on North's lips. A new star to be named. A new beacon of light and hope within the night sky. Though she'd never live to see it, just knowing that it would one day come into existence filled her with warmth. Warmth which radiated through her body like the touch of something wondrous.

Alexander had turned away from her, had concluded the meeting with a clap of his hands and was now answering questions from nearby staff.

'Well, that's exciting,' Elijah leaned in to grin at her. 'A new star, huh? That doesn't happen every day.'

'I was so certain it would be a black hole.'

'Maybe they'll let us name it,' Elijah laughed.

'Doubtful.'

'I'd put forward the North Star but I'm pretty sure that's already taken,' he joked.

'Seven.'

'Huh?'

'Pick me up at seven,' North explained shyly. 'For the cinema. Then we can get there and check the times and mill about a bit.'

'Sounds good to me.' Elijah was beaming.

*

A new star.

North looked at her computer screen but couldn't focus on any of the numbers displayed on it. She kept thinking about how the death of something glorious would ultimately result in the birth of something equally brilliant, equally radiant. There was a wonderful symmetry to that. A symmetry that Kelly would have loved. She'd have probably started singing 'Circle of Life' the moment North told her about it.

The ache in North's chest never eased. So many souls now clung to her back, pushing her down with the weight of their loss, but somehow she was still standing. Somehow she existed from each second to the next, enduring along with time, along with the rotations of the earth.

Soon it would be night and North welcomed its arrival. Not so that she could gaze up at her beloved moon as usual but so that she could sleep. For the first time in what felt like an age she was ready to sleep, ready to close her eyes and face the darkness because it wasn't all consuming, because sometimes out of darkness came light.

Acknowledgements

Firstly a massive thank you to the wonderful team at Aria; Sarah, Yasemin, Nia and Caroline. I appreciate all the ongoing support and enthusiasm for myself and my work.

To my husband, Sam, thanks so much for listening to every character related ramble as I worked through this book, also for helping me fine tune the logistics of North's career. Which reminds me – we really need to fix our telescope!

Whilst writing this book I developed a strange addiction to Twister lollies and definitely couldn't have reached any of my deadlines without them!

Rollo, you were poorly during the latter stages of this book but even cone clad you managed to stumble your way up to my writing room to give me your enduring support and soundtrack of snores. I love you to bits you silly, fluffy man and am grateful for every day we get to spend together.

Finally to you, dear reader. Maybe this is the first book of mine you've read or perhaps you've been with me on my writing journey for some time, either way, thank you. For me there is no greater satisfaction than knowing that my books are being read and enjoyed. I hope that you'll stay with me as I continue writing.

About Carys Jones

CARYS JONES loves nothing more than to write and create stories which ignite the reader's imagination. Based in Shropshire, England, Carys lives with her husband, two guinea pigs and her adored canine companion Rollo.

Find me on Twitter
https://twitter.com/tiny_dancer85

Find me on Facebook
https://www.facebook.com/CarysJonesWriter/?fref=ts

Visit my website
http://www.carys-jones.com/

A Letter from the Author

Dearest Reader,

Thank you so much for reading my latest book, I hope you enjoyed it! If you did, please let me know by leaving a review online or getting in touch with me on social media – I'm on Twitter and have an active Facebook page – just follow the links below. These are also the places where I'll promote new releases if you want to keep up to date with me and my work.

Writing is quite a lonely pursuit, though I do have my handsome dog, Rollo, for company. Hearing from readers truly does brighten my day so do reach out, don't be a stranger!

Until next time. Happy reading!

Love,

Carys xoxo

Find me on Twitter
https://twitter.com/tiny_dancer85

Find me on Facebook
https://www.facebook.com/CarysJonesWriter/?fref=ts

Visit my website
http://www.carys-jones.com/

Also by Carys Jones

Find out more
http://headofzeus.com/books/isbn/9781786692481
http://headofzeus.com/books/isbn/9781786692498
http://headofzeus.com/books/isbn/9781786692504

First published in the UK in 2017 by Aria, an imprint of Head of Zeus Ltd

Copyright © Carys Jones, 2017

The moral right of Carys Jones to be identified as the author of this work has been asserted in accordance with the Copyright, Designs and Patents Act of 1988.

All rights reserved. No part of this publication may be reproduced, stored in a retrieval system, or transmitted, in any form or by any means, electronic, mechanical, photocopying, recording, or otherwise, without the prior permission of both the copyright owner and the above publisher of this book.

This is a work of fiction. All characters, organizations, and events portrayed in this novel are either products of the author's imagination or are used fictitiously.

9 7 5 3 1 2 4 6 8

A CIP catalogue record for this book is available from the British Library.

ISBN (P) 9781035906222
ISBN (E) 9781786692504

Head of Zeus
First Floor East
5–8 Hardwick Street
London EC1R 4RG

www.headofzeus.com

Printed and bound by CPI Group (UK) Ltd, Croydon, CR0 4YY

Printed and bound by CPI Group (UK) Ltd, Croydon, CR0 4YY

20/03/2026

02075568-0004